Behind the last float came [...] top hat riding a unicycle. A [...] "thrills and chills" spiel and [...] Circus's evening performance at [...]

Clowns threatened shrieking children with buckets of water, only to shower them with glitter. Others galumphed along in baggy pants and size-forty shoes, flinging candy from cardboard tubs. Aerialists swung from trapezes suspended from a chrome frame bolted to a flatbed trailer. And a lady magician and her older mentor in black satin capes strewn with moons, suns and stars made cards appear, multiply and vanish with a flick of their wrists.

Hannah's nape prickled at the sensation of being watched. An inexplicable kinesis pulled her gaze to the older magician.

His eyes were locked on hers; his gloved hands repeated the card trick's sequence effortlessly, as if performed by a machine. His shoulder-length, dark auburn hair, feathered at the crown and temples, contrasted with the wattled neck of a man well into his sixties.

David startled her by asking, "Do you know that guy?"

She gestured uncertainty. Lots of Chicago nightspots booked touring magicians. That could explain her vague feeling of recognition, but not the one telegraphed by the man's expression and unrelenting stare.

You're imagining things, she thought, turning away, then risked a peripheral glance at the magician's caped back. See? It was only an illusion, like the cards' disappearance.

Absently, she chafed her arms to stave the goose bumps tripping up them.

Suzann Ledbetter

North of Clever

MIRA

MIRA

ISBN 1-55166-848-3

NORTH OF CLEVER

Copyright © 2001 by Suzann Ledbetter.

Visit us at www.mirabooks.com

Printed in U.S.A.

In memory of Frederick M. Bean,
who left this world too soon,
with too many stories untold.

Abiding appreciation to the legions
whose guidance and advice was desperately needed
and graciously given: Christian County (MO)
Sheriff (ret.) Steve Whitney; Christian County (MO)
Sheriff Joey Matlock; Cpl. Todd Revell, Major Hal Smith
and all Springfield (MO) Police Department personnel
involved in the Third Civilians' Police Academy;
Rick Imhoff, vice president, Empire Bank, Springfield, MO;
Ellen Wade, R.N.; Janice Cooper, MT (ASCP);
Candace Ford, MT/BS HEW; Murray Hill, director,
Animal Education, Protection and Information Foundation,
Fordland, MO; fellow writer and black powder rifle expert
Richard "Dick" House; black powder rifle expert
Jay Hesselton; Paul Johns, my ever-dependable, eagle-eyed
first reader; Ray Rosenbaum, who is like a father to me,
as well as a mentor; fellow writer and separated-at-birth
twin,+ Ellen Recknor; Lois Kleinsasser, aka Cait London,
who drove eighty miles round-trip to loan a printer
when *both* of mine went kaput at zero hour;
Dianne Moggy, Martha Keenan and Miranda Stecyk,
MIRA Books; and, as always, business partner extraordinaire,
Robin Rue, Writers House.

1

Until five minutes ago, Hannah Garvey had never considered the advantages to being the sole surviving member of a family small enough to have held reunions in a convenience store's rest room.

Amazing how getting caught in flagrante delicto with the Kinderhook County sheriff when his parents dropped in for a surprise visit could change one's perspective.

Hannah's great-uncle Mort had often said, some things were funny "ha-ha," and others were funny "hmm." Being horny, naked and trapped in a shower recently occupied by an equally horny and likewise naked David Hendrickson wasn't destined to be funny "ha-ha" anytime soon.

In this lifetime, for instance.

From what she'd overheard, neither Ed nor June Hendrickson had explained how they'd set out from Florida for Toronto and wound up on their eldest son's porch in the central Missouri Ozarks at the freakin' crack of dawn.

Only fair, Hannah supposed, since neither had inquired whether David often answered his door wearing nothing but a homicidal expression, a towel and a woody the size of a Louisville Slugger.

She further supposed she couldn't fault him for not shooting the then-unknown intruders as he'd promised when he stormed out of the bathroom. Taking his parents out of the world they'd brought him into thirty-six years ago because their timing was worse than their ability to read a road map might have been a little excessive.

Hannah pulled on the black sweater and pants that had been de rigueur for the previous night's semi-felonious activities. Breaking and entering a motor vehicle and committing a noninjury assault with her own were unquestionably illegal, but so was framing the county sheriff for murder.

In her opinion, all's well that had ended well, even if some statutes, several law enforcement officers of her acquaintance and her Blazer's front end had gotten slightly bent out of shape in the process.

Wiping the steam from the bathroom mirror exposed a mass of shoulder-length, towel-dried hair about six shades darker than its natural brownish auburn. Pouches beneath her eyes from sleep deprivation, a scowl indicative of sex deprivation and dual, dark mascara smudges completed the perimenopausal Goth look.

Whimpering softly, Hannah squatted on her heels and opened the vanity cabinet's doors. A visual survey revealed that male sheriffs with quasimilitary haircuts don't own hair dryers. Male sheriffs who've been divorced for three years and have no children don't have bottles of baby oil lying around, either.

Then again, the unopened box of maxi-condoms, but no maxi-pads, tampons, diaphragm containers, whips or chains was a definite plus.

In the process of discovering that Vaseline Intensive Care Lotion stings like hell but does remove waterproof mascara, she jumped at a knock on the bathroom door. A familiar baritone asked, ''Are you decent?''

''No.''

A two-beat pause. ''Well, is it okay if I come in?''

She consulted the mirror. ''Yeah, but it's risky, unless you have a cross in one hand and a wooden stake in the other.''

The undaunted, living, breathing, albeit no longer naked epitome of Michelangelo's statue waltzed through the door. Not that a T-shirt and jeans shaved any points off David's overall lust-o-meter score. Hannah just wouldn't have minded another peek at six feet three inches of original sin.

For posterity, if nothing else. After all, on at least three occasions, experience had shown that God had taken the vow of celibacy she'd made after her last romantic disaster a lot more seriously than she had.

David snuggled up spoon fashion, pressed his head to hers and squinted at the mirror. ''So your hair's a little damp and mussy. I think it's kind of sexy.''

''I think you ought to trade Rambo in on a Seeing Eye dog,'' she said, referring to his rottweiler, who was trained to snack on strangers who thought Beware of Dog signs didn't include them. "Come to think of it, why didn't Rambo bark when your parents drove in?"

Better yet, why hadn't the beast treed them for an hour or two?

"I suspect Rambo barked like sixty, until he recognized them." A lazy grin crawled across David's face. "I can't imagine why we didn't hear him."

The image of David's slickly wet, hard-muscled body shimmied behind Hannah's eyes. She visualized the steam swirling around them…his arms crushing her to his chest…the hungry tenderness of his kiss…water channeling erotic paths of least resistance…

Hannah leaned back into his embrace. Her voice deepened to a husky whisper. "Are you thinking what I'm thinking?"

"Yep." He retreated a step. "Mom's probably pretty close to having breakfast ready by now."

This from a man who'd demonstrated an uncanny and annoying ability to read her mind? Either David's internal satellite dish was malfunctioning, or Mother Hendrickson was scrambling signals, along with the eggs.

Hannah turned from the sink, braced an arm on her chest and propped an elbow on it. An index finger tapped her chin. "Do you know what this bathroom needs?"

"Huh?"

"A window. The room would be ten times brighter if it had one."

David stared at her as though she'd switched from English to Serbo-Croatian.

"By golly," she said, "if this were my house, I'd grab a saw and get right to it. Really, how long would it take—"

"Only one problem, sugar. All the walls are of the interior variety."

"Oh." Hannah gandered at the ceiling. "Well, then…"

David shook his head. "Old farmhouses with sheet-metal roofs aren't prime for skylights, either."

Frowning, she asked herself, what would Steve *"The Great Escape"* McQueen do?

David rested his hands on her shoulders. "Look, I realize this is sort of embarrassing—"

Sort of?

"—but I figure a gal who's been involved in two murders, an assault with a deadly weapon, a pot bust and a bogus, second-degree manslaughter charge against me ought to be able to take this in stride."

"Stride is precisely what I'd like to do, Hendrickson. Straight out the front door to my Blazer and outta here."

"We're adults, Hannah."

"Speak for yourself. I may be seven years older than you, but I feel like I'm back in junior high."

"Same here." He kissed her forehead. "But bear in mind, I'm the one who's gonna get razzed by my folks, all three of my brothers and every aunt, uncle and cousin in creation from now until doomsday.''

Her smile hid a tug of sadness. She'd never had any siblings, and gossipy relatives hadn't been a problem for a long, long time. ''Okay, Sheriff. Onward and upward.''

'''Atta girl.''

A fluttery sensation, like pterodactyls taking wing, commenced in her belly as David steered her down the short hallway to the living room and toward the kitchen. Normally the aroma of bacon frying would send Hannah's taste buds into orbit. Instead, she wondered if asking for Maalox on the rocks would be too obvious.

June Hendrickson, a statuesque woman with bone structure rivaling Maureen O'Hara's, and Ed, a white-haired, slightly stooped and shorter version of his eldest son, greeted Hannah as though she'd just arrived—through the front door.

''Pull up a chair,'' Ed said, folding the newspaper he was reading and laying it aside.

''How do you take your coffee?'' June asked. ''Black? Well, that's simple enough.''

In a blink, steaming mugs appeared before Hannah and David. June topped off hers and her husband's, then rinsed the carafe for a fresh pot. ''Bacon and toast is a poor excuse for breakfast, but there's only one egg in the fridge and I couldn't find a speck of flour to make biscuits.''

Hannah would need more than eggs and flour to

whip up a batch of biscuits from scratch. Divine intervention, for starters.

Being treated like an instant member of the family rather than Vampira the Slut didn't put her completely at ease—nothing short of a tranquilizer dart could do that—but her piano-wire nerves were beginning to slacken, when she noticed Ed's gaze slide from her face to her ensemble and back again.

"You work under my son, do you?"

Coffee whooshed down Hannah's windpipe. Coughing and slapping her chest, she croaked, "Excuse me?"

"Hannah isn't in law enforcement, Dad. She's the operations manager at Valhalla Springs."

"That retirement village out on Highway VV?"

Her respiration not yet stabilized, a nod sufficed as confirmation.

Ed's woolly eyebrows rumpled. "Why would a pretty young lady like you want to ride herd over a bunch of old codgers?"

She'd posed a similar question when Jack Clancy had offered her the job. It had come within hours of her impulsive resignation from the Friedlich & Friedlich Agency in Chicago, where she'd spent twenty-five years crawling up the career ladder from receptionist-grunt to advertising account executive.

Her professional relationship with Jack, a renowned resort developer headquartered in Saint Louis, had quickly evolved into a close friendship. When Hannah called him to announce her departure from the agency, she expected a string of expletives, allusions that the black cohosh capsules she swallowed morning, noon and night weren't working worth a damn and long-distance sniffles and promises to stay in touch.

To the contrary, Jack somehow—and to this day, Hannah wasn't sure how—coerced her into managing the retirement community he'd built twenty-two miles south of Sanity, the Kinderhook county seat.

In answer to Ed's question, she shrugged and said, "I was tired of living in Chicago and tired of the advertising industry rat race. When Jack Clancy made the offer, I couldn't think of any reason to refuse."

June set a platter of crisp bacon and buttered toast on the table. "Jack Clancy?" She waggled a finger at Ed. "Didn't Patrick and IdaClare have a boy named Jack?"

"You know IdaClare?" David asked before Hannah could. Ed gestured an affirmative. "Me and Patrick used to swap lies at cattle auctions, here and yonder. Most big ranchers wouldn't tip their hats to a pharmacist with ten or twenty Herefords grazing behind the house. Clancy didn't care who you were as long as your check was good."

June added, "We didn't know Patrick had passed away until Ed saw a handbill about the ranch being for sale." She sighed and patted Hannah's hand. "And here you are, working for their son and sleeping with ours."

"Mom! For Christ's sweet sake."

This time a chunk of toast lodged in Hannah's throat. Survival instinct screamed Heimlich maneuver, but a slug of coffee cleared her airway.

June said, "All I meant was that it truly *is* a small world."

"Yeah, but...Jesus." David massaged a temple. "We aren't— I mean, we haven't—" He glared at Hannah when her foot clipped his shin under the table, the universal code for *Let's play this one cool, shall we?*

Ed's fork probed the bacon heap for another strip that met his sandwich specifications. "You were in advertising, huh?" His tone suggested a close relationship to sewage treatment. "Don't know if David told you, but before we retired, me and June owned six pharmacies.

"Started out with a drugstore in Saint Joseph— that's where David and his brothers were born, though it took so long for him to get here, we'd about given up on having kids. Then we bought this store and that one in the area when the owners went out of business, or went to the sweet by-and-by."

Hannah squelched a grin. A square jaw and blue eyes weren't the only things David had inherited from his father.

"The big dogs," Ed continued, "Wal-Mart and the like, cropped up in the seventies and early eighties. Losing some prescription trade didn't hurt as much as sundries sales going down the tubes."

He paused, his expression inquiring whether Hannah needed clarification.

"By sundries," she said, "you mean over-the-counter meds, health and beauty aids, gift items, greeting cards, etcetera. The meat-and-potatoes, with prescriptions being the gravy."

"Smart cookie." His fork stabbed the air between him and David, as if his son should note that the woman he wasn't sleeping with had brains, too. "Anyhow, I figured if it pays to advertise, we'd better do some. We hooked up with this outfit in Kansas City—the uh…" He snapped his fingers. "Well, I can't conjure the name, but we'd have been better off chucking our money down a snake hole."

Hannah wavered between defensiveness and the knowledge that all agencies are not created equal. "What was their concept?"

David laughed. "'Ed, Your Old-Fashioned, Down-Home Friendly Pharmacist.' They duded Dad up in a bow tie, suspenders, sleeve garters and a derby hat, and stuck him in front of a TV camera."

In industry parlance, a mom-and-pop. She'd lost accounts and a few clients over her refusal to use the hokum approach, but as her grandmother Garvey told her, "You've gotta stand for somethin', or you'll fall for anything."

Of course, the gall-bitter old crone had also said that Hannah and her mother, Caroline, weren't worth spit in a drought.

June's coffee mug banged the table. "Those commercials were as much an insult to our customers as to Ed. Like northern Missouri is chock-full of half-wit hillbillies. Why, the next thing, they'd have gussied me up in a Miss Kitty outfit and told me to do the Can-Can on the counter.''

Ed drawled, ''Well, darlin', you've got the gams for it, sure enough.'' Food bulging his cheek, he said, ''Water under the bridge. Wasn't long before that city slicker agency went kaput. Me and June held our ground then sold out at a profit.'' A shoulder hitch implied retribution was his; end of story.

''The agency you worked for,'' June said. ''Didn't you say it was in Chicago?''

Hannah nodded.

''Are you from there?''

''I'm a native Illinoisian, but from the southern end of the state. Effindale—a small town you've probably never heard of.''

Suffixes spray-painted beside ''Effin'' on city-limit signs captured the essence of the bleak, jerkwater burg Hannah ran away from at the age of eighteen, after her mother died.

Cancer was the cause inked on Caroline Garvey's death certificate. Thirty-six years of suicide on the installment plan was nearer the truth.

June said, ''We visited Chicago several times for pharmaceutical conventions. It was too big for my liking, but oh how I loved to shop on State Street.'' Rapture flushed her cheekbones. ''It sounds crazy, I know, but I used to dream I was accidentally locked inside the Field Museum for days and days.''

Ed grunted. ''That's funny. I used to dream you were, too.''

''Well, if I had been, you'd still be driving around the Loop trying to find the road back to Saint Joe.''

''Nah.'' Ed grinned at Hannah. ''I've let my bride think I don't know up from down for going on forty-three years now. Makes her feel useful, 'specially now that the boys are grown and gone.''

David said, ''When Mom was due to have Dillon, I guess that's why you took me, Daniel and Darren to Aunt Mary and Uncle Pete's in Nebraska…by way of Sioux City.''

Ed sat back and crossed his arms at his chest. His lips compressed then smacked. ''You ever gone back to Iowa?''

''Nope.''

''Then if it wasn't for me, you'd have never been there, huh.''

David resembled an actor thrown by a costar's ad-lib. ''Where the heck did you pull that one from?''

''Danged if I know, son. But I reckon it's a keeper.''

Hannah laughed, yet felt a pinch at her heart she thought she'd outgrown. Television had been her window on a world where children knew who their fathers were, mothers vacuumed between kaffee-klatsches with neighbor ladies and kids didn't hide behind the stacks in the school library at noon because Mom drank the lunch money again.

An advanced-English class in high school had introduced Hannah to Friedrich Nietzsche. Before her teacher was fired for promoting pinko-Commie rhetoric, Hannah adopted "What doesn't kill me will make me stronger" as her credo. Not the most uplifting sentiment on record, but an improvement over the Garvey family motto: Life sucks then you die.

The wall phone rang, the jangle startling them all. David snatched up the receiver, said, "Sheriff Hendrickson" and continued into the living room, pulling the cord taut.

Hannah sighed and gripped the table edge. "It's truly been my pleasure meeting you, but I'd better head for Valhalla Springs." She winked at Ed. "I had no idea when I took the job that senior citizens can be a bit on the ornery side."

"Well, now, hon, just 'cause there's snow on the rooftop don't mean the fire's out in the chimney."

Hannah chuckled. "I know a retired postal supervisor who probably has that tattooed on him somewhere."

David's cop face was in evidence when he reentered the kitchen and cradled the receiver. He ignored the eyebrow Hannah arched in "What's up?" fashion. He didn't volunteer anything as he walked her to her truck, either.

No biggie. Just because they had the hots for each other and eight hours ago she'd saved David's migh-

T-fine butt from life imprisonment for a crime he didn't commit didn't mean sheriff's department business was any of hers.

Besides, if the call concerned anything interesting, such as a homicide, or UFO landing, the Valhalla Springs grapevine would have all the details.

"Do you know how long June and Ed plan to stay?" she asked.

"'Fraid to ask." David opened the Blazer's door for her. "But I did find out why they took a notion to come."

He planted his forearms on the window ledge. "Shortly after they crossed from Florida into Georgia, Mom's radar picked up bad vibes with my name on them. When it was her turn to drive and Dad's to nap, she cranked a left at Savannah. Next thing he knew, they were on the outskirts of Nashville."

From her vantage point, Hannah couldn't see the dings in her front bumper and headlamp casing from last night's escapade. "Are you going to tell your mother what set off her radar?"

"I have a choice? A man doesn't stand a chance against women's intuition."

"Is that a complaint?"

"Hardly." He leaned in and kissed her, a bone-melting, toe-curling, tongue-intensive lollapalooza that reestablished his title as the world's best.

Kisses were to her libido what arrows were to Achilles' heel. A man could be a maestro at parry and thrust, but who cared if he smooched like a salamander.

David didn't. David's lips should be registered with the FBI as lethal weapons.

Hannah's were still thrumming when she wheeled her truck around in the yard and waved goodbye. The air drifting through the open window felt cool and heavy, like a breeze filtered through sheets pinned on a line to dry. Her eyes swept the wildflowered meadow rife with bumblebees, then raised to the knoll and the skeletal A-frame David was building there. When it was finished, the view would be spectacular in any season.

The lane curved up an incline and into a tunnel of trees impervious to sunlight. At its intersection with Turkey Creek Road, a tar-caulked two-lane that carried more milk tankers and hay balers than cars, Hannah remembered café owner Ruby Amyx saying that David lived "at the corner of East Jesus and plowed ground."

Ruby had not exaggerated.

All of a sudden the joke about them being too preoccupied to hear Rambo bark when Ed and June arrived didn't seem so funny.

Hannah told herself she'd spent too many years in Chicago where barred windows and doors and rooftops fraught with concertina wire were the cost of doing business. That she'd seen too many movies where bad guys armed with AK-47s snuck up on the good guy's secluded lake cabin, hunting lodge or middle-of-nowhere ranch house.

Now, really. What was there to worry about? David had been a law enforcement officer in Tulsa for ten years before he became the Kinderhook County sheriff.

Sanity, a three-stoplight town and home of the Curl Up and Dye Beauty Salon and Sid's Factory Furniture Universe, had a closer kinship with Mayberry than Chicago.

And movie bad guys always shot the shit out of walls, furniture and major appliances, but only winged the good guy in a shoulder or thigh. The wound might bleed profusely, but never hindered the hero's ability to pick off the assassins with a small-caliber pistol.

Like everything else in life, there were two ways to look at anything. "Nice guys finish last," for example. On the one hand, it meant the John Goodmans of the world were destined to lose out to the Brad Pitts. On the flip side, good guys have inherently better aim, and the number of bullets in their weapons exactly equals the number of bad guys involved in any given assault.

Of its own volition, the phrase's third connotation popped into Hannah's naughty little mind. Speculating on how nice a guy David might be, and the odds of her ever finding out, she almost drove past the retirement community's brick and wrought-iron gates.

Chert pinged off her truck's undercarriage. Hannah

smiled at the faces goggling from an outgoing Valhalla Springs' shuttle bus's windows, as if two-wheeled entrances were part of her job description.

She held the Blazer's horses to a repentant fifteen miles an hour, though its engine lugged up the hill leading to her cottage. The shake-shingled roof peaked on the horizon, then the mellow brick facade, then the toasty brown, cedar porch posts—

The vehicles parked in the circle drive fronting the cottage must be a mirage. Figments of her imagination. Tools of Satan.

Hannah squeezed her eyes shut. Made a wish. Suggested an alternative. Counted to three.

IdaClare Clancy's Lincoln, Delbert Bisbee's turquoise Edsel Citation and Leo Schnur's orange convertible Thing had neither vanished nor exploded into mushroom-shaped fireballs. All were unoccupied.

Well, why wouldn't they be? Why wait in their respective stuffy ol' cars when Delbert carried a lockpick gun in the trunk of his?

2

Hannah started to pull the Blazer into the cottage's detached garage then thought better of it. When IdaClare and Company were in the vicinity, a get-away vehicle should be readily accessible.

Stepping from her truck, she breathed in the sweet scent of fresh-mown grass. Squinted against sunshine unfiltered by city smog. Smiled at birdsong performed on leafy, overhead stages and a golfer's huzzah drifting from the course's fourteenth green.

A yodeled *bur-rur-rurf* warned of an incoming giant Airedale-wildebeest. Before Hannah could dodge away, Malcolm planted his paws on her shoulders and smothered her with kisses.

"Yes, yes, I missed you, too, doofus-dog," she said, staggering under eighty-five pounds of unbridled affection. "But that's enough. Get down."

Slurp. Nuzzle. Slurp.

"Damn it, Malcolm." She crooked an arm in front of her face. "Will you freakin' *heel* already?"

Malcolm didn't know from heel, but all fours did find asphalt. His speckled haunches twitched in op-position to his blond, feathered tail. The sum of his other parts—a black lopped ear and an upright one, black-mustached muzzle, blond lionlike ruff, gray-and-tan fleece coat and a nobody's-home gleam in his eyes—suggested a genetic experiment involving a sixteen-speed blender.

Hannah tried to look stern. The company Malcolm had been keeping, namely Itsy and Bitsy, IdaClare's pink, psychotic teacup poodles, was having a bad influence. The beady-eyed pot scrubbers on legs were the closest thing to grandchildren Jack's mother was likely to have, and she spoiled them rotten.

"No more jumping up on people, big guy," Hannah said. "Just because the Furwads from Hell are allowed to be obnoxious doesn't mean you can."

Moomph. In Malcolm-speak, that response had myriad permutations. Hannah took it as agreement.

He escorted her to the front porch, his butt bumping her thigh every third step. The leash she'd bought was a waste of money. Rescued from a crew of slimeballs who operated a puppy mill and sold dogs for lab animals, Malcolm never strayed far from her side or beyond his wooded relief station behind the cottage. Though he took the "watch" in watchdog literally, anyone who threatened Hannah might bring out his inner Cujo.

At the door, she said, "You'd better stay out here, Malc. The gumshoe gang tends to table-dance when you're around and I'm out of scratch remover."

He whined, slumped against the wall and slid downward to the porch planks, a large, boneless mass of canine dejection. It was a masterful performance, but Hannah didn't buy it.

Two steps into the living room, a cinnamon-sugar aroma hooked her by the nose. The unique quality to the senior Sherlocks' constant breaking and entering was the hideously fattening baked goods they always brought with them.

A stronger woman would tell them to take their goodies and not darken her door again unless invited. Hannah's shoulder bag sailed over the office nook's railing and clunked on the desk. Sneakers yipping on the hardwood floor, she shuffled toward the kitchen like a spellbound captive into a sorcerer's lair.

"Hannah?" IdaClare called from the breakfast room. "Is that you, dear?"

Leo Schnur, Delbert's best friend and a dead ringer for Mr. Potato Head, waved from the half-wall divider. "Come in, come in. It is the party we are having," he said.

A platter of homemade cinnamon rolls spiked with lighted candles provided a centerpiece for the pub table. Coffee cups, goblets of orange juice, plates, napkins and silverware were arranged buffet style. The instigators stood behind it like a Rotary Club's board of directors posed for a newsletter photo.

Delbert was clad in a typically radioactive ensemble consisting of a lavender-striped shirt, puce-plaid Bermudas, sandals and orange socks. His scowl said Hannah should be grounded for a month for staying out all night with that Hendrickson boy.

IdaClare's smile looked forced, too, and her face was flushed as pink as her pouffy hair and polka-dot scooter outfit. By contrast, Marge Rosenbaum, attired in her lucky golf culottes, a sailor top and a visor, was a picture of perkiness.

Rosemary Marchetti's transformation from a graying *nonna* of nine to a pixie-haired, hoop-earringed vamp was as recent as it was disconcerting. Her tourniquet-tight spandex leggings did nothing to minimize her girth, and a sweetheart-necklined overblouse greatly maximized her bazooms. The tectonic vista was being bifocally appreciated by Leo, whose Banlon sports shirts, Sansabelt slacks and wingtips were reminiscent of a 1968 Sears Father's Day sale circular.

"What's the occasion?" Hannah asked. "Somebody's birthday?"

Leo's belly cha-chaed with laughter. "Oh, is better than that. Birthdays, they come, they go, every year, God willing, but not the—"

A horrific wail had everyone clapping their hands over their ears. Delbert yanked a chair from under the table and climbed aboard. All skinny, five-foot-four inches of him stretched on tiptoe to reach the ceiling-mounted smoke alarm.

The plastic cover flopped open. Delbert's knobbed fingers wrestled with the battery. A plaster crumb blizzard sparkled like fairy dust in the light from the deck's French doors.

Hannah yelled, "Don't—"

Silence fell. Then the battery, the alarm's lid, a variety of internal components, the housing, two chunks of Sheetrock and a few, wispy tendrils of R-80 insulation.

Arms aloft, Delbert's head lowered between them. He pondered the mess on the floor and said, "Oops."

Hannah's palm slid from her ear to her brow, anticipating a migraine similar to the one she'd had when Delbert changed a lightbulb in her bathroom and shorted out all the fixtures.

"If I've said it once, I've said it a hundred times," he muttered, stepping down from his perch. "They just don't build 'em like they used to."

Leo nodded. "Ach, the worksmanship, it is shoddy, these days."

IdaClare squeezed between the bar stools and the table. "I'll fetch the broom and dustpan. Marge, you and Rosemary blow off the plates. Leo, take those napkins out on the deck and give them a shake."

She paused in the utility-room doorway. "Well, don't just stand there, Delbert. Apologize to Hannah and be quick about it."

The home wrecker's grin held no trace of remorse. "Don't you worry about a thing, ladybug. Soon as everybody vamooses, I'll grab my toolbox out of the Edsel and—"

"No!" Hannah flinched and patted his arm. "I mean, uh, that's why Valhalla Springs has a maintenance department. I wouldn't want Bob Davies to think I had you fix it because he wouldn't do a good job."

"Hmmph." Delbert flicked plaster dust off his shoulders, earning a dirty look from IdaClare. "Everything's politics. You can't even do a friend a favor lest somebody gets his nose out of joint."

"Sad but true," Hannah agreed.

He surveyed the crater in the ceiling. "We'll do it your way, but give me a jingle when Davies shows up so's I can supervise. Being female, you don't know a molly from a two-by-four."

If the self-proclaimed Renaissance man weren't so adorable, she'd take exception to Delbert's routine misogynistic remarks. In truth, she did a little, but they were as much a part of him as bowed legs and the soft heart he hid behind a crotchety attitude.

She was about to ask again what they were celebrating when IdaClare said, "All right, gather round now. Leo and Rosemary have an announcement to make."

Hugging Rosemary around the waist, Leo raised a goblet of juice. "Who but with friends does a man share the news that he got lucky last night?"

Rosemary bopped him in the chest. "What he's trying to say is—" She made cooing noises and thrust out her hand. Rainbow sparks glinted off a diamond solitaire banded in platinum. "We're getting married!"

"On one knee I did not go down," Leo admitted, his round face wreathed in happiness. "The getting it up is not so easy at my age, but my Rosemary, she said it was a little thing and did not matter.''

Hannah added her congratulations to the chorus, noticing that IdaClare was less than enthusiastic. Probably old news to her, Hannah thought, watching her pluck the candles out and snuff them in a bowl of water.

Delbert clasped Leo's hand. "You damn fool. Retire where there's twelve setters for every pointer and what do you do? Go all moony-eyed over Rosie and take yourself off the market.''

"Ah, but the more the merrier for you, yes?''

Delbert chuckled. "Like you were competition, Schnur.''

"I'm so excited,'' Rosemary said. "We're going to have a real ceremony, too, just like I've dreamed about since I was a little girl. No insult to my first husband, God rest him, but the war was on and there wasn't time for a wedding before Ilario shipped out overseas. Leo and his first wife barely escaped Germany ahead of the Nazis.''

"A second chance we have.'' Leo smooched his bride-to-be. "Whatever my Rosemary wants, she gets.''

Tears misted Hannah's eyes. If they were any example, maybe love was wasted on the young. Or underappreciated by them.

"May you live long and prosper.'' Delbert took a plate from the stack. "Let's eat.''

Marge said, "You're about as romantic as a stump, Bisbee."

"Oh yeah?" Delbert leered at her. "I suspect you know better than that."

Marge's mouth clamped shut. She whirled and stomped off to get the swivel chair from the office nook. By her reaction, she was a former member of Delbert's harem. The retired postal supervisor had five ex-wives, and at sixty-seven, a social calendar George Clooney would envy.

The wannabe detectives took their customary places around the table. As usual, Hannah availed herself of the bar stool nearest IdaClare and behind Leo's shiny head. Marge placed the desk chair as close to Rosemary and as far from Delbert as the table legs allowed.

Between bites of a pastry Hannah might as well have slapped on her hips, she asked, "Have you two set the date?"

Rosemary leaned back, wiping icing from her lips. "Sunday evening, just before sunset at Lake Valhalla Springs. We'll have a reception afterward at the community center."

"That," Marge said, "is what I call romantic."

A whorl of cinnamon dough dropped onto Hannah's plate. "*This* Sunday? As in, three days from now?"

The betrothed's heads bobbed in unison. Leo said, "Patient we must be. The bingo tournament, it is tomorrow night at the center and Saturday is the potluck dinner dance.''

"But—"

"Don't waste your breath, dear," IdaClare said. "I've already told them they've lost what minds they have left."

If bickering were an Olympic team event, this bunch would bring home the gold, yet IdaClare's tone was knife-edged not teasing.

Ye gods, was she jealous? Of Leo? A mental head-shake divested Hannah of that idea. IdaClare had been a widow for almost a decade, but would wear her gold wedding band to the grave. Something was wrong, but it wasn't unrequited love for a rotund, bespecta-cled, former insurance executive.

Rosemary said, "You *also* told us we had to wait three days for a marriage license. I called the county recorder this morning and she said the circuit court judge would grant us a waiver."

IdaClare huffed. "A judge bending the law to suit *you* doesn't make *me* wrong."

"Well, it doesn't make you right, either."

IdaClare hooked a forefinger with her thumb and took aim at the raisin on the rim of her plate. Delbert forked her ammo and popped it in his mouth. Quietly, he said, "Truce."

Hannah jumped in with, "What about a minister? Flowers? Music? Caterers? I'm not trying to discourage you, but a traditional wedding in three days? I had friends in Chicago who spent a year on what they called a simple outdoor ceremony.''

Rosemary laughed. ''There's the generation gap for you. You youngsters just think time flies. Old fogies like us know it does. Waste it, or squeeze the daylights out of it, it never comes back.''

''Money does not buy the happiness,'' Leo said, ''but flash some and the peoples' rears, they are put into the gear.''

His fiancée pressed her forehead to his cheek. ''Most of all, it's rare to find true abiding love once in a lifetime, much less twice. When what you want is right in front of you, what's the sense in waiting to have it?''

Leo murmured something in German. Rosemary whispered in Italian. Hannah looked away before she bawled all over the back of Leo's three-X-size shirt.

A message slip on the bar caught her eye just as Delbert said, ''Well, if we're gonna have a shotgun wedding, the best man has to go to town and rent a penguin suit.''

''What are you complaining about?'' IdaClare stacked plates with clattering fervor. ''Rosemary asked me to be matron of honor, then said I have to wear *blue,* which she knows I don't have a stitch of in my entire closet.''

''I've waited fifty years for a blue-and-ivory wedding,'' Rosemary said. ''It's not my fault everything you own is pink.''

Marge fell in behind IdaClare, carrying the platter

laden with cups and silverware. "I promised Rosemary I'd help her run errands today, but you and me and Hannah can go dress shopping tomorrow. Wouldn't it be fun if we found matching outfits?"

"I am not a child, Marge Rosenbaum. Don't you dare wheedle at me like I am. Hannah doesn't need to buy a thing. There's more blue in her closet than Carter has oats."

Hannah looked up from the message slip written in penciled hieroglyphics. "The guests are supposed to wear blue, too?"

"Oh my Lord." Rosemary slipped behind Leo and took Hannah's hand in both of hers. "In all the excitement, I completely forgot to ask if you'd be a bridesmaid, didn't I?"

"Me?"

"Yes, you. Coming here for meetings is how Leo and I got better acquainted. Of course we want you to be in the wedding party."

Yeah, well, always the bridesmaid... Hannah could teach a course on the subject—graduate level. "I'd be honored," she said, and meant it.

"Perfect." Rosemary kissed her fingertips. "Everything is going to be *assolutamente perfetto.*"

"Careful," Marge warned. "Don't count your chickens before they hatch."

The odd remark registered a faint blip on Hannah's internal-radar screen. Why, she didn't know and was afraid to ask.

"To the courthouse we must go," Leo said, "or it's bupkis we'll have on Sunday."

IdaClare waved, but told none of them goodbye. Hannah finished clearing the table while IdaClare washed dishes as though performing neurosurgery.

Taking a towel from the drawer, Hannah dried the goblets and most of the coffee cups before IdaClare said, "All a man Leo's age wants is a purse or a nurse, but will Rosemary listen? I should have known she'd taken leave of her senses when she started sashaying around in those hot pants and that gypsy haircut."

Hannah didn't respond.

"Neither of them has given a thought to what marriage will do to their pensions, wills, investments." IdaClare's expression went from snippy to dour. "Time flies, my foot. Marry in haste, repent in leisure is more like it."

Silverware clanked to the bottom of the rinsing sink. "Six children they have between them. Not a one is coming to the wedding. Marge says they're all having a hissy about it. Leo's older son is threatening to have him declared incompetent, and who could blame him if he did? Why, if Patrick Clancy were here, he'd give them—"

IdaClare glanced at Hannah then away. Stoic to a fault, she sniffed and gazed out the window for a long moment. Presently the glass reflected her wan smile. "If Patrick Clancy *were* here, he'd slap me on the rump and tell me to stop acting like a foolish old woman.''

Hannah slipped an arm around her. IdaClare stiffened, too angry with herself to accept sympathy. "I'm sorry, dear. I know I've been a sourpuss all morning, but you couldn't—''

"Possibly understand why," Hannah finished for her.

She moved to start shelving the glassware. "How would I know how it feels to see a close friend pair off, making me the third wheel? Not that I'm envious or anything. Much as I might like the guy, I wouldn't stoop to pick up his underpants from the bathroom floor. In my heart, I'm genuinely happy for them."

Swiping a renegade droplet off a goblet's base, Hannah continued, "No, I have no experience with the nasty habit weddings have of reminding me I'm alone, content as I am most of the time to be that way. Or with the anger of being an emotional hypocrite."

She refrained from mentioning the pang attached to "Will you marry me?" being nothing but a line of dialogue in movies or novels. It was a small comfort that those four momentous words never being spoken to her had saved a fortune in attorney fees.

Very small.

Hannah's longest lasting relationship, a ten-year love affair with Jarrod Amberley, a London-based, European-antiques dealer, had convinced her that whoever coined the phrase "First comes love, then comes marriage'' was a jump-rope fanatic not a soothsayer.

She acknowledged, however, that "First comes love then comes abandonment, depression, loneliness, chocolate binges and zits'' didn't rhyme worth a crap.

IdaClare rinsed the platter, then turned from the sink. Her expression was a mixture of relief, amusement and the leeriness people have when innermost feelings are exposed but they're uncertain whether to confirm, deny or stay mum.

"On top of all that," Hannah said, building a crooked coffee-cup tower in the cabinet, "how would *I* know how aggravating it would be for a bride to develop this sudden *blue* fetish.''

IdaClare made percolator noises, then burst out laughing. "Dear God in heaven," she said, patting her pink, lacquered coiffure. "With *this* hair? For two cents I'd have Dixie Jo down at the Curl Up and Dye tint *it* blue, too. I'd sooner look like a Smurf than a walking baby shower.''

The irrepressible, take-no-prisoners Queen Bee of Valhalla Springs was back. IdaClare probably wouldn't make good on the threat, but if she did, what the heck? As Delbert once said, "The best thing about being a senior citizen is you can call a son of a bitch a son of a bitch to his face instead of just thinking it.''

IdaClare said, "It's no wonder my son believes you hung the stars and the moon, dear.''

"I'm pretty fond of Jack, too, you know. Have

been the more than fifteen years I've known him—give or take a few million differences of opinion.''

IdaClare ripped paper towels from the spool and dried her hands. ''I'd swear you two were made for each other, except for him being gay and all.''

Hannah's jaw dropped. To the best of her knowledge, Jack's mother had never made reference to his homosexuality, even to him. Wait'll he heard about this one. He'd laugh himself into a hiatal hernia.

''That Sheriff Hendrickson is a sweet young man, too, though,'' IdaClare went on. ''Not as fine a catch as my Jack, mind you, but there's no sense carrying a torch after the sun rises.''

Great-uncle Mort, the king of screwball homilies, would have been the toast of happy hour at Night Al's Bar & Grill with that one.

IdaClare retrieved her diamond cocktail ring and plain-Jane Timex from the windowsill. Peering at the watch face, she consulted the microwave's clock-timer. ''Mercy sakes alive, you'd better freshen up, and hurry. The Eppincotts will be here any minute.''

''The who?''

IdaClare bustled to the bar counter. Her hand polished then slapped the Formica. ''Where *is* that note? I left it right here, where you'd be sure to see it.''

Hannah produced the illegible message slip. ''This one?''

IdaClare knuckled her hips. ''Yes, that one.''

''Oh, I found it.'' Hannah held the paper at arm's length, then reeled it in. ''I'm just not as good at deciphering someone else's handwriting as I used to be.''

IdaClare's eyes crinkled at the corners. She removed a pair of half glasses from her scooter-skirt pocket. ''See if these help.''

To appease her, Hannah slipped the drugstore specs on her nose. Like magic, the tiny, blurred lines assembled themselves into words and numbers.

Well, hell. Next thing, she'd trade in her spike heels for Soft Spots and coil her hair into a bun. Toss in a hot flash and a night sweat and David would go freakin' wild with passion.

''Now don't be upset, dear,'' IdaClare said. ''Just think of it as your arms being too short. It happens to everyone sooner or later.''

Yeah. A lot sooner when you already have a seven-year head start on the man you maybe, might be, sort of in love with.

Hannah surveyed the living room with a wary eye, and it only half-open. The leather couch she was sprawled on looked familiar. Ditto the love seat, club chairs, the antique trunk reborn as a coffee table and the wineglass on it.

All clues pointed to an impromptu nap, not the residual effect of an alien abduction.

Malcolm's big, squarish head brinked cushion-level. She stroked his lop-ear. He tooted in ecstasy.

''Good God.'' Hannah scrunched in a corner of the

couch, batting at the air. "No more nachos for you, sport."

The phone rang. Malcolm went into attack stance, ready to pounce on something, he just wasn't sure what. At the phone's second ring, he *burfed* and raced for the front door.

Hannah vaulted over the end of the couch. Leaning over the office nook's railing to snag the receiver, she yelled, "Shut up, you idiot," then said into the mouthpiece, "Valhalla Springs, Hannah Garvey speaking."

A hum indicated the connection hadn't been broken. She heard no heavy breathing other than her own. All tenant cottages had emergency panic buttons and intercoms for instant contact with Dr. Pennington, the development's full-time doctor. Besides the gumshoes, it was unlikely the office's telephone number was programmed into anyone's speed dial.

"Hel-lo?" Hannah singsonged.

"Does that mean it's okay for the idiot to talk now?"

She laughed. "Sorry. Malcolm's still a little hazy on the difference between the doorbell and the phone."

David said, "If Malcolm were any hazier, you'd have to mow him once a week."

"Did you call just to insult my dog?"

"No, ma'am. I called to ask how your day went then to bitch about mine."

"Sounds fair." Hannah swung her legs over the railing and pulled out the desk chair.

"Did I wake you up?" he asked.

"Technically, no." She tipped back in the chair and crossed her ankles on the desk. "I conked out on the couch for a while, but I've been up for one, maybe two minutes, now."

"Public servants don't get naps."

"Among other things."

David snorted. "Yeah."

Hannah imagined Ed and June nearby, pretending to be oblivious and hanging on their son's every word. "How are your folks?"

"Fine. Dad hit the bunk in the travel-trailer before I got home. Mom heated some supper for me, then she went to bed, too."

Hannah twirled the telephone cord around her finger. "Did they, uh, say anything about me?"

She heard the smile in David's voice. "Mom wanted to know when and how we met, if you'd ever been married, had any kids, and what year you graduated from high school. Dad said you were nice and had a good head on your shoulders and for Mom to stop being so nosy."

Kiss of death. June Hendrickson was estimating the ticks left on Hannah's biological clock. "Nice" and "good head on her shoulders" were fatherly euphemisms used when "Why don't you try thinking with your brain instead of your dick, son?" might seem a bit tactless.

David said, "They're hitting the road for Toronto in the morning."

"So soon?" Hannah winced at the happy uptick in her tone.

"Uh-huh. Rambo isn't who they came to visit, I'm way behind at the office and, with Dogwood Days starting tomorrow, I'll be gone more than I'm home."

Banners advertising the festivities had furled above First Street in Sanity for over a week. Valhalla Springs's Events Committee was providing shuttles between the development and the county fairgrounds, but Hannah had been too preoccupied to ask what Dogwood Days entailed.

"I'll tell you about it when it's my turn to gripe," David said. "Unless nothing happened to you today worth griping about."

"Well, let's see…" She gazed up at the ceiling's beams and the paddle fan suspended from a rough-hewn joist. Assorted traumas arranged themselves in chronological order.

"Leo and Rosemary's engagement party was in progress when I got home this morning. Need I mention, it was in my breakfast room?"

"Where else? The Mod Squad won't stop busting in until you take their keys away from them or change the locks. Again."

When the gumshoes appropriated Hannah's breakfast room as their investigative headquarters, IdaClare had duplicated and distributed keys for round-the-clock access. Hannah retaliated by changing the locks, but hadn't told David about the lock-pick gun Delbert mail-ordered from Private Spy Supply Company. Cops frowned on private citizens possessing burglary tools, and if David confiscated it, Delbert would just order another one anyway.

"The candles IdaClare stuck in the cinnamon rolls set off the smoke alarm," Hannah continued, "which Delbert fixed, only now there's a big hole in the ceiling where the smoke alarm used to be.

"Then Rosemary asked me to be a bridesmaid, IdaClare forgot to tell me about not one but two tour appointments she'd scheduled for this afternoon, and a pipe burst in the wall between Wiley's Newstand and Pop's Malt Shoppe in the commercial district."

Hannah answered David's questions about water damage, which had been extensive, adding, "Juaneema Kipps insists that her cottage be relandscaped with fountains installed by a feng shui master to stimulate her chi, and as of midafternoon I can't zip my fat jeans."

"Holy Moses," David said, followed by resonant swigs from a beverage container and a gulp.

Hannah's eyes pegged the wineglass on the trunk. It was almost empty and the wine likely warm. As soon as Malcolm solved the phone versus the doorbell mystery, sommelier lessons were in order.

"Are there any upsides to go with all that?" David asked.

"Umm...yeah." She gnawed a lip. "But you were a participant."

His baritone dropped an octave. "Sugar, if I wasn't dead tired and on my second beer, I'd drive out there and finish what we started. But I'll be glad to give you my good news, bad news and worse news in the manner of misery lovin' company."

His banter didn't quite mask an underlying tension. If slugging back a couple of post-duty brewskis was standard operating procedure, Hannah wasn't aware of it.

She rearranged her legs and wriggled to relieve her numbing feet and glutes.

"Okay, Hendrickson. Your turn."

He cleared his throat. "The good news is, Dogwood Days kicks off with a parade. Some of the performers from the Van Geisen Circus are joining in, and we have front-row seats."

Some kids never outgrow the circus—present company included. "What time will you pick me up?"

"Noonish. We can pig out on hot dogs and funnel cakes and cotton candy at the fairgrounds after the parade, if that's all right with you."

A date with David, a circus and acres of junk-food vendors. Hannah's mouth watered at the thought until another elbowed in beside it. "Definite good news. So, what's the bad?"

"Woman, you add two plus two so fast, it's scary." He sighed, long and low. "Dogwood Days being second to the county fair for drawing a crowd means I have to politic and out-handshake Knox while we're there."

Jessup Knox, the owner of Fort Knox Security, was opposing David for sheriff in the August primary. The blowhard good ol' boy had no law enforcement training but was native to Kinderhook County, related to half the population and adept at innuendo, scare tactics and spin-meistering.

"Not a problem," Hannah assured. "While you press the flesh, I'll pass out bumper stickers. Jessup the Jerk doesn't stand a chance."

"Oh yes he does." Anger laced David's voice. "First I come within an inch of being charged with second-degree manslaughter—"

"Which you didn't commit," Hannah broke in. "And were totally exonerated of."

"By the court, sure. Public opinion is something else altogether. Stuart Quince tricked me into a suicide-by-cop scenario, but homicide in self-defense is still homicide. There's some who think bulletproof vests make cops invincible, like they are on TV, and that wearing one gave me an unfair advantage over Quince from the get-go."

Hannah said, "What, they've never heard of a head shot? Cop-killer bullets? Quince didn't care if he killed you, as long as he got killed in the process."

"That's true, sugar, but Jessup Knox is going to hang Wyatt Earp's six-shooters on me regardless. If that wasn't bad enough, as of this morning, Quince's widow filed a million-dollar wrongful-death suit against yours truly and the sheriff's department."

"Shit."

"I said a lot worse when I heard about it."

Hannah guessed that was the topic of the telephone call David received that morning at breakfast. After David was proven blameless in the death of Stuart Quince, a felony clause in his life insurance policy nullified a hundred-thousand-dollar survivor benefit payable to his estranged wife, Lydia.

It wasn't fair for Lydia to suffer financially because her husband chose the sheriff to be his executioner, but suing David personally, as well as the department, was a lousy way to even the score.

"Lydia can't win," Hannah said. "Can she?"

"The department carries liability insurance, but win, lose or settle out of court, the taxpayers foot the bill. A fact Knox will embroider to the hilt."

There was nothing David could do about it, either. Whoever said, "Sometimes the best offense is a good defense" failed to consider that the defense rarely puts points on the scoreboard.

Hannah sat up straight in the chair. "If there's such a thing as justice, a circus elephant will stomp your unworthy opponent in the dust tomorrow."

"Be careful what you wish for, sugar. I didn't use to be superstitious, but lately we've had enough trouble in Kinderhook County to last me a good long while."

3

The mantel clock read 11:41. David had said he'd pick her up around noon. Unless a crime wave had occurred without Hannah's knowledge, he'd be there any minute.

Across the conference table, Nate Tuchfarber squinted at the three-page tenant agreement as if it were a proctology instrument and to sign it was tantamount to bending over and coughing on command.

His wife, Zona, shot sidelong laser beams at Nate's right temple, twiddled her necklace and tapped a toe against the table's pedestal. The hurry-up body language had no effect on Nate, but Hannah's nails hyphenated her palms and she began to rethink her views on primal-scream therapy.

The Tuchfarbers were the second couple she'd toured through Valhalla Springs yesterday, and Nate the second husband that morning to develop commitment phobia.

Their search for a retirement community had taken them from California to south Texas to Florida's Gulf Coast. Zona said sunshine and balmy climes were great for oranges, but wanted a place where a calendar wasn't needed to distinguish June from January.

She'd been enchanted with Main Street's Victorian brick shops, stores, eateries and boardwalks shaded by striped awnings. Nate said Valhalla Springs's golf course was subpar, his health club in Boise put the community center's indoor lap pool and workout rooms to shame and that he'd seen puddles larger than the lake.

Reverse psychology in spades. Hannah knew the retired transportation manager for Albertson's, Inc. was as eager as his wife to move into the stucco and timbered cottage at 2209 Mayflower Drive. At this rate, however, it would qualify as a historic home before they laid claim to it.

Malcolm, who was snoozing on the porch, *moomphed* at a vehicle turning into the driveway. Hannah's head bowed and pivoted for a surreptitious peek outside. A blue-and-white cruiser rolled up behind the Tuchfarbers' rented Buick.

"For pity's sake." Zona reached over and yanked on the paperwork. "Gimme that."

Rudely awakened from his stupor, Nate examined his empty hands. "What do you think you're doing?"

"What I should've done a half hour ago." Zona's seismographic signature filled the agreement's lower line. "Cautious was yesterday, Nate. Today you're being stubborn."

Heaving a sigh, he took the pen Zona offered. "All

right." His tone guaranteed an "I told you so" if she dared complain about anything in the future.

Hannah excused herself to answer the door. Having already scoped her visitors through the screen, David said, "Sorry to barge in. I'll help Malcolm hold down the porch till you're ready."

She whispered, "And miss an opportunity to charm a couple of new voters?" Swinging the screen door wide, she upped the volume. "Interrupting? Why no, of course not, Sheriff Hendrickson. It's always a pleasure to see you."

Removing his Stetson as he stepped inside, he muttered behind it, "Gee, can't you lay it on any thicker?"

"Yes."

"Forget I asked."

As Hannah made the introductions, Zona inventoried David's black polo shirt and jeans, Western-tailored canvas sportcoat, the gold shield pinned to the pocket and the holstered Smith & Wesson riding his hip. Her gaze diverted to Hannah, obviously adding one plus one, then intrigued by and approving of the answer.

Hannah's private side cringed. Hers and David's relationship wasn't a secret, but a veritable stranger's at-a-glance diagnosis was unsettling.

Nate stood and extended his hand. "Get a lot of calls out here, do you, Sheriff?"

"No, sir."

Which was true, though the most recent involved

busting IdaClare and the Every-Other-Tuesday Bridge Club for pot possession.

"I wish the department had the budget to hire a half-dozen more deputies," David said, "but what we have stay as visible as they can."

Nate smirked. "The one with the radar gun parked behind your election billboard on the highway wasn't what I'd call visible."

David's eyebrows crimped. "You weren't speeding, I hope."

"On that road?" Nate made a roller-coaster motion. "You'd have to be nuts to put the pedal to the metal along there."

David nudged Hannah, as though she'd forgotten their first meeting, the speeding ticket that resulted or the lecture he'd delivered with it. "Well, Mr. Tuchfarber, if everyone felt that way we wouldn't need traffic control officers."

"Let's go, Nate," Zona said. "We've taken enough of Hannah's time, and you promised me lunch at that cute little café on Main Street."

"Nellie Dunn's," Hannah said. "I can personally vouch for the huevos rancheros."

"What's the rush?" Nate's natural frown deepened as Zona gathered up the new-resident packets, keys, garage-door openers and directories. "I want to ask the sheriff—"

"Save it for the open house, Memorial Day weekend." Zona smiled at David. "You and Hannah will come, won't you?"

Hannah ignored David's *How'd she know?* look. "We're both subject to duty calling, but we'll do our best."

"Wonderful." Zona tucked her arm through Hannah's and started for the door. "We'll fly back to Boise tomorrow, so I'll phone no later than Monday with the paint colors I want for the living room, dining room and bedroom."

Hannah said, "Then I'll go ahead and have maintenance schedule the job for—"

"What open house?" Nate blustered, practically stepping on their heels. "Memorial Day's only three weeks off, Zona. No chance in Hades we can move here that fast."

"Oh, really? Who do you think organized twenty-three transfers to twenty-three different towns in five different states? The moving fairies?" Zona bumped the screen door with a hip. "Nice meeting you, Sheriff." She winked at Hannah. "We'll be in touch."

Nate stalked to their rental car. "Soon as we get back home, you're going in for a checkup. The way you're acting, you're taking too much of something or not enough of something else."

Zona's reply was lost in the slam of car doors.

Hannah spun around and slumped against the wall. "Forget FedEx. If it absolutely, positively has to be there overnight, call Zona Tuchfarber. Ten bucks says the moving van is in the driveway before the paint dries."

David studied her for a moment then chucked her

under the chin. "Listen, you've put in a full day already. If you're too tired to go to town, say so."

"Meaning, I don't look so great."

His face was a picture of bewilderment. "You look terrific. You always look terrific."

"I don't know..." Feeling her deadpan expression unravel at the edges, Hannah surveyed her bouclé-knit tank sweater, short-sleeved safari jacket and walking shorts. "Maybe I should change into something more colorful. And blusher. I definitely need more blusher."

She peered up through her lashes, tracing the crease in his sleeve with a fingertip. "Or maybe all I need is a battery recharge. That is, if you can spare a few volts."

"Ornery." David's arm hooked her waist. "You are pure-de-ornery, Miz Garvey." His lips teased hers, parted, then took possession, opening and closing with each sensuous stroke of his tongue.

"How's that?" he murmured.

Hannah's eyelids fluttered but wouldn't quite open. "Mmm, well...I'd, uh, give it an eight."

"Oh, yeah?" The Stetson hit the floor. His hand slid up her cheek, fingers raking back her hair. "What the hell. If you've seen one parade, you've seem 'em all."

"Except you're the one who's supposed to be seen, David."

Hannah sidled from his embrace. "Can't let Jessup Knox have the spotlight to himself."

"I know." His arms fell to his sides. "But as if I needed it, rack up another reason for me to despise that brass-plated idiot."

During the drive into Sanity, the cruiser's air conditioner was at its standard left-of-Antarctica setting, but the vapor whistling out of the vents was more refreshing than frost-biting.

Between the Quince shooting and the lawsuit stemming from it, Hannah knew David was literally sweating the public reception he'd receive, but he didn't own a monopoly on nerves. Her own crackled at the prospect of being identified as the hunky bachelor sheriff's new "lady friend."

Ranking herself near the top of the gossip hit parade wasn't egotistic or self-indulgent. Election or no, sex beat death and taxes as topics for discussion any day of the week.

Too bad they weren't having any.

David caught her eye and smiled. He adjusted to a one-handed grip on the steering wheel, his free hand taking hers. Finding a comfortable resting place was no easy task. Not with a metal citation book wedged between the seat, the console's communications equipment, siren and light-bar control box and assorted, law enforcement gadgetry taking up the rest of the available space.

"We're going to have fun," Hannah said.

"Yep. Every chance we get."

"In case I neglected to tell you, you look pretty terrific yourself, Sheriff."

He squared his shoulders. "Think so, huh?"

Naked, hot and hard was his best look, but this wasn't the time or place to mention it. "I just sort of presumed you'd be in uniform."

She'd seen him only once in official, razor-creased midnight blue, with a black clip-on tie tucked in his shirt placket and light glinting off his collar's insignia, nameplate and badge. At the time, her thoughts, which revolved around him being a big, stupid ticket-happy jerk face, hadn't blinded her to David's born-to-wear-a-uniform physique.

"I presumed campaigning in uniform was the way to go, too," he said. "No sooner than I got to the office, Claudina nixed it and sent me home to change clothes."

Claudina Burkholtz, the department's chief dispatcher—and part-time waitress at the Short Stack—had been David's campaign manager until a few days ago. As a single mother of three, and the odds of Jessup Knox winning the primary and general election on the rise, Claudina couldn't risk her job and health insurance on the outcome.

Hannah worried whether the Knox camp was fooled by Lucas Sauers, David's personal attorney, taking over the campaign's helm—in name only. Knowing Claudina, a clandestine advisory position was a larger charge than running the show, but secrets were as impossible to keep in captivity as unicorns.

"Don't let it go to your head," Hannah warned, as if David ever noticed feminine backward glances, "but I think you look great in uniform, too, and wearing it would have emphasized who's the sheriff and who's the wannabe."

"Except, according to Claudina, that's your basic two-edged sword. She says in street clothes I'm more approachable and less of a fall guy for anyone with a hate-on for cops, for any reason, anywhere in the U.S. of A."

Hannah countered, "No offense to Claudina, who is a very smart, very shrewd woman, but I think she's doing the mountains-out-of-molehills thing."

"Oh, you do, huh." The creases deepened at the corners of his eyes. "I reckon that explains your heartwarming reaction to my uniform the first time we met."

Hannah opened her mouth to protest then shut it. Okay, she *had* associated David with Vic Brummit, her hometown's chief of police and stereotypical, jackbooted thug. She also thought she'd disguised that initial animosity with poise, charm and unflagging good humor.

Apparently not.

His attention diverted to radio chatter—to her untrained ears, so much staticky, nonsensical garble.

Hannah tensed, staring out the side window at horses grazing in a lush, undulating field. Any second now David would release her hand, unhook the microphone and thumb the relay button. Lights and sirens would switch on, the Crown Vic would feel as though it were levitating, then respond to a floor-boarded accelerator.

Adrenaline zinged through her as it had last week when she'd ridden along on what was supposed to have been a routine complaint call at the home of Stuart and Lydia Quince. Since that night, the scanner Delbert bought Hannah and each of the gumshoes had become little more than a dust catcher.

Eavesdropping on police calls wasn't the same as watching *Cops* on TV without the video portion. David's radio identification was Adam 1–01. Monitoring his every move invited paranoia acute enough to make Saint-John's-wort a food group.

What Hannah couldn't ignore were the subtle changes in their relationship. No one emerged from a crisis unscathed. The shooting and its aftermath had brought them closer, but had also erased any degree of separation between David's personal and professional life.

He'd made scant reference to his first marriage, or his ex-wife, but had mentioned Cynthia's snide distinction between "A cop is my husband" and "My husband is a cop."

Hannah had discounted the remark as a bitchy, verbal knee to the groin, much like calling Jarrod Amberley's antique auctions "used furniture sales."

Reality had struck with the sound of a gunshot. The agonizing, helpless minutes of not knowing whether David was wounded or dead; the dizzy relief when he reappeared out of the darkness; her intimate understanding that when a badge becomes a target, deadly force means kill or be killed.

On-duty, or off, visible or concealed, a cop's shield and his gun represented a readiness to serve and protect, unbound by clocks, calendars or circumstances. Hannah had just begun to comprehend that, like most bitchy remarks, the former Mrs. Hendrickson's had wrapped truth in layers of barbed wire.

When half a couple was a law enforcement officer, the job was a constant third party in the relationship. That's the facts, ma'am. Love him, love his job, for the two are virtually inseparable.

Could she live with being first in David's heart, and second to his oath of office? The Kinderhook County courthouse was thousands of miles closer than London was to Chicago, but if she'd learned anything from her relationship with Jarrod, the man you loved never being there for you caused distance unrelated to geography.

David's chuckle jerked Hannah back from the uncertain future to the present. "It sounds like Deputy Vaughan may miss out on parade duty."

She blew out a breath. Thank God. Whatever the dispatcher had said, it was still a beautiful, nonfelonious day in the neighborhood. "What happened? All I heard was gibberish and static."

"That's 'cause you're a civilian." Ignoring the single-digit salute rising from their clasped hands, he said, "Vaughan did a check-the-well-being out at Ute

Hensley's farm and left his patrol unit's door open. Ute's pet sow took it as an invitation to climb in and make herself at home.''

Hannah's nose wrinkled. The stench of hog on the hoof was as breathtaking as it was unforgettable.

''Dinner—that's the sow's name—won't budge, and Ute says he'll take a shotgun to anyone who tries to zap her with a tranquilizer dart.''

''Well, if it were me,'' Hannah said, ''I'd zap Ute, then the pig.''

''Not a bad plan, except Ute is about nine hundred years old and tends to hold a grudge. Since Dinner has carjacked visitors before, dispatch told Vaughan to take her for a ride to the feed mill and back.''

''You're kidding.''

''Scout's honor,'' David said. ''That's all the pig wants, and chances are she'll evacuate the unit afterward of her own volition.''

Hannah threw back her head and laughed. ''Occupational boredom isn't a problem for you, is it, Sheriff?''

''Not often,'' he allowed, grinning. ''But keep in mind, these kinds of hostage situations don't come along every day.''

By virtue of signage, Highway VV became First Street at Sanity's northern and southern city limits. Strip malls and franchises had rendered the southern end a replica of countless others from coast to coast. While tourists might appreciate a Holiday Inn Express's consistent proximity to a Wal-Mart, a Jiffy

Lube and a KFC, the arrangement purveyed an eerie hamster-wheel effect, as if, regardless of how far, or what direction you traveled, you always circled back to the same McDonaldLand.

The county seat's hill-and-dale terrain wasn't conducive to secondary-road construction to alleviate congestion on the main drag. None had been needed until twenty-some years ago when several manufacturing plants descended to take advantage of federal rural-development grants.

The cloverleafs and four-lane alternate routes promised by the Missouri Department of Transportation had yet to materialize. As they had since Sanity's founding fathers staked out the original boundaries, the natives left complaints to the come-heres, who'd sought a relaxed, small-town atmosphere, then were appalled by the locals' flair for laissez-faire.

David circumvented the traffic snarl caused by parade roadblocks with a nifty series of turns through residential neighborhoods. As they neared the square, his hand slipped from hers and his features took on a Mount Rushmore mien.

He scanned the spectators who lined the sidewalks like a gigantic game of Red Rover. Hannah followed his gaze, knowing her powers of observation were to David's what a window was to a microscope.

They parked parallel to the antiquated courthouse in a driveway reserved for transporting prisoners to and from the third-floor jail. Hannah was surprised by the number of children capering on the lawn. School hadn't dismissed for summer vacation yet.

David said, "When the boys who'd played hooky on Dogwood Days grew up to be school board members, they voted to make the first Friday in May a half-day holiday.

"Their kids got rickeydoed out of the hair-curling terror of bumping into Mom between the Macedonia Free Will Full Gospel Church's slice o' pie booth and the donkey rides, but it's saved school attendance clerks a ton of paperwork."

Hannah volunteered to woman the canvas tote bag full of *Hendrickson for Sheriff* bumper stickers, pamphlets and emery boards so David could distribute howdies and handshakes. Near a section of portable bleachers reserved for the parade's VIPs, David stopped to affix a foil, badge-shaped sticker to a little boy's T-shirt.

Eyes wide, the child fingered the shiny shield and lisped, "Am I a real deputy now, Misther Theriff?"

David knelt down, asked the boy's name, then told him to raise his right hand. "Eric Peter Worley, do you solemnly swear to uphold the law, to mind your mama and try your best to do what your heart tells you is right?"

"Yeth, thir."

"Then I hereby grant you the extra-special rank of Deputy, Junior Grade." David ruffled Eric's hair. "Now don't go arresting anybody, but if it's okay with your mom, show that badge to Mr. Taylor at the refreshment tent and he'll give you a free sno-cone.''

"Free? Wow!'' The boy took off running, then hollered back, "Thanks, Misther Theriff.''

In seconds, David was hip deep in boys and girls clamoring to be deputized. Even without sno-cones as incentive, children gravitated to him, as if they saw through the exterior trappings and sensed he was just an oversize kid.

What a wonderful father he'd be, Hannah mused, then corrected herself. "Father'' corresponded to George C. Scott in *Patton*. Like Ed Hendrickson, David would be a daddy long after the abbreviation to Dad.

Her maternal instinct had flared in her mid-twenties and fizzled before thirty. Pretty much, anyway. She'd attributed subsequent outbreaks to the idyllic, idiotic image of telling Jarrod she was carrying his child, whereby his froggy eyes moistened with tears and he swept her into his arms and smothered her with kisses. Reason dependably ripped that frame from her mental View-Master. The replacement portrayed Jarrod silhouetted against the clouds, his arms flapping and nose pointed toward England.

Hannah doled out pro-Hendrickson paraphernalia to the voting-aged, trying to imagine herself forty-plus and pregnant. Snuggling an infant morphed into clomping into an auditorium on a walker to attend his or her high-school graduation.

"No way, no how.''

"I beg your pardon?" said a well-dressed brunette, her hand extended for an emery board.

"Uh, no way, no how can Sheriff Hendrickson thank you enough for your support."

The woman backpedaled and beat a somewhat hasty retreat.

A bass drum's rhythmic thunder and strains of "Let The Good Times Roll" sent people flocking to the curbs, juggling drink cups and camcorders. David pointed to a vacant space at the bleachers' center section. Hannah climbed the rickety planks, lobbing hellos at other occupants and trying not to mash their toes or deck anyone with the tote bag.

Jefferson Davis Oglethorpe, the septuagenarian, perennially losing Democratic candidate for sheriff, tipped his straw boater. "I'm so pleased you could join us for the festivities, my dear," he said in a honeyed, grandson-of-the-Confederacy drawl.

Stifling an impulse to curtsy, Hannah smiled at the old gentleman who was as easy to like as dislike. He had the means to buy an election, but was content to yank the county commission's chain and dispense myopic views of the Civil War and the ongoing family feud arising from it.

A voice at the top row called out, "Hey there, Dave. Glad to see you back on the right side of the law, ol' buddy."

Tense chuckles rippled through the stands. If looks could kill, Hannah's would have vaporized the smarmy, Elvis-pompadoured speaker.

"Sorry to hear you don't believe in innocent until proven guilty, Jessup," David said. "Much less innocent after proven innocent."

Knox responded to murmurs of agreement with, "Aw, I was jes' joshin' the boy. Can't y'all take a joke?"

David sat down, rested his Stetson on a knee and played deaf.

"You're a saint," Hannah said.

"Nope. If I'd said what I was thinking, I'd have started with A for asshole and worked my way through the alphabet."

She contemplated the possibilities. "X would have been a tough one. Let alone Z."

The muscle stitching in David's jaw relaxed. A decent facsimile of a grin appeared. "Any word with more'n three letters is tough for Jessup."

Cheers and camera flashes greeted the Sanity High School marching band giving "Born in the U.S.A." their all. The parade's staging area was less than four blocks away, but the musicians, baton twirlers and cheerleaders were already sweating in their kelly-green, silver-and-crimson uniforms.

Miss Dogwood Days and her preschool princesses followed in a convertible Corvette, then a mirror-polished fire truck. Next was the Kinderhook County Saddle Club in spangled, equestrian splendor, and homemade floats sponsored by civic groups, the 4-H, Boy and Girl Scout troops and various churches. Hannah clapped until her palms stung. The noisy explosion of hometown pride triggered memories of clambering up on Great-uncle Mort's shoulders to wave and laugh and forget about being a no-account Garvey crawling with cooties and wearing a stranger's hand-me-downs.

Behind the last float came a man in a red tuxedo and top hat riding a unicycle. A megaphone amplified his "thrills and chills" spiel and an invitation to the Van Geisen Circus's evening performance at the fairgrounds.

A pair of Asian elephants in tasseled livery rounded the corner. Second-story windows reflected their shapely, blond riders clad in electric-blue chiffon and sequins.

Clowns threatened shrieking children with buckets of water, only to shower them with glitter. Others galumphed along in baggy pants and size-forty shoes, flinging candy from cardboard tubs.

Aerialists swung from trapezes suspended from a chrome frame bolted to a flatbed trailer. A lady magician and her older mentor in black satin capes strewn with moons, suns and stars made cards appear, multiply and vanish with flicks of their wrists.

Acrobats tumbled and cartwheeled. Jugglers' rings and bowling pins gyrated in a blur of whirling motion. Trick cyclists executed wheelies and flips, sure to inspire an epidemic of skinned knees and elbows.

Hannah's nape prickled at the sensation of being watched. An inexplicable kinesis pulled her gaze to the older magician.

His eyes were locked on hers; his gloved hands repeated the card trick's sequence effortlessly, as if performed by a machine. His shoulder-length, dark auburn hair, feathered at the crown and temples, contrasted with the wattled neck of a man well into his sixties.

David startled her by asking, "Do you know that guy?"

She gestured uncertainty. Lots of Chicago nightspots booked touring magicians. That could explain her vague feeling of recognition, but not the one telegraphed by the man's expression and unrelenting stare.

You're imagining things, she thought, turning away to watch the cyclists do back flips off each other's tires. The man wasn't even looking at you. Probably at Mayor Wilkes or that pathetic imitation of the king of rock 'n roll hooting and hollering behind you.

Hannah risked a peripheral glance at the magician's caped back. See? It was only an illusion, like the cards' disappearance.

Absently, she chafed her arms to stave the goose bumps tripping up them.

4

The Kinderhook County fairgrounds were on an elevated plain, a mile or so north of Sanity's city limits. On two sides the land was bounded by a national forest. Old Wire Road demarked the third. To the east, a limestone escarpment beetled over Jinks Creek, a popular site for amateur rock climbers and EMTs summoned to transport party-hearty bubbas with delusions of Spiderman.

Man-made structures were few and functional: creekside pavilions as long as boxcars, a rodeo arena, baseball diamond, dual-purpose cinder-block snack bar–rooftop announcer's booth, rest room–dressing room facilities and storage sheds.

Hannah gulped down a childlike squeak at the red-and-yellow-striped circus tent dominating the grounds. Flags screen-printed with clown faces, elephants and snarling tigers waved from twin spires. Between the tent and parking areas were scores of arts-and-crafts booths, vendors, a petting zoo and pony rides. Portable stages accommodated a gospel trio, a bluegrass quartet and a local garage band.

"No carnival rides?" Hannah asked, a rhetorical

question since there wasn't a Ferris wheel or Tilt-A-Whirl in sight.

"Sorry, sugar. We had complaints out the wazoo about the carnival the Dogwood Days committee hired last year. Pickpockets, rigged games, supplying alcohol and drugs to minors—you name it. No charges were filed against any of the carnies, but the committee decided Van Geisen was a safer bet."

Oh, well. David's kisses induced enough vertigo on terra firma. Hannah relegated making out within reach of the stars to a thick, mental file folder labeled Wishful Thinking.

A teenage parking attendant pointed his orange baton at a section reserved for county law enforcement vehicles, off-duty officers moonlighting as security guards and a first-aid tent.

"Hey, Gary." David held a five-dollar bill out the cruiser's window. "Going to have a good crowd, it looks like."

"Parking's only a buck, Sheriff." The young man's swagger was as reflexive as his wariness. "It's free for you'uns behind the ropes."

David waved the bill. "Aw, this was just cluttering up my pocket anyhow."

Gary hesitated, as if expecting entrapment. "If you've got it to burn, dude." He stuffed the money into the nail apron tied around his waist with a muttered "Thanks."

"Don't mention it." As the cruiser rolled forward, David said, "On second thought, drop a hint on Jessup when he gets here. Nothing makes him happier than one-upping me.''

While the Crown Vic's heavy-duty suspension heaved into and out of fresh and fossilized ruts, David explained that Gary was a high-school dropout and repeat juvenile offender, earning a GED at Sanity's Alternative High School.

''It's a new program to turn kids around before they're too far gone to make something of themselves. Trouble is, too many folks think any slice of the school budget spent on 'bad' kids somehow cheats the 'good' ones.''

''Oh but for the grace of God go they,'' Hannah said.

''Amen to that. Bret Janocek, the teacher who started A.H.S, sweet-talked the committee chairlady—who happens to be his grandmother—into letting students collect parking fees and splitting the proceeds.''

''Sharp man this Janocek,'' Hannah said. ''How much do you think Knox will donate to the cause?''

''Knowing Gary, he'll say I gave him a ten, so Elvis ought to up the ante to—''

David's mouth flattened. He wheeled the cruiser into an open space and stabbed the window's control button with his thumb.

An obligatory *What's wrong?* sprang to Hannah's mind, but she recognized that an internal argument was being waged. Three seconds before curiosity reached the statutory limit, David reached over the seat for his Stetson. "I'll be right back."

Peachy freakin' keen. The last time he told her that, it had been prefaced with a "Sit tight" and followed shortly thereafter by gunfire.

Hannah took the absence of the former and David's hand drawing out his wallet, not his service revolver, as permission to exit, prop her elbows on the roof and snoop.

Except the distance was too great and incoming cars too loud to eavesdrop on his conversation with Gary. Due to David's superior height and bulk, it looked as though he were talking and gesturing to himself.

Presently, he clapped Gary's shoulder and strode back to the cruiser. "I'm starved," he said in lieu of an explanation. "Let me stick a bunch of election claptrap in my pockets, then we'll see about some food."

They were walking hand in hand through aisles of manure-smeared farm trucks, mini-vans, motorcycles, beater sedans and upscale imports, when Hannah said, "Eric Peter Worley would be proud of you."

David voiced the inevitable "Huh?"

"And the longer I hang out with you, the better I'm getting at this detective shtick."

"Guess I'll have to take your word for it," he said, "since I don't have a clue what you're talking about." He frowned down at her. "I have a strong inkling I'm about to find out, though."

Hannah sighed. "It's elementary, my dear Hendrickson. You realized the twenty bucks Gary might liberate from Jessup Knox—as well as anyone else Gary might shine on in a similar fashion—would result in a snotty remark from Jessup concerning it turning up in Gary's pocket.

"Further realizing the good cause didn't justify the means, you told Gary you were wrong to suggest it, told him not to do it and gave him a twenty to make up the difference."

David chuffed. "You snuck up behind—"

"No, I didn't, and I'm not finished yet." Her index finger pronged skyward in proper Sherlockian style. "Therefore, you showed Gary that even sheriffs screw up, a mistake can and should be rectified, and in a subtle way, that you trust him not to steal yours or anyone else's money."

She grinned. "Thus, Deputy Junior-Grade Eric Peter Worley would be proud of you."

David's jaw worked like a cow gnashing her cud.

"So?" she said. "How'd I do?"

Another Cro-Magnon grunt. "You were scary enough when your hunches couldn't hit the broad side of a barn."

If memory served, her hunches carried a five hundred batting average. Okay, the high four hundreds. Even Mark McGwire smacked it foul and struck out on occasion.

She said, "Assuming that's cop-speak for 'Jeez,

you're absolutely right,' I also have a hunch that Gary will still try the ten-begets-twenty on Jessup Knox.''

"Oh, yeah.'' David's chuckle lacked humor. "Am I an inspiration to the youth of today, or what?''

"Trust me. The kid would have thought of it all by himself. Hustling is addictive and it doesn't have to be illegal to be fun.''

"The devil you say.'' He looked at her as though expecting a confession. Surely he knew her better than that.

She made a mental note to phone Bret Janocek at A.H.S. on Monday. An internship and a college scholarship were available through the Friedlich & Friedlich Agency to help young people who needed a break in their favor to prove themselves, and prove everyone else wrong.

If Gary was interested in hustling advertising copy for fun and profit, the fund's founder—an anonymous former account executive—would give him that break. What he made of it was up to him.

Hannah gandered at the overnight village of staked canopies, wood-and-canvas booths and food vendors' mobile kitchens arranged in block formation. Crafts ran the gamut from kitschy crocheted pot holders, home-fired ceramic elves, appliquéd shirts and blown-glass menageries, to oil-painted forests primeval, hand-carved mantels, collectible Christmas ornaments and lamps with gorgeous, leaded-glass shades.

"What'll it be?'' David asked. "Bratwurst and

kraut? Hickory-smoked barbecue? Hoagies? Fried catfish and all the fixin's?''

Hannah inhaled scintillating smells, along with ten-million, free-range fat grams. ''Okay.''

He laughed. ''In that case, let's start with whatever's closest and eat our way toward dessert.''

''Good plan.''

And it would have been if her stomach hadn't wimped out between the ribs, coleslaw and corn-on-the-cob course and a humongous slice of four-cheese pizza.

David hadn't fared much better. The poor guy couldn't take a bite without someone homing in on his side of the picnic table to lodge a complaint or wish him well—and give Hannah a not-so-casual inspection.

A middle-aged man in Sunday overalls and a straw cowboy hat was discussing last year's rash of hay-barn arson fires. Hannah left the serrated pizza crust to the flies, braced an elbow on the table and stretched out her legs on the bench. She felt at one with whomever coined the phrase ''a glutton for punishment.''

Farther down the grassy lane, fairgoers stood three deep watching a woman in a coal-scuttle bonnet, apron and calico dress pour batter through a funnel into a vat of boiling grease. A younger assistant, also frontier attired, scooped a golden-brown Gordian knot of a confection from the kettle. She sifted a blizzard of powdered sugar over it, then passed it to the cashier.

An oven-warm, glazed doughnut aroma wafted from the cook tent. Hannah pressed her quivering lips together before any drool could escape.

The table juddered. David stood to shake hands with Mr. White Hat. Hannah returned a "Nice meeting you," then her gaze drifted to a booth built to resemble a porch, where a woodcarver held court in a high-backed rocker. His whittling and storytelling had drawn a rapt audience...except for an auburn-haired man staring at Hannah.

The distance was greater than during the parade and he'd doffed his celestial cape, but there was no mistaking who he was.

"Hannah," David said. His tone indicated repetition.

She started, snapped "What?" then stammered an apology.

He took a long look over his shoulder and back again. "Care to tell me what's up?"

The man had vanished. Such was a magician's stock-in-trade, wasn't it? "Nothing's up, David. I just thought I saw someone I knew."

He said, "Uh-huh," but she heard, "Bullshit."

Whatever they had, it wasn't a failure to communicate.

They stacked their lunch trash and dumped it in a hooded barrel. David lowered his hat brim to eyebrow level and offered his hand, which she took.

Gasoline-powered generators added an offbeat clatter to strains of "He Has Made Me Glad," a harmonica grieving "I'm So Lonesome I Could Cry" and a thumping hip-hop tune.

Friends hugged dead center in the walkway, teenagers shuffled along like a boredom support group, men guffawed at their own jokes and their wives laughed, as though they couldn't recite the punch lines in their sleep.

David and Hannah meandered through the crowd, him lending an ear to anyone wanting to bend it, while she sorted blondes, brunettes, the bald and the gray from carrottops, Titians, genetic auburns and unnatural hennas.

David was deputizing a Hispanic brother and sister when Hannah sensed the watcher's presence. She finger combed her hair as if she hadn't a care in the world. Her head swiveled with the motion, her palm shielding her eyes.

The man was out there. Gut instinct confirmed it. Dropping all pretense, Hannah weaved on the balls of her feet, visually searching the nooks and crannies and shadowy caverns between structures.

Clad in a black turtleneck and trousers, he was lurking in the shade cast by a drink vendor's trailer. Hannah's heart banged against her ribs. Who was he? What did he want?

She took a step toward him. For a moment, a joyful, terrible longing softened his features. Then he whirled around and was gone.

Hannah stared at the spot, willing him back. Her brows knitted as she pondered the line between

watching and stalking, and wh
than afraid.

Rosina, the younger of David's
on the hem of Hannah's jacket. "W
d'you gots?"

Hannah spread her hands. "Sorry,
don't have any. I'm just the sheriff's hel

The child's huge, dark eyes expressed precisely
what she thought of that answer. The family departed,
the mother lecturing her daughter in Spanish. It
sounded like a lullaby compared to some Hannah had
received when she was Rosina's age.

"Let's check out the dunking booth," David said.
"Jimmy Wayne's shift ought to be starting about
now."

Hannah smiled agreement. The urge for a last look
at the shadowy recess where the man had been was
almost too strong to resist.

Jimmy Wayne McBride, David's handsome-and-
knew-it chief deputy, was teasing a twenty-something
blonde from his perch inside the wood-and-wire en-
closure. Her skintight jeans and midriff top left nothing but minor details to the imagination. A cascade
of palomino curls tumbled to her nipped waist.

If that wasn't reason enough to hate her, not a
molecule of arm flab jiggled when Baseball Barbie
threw a sissy-girl pitch at the release mechanism.

"Gosh darn it." She stamped a foot. "I wanted to
be the first, Jimmy Wayne."

Hannah meowed. The girl hadn't been born yet

e'd had his first. But, gosh darn it, *somebody* d to be Jimmy Wayne's nine hundred and sixth.

Or so Horndog McBride would like everyone to think. From what Claudina had told her, the lanky, career county mountie with the gunslinger mustache and dimples wasn't as love 'em and leave 'em as the reputation he fostered. Nor would David have chosen a mattress maestro for his second-in-command.

Besides, Kinderhook County's population was only about thirty-two thousand.

In the spirit of contributing to another good cause, David bought five chances to drown McBride from the Sanity Police Department D.A.R.E.—Drug Abuse Resistance Education—officer in charge of the booth. Balancing four, grime-gray softballs on his crooked arm, David yelled, "Head's up, Miz Garvey," and tossed her the fifth.

She caught it on the fly, protesting, "You're not roping me into—"

"C'mon, Hannah," Jimmy Wayne jeered, his fingers waggling. "Give it your best shot. I ain't had a good laugh all day."

Fighting words to a die-hard tomboy.

She stepped up to the chalk mark. Spit in her hands. Crouched into a pitcher's stance. Tongue clamped between her teeth, she inhaled on the windup and let 'er rip.

Clack. The ball clipped the top of the target. The booth's trapdoor seat wobbled, but didn't break away.

Well, hell.

"Whoo-eee." McBride swiped his brow with his sleeve. "I do believe my life flashed before my eyes." He motioned at David. "Give her another one, boss. There were some sweet by-and-bys in that rerun I wouldn't mind seeing again."

Hannah laughed, her hands raised in surrender. "Uh-uh, it's your turn, Hendrickson. Show me what you're made of."

His grin was pure lechery. "Can't say I haven't tried before now, sugar."

He took off his sports coat and gave it to her to hold. Losing the shirt would give greater freedom of movement, but Hannah refrained from suggesting it. The object was to get McBride wet.

Backing away a couple of yards, she sidled over until she had the best perspective for a full-body ogle. Baseball Barbie was positioned on David's opposite side. The haughty gaze she leveled at Hannah was answered by a telepathic response that ended in "and the horse you rode in on."

David's opening pitch thumped the canvas backstop. His holster had interfered with his aim. Maybe Hannah should offer to hold it for him, too. Then again, maybe she shouldn't waste her breath.

"Yeehaw, that's showing her." Jimmy Wayne grabbed the board seat a second before his whooping butt boogie would have keeled him into the tank.

Muscles flexed in David's shoulders and rippled across his back. He wouldn't miss twice. Hannah was cringing in sympathy for the target about to be splintered, when a soft voice behind her spoke her name.

She turned, a "Yes?" dying in her throat.

The magician's eyes searched her face. "Your birthday is March 28, isn't it." It was a statement not a question.

She nodded, her mind at once buzzing and completely blank, as if she'd been hypnotized.

"Your mother's name was Caroline Angelina Garvey and you grew up in Effindale, Illinois."

Dizzy, her knees threatening to buckle, Hannah forced out "Who are you? How could you know—"

Callused hands, the fingers swollen and knuckles misshapen, cradled Hannah's chin. "AnnaLeigh said I'd find you someday. I never stopped lookin', sweetheart. Never once in all these years."

Tears welled in his eyes and trickled out the corners. "You don't remember me, do you? I'd hoped you would, but it was too long ago...."

His smile was wistful, yet an inner radiance suffused the lines and seams riven on his face. He gathered Hannah in his arms. "It doesn't matter," he crooned. "Nothing matters now that I've found my little girl again."

5

Hannah pushed the man away, clutching David's jacket like a shield. "Are you trying to tell me you're my *father?*"

He blanched, his dark brown eyes imploring and desperate. "I know it's a shock, sweetheart, but—"

"My father, the circus magician." Four decades of anger, confusion and unanswered prayers boiled up from within. She tipped back her head. Laughter racked out in dry, throaty bursts. "That's rich. God, is that *ever* rich. Helluva disappearing act you pulled on me and Mama, but never once—not once—did it occur to me that my dear old absentee daddy was a magician."

John Doe was the name on her birth certificate. When she was little, she'd imagined that Bambi was her brother and that their father had been shot by a hunter, then the story changed to the mother deer being killed to make it sadder.

Later, she tried to hate the shadow-man who hadn't wanted her, only to decide that blind people must be incapable of hatred. Jesus was the face of good. Hitler epitomized evil. Without a tangible image to dredge up, Hannah might as well have despised the air she breathed.

A late-night, black-and-white movie had filled the void for a while. She'd sat transfixed, enthralled, by the planes of Jack Palance's face. His cold slit eyes and thin lips belonged to a father who'd throw his child and her mother away like yesterday's newspaper.

She'd shoplifted copies of *Silver Screen* and *Photoplay* from newsstands, cut out every picture of Palance she could find and glued them in a notebook she hid under a sofa cushion. Whenever she flipped through her "slam book," Hannah told herself she'd rather not have a daddy than have one like him.

The magician looked nothing like Jack Palance. White rimmed the roots of his dyed auburn hair. His face was an elongated oval, the chin shallow and blunt, and his skin as creased and crosshatched as heirloom linen.

"Please, Hannah." He moved closer. His features constricted with such yearning, a twinge of pity nicked her protective shell. "All I want is a chance to explain."

David's hand clamped the man's shoulder. "Then start with me, mister. Let's see some ID."

Startled, the man glared up at David. His arm winged with deliberate slowness. He fished his wallet from his trouser's pocket with two fingers.

David took the driver's license and waved it toward a drenched but intimidating Jimmy Wayne McBride, standing well behind him. "Why don't you go keep my deputy company while I talk to this lady."

The magician looked to Hannah as though expecting her to intervene, then turned on a heel and strode off.

Her breath coming in sour gasps, she wanted David to hold her, to stroke her hair and tell her it was okay to wish old wishes had expiration dates, but she couldn't tear her eyes away from a candy wrapper smashed in the grass.

A shock, the man had said. *All I want is a chance to explain.* Where would he start? With why he'd abandoned Caroline and his daughter? Or work backward from what gave him the right to ambush her, forty-three years after the fact?

Until David reached out, a handkerchief flashing white in his palm, Hannah hadn't realized she was crying. In a gentle yet firm voice, he said, "I'll trade you."

She exhaled a shuddery sigh, then another. Lips curving into a wan smile, she brushed the wrinkles from his sports coat, wondering how he always sensed when to lend comfort and when to just wait for her world to resettle on its axis.

"I'm okay." She held out his jacket. "Or will be after I smear mascara all over your hankie."

That killer, exclusive-to-her grin crept across David's face. "Then I reckon you might as well honk a few into it, too, while you're at it."

Hannah laughed, her mind scrolling through all

those women's magazine articles she'd read entitled "I Knew I Was in Love When..." None of the answers ever included: *He gave me his nice clean handkerchief and told me to fill 'er up.*

There couldn't be a more absurd, inappropriate, inopportune time to want to jump into his arms and shout, "I love you, David Hendrickson."

Not now. Not in the midst of an emotional cyclone. Not in front of rubberneckers hoping the FBI's Ten Most Wanted was about to be reduced to nine. And not to Sheriff Hendrickson, jotting vital statistics gleaned from the man's driver's license into the spiral notebook he'd taken from his coat pocket.

He looked up. "Are you okay to answer some questions?"

She nodded. Strange, how the businesslike shift felt like ballast.

"From what I overheard, the fellow over there claims he's your father."

Hannah reiterated their conversation, adding that she didn't know who the AnnaLeigh was he'd mentioned.

"Does the name Reilly Boone mean anything to you?"

It didn't, but Hannah allowed long-term memory to take a crack at it. "No, but I never knew my father's real name. My mother refused to tell anyone."

"Any idea why?"

"No." She shrugged. "After a while, I stopped

asking. As much as it upset her, I figured she must have had her reasons.''

''Uh-huh. I suppose she did.'' By David's tone, nothing justified that kind of secret being buried with her.

Hannah had asked again, the day before Caroline died. Her mother had turned away, her back bowed, her legs drawing up in a fetal crouch. ''You're mine,'' she answered just as she always had. ''That's all that matters.''

David said, ''Have you ever seen Reilly Boone before today?''

Another simple question that should elicit a simple response. ''Like I told you during the parade, I don't think I have, but there is a—a *familiarity*.''

''You've seen him several times since the parade though, haven't you.''

It was an accusation and it angered her. She suddenly knew why David had worn his hat tipped forward after they finished lunch. He'd spotted Boone, too, and had watched him watching her.

The spy versus spy versus spy scenario would be comical if it wasn't so overbearing. IdaClare and Company would be crushed when they found out they'd missed an opportunity to make surveillance a tag-team event.

''I can't speak for you, Sheriff, but I only saw Mr. Boone twice.''

His hackles raised almost visibly. Good. It evened

the score and the attitude. ''Why didn't you tell me the first time you saw him?''

''For the same reason you didn't tell me.''

''And what might that be?'' David said. ''Seeing as how you can read my mind and all.''

''Because he kept his distance, and he didn't appear to be a threat.''

Gray overwhelmed the blue in David's eyes. In them, her judgment rated a solid zero. After all, between the two of them, she wasn't the one wearing a badge. ''How about when Boone accosted you? Did you feel threatened then?''

''Accosted?'' Heat warmed her cheeks. ''Reilly Boone didn't threaten me at any time, in any way. Got that?''

''Did he ask you for money? Try to get you to go off somewhere with him?''

''No, he did *not*.''

David gestured frustration. ''What's going on, Hannah? Why are you being so defensive? A total stranger—''

''Knew my birthday. Where I was born. My mother's middle name.''

''That's public record. Easy for anyone to find. Easier than ever these days, thanks to the Internet.'' David's voice softened. ''Your mother's full name is probably on her grave marker.''

''Oh no, it isn't. Not even a middle initial. She hated Angelina. My grandmother mocked her, called her Angel whenever Mama did the slightest thing wrong. I'd all but forgotten she *had* a middle name.''

David's sigh must have originated between his toes. He stowed the notebook, pen and driver's license in his pocket and took her hands in his. ''Look at me.''

She shook her head.

''I'm not the enemy.''

''Then why does it feel like it?''

''C'mon, sugar. That guy knocked you for a loop, I'll grant you that. But you have more sense than six people put together. Just because some two-bit magician rattled off a few stats about you and your mother doesn't mean he's your father.''

''Of course it doesn't. Except public record or not, why do the research?''

''Maybe he didn't,'' David said. ''Maybe Boone lived in Effindale when you were a kid, or has relatives there.''

A valid argument on the surface, but ''Grandma Garvey, Great-aunt Lurleen and Great-uncle Mort died before I started high school. My mother has been dead for twenty-five years. I left Effindale a month after her funeral. Other than visiting the cemetery on my way to Valhalla Springs, I've never been back.''

''Okay,'' David countered, ''but you've said yourself that the smaller the town the longer the memory. When nothing newsworthy trips their trigger, 'I wonder whatever became of such-and-such' is a gold-plated tongue wagger.''

"True, except I'm in Kinderhook County, Missouri, not Effindale, Illinois. Nobody knew where I went when I left there. Nobody knows I live here now. So how did Reilly Boone pick me out of a crowd at the parade?"

David's thumbs kneaded the backs of her hands, strumming the fine bones and veins in a rhythmic motion that should have been soothing. "I can't answer that. I've just seen too many folks flimflammed by con artists posing as long-lost children, parents, spouses—even high-school sweethearts—to swallow what that guy's feeding you."

"Well, thank God you're here to save naive, stupid-assed me from making a fool of myself."

David's arms dropped as though he'd been slapped. "That's not what I meant."

"Sure it is," she said. "And you're right. But that doesn't necessarily mean I'm wrong to want to hear what else Boone has to say."

Hannah regretted hurting him, but raw emotion defied, even abhorred, calm, cool logic. "This is going to sound crazy, but whoever Reilly Boone is, and despite all the facts he could have thrown at me, he *knew* Angelina was the key to my skeleton closet."

Reilly Boone walked between David and Hannah to the circus's "backyard" where his motor home was parked. Boone wanted privacy for their talk and they'd agreed.

Silence had tagged along with them after he said,

"If I had it to do over again, I wouldn't have grabbed you the way I did," and apologized for frightening her.

Hannah didn't ask if any hindsighted regrets applied to forty-three missed birthdays and Christmases. Of the many attitudes at her disposal, hostility probably wasn't conducive to a budding father–daughter relationship.

Not that she believed Boone was her father. Tens of millions of people had brown eyes and moles at the cusp of their jawlines. Noses with a slight bump below the bridge weren't rare, either.

The circus tent loomed like a striped, geometric mountain of stretched canvas. Open flaps exhaled the scent of scalped grass, manure, fresh hay and the musk of animals who earned their keep under thousand-watt spotlights.

Along the midway, townies chatted with performers dressed in workaday T-shirts and jeans. Three stair-step kids straddling an elephant's howdah yelled, "Che-eese," while the trainer snapped a three-dollar souvenir Polaroid they'd beg their parents to buy.

Being on home turf cured the magician's reticence. He nattered on about American Indians performing ceremonial illusions centuries before the *Mayflower* docked. Pointing to a poster attached to the ticket booth, he told them the first trapeze artist was Jules Leotard, who originated the three-man "flying" routine, but was immortalized for the full-body costume he invented.

"Know what the Ringling Brothers was called back in the 1880s?" he asked.

"No," Hannah said, and couldn't have cared less.

Voice pitched like an announcer's, Boone said, "Ringling Brothers United Monster Shows, Great Double Circus, Royal European Menagerie, Museum, Caravan and Congress of Trained Animals."

"I'd have paid to see that myself," David said. "With all that printed on them, folks must have needed two hands to carry the tickets."

Boone asked if Hannah was coming to the show that evening. She said no. If David had planned on it, fine. What they did with their evening was their business, not Reilly Boone's.

He pointed to the small top—all tents being tops in circus parlance—known as Clown Alley. Adjacent to "the spec," an open area with the same purpose as a theater's wings, was the cookhouse trailer and dining hall where workers and some performers took their meals. Tonight's bill of fare smelled like fried chicken, yeast rolls and apple pie.

David asked, "How long have you been with the circus, Mr. Boone?"

"Reilly will do, lest somebody thinks I'm putting on airs."

David nodded. Hannah's mouth crimped.

"I was a first of May—that's circus lingo for a greenhorn—by the time I turned fifteen." Reilly smiled. "Any man that says he'd druther swing a pick in a Kentucky coal mine as shovel up animal dung is either lying or too dumb to understand the difference.''

Reilly looked at Hannah, then away, as though consciously editing remarks before making them. ''Slow but sure, I'd worked up to assistant handler, then I wintered with a magician and his missus. I caught his trade real quick, but it took another year and a half practicing every spare I got before I had a ring-three act. A couple-three more skipped by before anybody'd book me center.''

The center ring was the largest and fronted the higher-priced reserve seats. Hannah assumed ring one was inside the main entrance. Ring three must be nearest the back entrance—the circus equivalent of Siberia.

''Don't s'pose you've ever heard of The Amazing Aurelius, have you?''

Honest David Hendrickson said no. Hannah, who'd waltzed by corporate gendarmes, maître d's and publicists at the drop of a name, fibbed. ''I most certainly have.''

''Well, that was my moniker for thirty-three years,'' Boone said.

''You performed in Chicago, didn't you? The Gale Street Inn? Or was it the Ford Center?''

''No...'' He seemed loath to disappoint her. ''The money's good, but I never had a yen for club or theater dates. Playing to the upper crust makes my collar itch and close-ups aren't my kind of act.''

So much for a logical explanation for her déjà vu.

"You said The Amazing Aurelius *was* your, er, moniker? Did you change it for some reason?"

Reilly stared into the middle distance. His expression resembled a career army officer reduced to sacking groceries to supplement a pension. "Arthritis changed it for me."

He rotated his hands, the fingers clawed, the knuckles more swollen than they'd been earlier. "Liniment helped a while. The doc gave me pills, but they tear up my insides. I take 'em when I have to, but you can't perform when you've got a gutful of ground glass.

"My wife monkeyed with the act, so the audience would think me assisting her with some of the setups and her selling the flash was how we'd always done it."

Glancing at Hannah then David, he made a *que sera sera* gesture. "AnnaLeigh's been the headliner since we signed on with the Van Geisens a couple of years ago. She sells it like I never could."

His lips curved up, but didn't engage the fantailed laugh lines at his eye corners. "Talent I got—or used to have—but nobody ever whistled and stamped their feet when the spotlight hit *me*."

His tone was light, but implications clanged in Hannah's mind. Reilly was proud of his wife's talent yet bitter about his disability and demotion from magician to magician's assistant. AnnaLeigh's beauty was also a source of pride—and perhaps jealousy.

The circus's backyard was a lively hybrid of a

K.O.A. campground, truck stop and zoo where roust-abouts and performers relaxed, caught up on daily chores, home schooled their children, practiced routines and socialized.

A convoy of tractor-trailer units, flatbeds, animal haulers, cab-over vans, pickups, travel trailers and motor homes were circled like a pioneer wagon train. One cream-colored behemoth stood out like a tuba in a string quartet.

The Amazing AnnaLeigh in gilt-edged, cobalt letters dominated the coach's sidewall. Silver and gold stars wreathed the windows, windshield and fender skirts. Only its roll-out awning and the enclosed trailer hitched at the back had escaped celestial adornment.

Several other vehicles bore Van Geisen Circus logos, with tiger, lion, elephant and clown decals. A pastel mural on the Flying Zandonatti Family's home-on-wheels depicted two aerialists gliding among the clouds.

From an advertising perspective, Mrs. Boone's rolling billboard was a dog and pony show.

''Some rig you've got here, Reilly,'' David said. He moved to inspect the motor home's snubbed front end. ''Must have set you back a buck or two.''

''Enough to retire on, but what AnnaLeigh wants—''

''Hey, Reilly.'' A sandy-haired, muscular man in cutoffs and a sweatshirt winked knowingly at Hannah.

"Sorry to horn in on y'all, but I need to talk to Vera and can't find her anywhere. You seen her around?"

"Check the ticket trailer," Reilly said. "Vera or Frank are bound to be there."

"He is, but she took off somewhere in the pickup. Didn't lock the trailer, leave a note where she went or nothing."

"Ain't like her not to lock up the till." Reilly opened the motor home's door. "Knowing Frank, she told him all right, and whatever she said went in one ear and out the other."

"Yeah." The man walked off, grinning. "That's what she'll say when she gets back, anyhow."

Hannah's eyes needed a moment to adjust from sunlight to the interior gloom. A faint formaldehyde odor lingered in the air, along with the scent of hair spray and a note of musky perfume.

Contrary to the garish exterior, the motor home's cabin was as impersonal as a showroom model and immaculate to the point of, well, anal retentive, if not obsessive compulsive. Hannah wasn't a slob, but the beer can crumpled in a corner of the galley's counter, mangled tube of saltines, bottle of club soda and antacid tablet's foil wrapper on the table wouldn't be as conspicuous in her kitchen.

Reilly insisted they take the cockpit's high-backed, swivel chairs, then he peered at the closed pocket door at the rear of the coach. "AnnaLeigh must still be napping. She was queasy when she got up this

morning. I told her to skip the parade, but nothin'
doin'.''

As he started down the hallway, Hannah said,
"Please, Reilly, don't wake her. Let her sleep."

"I was, uh—" He waved at another door. "The
donniker's this a'way, too."

In other words, such as plain English, the bathroom.

David laid his hand over Hannah's. "What do you
think about postponing this until later?"

Splaying her fingers, she captured his and curled
all ten into a fist sandwich. "You really don't have
to stay."

His head tilted in a speculative pose. "Haven't we
already had this conversation?"

"Uh-huh."

"Thought so. How'd it come out?"

"You're here, aren't you?"

David knew she was teasing, but his expression
shifted to pensive. "Yeah, but I wouldn't mind waiting outside to give you and Reilly some privacy."

Hannah nibbled on her lower lip, weighing the pros
and cons. God only knew what, if any, family secrets
Reilly might spill. What would David think of her
if...

The coach vibrated with Reilly's approaching foot-
falls. Hannah clamped David's fingers. "This is a
trust thing, isn't it?"

"Kinda."

"Then stay. I'm sick to death of secrets. All keeping them does is make them a bigger damn deal than whatever they're trying to hide.''

Reilly offered them soft drinks, which they declined, then seated himself on a built-in lounge. Leaning forward, he propped his elbows on his knees. Muffled laughter, barking dogs and an engine revving seeped in through the motor home's sidewalls.

"I, uh, gotta tell you, this ain't the way I imagined our get-together. I don't know where to start.''

Hannah curbed the impulse to prompt him. According to Parkinson's Law, volume expands to fill a void. Its applications weren't exclusive to walk-in closets and chocolate binges.

Reilly's eyes remained downcast, but his features softened. He smiled the way people do when a memory resurrects a special time, a place, a person.

"Caroline Garvey was the closest thing to an angel I've ever seen before or since," he said. "Skin as cream-white as milk, big hazel eyes and copper-colored hair clean down to her waist.''

His gaze flicked to Hannah. "I know what your grandma would say to that, and it'd be pure meanness. At seventeen, Caroline was so pretty, just looking at her made my heart swell too big for my chest.

"Nobody believes in love at first sight lest they've felt it. Sure, when we ran away together, we were too young and stupid to realize how young and stupid we were, but...''

Reilly's fingertips joined. The knuckles flexed like a five-legged spider on a mirror. "She hated school, hated her folks, hated Effindale so much that any road to anywhere was an adventure waiting to happen.

"Except we never stayed in one place long enough for her to have one. Regular people just *think* all they do is work, eat and sleep. Ain't no such thing as weekends and holidays in the circus. Nothing real glamorous about bunking with critters that don't know day from night, and bathing the best you can hunkered over a washtub."

Hannah heard her mother yell, "Quit whining about the water being cold and set yourself down in that tub, missy. The gas company'll have their money in a day or two. This is the Ritz compared to when I had to splash off in a damn ol' rusty bucket."

She'd always assumed her mother was referring to her childhood home's lack of indoor plumbing. No matter. If asked, Caroline would have dodged the specifics, Hannah's bullshit detector would have hit high C and she'd have had another secret to stew about.

"Worst of all," Reilly said, "Caro was terrified of the animals, and once they smell fear there's no mercy in 'em. Got to where every time one looked at her crossways, she'd beg me to beat them, make 'em more afraid of her than she was of them.

"I didn't understand then, but it was more than fear talking. Caro was worn-out, homesick..." He paused, again grappling with memories that time hadn't dulled.

Hannah squirmed in her seat, as if posture were an antidote for sympathy. She shouldn't have come. She didn't want to feel sorry for Reilly Boone. Didn't need more evidence of her mother's shortcomings.

"The circus was home to me," Reilly said, "but for Caroline? Well, it was like somebody'd dropped her smack in the middle of a foreign country. First, she tried too hard to get along, then she wouldn't give anybody the time of day. I nagged her to do this, do that, lost my temper, babied her, then just kept my distance, thinking that's what she wanted.

"We were playing a date in northern Michigan when Caro said she couldn't hack it another day." Reilly's expression was as thunderstruck as it must have been at the time. "The top was going up. I was dug in, haulin' back on the rope. The canvas boss was hollerin', 'Take it, make it,' and there was Caroline, all scrubbed and pretty as a picture, tellin' me it was the circus or her."

He wiped his brow with the back of his hand. "What was I s'posed to do? Tell the gang to take five? I said we'd talk later, after the show. Unbeknownst to me, she'd already hitched a ride off some yahoos that lived downstate."

Hannah said, "Do you mean my mother hitchhiked all the way back to Effindale?"

He nodded. "Left before I knew she was gone. We were saving our pennies to get married on, after the season ended. The money was half hers, but all she took was clothes and a stuffed puppy dog I gave her."

Lies. Had to be. From the *Romeo and Juliet* beginning to the *Tom Sawyer* end. That, or Reilly's memory was ungodly selective. Young and stupid, yes, but Caroline wouldn't have left him and the mon—

An image flashed of a ratty toy spaniel dangling from a ribbon thumbtacked to the wall in her mother's bedroom. The dog's tongue and a glass eye were missing, and the fur had faded to a sickly yellow, but Hannah would sooner steal the baby Jesus from the crèche on the First Baptist's Church lawn at Christmas than lay a curious finger on Caroline Garvey's second-most prized possession.

Reilly paced between the door and the galley. "I didn't know Caro was pregnant until months after you were born. I quit the circus. We tried to make a go of it, but I couldn't keep a job, couldn't settle down. Caro said she'd be damned if she'd compete with a mistress I cared more about than her and the baby."

"Meaning the circus." Hannah snorted derision. "Well, I guess you proved Mama right, didn't you?"

"Easy, sugar," David said.

Easy? she thought, glaring at him. That's precisely what it was for Reilly to dump his teenage lover and their child to fend for themselves.

"I had to make a living, Hannah. For you and Caroline." Reilly halted, his face flushed scarlet. "I didn't know but one way to earn it."

"Correction," she said. "There was only one way you chose to earn it, Reilly."

"We *loved* each other. All we needed was a place where both of us fit."

He slumped against the doorjamb, gazing out the

porthole window as if he was still looking for that mystical place where a vagabond and a small-town girl could live happily ever after.

"Caroline promised, if I quit animals for any other kind of an act, she'd go back on the road with me...as my wife."

David and Hannah exchanged glances. He'd already told them he spent three or four years learning the magician's trade.

"I broke more promises than she did," he said. "I got lonesome, too. The same as her, booze helped me forget. Made me sleep. Tricked me into seeing Caro's face on every girl I was with."

He dug out his billfold for the second time that afternoon. "You were four, going on five, the last time me and your mother were together. We told each other everything we'd done, hoping it'd wipe the slate for a clean start."

Hannah laughed. She couldn't help herself. "Whose brilliant idea was that?"

"Ours." Anger flared in his eyes. "And both of us paid the price a hundred times over."

Hannah examined the cropped, wrinkled photographs he offered. All were taken from a distance. The gangly kid in each was scarcely an inch tall and recognizable as female only by her clothing and lopsided pigtails.

"I presume these are supposed to be me, but—" She squinted at the junkyard dog of a bicycle the girl was astride. Mismatched tires. One fender blue, the other red, attached to a boy's green spray-painted frame. There couldn't be two of them in existence.

"You bought me ice cream," she whispered. "At the park."

Reilly knelt on one knee on the carpeted riser. "I sure did, sweetheart. An Eskimo Pie *and* a Drumstick. Then you wanted to play on the swings." Lower lip trembling, he said, "Higher, mister. Make me go higher."

Tears spilled down her face. "Why didn't you tell me who you were?"

"Because you didn't remember me," he said softly. "And because I couldn't stay."

David said, "Those pictures were taken over several years."

Reilly nodded, shuffling through them. "After Caroline and I split up for good, I still sent her money, care of General Delivery, but she wouldn't answer my letters. Only way to know if my little girl was all right was to sneak into town and try and see for myself.

"That day in the park was the next-to-last time I went back." He smiled. "You were smart. Too smart. If I'd kept popping up outta nowhere, you'd have recognized me and started asking questions."

Hannah dashed the tears from her eyes. "What if I had? Didn't I have a right to know who you were?"

Reilly struggled to his feet. "I was going to tell you when you turned eighteen. We played some late dates that year, so it was almost Thanksgiving before

I got to Effindale. When I saw an old man was living in your trailer, I asked around town about Caroline.''

He jerked his chin at David. ''Spent a couple of nights in the slammer there, too, after I punched the bastard that said, 'Caroline Garvey? Why, that no-account whore done drunk herself to death last spring.'''

His eyes returned to Hannah's. ''Nobody knew where you'd gone, sweetheart. But like I told you, I never stopped lookin'.''

Hand aloft, her head wobbling from side to side, Hannah said, ''Those pictures are too small and blurry for me to identify anything except the bicycle. That day in the park, I was nine, maybe ten years old. How could you possibly have recognized me today?''

It must have been the angle of the light filtering through the windshield curtain that erased decades of rough-and-tumble living from Reilly's face. He studied Hannah, yet seemed to be looking through her, past her, beyond her.

''Mirrors lie. They reflect what we want to see, what we're used to seeing. I don't expect you to believe me, but you are the spittin' image of your mama.''

''No. I'm not.'' Hannah turned to David. ''You've seen Caroline's picture on my dresser. I don't look anything like her, do I?''

''Well, now—''

The motor home's door jerked open. AnnaLeigh Boone, her complexion more ashen than olive, stopped in her tracks. She glowered at Hannah, then David.

Reilly's head swung toward the hallway and back to his wife. "Where the hell have you been? I thought you were sleeping off a bellyache."

"I, er, I—" AnnaLeigh slid away from him. "Vera needed something from town. I went with her." She struck a regal pose. "Is that all right with *you?*"

"Sure, hon." Reilly noted the absence of a purse or packages. "It just seems funny—"

"I don't mean to be rude," AnnaLeigh said to Hannah, "but you'll have to excuse us. We have a show to get ready for."

"What's eating you?" Reilly gripped her arm. "Rude ain't the half of it. This is Hannah. My *daughter.* And her friend, Sheriff Hendrickson."

The color returned to AnnaLeigh's aristocratic face in a rush. Dithering with the tails of the oversize shirt knotted at her waist, she appeared to be thinking six things at once.

"I'm so embarrassed, I could just die," she said, and shook hands with her guests. "Reilly's terrible about dragging lot lice home with him, and I thought he'd gone out and done it again."

"Lot lice?"

Reilly's barroom laugh nettled the broken capillaries in his cheeks. "It sounds bad, Sheriff, but it's what we call hard-core circus fans. They've got clubs and newsletters—the whole ball of wax. Love to visit and swap stories."

AnnaLeigh appraised Hannah as one would a child, although they were about the same age. Or, a quiet vibe suggested, as one might gauge a rival.

From her whiplike black braid to the ruby toenails peeking from her designer mules, The Amazing AnnaLeigh projected haughtiness. It didn't quite conceal the high-voltage anxiety humming beneath the surface. Her hooded sloe-eyes didn't mask repeated glances at the shield pinned to David's jacket, either.

"I've told Reilly since the day we met, if it was meant for him to find you, he would," she said. "But I can hardly believe you're really here."

Her breath caught, the quaver in her voice reflecting genuine happiness. "It must be like a miracle jumping up in the middle of a hailstorm for you, though."

Miracle was a tad strong, but the hailstorm analogy was on target.

AnnaLeigh allowed Reilly's arm to encircle her waist. "This lady's more than my wife and my partner. She's been my salvation for going on fifteen years. Broke me of all my bad habits." He chuckled. "Well, most of 'em, anyhow."

Spotlighted by their smiles, Hannah fidgeted at this bizarre edition of a fairy tale. If Reilly was her father, then AnnaLeigh was her stepmother—with or without the wicked connotation.

What she wouldn't give for a fairy godmother to conjure up a coach-and-four and get them the hell out of here.

"This calls for a celebration, but we don't..." AnnaLeigh clapped her hands. "Hey, we can pretend club soda is champagne, can't we?"

While AnnaLeigh played hostess, questions and replies were volleyed back and forth regarding Hannah's job at Valhalla Springs. The conversation didn't lag, but the drink-dispensing seemed to take longer than it should have.

Hannah lofted her glass and downed the hatch before Reilly could offer an unwanted, albeit eagerly anticipated, toast. All four almost swallowed their ice cubes when someone pounded on the door.

"Where's the fire?" Reilly yelled to the unseen visitor. Head craned around the jamb, he paused, then said, "Can't you see I'm— All right, all right." An over-the-shoulder "Back in a minute" preceeded his exit.

David slapped his thigh. "Well, I reckon these people do have a show to put on."

Who needs a fairy godmother when Hendrickson's on the scene?

"Yes." AnnaLeigh glanced at the door. "We do need to get changed."

Hannah left hers and David's glasses on the counter, turned, then started when AnnaLeigh materialized beside her. She encased Hannah's hands in an icy grip. "You will come to the show tonight."

Her eyes bored into Hannah's. Something tickled across Hannah's palm and her fingers closed around a slip of paper.

"I'll get you seats," AnnaLeigh whispered. "Front-row center. Vera Van Geisen will have passes for you at the ticket trailer."

Hannah didn't argue, but the section reserved in advance for Valhalla Springs' residents would do just fine.

AnnaLeigh kissed her cheek, then the other. "I know you won't let me down."

6

David leaned against the cinder-block rest-room building to add Reilly Boone's Texas trailer plate numbers and the motor home's make and model to his notes.

The building's interior walls amplified voices like an echo chamber—teenage girls, by the pitch and language. Hannah must be either rolling her eyes so far back she could see her brain, or stuffing her fist in her mouth to keep from screaming.

David surveyed the Dogwood Days section of the fairgrounds. Twilight came early in river valleys. A majority of the booths were shuttered, or in the process. Folks arriving for the circus wouldn't fit a vendor's definition of a live one. Some would dawdle and shoot the breeze, but weren't about to lug around a quilt, an oil-painted saw blade or a flat of baby begonias all evening.

A giggly trio scuffled out the rest room's exit. They looked at David, quick-stepped several yards, then burst out laughing, grabbing each other's jacket sleeves and running for the generator-powered halogens illuminating the big top.

David doubted if Hannah had been a giggler at their age. Not sourpussed and serious, either. More likely the type a guy could tease and talk to about nothing and everything, then whip his butt shooting hoops.

"She still is." David chuckled. "Except I figure I could take her in a round of horse."

"Talk to yourself often?" Hannah inquired, her hip-cocked stance backlit by the interior light.

"Nope." David pushed off from the building and stuck his notebook in his pocket. "Just thinking out loud. Different thing altogether."

She'd brushed her hair, the mascara smudges were gone and her lips were glossy, as though freshly licked. The strain of a hellacious afternoon showed, but Hannah was nearly as bullet proof as she thought she was. It was the gleam in her eyes that worried him.

Her hand slipped into his. They walked toward the crowd stockpiling snacks, souvenirs and balloons that would eventually swim for the ceiling like mutant tadpoles.

David said, "I don't suppose you know where the Boones are scheduled in the program, do you?"

"No." She looked up. "Why?"

"I need to go by the courthouse." That much was true. "It shouldn't take long, but we might miss a few of the opening acts."

"Oh?" She raked her fingers through her hair—a tip-off that something was stewing underneath. "Um,

well, I could stay here… You know, save you a
seat?'' Her voice hiked a notch. ''That way, if you
get stuck at the office for some reason, no problem.
I can catch a ride home on the Valhalla Springs shuttle.''

Suspicions confirmed. Hannah wanted shed of him
for a while, too.

''Sounds like a plan,'' David said. ''On one condition.''

She laughed. ''No guarantees, but I'll do my best
to keep Delbert off the high wire.''

''That isn't the condition I had in mind.''

A short pause. ''I'm not going to like it, am I.''

''I don't know why not,'' David said. ''Just tell me
why AnnaLeigh had you in a death grip before we
left the motor home.''

Another pause, a second laugh, but this one anx-
ious. ''My, my, how you do exaggerate, Sheriff.''

''Could be.'' He shrugged. ''Come to think of it,
I'm probably exaggerating any need to traipse off to
the courthouse, too.'' He squeezed her hand. ''What
the hey. I'll stick around till the show's over, take
you home, *then* go by the office.''

She didn't deserve the rope-a-dope, but something
was up, and he wouldn't trust Reilly or AnnaLeigh
Boone if they'd been baptized in the River Jordan by
Billy Graham himself. Hannah didn't trust them either, but that would only encourage her to play along.

''Shit.''

He grinned. "Remember, you're the one who said you were sick of secrets."

"Don't quote me back to me." A sigh preceded capitulation. "AnnaLeigh slipped me a note asking me to meet her in the parking lot by the pony rides after the show. Alone. Specifically, no cops. She said she needs my help."

"Where's the note?"

"One flush closer to the sewage treatment plant."

Terrific. "All right, I'll make sure I'm back from town way before the grand finale."

"No cops was underlined, David." She spun around to face him. "And you didn't see the look in AnnaLeigh's eyes when she slipped me that note."

"Tell me about it."

"She was scared. Angry. A little desperate—make that more desperate than she let on, to ask the apparent prodigal daughter for help."

David maintained his composure, but not without effort. *Apparent* prodigal daughter? He'd suspected Reilly had hooked her with that day-at-the-park story. The son of a bitch.

Hannah leaned in to tap his badge. "Finding out who AnnaLeigh is afraid of is why you'll promise not to skulk around and spy on us, and why I promise to tell you everything she says afterward."

"Well, now, the who is pretty evident, isn't it?"

"Yes, but I want to hear it from her."

"It isn't smart to meet anyone alone at night in a parking lot," David said.

"Except telling the person you're meeting that the sheriff knows where you are, who you're with and that she has five minutes to spill her guts is a verbal seat belt."

David couldn't have agreed less. Priorities reshuffled. The argument Hannah expected would waste precious time. A swift concession wouldn't fool her for a second.

He served. She volleyed. He protested, grunted and groaned, then said, "Okay, but Ms. Amazing had better talk fast. Five minutes is all she's going to get."

"Promise?"

"That I won't spy on you?" He kissed the top of her head. "Promise."

Inside the big top, old-fashioned calliope music tootled from a Surround Sound system. The air was muggy with body heat radiating from a thousand spectators, the smell of roasted peanuts and buttered popcorn and the pulsating excitement a live performance generates.

The Valhalla Springs contingent was larger than Hannah had anticipated. Or maybe it just seemed that way when a section of the grandstand erupted in "Yoo-hoos," "Here we ares" and waving arms.

Relief whisked through her. IdaClare and Company knew nothing about Reilly Boone. With them, and without David's presence to remind her otherwise, Hannah could act like everything was hunky-dory. Bring on the clowns, the daring young men on the flying trapeze, flame-jumping tigers and acrobats extraordinaire, and it might become a self-fulfilling prophesy.

At that realization, Hannah didn't know whether to laugh or curse. *Have to go to the office,* my foot. David's decampment was as perceptive as it was strategic. For her, it provided a much-needed diversion. For him, a chance for a private background check on Reilly—which David had been itching to do from the moment he'd seen Reilly's ID.

The rat. A wise and wonderful one, but a rat, in or out of uniform, was still a rat.

Fine and dandy. If he wasn't forthcoming with Reilly's records, she'd renege on her tell-all promise. AnnaLeigh might not divulge anything worth repeating, but David, whose word was law in more ways than one, wouldn't know that.

"'Ey, ladybug," Delbert said. "What's with the cat-that-ate-the-canary look?"

"This is my happy face."

"Uh-huh." He followed her gaze to the sliver of bleacher between the steps and his gold-over-yellow, houndstooth-check posterior. Motioning "scoot over" to Marge Rosenbaum and the others seated on his right, he bellowed, "For the love of Mike. Slap those knees together, girls, and give us some room down here."

Every woman within earshot, which was approximately half the arena, sat bolt upright. Hannah slunk onto the sudden six-foot space beside Big Mouth Bisbee and tried to make herself small.

IdaClare, seated behind them, locked a middle finger and thumb into a semi-obscene OK sign and zeroed in on Delbert's skull. Ready...aim..

"Yeow-w-ww." He clapped his hand to the thunk site, his mauve turtle-necked neck craning eighty degrees. "What the *hell'd* you do that for?"

"Behave yourself." IdaClare's tone could still stop her fifty-year-old, entrepreneur son in his tracks. "Or I'll send you to the car."

"Oh, yeah? Bean me like that again and you'll walk home, you crazy old bat."

Hannah said, "I take it you guys didn't ride the shuttle?"

Delbert huffed out his chest. "No, and this is the thanks I get for running a jitney service."

"Careful," Marge warned, "or IdaClare will thunk you for lying." She leaned over to see past Delbert's akimboed arms. "He volunteered to drive this afternoon when we went by your cottage to ask if you wanted to go shopping for bridesmaid dresses."

Rosemary, sandwiched between IdaClare and Leo, said, "We forgot all about you spending the afternoon with your sheriff." She paused for a beatific smile and a dreamy sigh. "So, we did the next best thing."

Hannah gestured as though wiping fog from a window. To Delbert, she said, "You were at my cottage this afternoon?"

"Durn tootin'. Good thing I happened by before

Bob Davies got himself in too deep, fixing that dimple in your ceiling.''

Dimple? If the crater in her breakfast room was a dimple, Pike's Peak was a hill with ambition.

Delbert's chin took a bow. "Don't you worry, ladybug. After I set Bob straight, we got the job done right.''

Hannah offered up a prayer to the god of Sheetrock, plus an all points bulletin to any and all deities, that she wouldn't find her maintenance supervisor's resignation impaled on her desk with a giant screwdriver.

Turning sideward, she asked IdaClare, "And what might be the next best thing to taking me shopping?"

The three female conspirators exchanged impish grins. Rosemary said, "Taking your *dress*." She didn't tack on "you silly girl." She didn't have to.

"We had the awfulest time deciding what you should wear to the wedding, dear," IdaClare said. "Marge held out for that darling silk suit with the peplum, until I pulled out the velvet gown at the back of your closet."

Clasping her hands to her bosom, she gushed, "I guess I don't have to tell you, the vote was unanimous."

Sometimes life's little ironies packed a sledgehammer wallop. Hannah had bought the dress eight years ago when Friedlich & Friedlich had been nominated for a CLIO. Jarrod, as usual, went AWOL at the last minute, so Jack Clancy had filled in as Hannah's escort.

Fueled by hope and a magnum of champagne, they'd ended up in Jack's hotel room, only to discover that love can't conquer all, no matter how badly you want it to.

Many times she'd almost thrown the gown away, then heard her Great-uncle Mort say, "Ya gotta take the bitter with the sweet." No bitterness was attached to the dress, or the memory. Sweet it wasn't, either, and would never be, but hers and Jack's friendship had endured, and that was close enough.

"Ach, it is elegant, you will be," Leo said. "The color, it is darker than my Rosemary had in mind, but is her—what you call it—her prerogative to change. Yes?"

IdaClare flapped a hand. "And the shop girl who helped us this afternoon was the sweetest thing. She slipped on your gown while Marge and I tried on our suits, then we all went outside to let Rosemary see the effect in natural light."

"Lovely," Rosemary assured. "Absolutely lovely."

Okay, God. Bob Davies's resignation I can live with. Wearing that dress to the wedding—wearing it *anywhere*—would be like a *Titanic* survivor saving her lifeboat ensemble for her next transatlantic cruise.

All I ask is for a twenty-four-carat excuse and instant liposuction so that *darling* silk suit with the peplum won't make my butt look like a beach ball with a ruffle stapled to it.

Rosemary squeezed Hannah's arm. "Would you believe, the florist had ribbon to match your gown, Marge's outfit and IdaClare's? She finished the bows for the candelabra on the spot *and* cut the streamers for the bouquets."

"An omen, it is," Leo said. "Right?"

Slowly, Hannah swiveled around and laid her head on Delbert's shoulder.

"You okay, ladybug?"

"Oh, yeah. This is my hunky-freakin'-dory face."

The Kinderhook County Courthouse was the architectural equivalent of a blind date with a nice personality. If not for its compass-point entrances and the cannon mounted on a concrete slab on the lawn, the boxy, three-story building would be mistaken for a warehouse.

David didn't mind its ugliness. He kind of admired the old bastion's refusal to fall down. What chafed him was the dire need for additional space and modernization, with no possible way to accomplish either.

A century ago, putting the sheriff's department and jail on the top floor had been smart thinking. At that altitude, yanking the bars off the windows to abet a jail break would have required six miles of rope and one helluva tall horse.

Time just had a nasty habit of turning a common-sense idea into a liability. A hoosegow built for antebellum criminals bordered on cruel and unusual punishment for their great-grandchildren. Shoehorning twenty-two departmental employees into offices designed for four and a part-time telegraph operator was a 24–7 nightmare. Those thoughts didn't lighten David's mood as he negotiated the courthouse's spiral staircase. His boots tolled on the concrete treads, the sound echoing like a dirge up the well and down the silent hallways.

His pace was brisk, but he suppressed the urge to break into his usual nonbusiness-hours vertical jog. A good sweat and an endorphin rush would relax body and soul, but he couldn't go back to the fairgrounds smelling like the north end of a goat.

Antique milk-glass globes suspended from tubular, brass fittings cast enough light to prevent barking a shin on one of the benches under the rotunda. Courtrooms and judicial offices dominated two-thirds of the top floor's square footage, but that branch of county government was as jammed up and jerry-rigged as the enforcement side.

As he had outside the building's east entrance, David inserted a key card in the electronic reader on the department's main door. After two tries, a green button granted permission to enter. Must be his night. Normally it took three and an uppercut to the control box.

David flipped on the light and closed the door to his office. Tony Kurtz and Nancy Aldecott, the night dispatchers, had seen his unsmiling face on the security cameras, but there wasn't time to be sociable.

Waiting for the computer to boot, he punched number eight on the phone's speed dialer. Marlin Andrik, chief of the Detective Division, answered on the second ring.

"I need someone I can depend on for about an hour's worth of surveillance," David said. "Any suggestions?"

"None you'd appreciate hearing." Andrik grunted. "Does this surveillance involve a certain redhead?"

"It does." David sat back and briefed him on the situation. "Obviously this is personal and confidential."

"As opposed to official and on the clock."

"Yep."

"And you don't want Toots or Ms. Boone to know I'm there—unless somebody makes a move."

David rolled his eyes at Andrik's nickname for Hannah. The detective had a private label for practically every person, place and thing, including David, though he didn't know what it was. "That's a 10-4, all frequencies."

"Okay," Andrik said in a thinking-aloud tone. "What if Ms. Boone says something nonthreatening but important?"

David would have his portable radio along, but communications via a private channel were anything but. "Leave me a voice mail. As soon as the tea party's over, I'll check with my cell phone. Anything major goes down, hit the radio, Code One."

"Will do." Andrik paused. "How's our girl holding up?"

"Not as well as she'd like me to believe. You know Hannah. Try not to bow too much and maybe you won't break."

"Birds of a feather." Andrik's voice implied his exclusion from the flock. Like he was the king of emote.

"Do you think this dude is Hannah's father?" he asked.

"It doesn't matter what I think."

"Meaning you don't, and she's convinced he is."

"Not exactly." The photos and that ice-cream story had been pretty convincing.

"Well, the drone's an asshole, any way you slice it." Andrik broke the connection.

David pushed back in his chair and swiveled to face the computer. A few keystrokes confirmed that the motor home and equipment trailer were registered to AnnaLeigh A. Boone and licensed to AnnaLeigh A. and-or Reilly J. Boone.

So, AnnaLeigh was the rig's sole owner. Unusual but not unheard of with their age difference. Same with the dual licensing, except the husband's name customarily preceded the wife's on such documents.

There were no outstanding wants or warrants. Boone had been ticketed for some non-accident traffic violations, but the odds of a citation rose in proportion to the number of miles driven per annum.

His arrest record began with two drunk-and-disorderlies within the past fifteen years. Hard to say whether AnnaLeigh had kept him mostly on the wagon or mostly out of bars.

David scrolled down to the next screen. *Christ.* He braced an elbow on the desk and his chin on the heel of his hand. Attempted manslaughter. Four aggravated assaults. Multiple assault-and-battery charges. Resisting arrest. Weapons violations.

Most had been plea-bargained down to misdemeanors, but twenty-five years ago, Reilly J. Boone did a stretch in the Illinois state prison for involuntary manslaughter.

He said he'd coldcocked the man who called Hannah's mother a whore. He just neglected to mention the guy didn't live to apologize.

David left the courthouse wishing tar and feathers hadn't gone out of fashion. From what Hannah had told him about the Garveys, it was a miracle she'd overcome her raising without adding a sixty-one-year-old ex-con circus bum to the gene pool.

Fifteen minutes later, David stood just inside the big top's entrance, watching Hannah applaud a bicycle-riding Doberman. As far as David was concerned, the lone, one-hundred-percent-true statement Reilly had made was that only those who'd fallen in love at first sight believed it could happen.

The Van Geisens' brass band halted the *ta-dah* for

the dog act's exit. The houselights dimmed. A soft drumroll accompanied triple spotlights chasing around the center ring's portable stage.

"Ladies and gentlemen," spieled Frank Van Geisen, the ringmaster. "Prepare yourselves to be bewitched, bedazzled and bewildered by the astounding...the astonishing...the Am-*aaazing* AnnaLeigh."

The band swung into *That Old Black Magic.* Polite applause escalated into cheers and wolf whistles. Being a red-blooded American male, a breeze sailed out of David's lips, too.

AnnaLeigh's full-to-bursting, low-cut, slit-up-to-here, filmy black and feathered outfit looked a lot more like a negligee than a costume. Her hair was a wild mane of frothy curls. The tip of a gold, chevron-shaped necklace pointed to her cleavage—in the manner of highway department signage alerting tourists to the Grand Tetons.

Reilly, decked out in black satin bull fighter pants, a short jacket, bow tie, white shirt and gloves looked like AnnaLeigh's butler.

Holy Moses. David's immediate future was a stone-cold certainty. First thing in the morning, the department's phones would ring like the bells of St. Mary's. Tomorrow's kiddie matinee and the evening performance would be as packed as a Hooter's grand opening. Come Sunday, every preacher in Sanity would deliver a version of a lust-not-in-your-heart sermon to the already doomed.

The Boones performed each illusion in practiced,

fluid tandem, yet AnnaLeigh seemed tense, her movements a split second off tempo. Her eyes constantly engaged the audience but avoided Reilly's.

And just who are you to judge? David thought. The nearest thing to a magic trick you ever did was a flea-flicker handoff when you played football.

David's gaze averted to Hannah. Now *that's* tension, old buddy. Even Delbert's wise to it, seeing as how he keeps glancing at her. In his own way, the old coot loves her as much as I do, but he's sensing something, or you couldn't peel his randy old peepers off AnnaLeigh with a crowbar.

Frank Van Geisen's stentorian voice subdued the applause. While Reilly pushed a low, wheeled cart to the front of the stage, the master of ceremonies extolled the dangers and death defiance of the infamous Bullet Catch.

Two propmen rolled out an upright sheet of smoky glass. About twelve feet behind it, two other workers aligned a six-by-eight-foot metal shield. The curvaceous outline painted in red on its facade left no doubt which Boone was the intended target.

Her expression solemn, AnnaLeigh lifted a black powder rifle from the cart and raised it horizontally above her head. A hush fell as she pivoted, displaying the weapon's brass-fitted stock, its long, blued barrel, its graceful, lethal beauty.

Lowering it to a present-arms position, with the butt supported by the cart, AnnaLeigh took a white horn from Reilly and poured gunpowder down the rifle barrel. Removing the ball from her assistant's gloved palm with a forefinger and thumb, she flourished it stage left, right and center, then dropped it down the barrel.

Drumsticks beat a snare roll associated with military courts-martial and executions. The cadence quickened and the volume increased when AnnaLeigh gave the rifle to Reilly. Turning, she glided past the glass barrier toward the shield.

Her feminine contours replaced the outline painted on the metal. The drummer stepped up to a rapid, unbroken riff. Reilly, his back to the grandstand, brought the rifle to his shoulder.

Sweat broke across David's brow. The image of Stuart Quince, silhouetted in a doorway, morphed behind his eyes. Rearing back his head, David blinked it away, his pulse racing in time with the drumbeats.

Line of duty. It was him or you. Get over it. *Get over it.*

A *boom* roared through the tent. The glass barrier exploded and white smoke billowed out of the rifle barrel.

AnnaLeigh's arms flew up. Her body hurtled backward. Flattened against the metal shield, she slid downward. A bloody smear marked the path.

"*AnnaLeigh...*" Reilly's scream ripped the stunned silence.

The rifle hit the stage floor like a second shot.

7

The acrid odor of gunpowder lingered in the air; the haze floated on invisible currents. Hundreds of pairs of eyes riveted on the stage, as if the blood, the crumpled body, the men restraining the beautiful lady magician's assistant were illusions.

It was all part of the trick, wasn't it? Any second, The Amazing AnnaLeigh would rise unhurt and smiling, and take a bow for having fooled them, frightened them into believing that what looked so real was only a little smoke and mirrors.

Horrified screams split the silence. Mothers clapped hands over their children's eyes. Men bolted to their feet. Fingers pointing to the center ring. Shouts of "Help her. Somebody help her, she's hurt" swelled to a garbled roar.

Costumed performers and workers huddled around the fallen woman. David leaped onto the stage, yelling orders into his handset radio. Behind him, two moonlighting Sanity P.D. officers hooked their arms in Reilly's. They half carried, half dragged him from the scene.

Dr. John Pennington, Valhalla Spring's physician-in-residence, raced down the aisle beside Hannah. On impulse, she started after him.

Delbert grabbed for her wrist. "Hey, where are you—"

Jerking free, she collided with another spectator. Her sandal heel clipped the edge of the riser and she fell, skidding on her side down the rough board steps.

At the bottom, Hannah pushed herself upright, vaguely aware of her stinging palms and the blood trickling from a scrape on her leg. Dodging propmen carrying portable screens to fence the back of the stage from view, Hannah's heart vaulted into her throat when the band struck up Ravel's "Bolero."

"La-dies and gentleman…" the ringmaster bellowed. Spotlights illuminated the aerialists posed in their crow's nests high above the floor. "Allow me to present the one, the only, the *mag-nif-i-cent* Flying Zandonatti Family."

"What are you doing?" Hannah shouted. "For God's sake, stop—"

"It's all right, miss." A sad-faced clown wrapped an arm around her shoulders. "Come with me. I'll take you to Reilly."

She shrugged off the embrace. "All right? What do you mean, it's all right? AnnaLeigh—"

"Go with him, Hannah. Please."

Startled, she whirled and looked up at David, standing above her on the stage. Behind him, security guards stretched canvas between them like a curtain. Silhouettes gestured, moved, enlarged and shrank, a surreal shadow dance in concert with the music blaring through the arena.

"How bad is it?" she asked.

"Doc Pennington's with her." David's voice was as grim as his expression. "An ambulance is on the way."

Marlin Andrik jogged through the rear entrance, an equipment case in each hand. Dressed in a navy sports shirt, jacket and trousers, he looked like an undercover Secret Service agent at a White House picnic.

The detective's eyes slid from Hannah to David. His telegraphed "Get her out of here" was as easy to read as a neon sign.

The clown's hand pressed the small of Hannah's back. She started forward, her mind searching for something to say and coming up empty.

Kneeling beside AnnaLeigh Boone, Doc Pennington sighed as though attaching an amen to a silent prayer. His eyes met David's. Checking for a pulse at AnnaLeigh's wrist and carotid had been automatic, but a veil of matted black curls couldn't hide the fact that half the woman's face was gone.

Glass fragments crunched under the physician's shoes. David looked at his watch, then wrote the time in his notebook. Junior Duckworth, the county coroner, would pronounce the official TOD, but there was no such thing as too much information.

Pennington said, "If you need me for anything…"

David considered asking him to take Hannah back

to Valhalla Springs, but knew she'd refuse. "Thanks, Doc. I'll let you know if I do."

Two EMTs raced through the back entrance. David shook his head and motioned them away. AnnaLeigh Boone had been beyond help before the ambulance was dispatched to the fairgrounds.

Andrik said, "As long as they're here, maybe they ought to stay a while." He waggled a thumb over his shoulder. "Let the lookie-loos in the stands think Ms. Boone is still among us."

David agreed, although the ruse would end when Junior Duckworth arrived. The three-term coroner's grandfather had founded Duckworth's Funeral Home back when hearses were called undertaker's wagons and horsepower was actual. Like his father and grandfather before him, Junior was the county's harbinger of death in a dark suit, white shirt and discreet tie.

Applause burst from the audience as Andrik plied the latches on his equipment cases. "Weirdest damn crime scene I've ever worked. Fuckin' noisiest, too."

"I can't say I expected them to go on like nothing happened," David said.

Andrik chuffed. "Better they did, probably. Shut down the show, and we'd be up to our asses in ghoulies trying to snag a peek at the corpse."

He pried the lens caps off two cameras and slung both around his neck. "Good news is, the forensics are pretty cut-and-dried. Not much doubt about the cause of death the weapon or the shooter."

Light strobed across AnnaLeigh's body, recording

its position from triangulated perspectives. With each shot, Andrik noted the frame number, f-stop setting and distance from the metal shield used as a focal point; a juggling act the Van Geisen counterparts would envy.

"When Josh Phelps and Cletus Orr get here," Andrik continued, "I'm turning the scene over to them. Phelps needs the practice, and Orr can supervise while we have a talk with Dead-Eye Boone."

He glared in the direction of the unseen ringmaster's introduction of the BMX-bicycle team. David couldn't hear the detective's remarks over the fanfare, but Marlin's mouth movements attested to a variety of compound and hyphenated obscenities.

"As I was saying," he shouted when the clamor abated a few decibels, "I don't know what to tell Phelps and Orr about canvasing witnesses. Never had eighty jillion to pick from."

David scanned the spectators visible above the top of the fabric screens. "How about concentrating on the upper and lower rows of each section? The grandstand had the closest, straight-on view, but that'll cover the angles."

Noticing flashbulbs wink like giant fireflies and the glinting off camcorder lenses, he added, "It wouldn't hurt to ask if some of them were snapping away while AnnaLeigh was loading that rifle, too."

A long-term addiction to Marlboros lent a cat-hawking-up-a-furball quality to Andrik's chuckle. "You're watching too much *Law & Order* on the tube, my man. Life would be good if real cops ever got that kind of a break.''

The EMTs stepped back to allow Junior Duckworth and a pimple-faced young man in a lab coat room to maneuver. Andrik nodded permission for the coroner to begin his examination. Duckworth's assistant—a new hire David hadn't met—looked as if he was tasting his supper for a second time.

Andrik said, ''Kid, if you puke, I swear I'll nail you for evidence tampering.''

Not the most compassionate attitude, but unnatural death was homicide until the evidence proved otherwise. A contaminated crime scene was the bane of a detective's existence and a boon to defense attorneys.

David volunteered to help the coroner roll AnnaLeigh's body over to expose the grisly exit wound at the back of her head. Tasting bile, he looked away. The day violent death by any cause didn't kick his gag reflex was the day he'd hang up his badge.

As would the gruff-talking, dour-faced detective wielding the camera. He'd just never admit it, even to himself.

''Whoa—hold it,'' Andrik said. ''Don't move.''

He took a penlight from his jacket pocket and aimed the beam at a black ball that had fallen from AnnaLeigh's mouth.

''Is that what I think it is?'' Duckworth asked.

''Uh-huh, and it hasn't been fired, either.'' Andrik picked up the round with a pair of tweezers and rotated it slowly. ''I saw a John Wayne movie once where he told the bad guys they were gonna eat lead. Always thought it was one of those—whaddaya call 'em—euphemisms.''

Duckworth cocked his head at David. "If Marlin has already bagged and tagged the slug that killed her, and that one hasn't been fired, how in the devil did it get in her mouth?''

David thought he knew but said, "I reckon Mr. Reilly J. Boone would be the best person to answer that question.''

"You can call me Johnny." The man's tone and word choice caused Hannah to wonder if others called him something else.

Antique steamer trunks, wardrobes, cots and dorm-type accoutrements crowded Clown Alley's stingy dimensions. The smell of grease paint, hair spray, rubbing alcohol, stale sweat and cigarette smoke pervaded the air. The top was a shambles, but an exotic and uniquely male one, in multiple.

Hannah winced, her grip tightening on the folding chair's seat. By any name, she'd have never recognized the clown cleansing the scrape on her leg as the man who'd stopped by Reilly's motor home that afternoon, looking for Vera Van Geisen.

"I was a first of May in Detroit back in '62 when the Great Wallendas human pyramid fell apart.'' Johnny paused. "Could be you're too young to remember.''

She smiled. "Could be you need glasses.''

"Could be you need 'em worse'n me, hon." He doused a fresh cotton ball with bottled water. "They always say a tragedy, like the Wallendas', happens in slow motion. Well, I'm here to tell you it does.

"One of them keeled off the wire, then another and another. Forty feet they fell. It was so high up, I remember thinking maybe they'd glide out of it, like birds."

Johnny clucked his tongue. "None did, a'course, and there wasn't a net to catch 'em."

Hannah's storehouse of primarily useless trivia confirmed that fact, but not the reason behind it.

"Ol' Karl Wallenda didn't believe in safety nets," Johnny explained. "No room for sloppy footwork when there's naught but hard-packed dirt down below."

He sat back on his heels. "The dead, the dying and the bad hurt were still lying around the ring like broken baby dolls when the Moslem Temple Circus's band struck up the cue to send in the clowns."

The performer's roundabout way of making a point reminded her of David Hendrickson. As did Johnny's eyes. They reflected good humor and wisdom, yet what they'd seen had aged them beyond their years.

"We don't expect regular folk to understand," he said, "but that's what 'the show must go on' means to us. There's respect and honor and a whole lot of things in it I can't explain. AnnaLeigh would've done the same...."

He dampened another cotton ball to render first aid

to the palms of her hands. Hannah watched a moment, then said, "She's dead, isn't she."

Johnny's back stiffened. "Was before she fell to the stage." The cotton ball hovered, trembling, his fingers wringing it dry again. "A blessing, I suppose. Better to take a short walk through the valley of the shadow than a cussed-long hike."

Like the one my mother took, Hannah thought. Caroline Garvey and AnnaLeigh Boone had nothing in common except their love for Reilly and early death.

"What went wrong, Johnny?"

"Hot-tempered, the both of them. AnnaLeigh thought if she yelled loud enough he'd listen. Things got worse between them when she—"

Johnny glanced up, then lowered his head. "AnnaLeigh isn't the first to die from the Bullet Catch."

The remark he'd bitten off must allude to Reilly and AnnaLeigh's marriage—stormy and on the decline, due to something AnnaLeigh had done. Or hadn't done. Except volatile personalities usually acted rather than demurred.

The second comment wasn't an answer, but a side-step similar to David's hedge about Doc Pennington and the ambulance en route.

"Frank and Vera will be on the horn with the people that booked us, soon as the show's over," Johnny said. "Hang around a killed house, and we'll lose more money than we'd have made. Might as well tear down tonight and hit the road.''

"Oh, really?" Hannah yanked her hand from his grasp. "Tell me again how the circus is just one big happy family. I'm sure Reilly will understand when you pull up stakes and leave him to grieve for his wife, alone. Hell, the show must go on, right?''

Johnny hurled the bloodstained cotton ball into the paper sack beside her. "Ask him, why don't you?'' He tore open a packet of gauze and rifled the makeup table for ointment and adhesive tape. "Ask him about the straw house we'd have had tomorrow afternoon and evenin'—folks packed wall to wall and in the aisles.''

The gauze, tape and medicine bounced in Hannah's lap. "While you're at it, ask him if he gave a damn about how the rest of us'll get by till another sold-out, two-day run comes along.''

Reilly Boone sat in a folding chair, his head bowed, his hands dangling between splayed knees.

"I'm truly sorry about AnnaLeigh," David said, "but we have to ask you some questions.''

Reilly nodded, his eyes locked on the ground between his shiny, square-toed shoes.

At the opposite end of the dining tent, Andrik parted company with the Sanity P.D. officer who'd escorted Reilly from the stage and kept him isolated. The detective signaled "no dice." Reilly hadn't told the city cop anything.

So be it. David hadn't expected a confession. That was another scenario TV writers loved, like car chases and entrapment, but they weren't worth the paper they were written on without hard evidence to support them.

He hooked a folding chair with his foot and dragged it over to face Reilly's. Up close and personal—what a friend you have in me. Andrik positioned another chair to one side—for now, an interested observer with a notebook.

"It took me a while to calm down enough to think straight," Reilly said, "but there's only one way the accident could have happened."

"If it's all right with you," David said, "let's start with how the trick is supposed to work."

Reilly sat back, glancing at Andrik as though just realizing he was there. "Guess I can kiss honor among magicians goodbye, huh?"

Andrik's scowl suggested what else he could kiss.

"The Bullet Catch is as old as the hills. Lots of variations to it, but mine's pretty near the original. You show the audience a real lead ball, then palm it and load the rifle with a gaffed round—a wax dummy. The firing chamber melts the wax, but velocity busts the glass sheet before it disintegrates.

"When the glass breaks, you stagger around until the smoke clears—like the impact knocked you for a loop. Then you go out to the front rows and show folks the lead ball clamped between your teeth."

"Back up a sec," David said. "Where does the wax dummy come from?"

"It's alongside the rifle's trigger guard on the prop table. You palm the gaff when you pick up the rifle."

David visualized the sequence. "What happens to the real ball after you palm it?"

Reilly appeared startled by David's sudden lack of intelligence. "What do you think happens to it?"

"I'm asking you, Mr. Boone."

Raised eyebrows inferred an apology. "Well, you, uh, slip it in your mouth when you walk back to the metal shield. If you didn't, there'd be nothing to show for the catch."

"I guess it doesn't matter where you aim the rifle," Andrik said, "as long as it looks legit to the audience."

"Oh, no, the shot's gotta be true. Once in a while, the gaff busts a hole in the glass, but it doesn't shatter. Aim high, low or off to the side, and the audience'll see the hole and know you didn't catch the bullet."

What a way to make a living. Russian roulette meets P.T. Barnum.

David said, "My granddad had an old cap-and-ball rifle. Nothing as fancy as yours, but he let me plink cans off the fence with it a couple of times when I was a kid. Besides missing everything I aimed at, I remember burning the bejesus out of my fingers on the firing chamber. One shot and the barrel was hotter than hell, too."

Reilly chuckled. "Kind of makes you wonder how

we got off enough rounds to send them British yahoos back where they come from.''

"It also makes me wonder why a wax round doesn't melt away to nothing the instant the hammer falls."

A sly smile curved one side of Reilly's mouth. "It would if you tamped down a full charge of gunpowder. The stuff in the horn is the genuine article, but I cut it with a nonexplosive that just looks like gunpowder."

He waved a dismissal. "Any good magician's supply house stocks it. I get mine and the gaffs from a wholesaler in Dallas."

That answered David's follow-up: whether Reilly molded, or bought the fake ammo. Andrik stole David's next two questions by asking, "Are the gaffs a hundred percent wax? Or are they formed around a pellet or a BB?"

"Pure wax," Reilly said. "The manufacturer colors 'em black to make 'em look real, but a solid core would be too dangerous, aiming dead square like I do."

David and Andrik exchanged a glance. Reilly had a bad case of "I" disease. By name or pronoun, AnnaLeigh hadn't entered the conversation once so far.

"I believe we're clear on how the trick should play," David said. "You being the expert, I'd be interested to hear what you think went wrong."

Something akin to grief washed over Reilly's face.

The gloves wadded on the table were wearing most of his stage makeup, but rouge still brightened his cheeks. Between it and the black satin suit, he resembled an aged Dracula in a B-grade vampire flick.

"AnnaLeigh woke up feeling puny. Headachy and sick at her stomach."

He addressed David directly. "She should have rested this afternoon instead of tearing off with Vera Van Geisen. Said she was fine, but she like to never got her makeup on, her hands were shaking so. Jumped astraddle of me every time I opened my mouth, too."

Reilly's gaze averted to Marlin's wedding band. "Know what I mean?"

Instant best friendship had broken out in a new place.

"I do," Marlin said. "Once a man says it, he's screwed, only not as often as he was before he did."

David prompted, "How did AnnaLeigh usually act before a performance?"

"Oh, she loved nothing better than being on stage. Truth is, from time to time I reminded her that the audience didn't come just to see her." He frowned. "Only tonight, when we were waiting to go on—well, she said she felt fine, but I know she didn't."

Reilly sat up straighter. "When the band cued us— I can't swear to it, 'cause I barely heard her—but AnnaLeigh whispered something like 'Let's get this over with.'"

David's molars ached from the pressure exerted on

them. A muscle spasmed at Andrik's temple, as well. Blame the victim predated the Bullet Catch by who knew how many centuries. Staying neutral when a suspect passed the buck was a trick in itself.

"It's my fault," Reilly said. "I should've scotched the finale and made her take an early bow. The audience wouldn't know the difference. Even if they did, they got their money's worth."

Head shaking, he watched bugs orbit the yellow bulbs strung along the length of the canopy. "She muffed the switch. Had to have. Dropped the lead ball down the barrel instead of the gaff."

His voice broke. Tears glistened at the corners of his eyes. "She must have known. Wax is lighter than lead, for Christ's sake. Why didn't she give me a sign that something was wrong? Stepped aside, or..." Reilly smiled as though unable to comprehend how his wife could have been so stupid.

"If you're right," Andrik said, "after she loaded the rifle, she'd have slipped the wax dummy in her mouth."

"Ye-a-h." Reilly hesitated. "Yeah, that's exactly what she'd have done. A born trouper, that's AnnaLeigh. Maybe she thought she could dodge the shot, then skip giving the audience a close-up. She could've just stopped at the end of the stage and held up the gaff, like she did the real one."

"Sounds plausible," David said, deferring to Andrik.

"Only one problem." The detective leaned forward, intruding on Reilly's comfort zone. "The coroner found a ball in your wife's mouth, all right. A lead ball. Not a dummy." He edged closer. "Want to know what I think?"

Panic sparked in the magician's dark eyes.

"I think your wife palmed the real ball, like she always did. I think she loaded the rifle with the wax slug and the powder, same as she had a thousand times."

The metal chair squeaked. Andrik's nose hovered inches from Reilly Boone's. "Know what else I think? That somebody preloaded that rifle with uncut gunpowder and a bona fide, hundred-proof lead ball."

A sneer that lesser men than Reilly had cowered from distorted Andrik's features. "Wouldn't be surprised if the lab determines the powder in that horn had a touch more of the nonexplosive in it than usual, too. You know. For safety's sake."

Pausing, he backed off a few inches. "Lotta good it'd do to set everything up so carefully, then blow yourself to shit when the hammer fell."

"You son of a bitch." Reilly leaped from the chair. "You think *I* did it, don't ya? You think I killed AnnaLeigh."

He grabbed David's sleeve. "It was an accident. An *accident*—you hear me? Okay, maybe I was wrong about the switch. It's the only thing I could think of. Only way that made sense."

His head swiveled from David to Andrik. "You gotta believe me. *I didn't kill my wife.*"

David clamped Reilly's wrist until he released his hold on David's jacket. "How about that manslaughter charge in Illinois, Boone? You pled not guilty then, too."

A pretty, brown-eyed woman scrunched on a chair with a bandage on her shin was the only occupant of Clown Alley when David ducked inside the flap. "Where's Chuckles?"

Hannah gave him a semblance of a smile. "His name is Johnny." She stretched, then reached back and tousled her hair. "He and the others went somewhere to change and take off their makeup."

David surveyed the clutter strewn across the mirror-backed tables. A paper grocery sack recycled as a wastebasket beside her chair rated a second look. "I thought that's what they did in here."

"Not tonight. It seems word is getting around that I'm Reilly's daughter. Bad form, I guess, to accuse him of murder right in front of me."

Her eyebrow arched. "Oh, and his timing sucks, too. He should have waited until tomorrow night to kill her, after the till was full from a two-day gig."

"Beg pardon?"

Hannah's voice was taut, higher than its normal alto. "Of all people, Sheriff, you should know that crime doesn't pay. At least, it doesn't sell circus tickets. Especially post facto."

The smart-ass patter didn't fool David. It came naturally—one among her many charms—but was knife-edged, as though spoiling to be said.

"How'd you bugger up your hands and leg?"

"Bugger up?" She laughed. "I haven't heard that since I was a kid." A fingertip connected the dots of old scars, barely visible except in her memory. "I was pretty good at tripping over my own feet back then, too."

Hugging her knees to her chest again, she asked, "Why didn't you tell me AnnaLeigh was dead?"

"Whoa." David hooked a thumb in his belt. "Is that the opening bell for another round of Garvey versus Hendrickson?"

"It is, and no mouth guards and gloves allowed."

There never had been. That was the beauty of their verbal sparring. "Okay, then, I don't know why I didn't tell you about AnnaLeigh. Maybe I was too deep in robo-cop mode to let go, even for you."

"Was it an accident?"

"No." David explained the mechanics of the Bullet Catch trick. "Two mistakes were necessary for it to have been an accident. That's at least one too many."

Hannah nodded. "The lead ball had to be mistaken for the wax dummy. Full-strength gunpowder had to be used instead of the diluted stuff."

"Right." Anticipating her next question, David said, "By Reilly's own admission, the rifle and powder horn always stayed locked in the motor home until he or AnnaLeigh gave them to the prop boss before their appearance on stage.''

Mental gears whirred inside that lovely, intelligent head, where logic and abstract thinking operated in tandem. Ruling out an accident left suicide as the only alternative to murder.

He, Andrik and Junior Duckworth had considered it, too—for about thirty seconds. It was common knowledge that suicidal females rarely used guns, fearing the pain, noise and physical destruction. Those factors weren't alleviated by another person's finger on the trigger. Nor would AnnaLeigh have arranged a meeting with Hannah if she'd premeditated her death.

''Can I talk to Reilly now?''

David shook his head. Hannah knew the answer before she asked. Rookies fresh from the academy had less practical experience in investigative procedure and the limitations imposed on suspects and witnesses than she had acquired.

What she didn't know was that Reilly hadn't mentioned her once. If she asked, David would be forced to break his promise never to lie to her. To protect her, he'd have to protect Reilly, as well.

''Is Reilly under arrest?''

''He's in custody, but hasn't been charged. Right now, he's en route to the hospital for a blood-alcohol test.''

''Why?''

David brought out Boone's rap sheet. Hannah skimmed the pages as one might a restaurant menu.

"A BAC eliminates a later claim of impairment by the prosecution, or the defense," he said. "With Reilly's history of alcohol-related arrests, we didn't have to twist his arm to get him to sign a waiver."

He refolded the paper. "No such luck with consent to search the motor home and trailer, though. Reilly said he didn't want strangers pawing through AnnaLeigh's things, or, and I quote, 'busting our props to smithereens.'"

David's tone had sounded snide and he regretted it. "Hey, it's a stall and a dumb one at that. Even if AnnaLeigh were alive and well, Reilly Boone is an ex-con. He can't legally own firearms and damn sure doesn't have a permit to possess or transport explosive materials. We'll have a search warrant as fast as the judge can sign it."

"Maybe they weren't his," Hannah argued. "Is there any law against an ex-con's wife owning firearms and explosives?"

"Hannah…"

"All right, all right. I'd have made a great defense attorney." She rested her chin on her knees. "I think I liked it better when you were holding out on me."

"Bull."

"Yeah, I know, but damn it. This mess is too bizarre for the *National Enquirer*." She gestured as though framing a banner headline. "Tragedy strikes reunion of the world's most dysfunctional family."

Her eyes raised to his. The sorrow in them hit like a roundhouse to the gut. David said, "If you let Reilly come between us…"

"Good God, David. You still don't understand, do you? He already has. I can't turn my back on him."

A voice in David's head howled *Why? What about me? What the hell has Reilly Boone ever done for you?* Above the pounding at his temples, a softer voice asked, *Do you love her? Do you trust her? Now's the time to prove it. Paternity isn't the only issue. Boone is her link to Caroline. A part of her will always be the guilt-stricken little girl who failed to save her mother from herself.*

David held out his hands, pulling her to her feet and into his arms. Rocking her back and forth, he relished, as always, how wondrous it was just to hold her.

Burying his face in her hair, he smelled citrus and coconuts and a pure Hannah scent and knew Reilly hadn't lied about that "heart swelling too big for his chest" feeling, either.

He said, "Okay with you if we just stay like this until—oh, a week from next Tuesday?"

"I wish." She tensed. "Forget I said that." A sigh pooled warm and moist against his chest. "Did all the wishes you made when you were a kid come true?"

David nuzzled the sweet spot below her ear. "Do anyone's? I can't even remember most of mine."

"Then don't be surprised if someday you wake up and find a pony in the front yard."

A boulder lodged in his throat. Shake it off. Keep things light. "Well, uh, how about a naked cheerleader? Seems I do recall making a couple of wishes of that persuasion."

Hannah stepped back and grinned up at him. If what he saw in her eyes now wasn't love, it was close enough to sustain him for a lifetime. "Thank you for always knowing."

"That's what I'm here for, sugar."

"Jehoshaphat," said a raspy voice. "If my goodbyes had taken this long back in '43, World War II would've been over before I boarded the ding-danged troop transport."

"Delbert's still here?" Hannah inquired, as if the old gent in the doorway were a hallucination.

"Yep. He got word to me after the show that he'd wait and take you home."

"From now on, Hendrickson, *I'll* do the driving when we go out."

Delbert waved *hurry up.* "C'mon, ladybug, before my gumball runs the battery down."

"Your what?"

"My gumball," he repeated, spacing the syllables.

"A mobile flasher," David said, "like unmarked cars use in an emergency."

"Handy as a pocket in a shirt, too," Delbert said. "It plugs into the cigarette lighter and has suction cups on the bottom." Fist smacking palm, he made a sucking noise, adding audio to the visual demonstration. "You can stick that baby on the dashboard, the roof, the—"

"You can if you're a law enforcement officer," David said. "Otherwise, it's illegal."

"Are you sure about that?" Delbert's eyes narrowed. "There wasn't one word about it in the Private Spy Supply catalog."

"There's a shocker." David grinned in spite of himself. "How about if I give you and Hannah a head start to the car. Then, when I get there, if that gumball is anywhere in sight, I'll prove it's illegal by confiscating it and citing you for impersonating an emergency vehicle."

Delbert grabbed Hannah's arm. "Don't just stand there. I've got sixty-three dollars and fifty-seven cents, plus shipping and handling, tied up in that thing."

David unclipped the handset from his belt and keyed the relay button. *Baker 2–03, this is Adam 1–01. Clear.*

He was about to repeat the call when Andrik's *Yo, 1-01* blatted from the speaker-microphone.

"What's the status on that search warrant?"

Phelps is en route to the hospital to serve—hang on, Sheriff. Static hissed for several seconds, then feedback screeched from the speaker. *That was Phelps on the cell phone. We have touchdown, Houston.*

A simple affirmative that Boone's copy of the warrant had been delivered would cramp Marlin's style. *I'll meet you at the motor home in two. –101, clear.*

David started from Clown Alley, then halted and turned. With a glance out the flap and the other at the top's opposite end, he strode toward the grocery sack resting beside the metal chair.

The clean side of Boone's rap sheet, creased into a druggist's fold, secured several bloodstained cotton balls. David hesitated, then slipped the packet into his jacket pocket.

8

At the intersection of Valhalla Springs Boulevard and Main Street, Delbert spun the steering wheel right then left, banking into a wide U-turn around the median.

It wasn't as sweet as Hannah's high-balling one-eighty in Price Slasher's parking lot last week, but the Edsel was longer, heavier and forty years older than her Blazer.

The rearview mirror reflected Marge, Leo and Rosemary's oval mouths and saucer eyes, which resembled a crash-test dummy class photo. Beside him, IdaClare tromped an imaginary brake pedal. One bejeweled hand batted at the dashboard she couldn't quite reach. "What in the name of Mary are you *doing?*"

Delbert thought she'd never ask. "In the P.I. trade, this is known as an R S and D operation."

IdaClare extricated the right side of her face from the passenger-side window's glass. "Operation, my foot. Pull another stunt like that and you'll need a pocketbook-ectomy."

"The R, it is for the reconnaissance, yes?" Leo asked.

"Correcto-mundo." Delbert killed the headlights. "To ascertain whether Hannah tucks herself in for the night or tears out for town again."

Marge asked, "Why would she do that?"

"Because she's too tenderhearted for her own good," IdaClare answered before Delbert could say, "Because that no-account rummy of a has-been magician has her half convinced he's her father."

He pulled off on the grassy easement and inched forward to a spot where trees would hide his car without blocking their view of the cottage. The living-room windows blazed with light from the ceiling fan's fixture. It was early yet—half past nine by his reckoning—but he'd told Hannah to hit the hay and she'd promised she would.

"If R is for reconnaissance," Rosemary asked, "what's the S and D?"

"Strategy and Deployment," Delbert said, "for Code Name: Gamma."

IdaClare shook her head. "That can't be right. If our first cases were Alpha and Beta, the next should begin with a C, not skip clear to G."

"No," Leo said, "it is the gamma after the beta."

"Well, if you're so smart," IdaClare said, wriggling around to rest her back against the door, "what comes after gamma?"

"The delta." Leo counted off on his fingers. "Then will be the epsilon, the zeta, the eta—"

"Enough already," Marge said. "It's all Greek to me, anyway."

Rosemary laughed. "Hey, that's a good one."

Delbert stifled a snarl as he shut off the ignition. Lord love a duck. Boone was using Hannah to get away with murder, and his operatives were auditioning for "Ted Mack's Amateur Hour."

He angled sideward in the seat. "What the hell's the matter with you people? Didn't you hear a thing Hannah said on the way home from town?"

"Of course, we did," IdaClare said. "I almost cried just listening to her."

Rosemary's dangling earbobs rattled with indignation. "The way Reilly Boone up and grabbed her this afternoon, I'm surprised Sheriff Hendrickson didn't haul him to jail right then and there."

"If he had," Marge said, "AnnaLeigh wouldn't be laid out in the back of Junior Duckworth's station wagon."

Delbert slapped the upholstery. "Mrs. Rosenbaum, I do believe you hit the nail square on the head."

"I did?" Marge looked to the others for edification. Shoulders rose in unison as four pairs of eyes swung in Delbert's direction.

"You said AnnaLeigh wouldn't have bought the farm if Reilly Boone hadn't met Hannah this afternoon."

"No, I didn't...did I?" Marge fumbled for her glasses, hanging by a neck chain. Setting them on her nose, she squinted at Delbert as though the exact quote were etched on his forehead.

IdaClare said, "Regardless of what Marge said, how does AnnaLeigh's death have anything to do—" She started, then froze. "Wha' waz-zhat."

"Oh, for the…"

Rustling sounds, faint and intermittent, steadily approached IdaClare's side of the car.

Marge shrank from the door. "I heard it, too."

"A skunk it is, prob—"

"Shh." Delbert glanced at the cottage. Bright as a bus station in a bad neighborhood.

Rustle-rustle. Snap…crunch.

Too big and cumbersome for a skunk, he thought. A deer, maybe? Nah. The woods were crawling with them, but they're light on their feet. As opposed to…

He swallowed hard. Judas Priest. A couple more clucks and he'd pull an egg out of his ass. So what, if Roscoe Hocking said he saw bear tracks on number eleven green the other day? That twit—

A furry blur loomed in the rear passenger window. Marge screamed and climbed Leo like a tree.

IdaClare launched herself at Delbert. "Save me!" Her knee frogged his thigh. They conked heads, his nose bearing the brunt of the impact. Delbert pushed her backward, yelling, "Get off, get off—you're breaking my leg."

Rosemary, howling with laughter, flapped a hand at the window. IdaClare twisted sideways, inflicting new agonies on Delbert, her savior. He craned his neck to see past her ax-handle-wide, pink-polyester rump.

Malcolm peered inside, tongue lolling and obviously thrilled to stumble upon a carload of playmates. *Burf. Bur-ur-urf.*

"Put a sock in it, Rosemary," Delbert said. "The rest of you, don't move a muscle." IdaClare crooned as she did to Itsy and Bitsy, "Aw, it's just widdle Malcolm—"

"If that mutt doesn't shut up, *you* can explain to Hannah why we're spying on her." An incomplete hush fell. Repressed breathing in multiple sounded like an obscene conference call. The Edsel's leather upholstery groaned with subtle shifts in weight. "Widdle" Malcolm whined and sniffed at the door cracks.

The cramp in Delbert's thigh spidered down to his calf. A sneeze tickled his nostrils. The armrest felt like a brick shimmed between his vertebrae. IdaClare's fanny wasn't his idea of a scenic overlook.

With a *moomph* of disappointment, Malcolm wheeled away from the car. He reversed for a last look, hiked a leg on the front tire, then bounded away into the darkness.

A symphony of creaking joints, grunts and muttered oaths accompanied the passengers' return to their seats.

Marge moaned and dabbed her face with a tissue. "Us kids used to play Swinging Statues when we

were little, but I don't remember staying still ever
being so *hard*."

Delbert kneaded his upper leg. "Try it with the
Venus de Milo in your lap." Realizing his mistake a
second too late, he tacked on a "just kidding" smile.

IdaClare said, "Are you insinuating that I'm fat?"

"No."

"Well, I should hope—" IdaClare squinted. She
wrenched her sweater around her and pouted.

Wasn't that just like a woman? Trust a female to
latch on to the worst half of a double-intended remark.

The ever-faithful Leo rescued him with, "The
Code Name: Gamma. Reconnaissance, we got. The
strategy and deployment we don't. All night we don't,
either."

Music to Delbert's ears, not to mention his bladder.
Except he couldn't remember where they'd left off.
The author of *Trade Secrets from the Masters of
Criminal Investigation* had an answer for nigh every-
thing, except what to do after being held hostage by
a stupid, slavering dog.

Modus always being as good an *operandi* as any,
Delbert began, "As I was about to say before Malcolm scared you girls out of your Supp-Hose, from
the scuttlebutt flying around while I waited for Hannah, it's pretty clear that AnnaLeigh's death wasn't
an accident."

Marge seemed to speak for the majority when she
said, "Do you think she was murdered?"

"I do, and it's about the slickest case of the pre-meditated variety I've heard of." Anticipating an argument, Delbert looked at Leo. "What's the last thing a killer wants?"

"To be caught."

"Okay, so what's the second to last?"

Furrows striped Leo's brow. He had a computerlike brain, but sometimes the files took longer to sort than others.

Rosemary suggested, "A witness?"

"You got it," Delbert said, astonished that she had. Then again, guess enough and you're bound to get lucky, eventually.

Marge argued, "But AnnaLeigh was shot in front of hundreds of witnesses. Us included."

"That's true." Delbert's eyes flicked to each of theirs in turn. For his operatives to ever be worth their salt, he had to let them deduce a few things on their own.

IdaClare gasped. "That's Reilly's best defense. Who's going to believe he *would* kill his wife with a tentful of people watching?"

She pressed her fingers to her lips and shuddered. "Lord, my skin's crawling just thinking about it."

"It's the ultimate illusion," Delbert said, "and Boone's had forty years' practice at them."

"A *huge* gamble, it is, to rely on the shadow of doubt," Leo mused aloud. "But if in his favor, it works…"

"Odds are it will," Delbert said. "The automatic

prime suspect in a case like this is the spouse. If Reilly'd bumped off AnnaLeigh in private, the cops would be on him like stink on Limburger. Doing it in public plays Billy Ned with logic.''

''Hide in plain sight,'' Marge said. ''I saw a movie about a nurse who was also a hit man for the Mob. No sooner had this FBI agent figured it out, than he had a heart attack. The last scene went from him stretched out in ICU to the head nurse telling the killer nurse how shorthanded they'd been and how glad she was the hospital had hired her.''

''That was the end?'' Rosemary clucked her tongue. ''Don't you just hate movies that leave you hanging?''

''Kind of, but I decided the agent must have faked the heart attack to catch the killer nurse in the act.''

''Sounds like what a G-man would do,'' IdaClare said. ''You know what they say. The FBI always gets their man. Or woman.''

Leo said, ''I think it is the Mounties what always gets them.''

''Oh, why don't you try out for *Jeopardy,* or something?''

Lacking a gavel, Delbert rapped the dome light with a knuckle. ''Keeping you on the subject is worse'n herding chickens. We've got a *real* killer to catch, for Christ's sake.''

Four shocked, contrite faces looked back at him.

''Sorry,'' he said. ''I guess I'm used to blowing off

steam in Hannah's breakfast room. Better sound absorption.''

His apology hung on the air until Marge, the peacemaker, said, ''I move that if Delbert promises not to yell anymore, we won't go off on tangents.''

IdaClare seconded. The motion carried unanimously, but a sense of ''What now?'' prevailed. Delbert featured himself the leader, with IdaClare second in command by virtue of her big mouth and being Jack Clancy's mother. In the past, Hannah had filled the parliamentarian role, but she was actually the group's glue and their rudder.

''I have a question,'' Rosemary said.

Delbert could have kissed her. ''Fire away.''

''Much as I like the crowd-as-cover scenario, and we all had ringside seats for the means and opportunity, what was Reilly's motive for killing Anna-Leigh?''

Delbert harrumphed. ''He was married to her.''

''Oh.'' Rosemary's eyes slid to Leo. He recoiled. ''Never, my beloved, would I harm the hair on your head.''

''Well, I'm no prude,'' IdaClare said prudishly, ''but the only thing amazing about AnnaLeigh Boone was how she kept that nightie she was wearing from falling off.''

''It was a bit much,'' Marge agreed. ''Especially for the circus.''

''The sex, it sells,'' Leo said.

"Yes," Rosemary said, "but AnnaLeigh is—was—a magician not a showgirl."

Delbert assumed they were meowing, then a mental picture of AnnaLeigh sashayed into his memory. "I think I see what you're getting at. Her costume distracted from the act, like a concert pianist strutting on stage in pasties and a g-string."

"Exactly."

"And Reilly had to know that," he went on, "since he'd been a headliner since Moses was in kneepants. So why'd he let her do it?"

"Besides that," IdaClare said, "he was her *husband*. Honestly, what man wants every other man in creation to ogle his wife like that?"

Rosemary adjusted her sweater's low v-neckline. "Well, the obvious answer to all three is, what right does a second banana have to tell the star what she can wear on stage?"

"Oh, please," Marge said. "I sincerely hope you aren't saying Reilly killed AnnaLeigh because her costume was too skimpy."

"It's the second-banana idea that smacks of motive," Delbert said. "In lots of ways. Being too crippled up to earn a living, Reilly needed AnnaLeigh a lot more than she needed him."

Marge laughed. "So he murdered his meal ticket?"

"Hell, yes, if she was making noise about trading him in on a newer model, and I'll bet the Edsel's title she was."

"That's pure speculation, and you know it," Marge said.

"Now who's yelling?"

Marge slumped in the seat. "I'm sorry, but I just can't go along with any of this. We don't know for sure whether the shooting was accidental or not, but what bothers me most is what you said earlier, about AnnaLeigh still being alive if Reilly hadn't introduced himself to Hannah this afternoon."

"That threw me, too," IdaClare admitted, "until we talked about witnesses. Then I realized Hannah was another, er, whatchamacallit..." She snapped her fingers. "Another red herring."

She held up a hand to ward off Marge's protest. "If it isn't logical for a man to kill his wife in front of an audience, killing her with his long-lost daughter *in* the audience really seals the lid on the pickle jar."

"Oh my God." Rosemary let out a wail. "I got so caught up in everything else, I completely forgot Reilly is Hannah's *father.*"

"I did as well," Leo said, shaking his head.

"Well, you can forget it all over again," Delbert said through clenched teeth, "'cause he isn't, and I don't want to hear another damn word about it."

Resentment churned inside him, stealing his voice, as it had when he'd escorted Hannah from Clown Alley, and Frank and Vera Van Geisen had swooped down on them.

"You're Hannah, aren't you?" Vera had asked. "Reilly's daughter?"

Delbert had just stood there, feeling like a cannonball had gutted him. He recalled how Hannah leaped to her feet after the shooting. He'd called her name, reached out to steady her, but she'd jerked away and run pell-mell for the stage.

Suddenly, it all made sense and no sense at all.

"Reilly talked about you for years, but we didn't know you were here until a few minutes ago," Vera gushed. "You poor, poor thing. How horrible this must be for you. Why, to find your father after *so* long and never even meet AnnaLeigh before it was too—"

"Reilly found me," Hannah countered. "I met AnnaLeigh when she returned from her shopping trip with you, and quite frankly, I'm tired of strangers assuming my business is any of theirs."

"Let's go." Frank Van Geisen nudged his wife. "The lady doesn't want condolences from the likes of us."

Later, during the drive to Valhalla Springs, what Hannah told Delbert and the others about her childhood and Reilly's absence from it was abbreviated, but it hurt Delbert to hear it. In his heart, she was the daughter he wished he'd had. He'd vowed then and there, if she couldn't be his child, damned if he'd let a murdering son of a bitch like Boone get away with claiming she was *his*.

"Delbert?" IdaClare said.

He cleared the bitter taste from his throat. "You're right about Hannah being a red herring. I'm as sure as I am the sun'll rise tomorrow that Reilly Boone has bided his time for weeks, maybe months, waiting for the perfect setup.

"Along comes Hannah and he spoon-feeds her a bunch of hooey about her and her mother. It's the easiest parlor trick in the world. Toss out a common this or that, stand back and let Hannah fill in the blanks for you, then *whammo*. Boone's an instant father and he has a fine, upstanding young woman for a character witness. Hannah and the county sheriff being a couple was a bonus."

The silence was as stifling as sea fog. Delbert's ears rang from the clamor he'd raised and the condemnations heard but yet to be voiced.

Marge scooted forward and laid her hand on his arm. "That's what this is all about, isn't it? Hannah. Not how AnnaLeigh died."

Delbert stared over his shoulder at Hannah's cottage, dark now, but for the glow from the porch light. God*damn*, how he hated getting old. Not so many years ago, he'd been as stout as pig iron, through and through. Now look at him. Every trifling thing that came along made him tear up like a doddering fool.

"Whether Reilly Boone is her father or not, Hannah believes he's innocent," Marge said. "Doesn't she deserve the benefit of the doubt?"

The question had eaten at Delbert for hours. No, he thought, not the question. The answer.

"Yes." He sawed a finger under his nose. "She does."

Marge gave his arm a final pat and slid back in the seat. Neither she nor anyone else cracked a patronizing smile, as people often do at an old man caught in the act of being a doddering fool.

He sucked in his gut, his backbone straightening along with his resolve. "Listen up. Deployment for Code Name: Gamma is as follows. First thing in the morning, you girls pay a call on the circus's females. Take 'em sweet rolls, make like a welcoming committee, and see what's humming on the grapevine—dirt and all."

"I'll drive," IdaClare volunteered, "and while we're in town, we'll pick up the rest of the things for the wedding."

Rosemary chuckled. "Oh, goodie. A two-fer."

Delbert's gaze focused on Leo, who cringed. "As for us, *compadre,* it's a deep-cover infiltration. Top secret. Briefing at my place, oh-seven-hundred, sharp."

"I don't like it," Leo said.

"How do you know? I'm not telling you until tomorrow what we're doing."

Leo's jowls sagged to his chins. "Yes, and of one thing I am sure. When you do, then I will *hate* it."

The incoming ambulance's siren stopped in midchirp seconds after the vehicle turned off First Street. Lights strobing, it accelerated up the slope to the porte cochere sheltering Mercy Hospital's emergency entrance.

David braked the cruiser and looked back over his shoulder. Paramedics jumped from the vehicle, threw open the rear doors and whisked the collapsible gurney from the bay.

According to earlier radio dispatches, the patient was a twenty-two-year-old pregnant female. Her first child had decided to be born while Daddy was on an all-night fishing trip with his buddies. Deputy Eugene Vaughn was en route to Jinks Creek to deliver the news and the father-to-be to the hospital ahead of the stork.

David's brother Daniel had told him—in strictest confidence—that watching the birth of his son combined an honest-to-God miracle with a horror flick, and Daniel wasn't sure it shouldn't remain a once-in-a-lifetime experience.

Normally David would laugh at the memory. At the moment, his mind was too clouded by thoughts of Hannah and Reilly Boone, the thin line between principle and self-righteousness, and whether or not he had crossed it five minutes ago.

Well, what was done was done. The result wouldn't be known until tomorrow. In the meantime, he had a homicide investigation under way and a crime scene and attendant witnesses hitting the road in thirty-six hours.

Evidence from the search of the Boones' motor home had made a nice two-plus-two motivewise...as long as David disregarded this, that and a couple of other things.

Dogwood Days had increased traffic on First Street a notch above typical for a Friday night. David turned north, surveying passing vehicles, their occupants, storefronts and parking lots. Gradually, neon-bright urban slid to shadowy suburban. With rural's near darkness just a hill or two away, David's back settled into a slough in the upholstery and his thoughts returned to AnnaLeigh Boone's home on wheels.

A mental alarm had sounded when he'd stepped inside. No signal, no words to the effect were needed to alert Marlin Andrik, waiting behind him, that something was off.

Little had changed in the cockpit and galley area since David and Hannah's earlier visit. A jar of peanut butter, loaf of bread and a gooey bread knife had been added to the crackers, club soda and medicine packet on the dinette table.

The first signs of disturbance were bottles of nail polish, makeup brushes, sponges and cosmetics fanned across the hallway diagonal to the bathroom. Inside, it looked as though an arm had swept across the small vanity, like a bachelor had done spring cleaning during a baseball game's commercial break.

The hall's built-in cupboard doors stood open, but their contents appeared undisturbed. Not so the bedroom, at the back. A quilted comforter, blankets and sheets slewed off one side of the mattress. A wadded silk negligee, the clothes the Boones had worn that afternoon and other apparel were jumbled on the floor. A clock radio dangled by its cord in front of the nightstand; the suspended lamps' shades were whomperjawed, exposing the bulbs.

Marlin said, "I do believe what we had here was a slight difference of opinion." He glanced back toward the galley. "Pretty well contained though, considering the size of this joint."

David squatted beside a corner of the bed and pushed the linens aside. A torn Polaroid of Anna-Leigh having sex with an unidentifiable male too muscle-bound to be her husband skimmed across the carpet.

Picking up the photo by its corner, David waved it at the detective. "I expect this might have annoyed Boone a tad."

Marlin whistled. "That'd do it for me." He dropped it into a plastic baggie. "How about we put the gloves on and see what else turns up in the course of our diligent search for explosive materials and firearms?"

Space being at a premium, Marlin decamped to the front of the motor home, leaving the bedroom, bath and hallway storage cabinets to David. The detective was searching the galley when David brought him an accordion file from the bedroom closet, the other half of the original photo and two additional Polaroids.

"Plumb courteous of Boone to rip these pictures more or less down the middle," David said.

"Would've been better if the photographer had put more of himself in the shots, though, so to speak."

Marlin squared the halves of the most damning

pose and scrutinized it. "Mrs. Boone was a beautiful woman."

"Yes, she was."

"Reminds me of a girl I dated back in college. Not AnnaLeigh's looks, but the expression on her face." Marlin altered the angle slightly. "Messes with a guy's mind when a chick falls asleep before he crosses the finish line."

David nodded a figurative agreement. "The resolution is too blurry to tell whether AnnaLeigh's eyes are completely closed or not."

The detective laid the photos on the counter. "Didn't Boone say something about her being sick this morning?"

"Upset stomach and a headache. It didn't stop her from marching in the parade, or going shopping with Miz Van Geisen this afternoon though."

"My wife could have ptomaine and still crawl to a shoe sale," Marlin groused. "Why does a woman with two feet need eight dozen pairs of shoes?"

He studied the pictures through a pocket magnifier. "No time–date stamp. No phone number tattooed on his dick. That would be too easy." His head moved up, down and side to side. "Yeah, this sure does mess with a guy's mind."

Marlin shrugged and stowed the photos in a Baggie. "So, what else you got?"

"Boone must have a Dracula fetish. Shirts, pants, even his briefs are all black."

"Did I need to know that?"

"Just being thorough," David said. "For the record, there are two more antique rifles, a can of gunpowder and a can of the nonexplosive stuff in a homemade compartment at the back of the bedroom closet."

"That's more like it. All I've come up with is a box of wax dummies in the fridge." Andrik's fingers delved his shirt pocket for his cigarettes. He hesitated, deliberated whether to use the sink for an ashtray, then decided against.

"What's with the file?" he asked as a surly armed robber would. "Where's the cash box?"

"Household records. Receipts, bills, the usual junk, with a couple of interesting exceptions."

"Such as?"

"Number one, it seems Mr. Boone never met a casino he could pass up. Played the ponies and dog races, too. Credit-card charges only show his stakes, not if he won, lost or broke even, but we're talking a thousand or more at a whack at the casinos."

Andrik reviewed the statements. "Well, he didn't win on dates where more than one charge is credited." He made throat noises. "Unless he got well again, before he cashed in for the night."

David gestured at the bottom of the sheets. "The fees tacked on for late payments are consistent, which is—"

"Hmm." Andrik shook his head.

"What?"

"I wonder why he gambled on credit. The circus

is one of the only legitimate all-cash businesses left. If a guy gets paid in cash, gambles in cash and wins, the IRS would have a helluva time collecting its share of the gains. Feeding the kitty on credit leaves a number trail.''

David said, ''I thought casinos always deducted taxes from the payout.''

''Sure they do. Just like all cocktail waitresses declare every penny they make in tips.''

''Okay, smart-ass.'' David produced more sheets from the file. ''Explain why the Boones racked up late fees when they had a little under a quarter of a million in the bank.''

''What?'' Andrik snatched the papers and scanned both sides. Discarding all but one, he held it up to the light fixture mounted above the sink. ''I'd bet Cattlemen's Union Fidelity in where-the-fuck's Molalla, Texas, is home-owned, but I don't like the printing.''

David peered upward. It looked okay to him, but that's what separated sheriffs from veteran county chiefs of detective divisions.

''Lower-grade paper than standard,'' Andrik said. ''Smaller font, letter-quality print, not boldface.'' An index finger zigzagged the length of it. ''Notice anything else?''

''No creases. Well, I'll be damned. Who mails bank statements flat instead of folded?''

Andrik made his respiratory-distress sound. ''Apparently, Cattlemen's Union Fidelity in where-the-fuck's Molalla, Texas.''

A potential motive and a probable motive for murder clicked in David's mind. Boone wasn't the first and wouldn't be the last husband to permanently rid himself of a cheating spouse, particularly if Anna-Leigh made a habit of it. Added to that, evidence of Boone's high-stakes gambling and off-kilter bank statements.

Money and infidelity—each a common motive for homicide. If they found AnnaLeigh's name on a high-dollar life insurance policy, the pope, Jerry Spence and Alan Dershowitz combined couldn't parlay an acquittal.

"My turn at show-and-tell pales by comparison," Marlin said. He wagged a thumb at the toiletries in the hallway, then at the peanut butter, bread and knife on the dinette. "Which came first, Charlie Chan? The sandwiches, or the slight difference of opinion?"

"Logic says the sandwiches."

"Uh-huh." Marlin gestured at a crumpled beer can floured in black fingerprint powder. "I found this laid up against the corner of the counter."

"I'm pretty sure it was there this afternoon, when Hannah talked to Reilly."

"Yeah, but get this. The prints match the postmortems taken from the deceased and the can's a loner. No full ones in the fridge, no empties in the garbage can under the sink."

"Why is that significant?" David asked.

"It may not mean shit. Could be AnnaLeigh was a one-brewski kind of gal and it's the last of a six-pack.'' He looked up at David. ''Except when was the last time you drank a beer and smashed the can in your fist?''

''Tuesday night.''

Marlin grunted. ''Being put on administrative leave doesn't count, boss. When, before that?''

''The last time the Rams fumbled on the two-yard line, I guess. I usually just chuck empties in the... trash.''

''Uh-huh, and nobody'd call you dainty.''

''Once, maybe,'' David said. ''Not twice.'' The hinkiness he'd felt when he entered the motor home crept over him again. Murder by the numbers should be basic math, not advanced algebra. ''What do you make of all this?''

''I dunno.'' Andrik's dark, hooded eyes swept the compartment. ''I just don't know.''

''Neither do I,'' David repeated to himself, as he'd admitted to Marlin an hour and a half earlier.

Noting the far-right slant of the cruiser's speedometer needle, his foot eased back on the accelerator. A mile or nine over the posted limit wasn't flying low, but even a sheriff in need of sanctuary should set a good example.

Hannah sipped from the mug, savoring the fragrance of hot lemon, cinnamon, nutmeg and sweet red wine. Chin tipped, she let the velvety warmth slide down her throat.

The thermal carafe on the deck beside her chaise

had been full when she'd come outside. Now a cup, cup and a half was all that remained.

Grinning up at the stars, she supposed she'd been curled up beneath them and the afghan her mother had crocheted for—golly, it had to be hours and hours. And really, it was a very small carafe.

Also really, she was freezing her butt off. Candy is dandy, but liquor is fickle. Warms the inner woman and leaves the outer one cold.

Just like Mama's afghan, Hannah thought. Her finger poked through a hole where Caroline had dropped stitches, or a cigarette. In keeping with idle hands being the devil's playground, a doctor had prescribed crochet as a cure for her three-pack-a-day habit.

Needlework had occupied Caroline's hands, all right. She'd worked that hook in and out, looping yarn in its crook to form wobbly stitches, a sputum bowl balanced on her thigh to catch the ash worms from the Chesterfield pinched between her lips.

But she'd finished the afghan. Gave it to Hannah on her eighteenth birthday. A month later, Caroline lapsed into a coma and died.

"I can't imagine how cold I'd be without it to keep me warm." Hannah sniffled and buried her nose on the nubby wool. "That's enough. Stop it right now. Wiping snot all over it is no way to treat an heirloom."

Retracting her neck to deepen her voice, she quoted Great-uncle Mort. "You can't keep sorrow from visitin', but you don't have to offer it a chair."

Malcolm scrambled up from the deck, startling her. Head swinging, he *moomphed* to the east, then to the west. Whatever he'd heard was probably in his dreams.

"Heel, big guy. Sit. Stay."

Toenails rat-tatted on the planks. He peeled out through the railing's open gate and cranked a right for the front yard.

A paragon of obedience. That would be Malcolm.

Hannah shivered, but wasn't ready to sissy out and flee inside. Stars were baby suns, weren't they? And a sixty-degree night in Chicago was balmy. Almost.

Careful to keep the coffee mug level, she drew up her knees, folding the afghan under her feet and chinking the gaps at her hips. Wine slopped over the rim and dribbled down her chest. "Aw, *hell.*"

"That glad to see me, huh?"

She jumped, flipping more droplets on her thigh. "David? What are you doing here?"

"I was about to ask you the same thing."

"I live here."

He stepped onto the deck, Malcolm dancing a crazed Watusi around him. *Burf. Bur-rur-rurf. Burf-burf.*

"Is that mutt ever going to get his timing down on when he's supposed to bark?"

Hannah laughed. "He's making strides. Last week, you were in the living room before he sounded the alarm."

"I reckon I have to give him points for hearing me

drive up. If he hadn't met me at the car, I'd have assumed you'd gone to bed."

David sat down on the adjacent Adirondack chair. He noted the carafe, the mug in her hand, and sniffed in its direction. "Let me rephrase the question I didn't quite ask. Why are you sitting out here in the dark?"

"I'm waiting for a sign from George Burns."

"Uh-huh."

"Nothing dramatic, like a lunar eclipse or anything. Just token reassurance that sticking my head in the nearest gas oven might be somewhat premature."

"Uh-huh."

"Could be I'm a weensy bit drunk, too."

David nodded. "Ye-ah."

"Want some mulled wine?" She waved the cup at him. "Hey, it's great stuff, lemme tell ya."

"I'm sure it is, but none for me, thanks."

"Suit yourself." She gulped down a mouthful, then smacked her lips. "Do you believe in God?"

For some reason, that gave him pause. "Sure I do. Haven't been a regular churchgoer for a long while, but I don't think that's the only place to find him."

"Ever seen the movie *Oh, God?*"

Comprehension flickered in his eyes. "Probably six or seven times."

Hannah blew a raspberry. "That's nothing. I bet I've seen it fifteen. Twenty, maybe. *I've* got the video. Mama and everybody were Baptists 'cause they brought food baskets to us every Christmas. But me? I'm a self-ordained Burnsian."

"Uh-huh."

"See, when I was a kid, God was this ancient, scary, bearded guy with a hawk nose and obs...obsid...really black eyes, and if I so much as kyped a cookie from Grandma Garvey's cookie jar, I was going to go to hell and that was all there was to it.

"Well, being doomed at an early age isn't much incentive to start behaving yourself. I mean, you can only hang somebody once, right?"

David agreed, but had the strangest expression on his face. Maybe it was the light—except it was dark.

"Anyway," she said, "after I grew up, I pretty much ignored the whole concept of religion, until I saw that movie. The original, you understand. Not the sequel."

Setting the mug down on the deck, she pushed herself up straighter in the chair. "In my opinion, that's how God ought to look, and act, and be. A nice old guy who's wise, has a terrific sense of humor and a touch of crustiness."

Hannah shrugged. "Kind of like Delbert, only with glasses and without the cigar and the attitude."

David burst out laughing—exploded, actually—rocking backward on his butt. His mouth gaped so wide, Hannah could have seen his tonsils had the deck lights been on.

"What's so funny? My religion? Huh? Is that it? Well, I'll put *mine* up against *anybody's* for comfort value, Hendrickson. Any-bod-y's."

"I'm sorry. Honest, I am. I swear, I was with you all the way, until you dropped Delbert into it, then—"

Forehead held in one hand, David batted the air with the other, motioning an intention to stop guffawing like a dork any second now.

Much, much later, David apologized again and told her he'd never again think of God without thinking of George Burns and, "I really do like the imagery. Especially compared to the one you had when you were a kid."

"Much less intimidating." Hannah gave him a shy smile. "I'll tell you something else, if you promise not to laugh."

"Cross my heart."

"Well…" She took his hand. "I think in a George-works-in-mysterious-ways way, I got my sign."

"Oh, sugar, that's—" David's eyes closed, the lids quivering and silence stretching to the edge of uncomfortable before he said, "I came here because I didn't like the way we left things tonight."

Catching his lower lip between his teeth, he inhaled slowly and exhaled in a rush. "I need something to hold on to. Not for just a little while. Long enough to make me stop feeling like…"

He shook his head in frustration. "Like I'm on a teeter-totter, and every time my toes touch solid ground, a bully at the other end hunkers down and up I go again."

The flutter in Hannah's belly clenched. She knew those bullies, too. Some were recognizable, some faceless; all queued like vultures at an emotional buffet.

Something to hold on to? Oh, yes. And definitely not for just a little while.

The light silvering the bedroom was enough for eyes accustomed to darkness. Hannah, in her over-sized nightshirt, and David, stripped down to his jeans, cuddled spoon fashion beneath cool sheets, his bare chest warm against her back, their arms inter-woven, their fingers entwined.

A glorious, gentle languor descended, a drowsy sensation of being adrift, yet anchored and safe and completely at peace.

"This is all I needed," David whispered. "All I want for now."

She nuzzled the stubbled cheek pressed to hers. Voice slurry, a misty veil closing over her, she said, "'member us talking before? The difference be-tween...making love for the first time, for the right reasons an'...for the wrong ones?"

"Mmm-hmm."

"And why, if we'd made love that night...it would've been...wrong?"

"Yes."

"That night...you 'member?"

"I remember, sugar."

"We should've...held each other...to sleep."

"I know." His lips brushed her temple. "That's why I'm here now."

She felt his heartbeat. His breath caressed her face.
The night wasn't cold anymore. No ghosts, no bullies.
Falling...falling...
"I love you, David."

9

Marlin Andrik cradled the telephone receiver. Three fingers drummed a riff on the handle. "Neither snow, nor rain, nor dark of night will keep me from nailing a perp's dick to a tree."

He swiveled around in his chair. Josh Phelps, the greenest bean in the Detective Division, sat on a cast-off desk opposite the one-way window in the interrogation room's door. The rookie's eyebrows raised expectantly.

All in good time, kid, Marlin thought, acknowledging his sadistic streak. Rank didn't have that many privileges and he was downright glib compared to Neimon Vestal, the chief he'd trained under. An investigator had to think, hear and see between the lines. "And it'll never happen," Vestal had preached, "as long as I stand over you, telling you what's shit and what's shinola."

Marlin lit a cigarette and inhaled. Watching another minute of his life go up in smoke, he chucked the pack and his lighter in his shirt pocket. Last one tonight, he promised his wife, Beth, in absentia.

He envisioned her curled up asleep, a petite, dark-haired Goldilocks, all alone in a too-big bed. Beth nagged him about not helping enough around the house, for being too strict with their son and too lenient with their daughter. Not a word was said about the hours Marlin worked and the Marlboros he inhaled by the carton.

Smart lady. He'd feel a lot less guilty about both if she did.

Phelps pointed at the terra-cotta saucer Marlin used for an ashtray. "You're going to burn the place down one of these days, Chief."

The Detective Division of the Kinderhook County Sheriff's Department occupied a midblock, narrow storefront across the street from the courthouse. To all who entered there, it was known as The Outhouse.

Marlin took another drag and surveyed the warped ceiling tiles, the fake walnut paneling and mangy carpet. Rust-seamed metal desks that might fetch ten bucks at a yard sale held computers and peripherals that relied on piggybacked surge protectors fed by three wall outlets. Cockroaches ran relays on the bathroom walls. Mouse turds rained down when file cabinet drawers slid open.

Oh, yeah. To see such splendor go up in flames would be friggin' tragic.

He jerked his head toward the interrogation room. "What's our drone doing?"

"Still staring at the glass."

After a final pull, Marlin stubbed out his cigarette. "Time to see if I can make him blink."

A sheaf of phony documentation was stuffed in the folder containing field notes, sketches and items found in the motor home. He'd been known to slam a boxful of closed case files in front of a suspect in the name of "mounting evidence" and the hope of scaring the truth out of him.

Reilly Boone wasn't the sharpest knife in the drawer, but he also wasn't a virgin to the system. Time was on his side. Bulking up the available paperwork would have to suffice as intimidation. Damn shame, too. A dirtbag's eyes going banjo at the sight of that box always gave Marlin a warm, fuzzy feeling inside.

"I thought we were waiting on the sheriff," Phelps said, his heels bumping the desk front.

"You thought wrong. We had enough manpower at the scene, and Hendrickson had personal business to take care of."

"Uh-huh." Phelps looked at his watch. "That's what I'll say next time I want to catch some zz's."

Marlin tapped the rookie's knee with a corner of the folder. "Lemme tell you something, Josh ol' pal. Nobody in the department logs more hours than I do—except David Hendrickson.

"Larry Beauford, the sheriff before him? In twelve years, Larry stuck his fat ass into four, maybe five major crime scenes. Not to help work them. To get his picture taken for the paper."

Marlin chuckled. "Beauford was fine to knock

back a beer with, but the man went to his grave believing a gun was optional on a burglary charge.''

Phelps's Adam's apple herky-jerked above his shirt collar. Marlin gave the rookie a moment to visualize demotion to a patrol unit. ''Relax, kid. It's Houdini I want to see sweat bullets.''

Hand resting on the doorknob, he added, ''By the way, the path to enlightenment is silent, grasshopper.''

Phelps looked like an elevator passenger ambushed by a monster gas pain.

''You know, like in 'Kung Fu.' The old TV show? The monk always called David Carradine...''

Phelps's face couldn't have been blanker if he were laid out in the front parlor at Duckworth's Funeral Home. Marlin wondered if Hannah ever dropped lines like that on Hendrickson, forgetting the gap between her age and his.

Bound to happen sooner or later. Wouldn't be pretty when it did, either. Toots was a helluva woman, but she had a temper to match her hair.

''Just keep your mouth shut and your ears open, kid. Think you can do that?''

''Yes, sir.''

Marlin flipped a switch to activate a video camera mounted near the ceiling of the interrogation room. He waited for the button beneath the lens to glow red, then entered.

A business card–size label on an interior wall warned that the room had constant electronic monitoring; the other cameras remained hidden. It wasn't a cop's fault if a suspect got bored and started talking to himself.

Isolated for nearly an hour, Boone hadn't let out a peep.

He sat up in his chair, a molded plastic bucket with no armrests. His eyes trailed Phelps to the corner diagonally behind him, back to Marlin, then down to the manila folder with BOONE, REILLY J. printed on the tab.

White stubble flecked Boone's chin and upper lip. Stage makeup puttied the lines in his face. His rumpled satin jacket hung limp at the shoulders, as though it were wearing him. In the harsh glare of the fluorescent lights, he looked like a man who'd sell his mother for a pint of Jack Daniel's.

The blood-alcohol test had been negative, though. Marlin hadn't expected a high content, only enough to infer that Boone had a snort of liquid courage before his wife's final finale. That he hadn't was yet another incongruity that disturbed Marlin's sense of order.

He ignored the camera humming above them, but said, "You understand, for your protection and ours, this interview is being videotaped and recorded, don't you, Mr. Boone?"

"Yeah." Boone glanced up. "It's okay with me."

Like he got a vote. He'd already waived his right to an attorney. Jailhouse psychology said a lawyer implied guilt, ergo, he who declined legal counsel must be innocent.

In reality, it meant zilch to an investigator. At any time, a suspect could whine ''I want a lawyer'' and end the interview. Everyone just danced until the fat lady sang, or the music stopped.

''Want another cup of coffee, Mr. Boone, or a soda? before we start?''

''No, thanks.''

Marlin removed his sportcoat and hung it on the cushioned chair with the padded armrests. Dressing down said they'd be there a while, and which of them had the home-field advantage. He sat with his back to the door, a position cops rarely took at any time, but if Boone got a notion to rabbit, he had to go through Marlin to do it.

Interrogation was an art, a science and improvisational theater larded with a heavy dose of bullshit. The irony that Marlin could lie himself blind to con the truth out of a suspect was one of the best parts of the job.

It was perfectly legal. Christ, it was essential. You just had to be smart about it.

For Josh Phelp's edification, Marlin had Boone repeat what he'd said at the scene: the Bullet Catch's setup, its various cheats and his theory about what went wrong.

When he finished, Marlin said, ''Your wife didn't cook very often on the road, did she?''

"No." Boone squinted in confusion. "What's that got to with anything?"

"Not needing much in the way of groceries explains why you had room in the fridge for a box of wax dummy cartridges."

"Oh, that. It keeps the gaffs from getting too warm, losing their shape. They sweat some when I take 'em out, but they soften up and dry out pretty fast."

"What would happen if they weren't thawed?" Marlin asked.

"Nothing. Being a touch harder when they're loaded doesn't matter. I don't think enough moisture condenses to foul the gunpowder mix either, but why chance it?"

Marlin made a note, though he could give a rip about the fake slugs. Boone was still in love with his switcheroo idea. Judging by Phelps's expression when Boone reiterated it, the rookie liked it, too.

Right about now, Phelps was thinking about no wax fragments being found at the scene and liking it even better. What hadn't occurred to him yet was that twenty-some people had walked all over the stage before it was cordoned off. That many shoe soles could pick up and carry off a pulverized Buick.

Marlin said, "So, you and your wife ate most of your meals in the dining tent."

"I did. AnnaLeigh pushed a fork around more than she ate. She said the cooks never met a meat they couldn't fry."

"How about tonight?"

"We didn't have time. AnnaLeigh slapped together a couple of sandwiches to tide us over."

Boone went pensive, wistful. "My little girl was visiting all afternoon." A shoulder hitched. "She's a grown woman now, but that's how I remember her. A gangly kid with big brown eyes and a Kool-Aid mustache turning cartwheels till she got dizzy and fell to a heap, then laughing at her own foolishness."

Marlin smiled back in spite of himself. He'd bet Toots could still turn a mean cartwheel. When Hannah laughed, for any reason, her chin tilted upward like a child's.

"Hey," Boone said, "you probably know her already. Hannah Garvey? She and the sheriff are—"

"We've met."

Phelps snapped to attention. There would be a lecture on confidentiality before he went off the clock. As far as Marlin knew, the rookie kept his trap shut, but his mother, Winona, was the manicurist at the Curl Up and Dye—Sanity's answer to CNN.

Hendrickson had been a juicy topic of conversation since the day he crossed the county line. He'd dated some, but rumors were flying about the bachelor sheriff's "mystery" girlfriend. Winona Phelps would trade her limited edition Bradford Exchange Christmas plate collection for the skinny on Hannah's relationship to a suspected wife killer.

Marlin said, "These sandwiches you had for dinner. Did your wife eat one, too?"

"I guess so. She took half of one into the donniker with her, whilst she put on her face."

"Was that before or after the argument?"

Boone recoiled. "What argument? AnnaLeigh gets cranky when she has to rush to get ready for a show, but we didn't fight about it."

"Then what did you fight about?"

"Tonight? Nothin'. How many times do I have to tell ya? We scarcely had time to say two words to each other."

Marlin slipped the taped-together Polaroids encased in plastic sleeves from the folder, then hesitated. The weather should be as predictable as Boone's reaction would be.

He'd deny he'd ever seen them. Deny they'd fought about them. Deny he'd killed his wife because of them. Why wouldn't he? A hamster would know better than to try to sell a crime of passion with a time-out in the middle of it.

Other than a messy motor home—"Jeepers, Detective Andrik, I told you, AnnaLeigh got cranky when she was rushed"—Marlin had nothing with which to stuff Boone's denials down his wattled old craw.

The alternative was to keep those aces in the hole until he received the preliminary autopsy report. A premortem bruise, an abrasion, fingernail residue—anything alluding to a scuffle—might pry the truth out of Boone, Reilly J.

Because a week or more could tick by before AnnaLeigh's number came up at the backlogged state lab in Columbia, Junior Duckworth had asked the Greene County medical examiner in Springfield for a favor.

Presumably, it was a slow night down in the southwest corner of the state. The M.E. had also been intrigued by the circumstances and the hunch Marlin asked him to follow up on. He'd promised to light fires under lab techs and forensic specialists and report any anomalies ASAP.

Now, if the friggin' phone would just ring…

Telling himself to have patience, Marlin returned the photos to the folder. "Maybe you and your wife were as lovey as dovies tonight, but you did argue sometimes, didn't you?"

Boone almost denied that, but thought better of it. "Yeah. Sure. Who doesn't?"

"What was your last argument about?"

"Jaysus, I dunno. What did you and your wife fight about last time you had one?"

"Money," Marlin lied. Intuition embellished it. "Before Beth went back to work, my money was our money. Now my money is our money, and her money is her money."

"Yours, too?" Boone stabbed a thumb at his chest. "Think I did that when *I* headlined the act?"

"Damned if I can figure out what comes over women when they start earning a paycheck. Goes to their heads for some reason."

"Ain't that the truth? Overnight, AnnaLeigh was the expert on everything. I was just along for the scenery. Even turned the fact I've been in this bidness my whole life against me.''

A tickle scratched at Marlin's throat. *Don't cough—gotta let the bad times roll.* Swallowing hard, he tightened his diaphragm, strangling in silent agony. *Bitch faster, dirtbag. I'm dying here.*

''I can't get through to AnnaLeigh that tradition is what the circus is all about. Folks *want* it to be the same as it was when they was kids. Why, they don't call it the greatest show—''

The cough ripped out, a spell-breaking hack Marlin failed to muffle with his shoulder. No loss. A Barnum & Bailey commercial wasn't what he was after.

''No insult intended, Boone, but if all lady magicians wear costumes like your wife's, you top-hat-and-tails guys are history.''

''Her choice.'' Scarlet crept up Boone's neck. ''A magician's supposed to sell the flash not *be* the flash. AnnaLeigh didn't used to be like that.''

''Like what?''

Boone opened his mouth, eyeballed the video camera, then pressed his lips together. Nix the fraternal order of the ball and chain. He'd remembered where he was, and why.

Marlin flipped through the file folder. ''What else didn't your *wife* used to do?''

No comment.

''Hey, she was a beautiful woman. Anybody…*everybody* could see that. She didn't hide her light under any bushels, did she, Reilly?''

"AnnaLeigh didn't dress like that, except on stage."

Paper rustled loud in the confined space. "I can't say I was surprised when I heard you'd argued about her flirting with other men."

"That's a *lie.*"

"Your wife wasn't a flirt? Or you didn't fight about it?"

"Both. I mean, neither."

Marlin riffled the edges of the requisition forms he'd added to the file. "Then all these people who said she liked to tease, and you had shouting matches an average of twice a week are lying. Is that what you want me to believe?"

Trembling so hard he appeared to hover an inch above the chair, Boone said through clenched teeth, "I don't give a fuck what you believe, Andrik."

A common but not particularly astute remark to snarl at an officer of the law. Marlin crossed his forearms on the table. "Well, now, that, Mr. Boone, *is* a lie. Maybe it's the first one you've told me. Maybe not. But I think you care very much what I believe."

He leaned forward. "Or you ought to start caring, quicker than you can pull a bunny out of your ass."

By increments, self-preservation nudged Boone's anger aside. "A'course I didn't like AnnaLeigh's costumes. Yeah, sometimes she carried joking around a little too far, too."

"What do you mean by 'too far'?"

The effort to repress his emotions contorted

Boone's features. "I'll be sixty-two years old before the month's out. If you were my age and AnnaLeigh was your wife, think *you* wouldn't get jealous once in a while?"

Answering a question with a question was no answer at all. "Waited kind of late in life to marry, didn't you?"

A squirm. A lengthy pause. "I was forty-six when me and AnnaLeigh got married."

Marlin termed that type of answer a "Paul Harvey." He mentally licked his chops. And now, for the rest of the story. "AnnaLeigh wasn't your first wife."

"No."

Nor his second, or he'd have specified. "How many times have you been married?"

Boone thrust out his jaw. "Three."

"Counting AnnaLeigh?"

"Uh-huh."

But not Caroline Garvey. From what Hendrickson had said, Boone had neglected to tell Hannah about wives number one and two.

"Any children?"

"Not by me." He blew out a deep breath, as if realizing evasion was a shovel not a rake. "Darla, the first one, had a boy from a previous marriage. The second, Jeannette, had a son and a daughter."

"How long were you married to each one?"

"Five years to Darla. Seven to Jeannie."

"Pay alimony to either, or both?"

"No."

Another flat no. Marlin consulted the clock on the back wall. Saturday was seventeen minutes old. He shook a cigarette from the pack, lit it and commandeered a foam coffee cup for an ashtray. "I want the year, county and state of those divorce decrees."

Boone's groan diffused the smoke billowing in his face. "There weren't any."

"Oh?" Marlin flicked ashes into the cup. "Then, among other things, that makes you a bigamist, doesn't it?"

"The hell it does." Hate smoldered in the man's dark eyes.

"They aren't called public records for nothing, Boone. You can explain how three marriages and no divorces isn't bigamy, or Detective Phelps can search a few databases on the computer."

With nothing more than names to go on, a records search could take a week or longer, but the drone didn't know that. God bless Bill Gates and the nerds who invented the Internet. They'd sent an interrogation's bullshit quotient into the stratosphere.

Boone leveled another "fuck you very much" look. "Darla was a bareback artist. Her regular mount pulled up lame. She had to ride one she was training.

"Something spooked it—noise, flashbulbs, coulda been anything. Darla lost her footing. The horse behind her reared, trampled her before she could roll out from under it."

Marlin's pulse stepped up, and not because of the nicotine hit. "What about your second wife?"

The man slouched as though grief-stricken. Painful

memories? Or feeling a noose tighten around his neck?

"Jeannie and three others performed the Spanish Web—prettiest circus act there is. When they twisted and looped on the ropes with the music, it was an air ballet."

His voice cracked. His gaze lowered to the floor. "We made a power run, a jump way off the regular circuit. Since we'd set up and tear down in a half day, the boss rigger didn't string the nets."

Marlin said, "Is that standard operating procedure?"

"Power runs is hardly ever done, any—"

"Answer the question, Boone."

"More common than not. The rigger has to have the performers' okay on it, though. *All* of the performers."

Marlin got the drift. Jeannette Boone, included. He motioned for him to continue.

"Jeannie was in the free spin, the finale. Only a loop in her teeth. Another thirty seconds and everything woulda been fine."

Boone's forehead glistened. "The turnbuckle on the rope snapped, and she—" He whirled to look at Phelps, then back at Marlin. "If we could've got her to a hospital, she'd have pulled through, but the closest one was a hundred miles away."

Shit on a pogo stick. Was Boone a friggin' serial murderer? Not a serial killer—wrong M.O. Those freaks stalked their victims and murdered them for thrills not personal gain.

"I know what you're thinking, Andrik, and you're wrong. I swear to God, they were accidents—just like AnnaLeigh."

Boone sprang from the chair, his arms extended. "I'll prove it to ya. Hook me up to a lie detec—"

Phelps rushed forward. "Sit down."

"Please, you gotta—"

"I said, *sit down.*"

Boone collapsed on the chair. "They were accidents. Both of 'em. Ask anybody." His plea alternated from Marlin to Phelps. "Ask Vera Van Geisen—her and Jeannie were friends. Or Johnny Perdue—he'll tell ya. Him and me go way back. Twenty years, at least."

Marlin said they'd talk to the clown and Mrs. Van Geisen, then asked for Darla's and Jeannette's dates of birth and birthplaces. Their social security numbers, Boone couldn't remember.

"Life insurance payouts," Marlin said. "Remember those?"

"There wasn't any." Again, Boone appealed to Phelps. "Insurance on circus performers costs double—triple—what it does regular folks."

"What happened to the kids?" Phelps asked.

"Huh?"

"Your stepchildren." The rookie held up three fingers, as if a visual aid were needed.

"Oh, them. Well, Darla's boy went back with her ex-husband. The bum Jeannette was married to first didn't want nothing to do with his. Her parents took custody of 'em."

Phelps said, "Convenient for you."

The human pendulum swung back to Marlin. "I tried to be a father to 'em whilst we were together, but—"

"It wasn't like they were your own flesh and blood."

"That's ri—" Boone winced, the derision in Marlin's tone registering a beat too late.

"Did AnnaLeigh have life insurance?"

"It was her idea to—"

"I'll take that as a yes. How much?"

"Two hundred thousand, but—"

Marlin whistled backward. "Third time's charm, eh?"

"I didn't—"

"Two hundred grand here, another two hundred large and change stashed away in Texas." Marlin sailed a plastic-sheathed Cattlemen's Union Fidelity statement across the table. "If you believe what you read."

Boone's complexion blanched whiter than the paper.

"Since I don't, I woke up the Molalla chief of police an hour or so ago, who woke up one of the bank's officers, who checked that account's balance on his laptop."

Marlin's glance at Phelps signaled, *Stand by for the dick-to-a-tree-part, kid.* He reached to circle the month-old date at the top of the statement and the six figures at the bottom. "According to Mr. Banker, this amount is off by two hundred thousand dollars. And the change.''

Eyes locked on the paper, Boone moaned, his head slowly shaking from side to side.

''C'mon, man. Think fast. You've had an answer for everything so far. Where'd all that money go? You didn't spend it on that rig you travel in.''

Unintelligible stammers sounded from Boone's throat.

''But now that AnnaLeigh's dead,'' Marlin said, ''that sweet ride is yours, free and clear, isn't it? The turpentine to wipe her name off the side might cost ten or fifteen bucks, but what the hell. The credit-life policy she took out on it will pay off the loan.''

Phelps planted his hands on the table. His nose was close enough to Boone's to count the pores. ''We know you're a compulsive gambler. What'd you do? Try to warm up the dice with some cold hard cash? Or were you as lousy at pickin' a pony as your first wife was?''

''You son of a bitch,'' Boone roared. ''I didn't kill her. I ain't never killed nobody.''

''Oh, yeah?'' Marlin yelled back. ''What about Sheldon Altman? You served ten years for beating him to death in a bar fight.''

''That was an acci—'' Boone shoved Phelps backward. ''Get outta my face, boy.'' He pointed at the video camera. ''Turn it off. I want a lawyer, ya hear me? Gimme a goddamn lawyer.''

10

Suspended in the fuzzy limbo between sleep and waking, Hannah wriggled backward to close the gap between her body and David's big, strong, almost naked, warm one.

Oh, yeah. It's so nice to have a man—

Grrmph.

One eyelid cracked open. A blast of sunlight slammed it shut. *Grrmph?* What did she have to do to get a "Good morning?" Buy the vowels?

Her arm slithered from under the covers. Thumb and forefinger in pinch position, she reached back in the vicinity of where David's butt should be and—

Hannah twisted sideward. Soulful, chocolate-brown eyes brimming with unconditional love gazed into hers. Bed linens exploded in giant wads of white. "What in the *hell* are you doing in my bed?"

Malcolm sprang off the mattress in a horizontal half gainer. He rotated into a belly flop, kaboinged off the floor and ran from the room as though his fur were in flames.

Just watching him made Hannah's head hurt. "Red, Red Wine" cranked up on her mental jukebox.

A hangover she could handle. A hangover with a Neil Diamond sound track was like getting the electric chair for jaywalking.

Taking extra care not to let her eyeballs bang around in their sockets, she noted the absence of a gunbelt slung from the corner of the sleigh bed's headboard. Bathroom, unoccupied. No handset radio, loose change, pager, wallet or keys on the nightstand.

Duty had called.

A visual shift brought the alarm clock swimming into view. Giant red numerals informed her that it was 9:88.

Hmm. Something seemed amiss, but she wasn't quite sure what. Then, before her squinted eyes, the numbers reconfigured to 7:33. She looked away and back again—7:34.

Yeah, well, too early was close enough.

She shuffled to the bathroom. Shuffled out a couple of minutes later. Shuffled on to the breakfast room's French doors to let Malcolm out before his bladder broke, then into the kitchen.

Where there was coffee. A whole pot. Brewed and everything. Beside it, a clean mug and a bottle of extra-strength headache tablets anchored a paper napkin.

Wish I could have stayed to hold you awake, was written in a hybrid of block and cursive script. *Love, David.*

Tummy flutters ramped into full-body tingles. Unlike most of the population—herself included—David didn't drop the L word indiscriminately. Hannah couldn't recall him saying he loved a certain movie, a restaurant, his job, a particular song. Not even his candy-apple-red and chrome pickup truck.

Then again, she thought, pouring a cup of coffee, they had spent the night together. Abstinence notwithstanding, how else would he sign a morning-after note? *Yours truly? Have A Nice Day* with a happy face in the exclamation point?

Three aspirin were shaken from the bottle and chased with a glass of water. From what little she remembered before zonking into a wine-flavored coma, *Professional Help Is As Close As the Phone* might have been appropriate.

Had she really told him George Burns was God, or had she dreamed it?

The ceramic pelican with a scrubbie in its beak looked askance at her. "All right, so I'm a little manic this morning. What else is new?"

The water glass smacked on the counter. "Wanna hear what *is* new? This time, I'm not going to be the first one to say 'I love you'—that's what. For once in my miserable life, *I'm* going to keep my mouth shut.

"Screw empowerment and liberation and taking the initiative. Been there, done that. Great for the boardroom. A big fat manipulative cheat in the bedroom."

She planted her hands on her hips. "You don't believe me? Okay, name one movie where the actress that gushes 'I love you, Reginald,' or Alphonse or whatever to pry an 'I love you, too, Daphne' out of him wasn't a certified psycho.

"Uh-huh. See? Well, no way, Jose Pelican. I've learned my lesson."

Hannah looked out the window, miles beyond the copse of trees, the sliver of lake winking in the sunlight, the distant, forested hilltops serrating the skyline. "I want to hear I love you. I want to be the one to say I love you, too."

Turning away, she picked up the coffee mug and the napkin. "Because this time it matters. This time I have to know it's real and not just a lover's knee-jerk version of 'You're welcome.'"

David aimed the squirt gun at his uniform shirt and squeezed the trigger. The iron's sole plate hissed on the damp fabric. The defensive, duck-butt maneuver was reflexive for a man wearing nothing but Jockey shorts and a pair of socks.

If Hannah were there, she'd tease him about a woman's work never being done, then point at the wrinkle he'd just ironed into the yoke.

On second thought, if Hannah were there, David wouldn't be standing half-naked behind an ironing board in the middle of his living room. He'd either have the good grace to put on his pants, or they'd both be horizontal, fully naked and in the middle of his bed.

He sighed, gazing out the window at a cottage twenty-six miles away that felt more like a million.

What he wouldn't give to still be in the middle of her bed, his arms wrapped around her, their bodies molded together naturally, instead of one conforming to fit the other.

Last night, when he called Claudina Burkholtz while Hannah was in the bathroom, Claudina hadn't asked why he wanted her to page him at 5:00 a.m. In all likelihood, she'd guessed where he was, guessed wrong about what he would be doing, and wrong again about why he was afraid he'd oversleep.

His internal alarm clock would have roused him in time to drive home, shower, shave and make his appointment at Terry Woroniecki's law office. The page was to guarantee he got a jump on Valhalla Springs' early birds, who might be inclined to chirp about his cruiser being parked in Hannah's driveway.

David could just hear her laugh. She'd say he was too protective and hopelessly old-fashioned, then remind him that sex and senior citizenship weren't a contradiction in terms. Being certain of Hannah's reaction hadn't stopped him from trashing thirteen paper napkins before he gave up trying to explain why he'd left, and simply told her why he wished he could stay.

More fun for her, he supposed, if he bared his provincial soul in person. And there was a slim chance Hannah would agree that Delbert's harem wasn't tacit permission for her to sleep with the sheriff, however defined.

David buttoned his shirt, remembering her as he'd

seen her last, lying on her side, her hair a tangled halo, one leg stretching for the footboard, the other bent at the knee.

A songwriter might liken her face to a child's, all innocence and vulnerability. Nothing wrong with the analogy, except he wondered why poets needed moonlight to see those qualities. Maybe they were just too busy hiding theirs to notice, or too preoccupied to look at other times of the day.

What David had seen in the morning gloam was no different than what he saw in sunshine—the woman he'd begun to believe he'd never find, and fallen in love with the moment he had, who whispered his name in her sleep.

Caffeine, pain relievers and a hot-as-she-could-stand shower reduced Hannah's hangover to a mild malaise. A second coat of liquid makeup and a heavy hand with the mascara wand lessened the oxygen-starved goldfish look.

Weeks removed from Henri of Chicago had wreaked havoc on her hair, but the wind was blowing outside. Maybe everybody would assume the funky, antennaelike strands protruding from her head hadn't sprung up until after she'd left the house.

With the tails of a white silk T-shirt and a striped oxford blouse tucked into her jeans, Hannah sat down on the bed to lace her boots. Her gaze averted to a photograph on the dresser. She toggled on the balls of her feet to reach it, sat down again, then looked back at the dresser. Hadn't the frame been beside the lamp instead of in its usual spot between it and her jewelry case?

She shrugged, then studied her favorite picture of her mother—not that she had boxes full to choose from. Where or when this one had been taken, Hannah didn't know. Nor could she put in words why it was her favorite. Trying to explain how the image seemed so here-and-now—how she felt part of it, as though she were standing just out of camera range—always made her sound like a street-corner mystic.

The breeze was brushing back Caroline's wavy, copper hair. She was squinting at the sun, her chin up and mouth open wide, laughing loud and long at something said or done. Or quite possibly, at herself.

Hannah's fingertip traced her mother's delicate brow, her regal nose, the heart-shaped contours of her face, in search of the "spittin' image" Reilly had seen.

There was a resemblance, but...Hannah stood in front of the dresser mirror. Holding the photograph at her temple, she studied the dual reflection. Caroline, in her early thirties and her daughter, at forty-three, could be cousins. No one would mistake them for twins. Even sisters.

Setting the picture in its rightful place on the dresser, Hannah frowned at it, then into the mirror. If she had a photograph of Reilly Boone and superimposed it on Caroline's, would she see herself in the composite?

"Why didn't you ever tell me his name, Mama? Did you hate him so much you couldn't say it out loud?"

Jefferson Davis Oglethorpe had told her about a long-standing feud with another family "whose name was blasphemy." No Oglethorpe, past nor present, had spoken it since the Civil War.

Hannah's lips pressed into a flat line. Forget it. Caroline's secrets were buried, sealed beneath a weathered granite stone.

Turning away, Hannah bent to strip the sheets from the bed. If the washing machine didn't drown the tiny, black, possibly hatchable things Malcolm had shed, she'd tumble dry them to death. Linens bundled in her arms, she paused in the doorway and looked back at the dresser top. "But how could you have hated Reilly *that much*, and kept the stupid stuffed dog he gave you before I was born?"

"Get a move on, Schnur." Delbert catercornered across Main Street. "We're already behind schedule."

"And whose fault is that?" Leo said, panting. "Oh-seven-hundred, you told me. Oh-seven-forty-six it was, before out of the bathroom you got."

Delbert rubbed his belly. It still felt like an alligator doing a death roll in there. Something he'd eaten? Nah. All he'd had for dinner last night was a jumbo bratwurst with sauerkraut and onions at the circus.

Maybe he'd caught a touch of whatever stomach bug was going around.

He did a mental fingersnap. Virus, hell. It was those ginseng capsules Maxine McDougal gave him when they went square dancing Tuesday night. Had to be. She said they'd improve his memory. Well, what good did it do to remember better if he never got out of the can?

Leo huffed up beside him. "Such a hurry you're in, to drive would have been faster."

Except both their golf carts were on the fritz and Delbert's car and Leo's orange Thing were too conspicuous. Some nosy Parker might wonder what they were up to.

Hannah, for instance. Brains and a suspicious mind were a bad combination for a female to have.

"I figured you could use the exercise," Delbert said, tugging down his golf cap against the wind. "No time like the present to whip you into shape for the honeymoon."

Leo's eyes widened behind his thick-lensed horn-rims. "But the wedding, it is tomorrow."

"Uh-huh." Delbert surveilled the immediate vicinity. "What's your point?"

If this were a weekday, twenty or thirty retirees would be strolling the boardwalk between the Flour Shoppe bakery and Wiley Viets's newstand. Being Saturday, most everyone slept in an extra hour or so.

Old habits die hard, Delbert thought. Some don't till you do.

On either side of Valhalla Springs' commercial district were four bronze-finished doors interspersed between the shops and stores. Beside each was a directory listing the respective volunteer committee offices and private ones occupying the second floor.

Jack Clancy, who'd surely inherited his smarts from his father, designed the entrances as fire breaks. The ground-level lobbies would slow the flames' spread. Water jets on the roofs and interior ceilings activated if smoke or excess heat tripped an adjacent building's alarm system.

Delbert stepped up to the door between Doc Pennington's clinic and Oliver's Apothecary. "Scoot over this a'way, Leo, and cover my flank."

Still mulling over how he might be whipped into shape for a honeymoon thirty-six hours hence, Leo obeyed without comment, until Delbert pulled the lock-pick gun from his duffel bag. "What is it you are doing?"

God save him from amateurs. "What's it look like I'm doing?" Tongue clamped between his dentures, Delbert inserted the gizmo's probe in the keyway.

"But at your house," Leo said, his tone puzzled, "before we left to come here, you told me you had the key."

Delbert finagled the device's triggers, his ears peeled for the sound of retracting tumblers. "Same difference."

"No, it is not." Leo hunkered down beside him.

"A key, it is like the permission, eh? This you are doing is the burgling."

"Oh, it is, huh?" Delbert gave him a dirty look. Leo was too intent on the lock's brass cylinder case to notice. "Well, then, I want my book back."

"What book?"

"My *Trade Secrets* book you borrowed. If you're not gonna read it, I want it back." The *thwick* of a disabled security pin was as sweet as Mozart. "And I know you're not reading it, or you'd know this isn't burglary, on account of we're not entering these premises with an intent to steal."

Clack. Gracing Leo with a smug smile, Delbert plied the lever and pushed the door open. "We're just borrowing a few things."

Leo preceded him into the lobby, then stopped short. His chins quivered as he visually climbed the stairway to the second floor. Spying the chairlift, he gestured, "Eureka," then noticed the sign above it.

Maximum weight, 220 lbs. Failure to comply with this restriction could result in serious injury or death. Thank you for your cooperation.

"Who was the lunatic what put stairs like Mount Everest in a building in a retirement community?" Fist aloft, Leo spun around. "It is the age discrimination. It is the fat people discrimination. And the handicapped people, and—"

Leo craned his neck to follow the finger Delbert

aimed at the opposite wall. "Oh." He cleared his throat, then a sheepish grin appeared. "The elevator, I forgot about."

Delbert clapped his shoulder. "I got just what you need for those senior moments, amigo. You can have the bottle of ginseng pills Maxine gave me."

"You mean the ginko biloba." Leo clumped toward the elevator. "I take it already. My Rosemary, she says it's good for the noggin."

Delbert scooted backward into the chairlift and lowered the armrests. Maxine had torn the label off the bottle, but he was sure he'd heard her right. "If ginko whatchamacallit is for your head, then what's ginseng good for?"

The elevator doors started to close. At the last instant, Leo stuck out a hand to stop them. "Is for the—" his gaze flicked downward "—you know."

Seconds ticked off, and so was Delbert. "No, I don't know, or I wouldn't have asked. Can't you finish a simple ding-danged sentence?"

Leo fidgeted and screwed up his face. The elevator doors rumbled from their side pockets. In a louder, more emphatic voice, he said, "Is for the...*you know.*"

Delbert pummeled the armrests. "Goddamnit, Schn—"

"Der männliches," howled through the narrow cleft between the elevator doors. "Is for *der männliches,* forsake the pities."

Delbert cogitated what little *deutsch* he could

sprechen. His eyebrows shot up. A strangling noise gurgled out. He looked down at his lap.

That's what gingseng's for? And Maxine Mac-Dougal thinks *his* needed it?

"Of all the sneaky, conniving— What kind of woman slips a fella you-know pills on the sly?" He fumbled for the chairlift's control lever. "A sixty-four-year-old nymphomaniac sex fiend, that's what. Well, by God, she's spent her last Tuesday do-si-doing with me."

The seat jerked and began its ascent. Delbert glanced over his shoulder and shifted the control lever to off. He didn't need help getting up *der* stairs, either.

A psychologist, a financial adviser, an attorney, a certified public accountant and Madame Rue, a psychic and tarot card reader, leased office space on the right side of the second floor's landing. All were based in Sanity, but provided their services to Valhalla Springs residents two or three half days a week, and evenings by appointment.

The development's Transportation and Travel Committee's office was to the left, as were the House-keeping Committee, Health and Liaison Advisory Committee and the rehearsal and storage area for the Valhalla Springs Thespian Society—a title Delbert couldn't pronounce without sounding like Daffy Duck.

Straight ahead were windows and the obligatory benches below them. Leo was sitting on the latter to

gander out the former. Without a doubt, Valhalla
Springs had more benches per capita than anywhere
in the world. Indoors and out, the lack of a place to
plop down one's behind to watch another bust his
climbing a flight of stairs was the least of a resident's
worries.

Leo gained his feet, but didn't smile, snicker or in
any way allude to their conversation in the lobby.
That's what best friends were for. Except Delbert
knew if the situation were reversed, he'd never be
able to keep his mouth shut about it.

Using the lock-pick gun on the Thespian Society's
door was like halving a turkey sandwich with a chain
saw. Then again, the props, painted scenery and costumes weren't what real burglars would consider hot-
ticket items.

"Yo, ho, ho." Leo brandished a plastic sword. "I
am the Zorro, here to save the day."

"Zorro didn't say 'yo, ho, ho.'" Delbert snatched
up a longer sword with a rubber sink stopper at the
hilt. "He wasn't a pirate, for Christ's sake."

"Then what did the Zorro say?"

Delbert planted his Hush Puppies in a fencer's
stance. "*En garde, señor.* Prepare to be mono-
grammed."

Their feints and jabs set papier-mâché mountains
atremble. Delbert scalped a shelf of wig stands. Leo
skewered a foil-wrapped, chicken-wire moon. *South
Pacific*'s palm trees toppled into a cardboard facsimile

of a Viking ship, which knocked the top rails off of
Oklahoma!'s painted foam corral.

"We'd better quit," Delbert gasped, "before we
break something."

Leo surveyed the damage, then blanched when he
saw the jagged hole in the moon. "Uh-oh. Already I
did, I think."

"No problemo, Bernardo." Delbert spun it a half
orbit. "See? Good as new."

Leo still looked guilty as he pulled a handkerchief
from his trouser's pocket. "So much fun it was, I
almost forgot why we are here." Mopping the sweat
from his brow, he frowned. "No, I didn't forget. The
why, you never told me."

"Did, too." Delbert rifled through an accordian-
shelved cosmetics case. "Not more'n a half hour ago,
during the strategy session on Code Name: Gamma."

Lipstick tubes, eyebrow pencils, metallic blue and
green eyeshadow and applicators clattered into the
duffel. He'd hoped for some white pancake makeup,
but the thespians hadn't gotten around to performing
Madama Butterfly, yet.

Oh, well. Black shoe polish had done the trick in
another caper. No reason white wouldn't work for this
one.

"At the strategy session, all you said was that the
mission, it is a deep-cover infiltration at the circus."

"Uh-huh." Delbert scooped the wigs from the
floor and began fitting them on the foam heads.

"Eavesdrop and snoop and like that," Leo said.

"Uh-huh."

"Then you pushed me out the door, and off we walked to here, but why we came you did not say."

"Criminey, Schnur. Do I have to spell everything out for you? Add deep-cover infiltration to a B and E at *Playhouse 90* and what do you get?"

The wigs' elastic linings conformed to the foam heads, but only two seemed stretchable enough for Leo's large skull. Delbert frowned. Neither the Lauren Bacall pageboy or the Betty Boop model would be an easy sell.

"The disguises," Leo said. An almost visible lightbulb glowed above him. "Here we came for the disguises."

"And make no mistake about it, they're critical to the success of this operation. Everyone working for Van Geisen's knows each other. The only way to beat 'em is to join 'em."

At Leo's solemn nod, Delbert held out the two wigs. "So, which it'll be, old buddy? Lauren or Betty?"

"Dead, I wouldn't be caught in those."

"It's slim pickin's," Delbert agreed, "but your head's too round for the rest of them, and there's no such thing as a bald clown."

Leo hunched his shoulders and folded his arms on his belly. "Lots of bald clowns there are."

"No, there's lots of *fake* bald clowns. All of them wear wigs to make them look that way. Going the fake bald route would be swell if we had a fake bald wig. Only we don't.''

If Leo were weakening, he was doing an admirable job of hiding it. He jutted an elbow at the shelf. ''Show me which one is yours.''

''I, uh…'' Delbert shifted his weight. ''Well, you see…''

''The hair you got, and I don't. Okay. But no such thing there is as a white-haired clown, either.'' Leo shook a finger at him. ''And otherwise, don't even try to tell me.''

He was right, but Delbert wasn't about to resort to wearing a wig. All his hair needed was a little color. Surely the mercantile had cans of that spray-on goop, or something he could dye it with.

''I'm way ahead of you on that one,'' Delbert lied. ''I guarantee, it won't be white when we're ready to deploy.''

He extended the Lauren Bacall model, his personal favorite. ''I'm not asking you to go to all this trouble for me, Leo. It's Hannah that needs our help.''

11

"A civil lawsuit deposition is like a mental hemorrhoidectomy," Luke Sauers said. "Without anesthetic."

The look David gave his attorney was sidelong and unamused. "Gee, thanks. I feel a lot better about it now."

Leaning against the trunk of Luke's BMW, their shoulders almost touching, the two men faced a graceful, two-story, rose-brick historic home.

The building had been remodeled for the offices of Sachs, Woroniecki and Pratt, Sanity's premier ambulance chasers. David had seen the "before" photos and saluted the owners for restoring the tumbledown relic, rather than bulldozing it and building a brick shoe box.

It was the only thing he'd salute Sachs, Woroniecki or Pratt for, but as the saying went, "Even a blind sow finds an acorn once in a while."

Along the walls and pooling on either side of the entrance was a thick bank of bush peonies. Their ruffled, white-and-pink blooms, as large as dinner plates, flavored the wind with their heady perfume.

A horn blared and brakes screeched beyond David's line of sight. His muscles tightened and his breath caught, then gusted out at the *ba-whump* of metal on metal. Failure to yield, he surmised, or following too close. Eight'll get ten, it's failure to yield. Rear enders seldom honk first and collide later. By the sound, it was a noninjury, if the individuals involved had their seat belts latched.

The responding Sanity P.D. officer would sort it out, hear an earful from both sides and cite the guilty.

David's thoughts returned to the ordeal ahead of him. "Care to explain what the rush is all about? The lawsuit was just filed a couple of days ago."

"We could have delayed," Luke said, "but it'll be more advantageous to drag our feet later, if necessary. The deposition is mostly a formality, the opening gambit to a chess match."

David needn't ask which were the pawns and which were the bishops.

Luke went on. "Terry Woroniecki, counsel for Lydia Quince, the plaintiff and not-much-bereaved widow, has forbidden his client to wed husband number two until the suit is settled."

"He did?" David knew he wasn't supposed to feel sorry for her, but happiness had been a stranger to Lydia and she deserved some. "Why?"

"Awfully tricky to convince a jury that a blushing bride incurred and is presumably still suffering a million bucks' worth of emotional distress, loss of service and companionship, etcetera, due to her first husband's wrongful demise.''

"Even if Woroniecki convinces them that I'm to blame for his death?''

"Anything's possible,'' Luke admitted, ''but a damage suit is a game of odds, and I'll bet this one never goes before a jury.

"Woroniecki knows we'll file motion upon motion to delay. The plaintiff won't mind stalling a few weeks—it'd be scandalous to walk down the aisle any sooner. Beyond that, she'll be hollering to get on with her life.''

David said, "Which means, she'll settle for the payout from the county's liability insurer.''

"Be more amenable to a settlement,'' Luke corrected. "Never underestimate the power of greed. Woroniecki's in particular.''

After a pause, he added, "Look, I know what you're thinking. Let it go to a jury. If they tell Mrs. Quince to fly a kite, the verdict will also exonerate you from all allegations of wrongdoing. Again.''

"Yeah, well, that does have kind of a nice ring to it, Luke.''

"Uh-huh.'' The attorney stabbed a forefinger at the building. *''J. E. Michaels versus Sanity Hardware, Inc.''*

David sucked air through his teeth. A jury had awarded fifty thousand dollars to Michaels, who allegedly injured his back when he fell through the hardware store's ceiling. That Michaels, a thrice-convicted burglar, entered the premises at 2:00 a.m. via a roof vent failed to sway the jury.

Luke said, "Then there's the cost of defending all parties to the suit—you, the sheriff's department and the county. The liability settlement is chump change by comparison."

Not to taxpayers it wasn't. David's morale sagged lower than his shoulders. "And folks who think I'm a trigger-happy SOB won't change their minds just because a jury says I'm Officer Friendly."

"An out-of-court settlement isn't an admission of liability or guilt, David. Merely an expedient."

In layman's lingo, if you're gonna get reamed anyway, you may as well bend over and get it over with.

"So, as my lawyer, you're betting the plaintiff wants a wedding more than she wants to be a millionaire."

"Yes."

"And as my campaign manager?"

"Don't ask."

"I already did."

Luke's expression slid to the far side of pessimistic. "If I'm right about the timing, it couldn't be worse. Jessup Knox will do his best to crucify you, and I wish to God you'd taken Hannah to bed on the night in question instead of out for dinner."

Correctly reading the look David shot him, the attorney said, "Make that on the night in question, I wish you'd taken Hannah out for dinner an hour earlier."

"Forget it, Luke. No insult intended, I know."

"None taken, but... Whew, brother. You have it bad, don't you?"

"Yep."

Luke grinned. "In case you have any doubts, which I would if I were the ugly, stunted wretch you are, from what I've seen, it's mutual." He adjusted the knot in his tie. "Only because Hannah met you first, you understand."

David's eyes drilled the lot's ruddy surface, scored to resemble paving bricks. The machine had answered when he'd tried to call her from his cell phone en route to the attorney's office.

Plenty of logical explanations for it. She could be asleep. In the shower. Outside horsing around with Malcolm the Wonder Dog....

Every instinct told him Hannah was awake, that the wall between them was on the rise and the next time he saw her, he'd be the sheriff again. The enemy. The man in uniform standing between her and the homicide suspect who said he was her father.

He couldn't compete. Didn't want to. Shouldn't have to. The echo of her voice sliced through his mind: *I can't turn my back on him.*

"For a guy in love with an exceptional woman," Luke said quietly, "you look more like your dog just died."

David pushed off from the car. Thumbs hooked in his gunbelt, he feigned avid fascination with the traffic flowing by on First Street. "AnnaLeigh Boone, that lady magician who was killed at the circus last night?''

"Yeah."

"Three or four hours beforehand, the shooter, her husband, Reilly, told Hannah he was her biological father.''

Luke's head whipped around. "Just like that?"

"Pretty much."

Confidentiality needn't be specified. That Luke was a trusted friend and David's attorney wasn't accidental. "No more than Hannah's mother told her about her paternity, she could have been a virgin birth."

Compassion and apprehension scrimmaged on Luke's hawkish features. Since he'd been adopted in infancy, his curiosity about his birth parents vied with reluctance to seek what he might regret finding. Or regret finding him.

"Is Boone her father?"

"From all appearances," David hedged. "Does it matter?''

"What the— Are you *serious?*''

David remembered the tears welling in Hannah's eyes when she recognized herself in those snapshots Reilly carried in his wallet. The wonder and resentment and love reflected in them, the joy and need and love shining in Reilly's.

His terse, selective biography of her upbringing preceded. "Hannah's forty-three years old. In all that time, she's never had so much as a name to attach to the man who fathered her. Homicide investigation aside, if she believes with her whole heart that Reilly Boone *is* that man, does it matter if evidence to the contrary comes to light?''

Hands clasped behind his neck, Luke shook his head, as though struggling to understand the question. ''If I'm hearing what you aren't saying, you've outdone yourself, my friend. That's a duke's mixture of leading, speculative, hypothetical, moral and ethical.''

Lawyers categorize. An argument between married ones must be fraught with objections, ''may it please the courts'' and plea bargains.

''Yes, it matters,'' Luke said. ''As if I'm telling you what you didn't already know.'' He smiled. ''And as if you wouldn't have trusted your gut had I told you it didn't.''

David nodded. ''Except at times like these I can't help thinking how much closer my gut is to my hind end than my head.''

A muffler barked asphalt, signaling County Commissioner Paul Gray's arrival. Riding shotgun was Ray Bob Oates, the commission's legal adviser and husband of Jessup Knox's baby sister's best friend.

Oates bailed from the car before the tires nudged the curbstone. The wind lifted the attorney's combover and held it aloft, flapping like thatch on a jungle hut. ''What kind of a sheriff's department are you running, Hendrickson?''

David stifled the impulse to say, ''The usual kind. You know, deputies, patrol units, lights and sirens…''

''That's precisely what a concerned citizen asked

me not five minutes ago," Oates yapped. "Clyde Corwin is fit to be tied about his lot getting broken into and his dogs poisoned again last night, and I don't blame him one iota.

"Crime is running rampant, *rampant* I tell you…"

David tuned him out, to mull over facts and implications. The county leased a scrap of ground behind Clyde Corwin's bankrupt gas station for an impound lot. In essence, the facility was a giant, post-and-wire fenced dog pen with vehicles parked in the middle of it.

Since there was no advantage to David's political opponent expressing his concerns directly, Citizen Knox was using Ray Bob for a mouthpiece. As usual.

"… and furthermore, Sheriff—"

"Take a breath, Ray Bob, before you suffocate," Paul Gray said as he rounded his car. The commissioner offered his hand to David, then to Luke—a courtesy Ray Bob hadn't extended. His hair had waved at them, though.

"Clyde Corwin is angry," Gray admitted, "but someone slipped his dogs knockout drops this time, not poison."

"I beg to differ," Ray Bob said. "A pinch too much of that dope would've killed them, sure as I'm standing here. It's pure luck those dogs are still alive and kicking."

Other than the pure-luck aspect, David tended to agree with Ray Bob. Corwin's pit bulls were inbred, untrained and vicious. Petitions circulated to ban the

breed countywide had failed to garner enough signatures. On three prior occasions, five of Corwin's dogs
had been poisoned.

"I'll look into it," David said.

"*Do* something about it." Ray Bob flounced off,
one arm winged and a hand clapped to his head.

Luke reached for the briefcase on his trunk. "Well,
gentlemen. Shall we go in and see how big a bite the
pit bulls in silk suits want to take out of us?"

By every indication, today's attendance at the fairgrounds would triple yesterday's. Hannah's Great-
uncle Mort would say Dogwood Days was "pullin'
'em in like flies."

A teenage girl with Cher-hair and matte black fingernails was collecting parking fees this morning. A
chubby boy who didn't look old enough to be in high
school, much less a student at the alternative one,
waved Hannah to the east parking area.

She spotted a patrol unit and Marlin Andrik's unmarked sedan in the reserved section, but not David's
cruiser.

Good. Avoiding Marlin while butting into a homicide investigation would be difficult. Sliding under
David's radar had proven almost as impossible as
sliding under him, personally.

His current whereabouts piqued her curiosity. Earlier, she'd moved the scanner radio from the bedroom
to the credenza behind her desk to eavesdrop while
doing as little of her job as she could get by with.

During those fifteen or twenty diligent minutes, no incoming or outgoing Adam 1–01 transmissions had hit the airwaves.

Phone calls to Delbert, then IdaClare, then the rest of the gumshoe gang had also gone unanswered. All five of them being AWOL seemed ominous, until Hannah remembered Leo and Rosemary's wedding tomorrow evening. No doubt IdaClare and Company had divided to conquer the prenuptial errand list.

Probably.

Hannah's Blazer seesawed over the uneven terrain like a box turtle taking a constitutional. Adult devotees of the-world-is-my-crosswalk persuasion strolled into the driving lane. Most held their children by the hand; some let their kids run unfettered, then yelled at them when they darted into Hannah's path.

She jockeyed into a space beside a panel van. A short, jowly dude in a wide-brimmed sombrero behind the wheel of a King-cab dually tapped his horn as he pulled in beside her. He grinned, then winked.

Jeez Louise. A frog with delusions of being a prince. Hannah stalked off, thinking an obscene gesture but not making it. The dude might consider it an invitation.

Ducking under the rope barrier, she heard whinnies on the wind and looked to her right. Five Shetland ponies harnessed to a giant wheel were clopping in a perpetual circle. Gonna-be cowboys and cowgirls kicked the animals' flanks, eager to giddy-up a gallop.

Meet me in the east parking lot by the pony rides after the show. No cops.

Hannah shivered, remembering AnnaLeigh's expression, the desperation in her eyes when she'd passed that note. Why had she wanted a secret meeting? Was she afraid of Reilly? Afraid for her life? If so, why exclude David?

Last night, he'd been concerned enough to send Andrik as a substitute spy, which explained the detective's arrival at the scene within minutes of the shooting, as well as his unrelieved navy blue clothing.

With her hair whipping across her face, Hannah strode toward the big top, on the lookout for a less monochromatically attired Marlin Andrik.

AnnaLeigh's death hadn't affected the need for answers to those questions. Just the opposite. She'd represented a threat to someone, a threat more imminent than she'd realized, or she wouldn't have delayed the meeting until after the show.

Someone—presumably Reilly—had found out about the rendezvous, panicked and killed AnnaLeigh to shut her up. Except how could he have known about it? Why would AnnaLeigh write a note, slip it to Hannah then tell Reilly about it?

A hollow gaped at her midsection. David, the county's top cop, had been standing less than six feet away at the time. How else could AnnaLeigh have gotten her message across in private?

"Except that doesn't explain why she'd have told Reilly," she said aloud to herself.

"Reilly Boone?"

Through a curtain of windblown hair, Hannah glimpsed a bespectacled, middle-aged man with two cameras slung around his neck. "Sorry if I startled you, Ms. Garvey. I called after you, but I guess you didn't hear me."

He extended his hand. "Chase Wingate, of the *Sanity Examiner*. Glad to finally make your acquaintance."

"My pleasure, Mr. Wingate." Which it was, disregarding the timing factor. She'd seen the county weekly's owner–publisher at a distance and spoken to him on the phone. He'd impressed her as being smart, professional and spinproof.

"If you're looking for Mrs. Clancy, she and her friends left about ten minutes ago."

Bells tolled a warning. The huge brass kind, symbolic of Mongol hordes about to descend yonder hill. Hannah shifted her weight. "I wasn't, but why do I have a feeling I should have been?"

The newspaperman winced, sucking air through his teeth. "I guess I shouldn't have said anything. When I saw you, you looked a bit peeved, so I assumed Vera Van Geisen had called you."

Uh-oh. "And why would she do that?"

"Well…" He chuckled, as people do when they know the humor in a situation is sure to be one-sided. "From what I heard, Mrs. Clancy and her friends brought doughnuts to the circus people. Everything was fine until Mrs. Clancy's poodles escaped from her tote bag.''

Hannah smote her forehead—hard. Stay calm. This story may yet have a happy ending. Such as, a Bengal tiger having snarfed Itsy and Bitsy for breakfast.

"Before anyone could catch them," Wingate continued, "the dogs made a beeline to where the elephants were having a bath." His hand shot up. "No one was hurt in the stampede, but security escorted Mrs. Clancy and her entourage from the premises."

Hannah's jaw worked pistonlike, manufacturing noise but not words. "Entourage," she croaked. "Define entourage."

"I didn't catch their names. One was a—er, full-figured woman with short, dark hair. The other was taller, and wearing a Valhalla Springs golf visor."

Rosemary Marchetti and Marge Rosenbaum. In cahoots with IdaClare, they were trouble in triplicate. But where oh where, were Dick Tracy Bisbee and his faithful companion?

Hannah pointed at Wingate's digital camera and the long-lensed, nine-millimeter Canon with the flash attachment. "I won't read about this little incident in next Tuesday's edition, will I?"

"Oh, it's tempting. I'd give a month's advertising revenue for a shot of those tiny poodles terrifying three, full-grown Asian elephants."

"But..." she said. "And there'd better be a but."

"The *Examiner* isn't a tabloid and humiliating people isn't journalism." His expression changed from amused to cagey. "Which is why we didn't print any details of Mrs. Clancy and her bridge club's pot bust. Other than in the court report, of course."

Mental bells clanged again, but this time they tolled for thee. Hannah's fingers throttled her shoulder bag's strap. "I must be going, but it was nice—"

"Care to comment on the rumor that Reilly Boone is your father?"

Her laugh was as fake as Wingate's casual tone. "Good Lord, I'd never even *heard* of him until yesterday afternoon."

The newshound arched an eyebrow. "Pardon the cliché, but my information came from a reliable source. And I did hear you say, 'That doesn't explain why she'd have told Reilly,' a moment ago."

"Then maybe you should rethink your definition of reliable while you're cleaning your ears." Hannah flashed a high-wattage grin. "Pardon the cliché, but I'll swear on a stack of bibles, yesterday was the first time I'd ever heard the name Reilly Boone in my entire life."

They parted, Wingate walking toward the main entrance and Hannah in the opposite direction. She sensed his over-the-shoulder glances.

The truth had turned her loose, but hadn't set her free. Yet another guiding principle bites the big one.

Activity along the midway duplicated the day before, with the exception of an elephant posing for pictures. Mrs. Jumbo obviously hadn't recovered from being traumatized by the Furwads from Hell.

The pachyderm stampede might also explain David's whereabouts. When he heard about it, he'd probably laughed so hard he had to be sedated. When Hannah tattled to Jack Clancy—a phone call she must record for posterity—he'd need a defibrillator.

Near the flagged cones dividing the public area from the private one, a medium-built man in a glen-plaid sports coat and slacks was talking to Frank Van Geisen. He was standing in shadow and his back was turned, but he looked suspiciously like Marlin Andrik.

She sidled toward the ticket booth, just as Chief Deputy Jimmy Wayne McBride's long, trousered leg arced over the hitch connecting it to the Van Geisens' travel trailer. Heart skittering in her chest, Hannah about-faced and ducked into the big top.

Dust hazed the air from a worker sweeping the stands with a broom. In the center ring, the daredevil bicyclists practiced loop-de-loops on a low-strung cable. Above her, a tiny girl in a purple leotard slid into the splits on the high wire. Propmen with tool belts slung around their hips moved equipment in preparation for the afternoon matinee.

Because appearing confident was the same as having some, Hannah followed the hippodrome track, her chin thrust out and arms swinging. Without the audience, the band playing, the colored lights and luscious smells, the arena seemed as shabby and forlorn as an aged film idol who'd fallen on hard times.

Exiting out a side flap, she skulked around generators, power cords, guy wires, trucks, transports and assorted living quarters and emerged…at a bare patch of ground.

No mistake. No errors of the geographic kind, anyway. The Flying Zandonattis' rig was on her right. To her left, the bullet-shaped Airstream. In front of her, a strip of churned, rutted earth marked where the Boones' motor home had been parked.

Hands jammed in her pockets curled into fists. *What more proof do I need that Reilly's my father? Daddy dear has run off and left you again, sweetheart.*

12

A young woman carrying a laundry basket entered Hannah's peripheral vision. She registered a lithe figure and strawberry-blond curls, then returned to editing the mental videotape of her first encounter with Reilly Boone.

In it, before he ever spoke Hannah's name, she told him to get lost or she'd have him arrested. As the stranger walked away, David asked who he was. Hannah had laughed and said, "Oh, just some crazy old man."

The End.

No ghosts of wishes past. No tales of star-crossed, teenage lovers. No faded, wrinkled photographs of a ragtag kid astride a one-of-a-kind bicycle. No unanswered questions. No gunshots.

Time took poetic license with all memories. Malicious intent could revise painful ones into cocktail-party anecdotes. Excise unwanted scenes, splice in hindsighted abridgments and replay in a continuous loop, until what should have happened became what *had* happened.

"The cops impounded AnnaLeigh's rolling castle

last night," a Southern-accented voice declared. "Kind of a surprise, you not knowing that."

The laundry basket was now on the ground between the blonde's feet. Hands on hips, she appraised Hannah like a used-car buyer seeing past the shiny wax job and noting every dent and nick the owner tried to hide. "It's just easier for you to believe the worst about Reilly, isn't it."

Assorted comebacks, both snide and obscene, halted at the tip of Hannah's tongue. She sensed the woman's remarks were dares rather than insults. Besides, they were true.

"Wouldn't it be for you?" she asked.

"Gawd, yes." The woman's laugh held more irony than humor. "If I were you, I'm not sure I'd give half an ear to any good his friends had to say about him."

"Yes you would," Hannah said. "And so will I."

Five minutes later she was seated at a portable, metal picnic table outside Gina Zandonatti's travel trailer. The trapeze artist had pressed a thermal mug of herbal tea on Hannah, then excused herself to check on her sleeping baby.

The steaming concoction was supposed to be healthful and invigorating. It smelled like the bottom inch of water in a vase of dead flowers.

Across from her sat Arlise Fromme, the fiftyish horse trainer who'd baby-sat Gina's fourteen-month-old son during her trip to the Laundromat.

"Gina gets a couple of hours away from the kids," Arlise had explained, "and I get a couple of loads of clean laundry. Better deal for me than Gina, if you ask me.''

Arlise sniffed at Hannah's cup and wrinkled her nose. ''Don't tell me you like that crap.''

Hannah smiled. ''It's safe to say I've never tasted anything quite like it.''

''Work around horses a while and you will.'' Arlise's grin exposed a mouthful of gold fillings. She was as short and stocky as Gina was tall and slender. The dark, cropped hair visible beneath her ball cap was heavily salted. Her shoulders were broad, her neck nonexistent, and quarter-carat diamond posts glittered at her earlobes.

Surrounding vehicles broke the wind and mellowed the odor of animal must and manure. Disembodied human voices combined with blue jays and crows filibustering their territorial rights and jungle sounds common to *National Geographic* documentaries. Two elephants were shackled near the creek bank, their trunks and massive bodies swaying gently to and fro, as if the water were playing them a lullaby.

Gina stepped out the trailer's door, a mug in one hand and another laundry basket balanced on her hip. The table sagged under the weight of the basket. Faint gurgles emitted from the baby monitor she positioned beside it.

''Nicky's either pooping in his sleep or trying to wake up,'' Gina said. ''We'll know which pretty soon.''

Because Arlise had mentioned ''kids,'' Hannah

said, "The little girl I saw practicing in the big top. Is she your daughter?"

"Francesca," Gina said, her face aglow with maternal pride. "My parents wouldn't let me near a high-line until I was six, but like Vincente says, our daughter is a born flyer."

"Yeah, and Nicky was almost born *on* the wire," Arlise said in the manner of a left-handed compliment. "It isn't enough that Gina's gorgeous, talented and college-educated. She can be nine months gone and look like she ate a big supper."

"You still performed while you were pregnant?"

"Sure." Gina took a towel from the basket and shook it. "Everybody does, for as long as they can. There's no such thing as maternity leave in the circus."

"Or pensions, 401–Ks, sick leave, paid vacations," Arlise said, rolling a pair of crew socks into a ball. "Some of the fancy-dance arena shows give benefits, but the competition's fierce, and—" She shrugged. "A circus just isn't a circus unless its under the big top."

Gina and Arlise exchanged approving glances when Hannah plucked another pair of socks from the basket. "Reilly feels the same way, doesn't he?"

"Most do that's been on the circuit since the Romans sicced the lions on the Christians," Arlise said. Her lips curved into a sly smile. "That's how the circus got its start, you know."

Hannah didn't, and would have preferred to remain ignorant.

"There aren't many independent outfits like Van Geisen's left," Gina said. "It's survival of the fittest. The big shows have either gobbled up or bankrupted most of the little ones. Every season it's harder to book enough towns too small for arena shows but large enough to pull in a decent house."

Lint flew from the dish towel Arlise snapped. "If Vera and Frank hadn't found an investor to back this year's run, me and Ernie wouldn't have signed on. Go belly-up in the middle of the season and it's too late to contract with another circus."

Her eyebrow arched. "I'd sooner jump off a building than say, 'You want fries with that?' for the rest of my life."

"Then you're all subcontractors," Hannah said, "not permanent employees?"

Gina explained that it was good for the owners to vary the acts, and good for the performers not to play the same towns year after year.

"And if the owner needs a certain type of act to fill the bill," Arlise added, "he'll pay more, or give 'em a cut of the profits."

"It does get scary sometimes," Gina said. "Acts have always moved around a lot, but there were dozens more circuses for my parents and Vincente's to pick from." She flipped Arlise with a hand towel. "And I don't want to sack hamburgers for a living, either."

Arlise retaliated with a pair of Jockey shorts. "That's the breaks, kid. AnnaLeigh—devil take her—could've had us on the road to fame and fortune by next season."

"Uh-huh, sure. The only place The Amazing AnnaLeigh's All-Girl Review would've taken us is to jail on a morals charge, then divorce court, then the welfare office."

Hannah re-ironed a washcloth with her palm. "AnnaLeigh was going to start her own troupe?"

"Reilly didn't tell you about it? Gawd, that's all she talked about. A Vegas showgirl–style circus. Strictly female—riggers to ringmistress to performers to animals."

In *Gypsy,* the bio-pic of Gypsy Rose Lee's life, a burlesque-era stripper named Miss Mazeppa sang a song entitled, "Ya Gotta Have a Gimmick." Its spirit and theme was the unofficial anthem of the advertising industry, as well.

Hannah automatically brainstormed a publicity campaign, magazine features, TV spots, cheesecake calendars, souvenir posters—the possibilities were endless. "Has an all-girl circus ever been done before?"

"No," Gina said, "and AnnaLeigh was determined to put it together by next season. Reilly tried to tell her most acts are husband and wife, male and female couples, or teams. It's impossible to replace half of one overnight."

Hannah must have looked unconvinced, for Arlise

said, "Take Gina and Vincente. He's the catcher during part of their act. When she comes off a triple somersault, she's a hundred and twenty–some pounds of deadweight, flying at about sixty miles an hour. He has to snag her wrists without losing his leghold on the trapeze or blowing a shoulder."

Hannah's eyes widened. "I never thought of it that way. I always thought the catcher had the easy job."

"Vincente makes it look easy." Gina said. "Most of all, I *trust* him to catch me. I'm not saying a woman couldn't do it, but if I signed on with an all-girl show, Vincente would need a new partner for his act, and...well, I didn't marry him and have children so we could go our separate ways half the year."

She glanced at the empty space where the motor home had been parked. "Reilly didn't like the all-girl idea, either. They argued about it a lot."

"When they weren't fighting about AnnaLeigh catting around on him," Arlise said. "Reilly's a man, which makes him stupid to begin with, but you just can't help feeling sorry for him."

Hannah's "Why?" earned glares from both women.

"He treated AnnaLeigh like a queen," Gina said. "Which might be why she thought she was."

Arlise shook her head. "It was the inheritance from her mother that stuck AnnaLeigh's nose in the air. Not that it wasn't already aimed that a'way. It wasn't nearly enough to start a show from the ground up, but nobody could convince AnnaLeigh of that—Reilly, least of all.''

Gina shoved the laundry basket aside and sat down on the bench. ''I can understand how much you resent him for not being around when you were growing up—''

''Does everyone in this freakin' circus know my life story? Most of which *I* didn't know until yesterday afternoon?''

''Hardly a day passed that Reilly didn't mention your name,'' Arlise said, her tone clipping the words like scissor blades. ''He'd see a kid in the audience and say she looked like you when you were that age.'' She turned to Gina. ''How often did he have a Hannah sighting? Once a month? Sometimes twice?''

Gina nodded. ''I remember them from back when I was a kid. It gave me nightmares about Daddy wading into this ocean of blond little girls trying to find me, but he couldn't.''

Her bright blue eyes met Hannah's brown ones. ''Reilly and my dad were close friends, but they didn't speak for months after Daddy yelled at him, told Reilly to stop driving himself and everyone else crazy saying he'd found you, then drinking himself blind when he was wrong again.''

Hannah couldn't swallow and could scarcely breathe. So, he really had searched for her all these years. And how it must have hurt when he mistook someone else for her.

Maybe Caroline had done her a favor. Spared her

the kind of agony Reilly had endured. Except, if Hannah had known his name and tried to find him, they'd both have been spared years—decades—of heartache.

Arlise said, "That's one thing I guess we have to give AnnaLeigh credit for. She got Reilly on the wagon and saw to it he stayed there. Well, she saw to it he didn't throw more than one leg over the rail, now and then, anyway."

"Yeah," Gina sneered, "and all he did for her was teach her everything he knew, let her boss him around like he was her servant and control all the money."

"That's why he gambled," Arlise said. "Want to geld a horse? Cut off his balls. Want to geld a man? Cut him off at the billfold. Parlaying a hundred bucks into a thousand was Reilly's paycheck."

By Gina's expression, those paydays were few and far between.

"Reilly told me they were partners," Hannah countered. "Not in a 'Wow, am I magnanimous or what?' way, but as though he genuinely believed it."

"Oh, they were. AnnaLeigh just sliced the pie like Francesca shares her cookies with Nicky." Arlise took a sip from Gina's mug and made a face. "Before arthritis ruined his hands, it was fifty-fifty all the way. His stage name was The Amazing Aurelius, but he always put in the contract that the billing should read The Amazing Aurelius and AnnaLeigh."

"Then when she took over the act," Gina said, "the split went to ninety-ten." Noticing Arlise primed to interrupt, she said, "Okay, I'm being kind.

Make that ninety-five–five. Reilly got no billing at all, and AnnaLeigh decided which tricks to do in what order, the music, costumes—"

"When he could take a dump," Arlise droned, "how much toilet paper he could have to wipe with…"

Chuckling, Gina cuffed the older woman's arm. "Shame on you. Hannah probably thinks we're awful enough, talking about AnnaLeigh like this."

"Why? Because she's dead? Well, I haven't spoken one bit more *ill* of her than I did when she was breathing." Leaning forward, Arlise shook a finger at Hannah. "And as long as I'm shooting my mouth off, I might as well go whole hog. If I'd seen AnnaLeigh yesterday, I'd have told her to her face exactly what I thought of her humping her brains out with that man the night before."

Hannah's jaw dropped so far her ears popped.

"That's enough, Arlise."

"No, it isn't. Hannah has a right to know why Reilly did what he did. Doesn't excuse it, but—"

Hiccups, then a yowl wended from the baby monitor. In the background was a rattling noise. Hannah imagined small fists shaking a crib's bars, like an angry prison inmate.

Gina kneaded Arlise's shoulder. "Would you mind?"

"Yeah, I mind," Arlise groused, but swung around on the bench. "And if you think taking care of the baby'll stop me from saying my piece, you're wrong.''

"I'll tell her," Gina said. "I just wanted to be a little—"

"Kinder?" Arlise finished as she pulled open the trailer door.

Gina rolled her eyes. "I love that woman like a second mother, but sometimes…"

"I wouldn't want her for an enemy," Hannah admitted, then smiled. "This is going to sound corny, but if you can judge people by their friends, Reilly must have done something right to have you two in his corner."

Gina switched off the cootchy-coos amplified by the monitor. Clasping her hands, she rested her chin on her knuckles. "He has his faults, but honestly, he's had more than his share of bad luck, too." A sigh streamed between her lips. "Better you hear it from me, I suppose."

"Hear what?"

"Short and sweet, AnnaLeigh was Reilly's third wife. The first two died in circus accidents. Or did, depending on who you ask."

"Oh my God." The bilious tea Hannah had drunk sloshed in her stomach.

"I know. It makes what happened to AnnaLeigh seem worse than it already does."

"Were they…shot?"

"No, Reilly performed with a boy apprentice back then. His first wife was an equestrian and the other an aerialist. As far as how they died, ask ten people and you'll get ten different stories—especially now.

"Usually, we protect our own. Punish them, too. Everybody thinks we're scofflaw gypsies, but circus people are too dependent on each other to abide trouble or troublemakers."

Pausing, Gina lowered her arms and splayed her fingers on the table. "Reilly's problems were personal, until last night. The drinking, the gambling, fights with AnnaLeigh and his jealousy—the circus has no secrets."

"But what he did about it," Hannah said, "or what he's *accused* of doing, brought trouble down on all of you."

"I'm afraid so."

"And I'm guilty by association."

Gina's eyebrows knitted. "You noticed?"

Hannah heard televisions and stereos blare at children on arbitrary house arrest. She surveyed the backyard's empty lounge chairs, the coffee drinkers huddled at the far end of the dining tent. Groups of three or four talked and laughed like birds on a power line, their backs turned to the Zandonattis' trailer.

Some things you never outgrow. Cooties, yes. Hopefully. Schoolyard politics? Never.

"When I took a shortcut through the big top and no one paid any attention," she said, "I thought it was because of my take-charge assertiveness." Pursing her lips, she made a sound. "I figured out while

I was standing over there itemizing all the reasons to hate Reilly Boone that I was a pariah, too.''

"I'm sorry, Hannah.''

"For what?'' The grin was forced but sincere. "Being honest with me and loyal to him?'' Hannah cadged another look around the backyard. "If the sheriff's department released him after questioning him last night, could he be staying with someone? Johnny, maybe?''

"Uh-uh. Reilly knows the score. Johnny would be the last person he'd ask for help. Reilly might get word to me or Alise, but even that's doubtful.''

Hannah thought, David would have let me know somehow if charges had been filed, but a suspect can be held twenty hours without them. That leaves three possibilities. Either Reilly is still in custody, or he's holed up in a motel room, or he's on a bus bound for Anywhere Else, U.S.A.

Would he run? With a prior manslaughter conviction on his record, two deceased wives, the third dead of a gunshot wound he fired at her in front of a thousand witnesses and being already tried and convicted of murder in his circus family's eyes, why *wouldn't* he run? Unless…

"Why is everyone convinced AnnaLeigh's death wasn't an accident?'' she asked. "If she and Reilly were as miserable as you say, he didn't have to kill her. They could have gotten a divorce. Or is there some circus taboo about that, too?''

Gina explained how the Bullet Catch was performed, which echoed what David had told Hannah the night before. "I wish I could believe otherwise," Gina said, "but the shooting couldn't have been accidental."

Rather than argue the point, Hannah reserved judgment until she had time to think about it.

Gina continued, "**But** as much as they fought, AnnaLeigh and Reilly loved each other very much. One or the other *threatened* to leave so often it got to be a joke. Some of the guys—Johnny included— had running bets on how soon they'd kiss and make up, and how soon after that Reilly would be looking for somewhere to bunk for a night or two."

Head shaking, Hannah spread her hands in frustration. "Lemme get this straight. Reilly treated AnnaLeigh like a queen. She had him by the balls and the billfold. They argued constantly, but a divorce was out of the question because they loved each other *so* much. Except last night, Reilly intentionally killed her in cold blood."

Arms folded on the table, she inquired, "Does that about sum it up, or am I missing something?"

Gina burst out laughing, then clapped a hand over her mouth. "The way you— Oh, gawd, I'm— It's not funny...I *know* it's not funny."

"Oh yes it is. That's the problem. I haven't heard anything that sounds like a motive." Hannah dipped her chin. "No, I'm not a cop, I just date the sheriff. But in my unqualified opinion, either something happened between AnnaLeigh and Reilly that you aren't aware of, or that you haven't told me."

"Something happened all right." Sadness and repugnance chased across the younger woman's features. Her voice quieted to a confessional tone and a reluctant one, at that. "The night before last—Thursday—we'd just crossed the Missouri border when the engine conked out on Arlise and Ernie's transport truck.

"Reilly's an even better mechanic than he was a magician, so we all strung out on the shoulder to wait. Long story short, Arlise drove their camper back to Springdale, Arkansas, for a new water pump, Reilly stayed behind to help Ernie fix the truck and the rest of us came on up here."

Hannah said, "With AnnaLeigh driving the motor home alone."

"Right. It was a short jump, an easy setup and our third consecutive two-day show, so the Van Geisens bought a couple of cases of beer to celebrate. It wasn't a wild party or anything. We had to roll out early the next morning for the parade."

Hannah nodded.

"Alise said it was after nine before Reilly and Ernie got the truck fixed. She followed behind them, and they were about fifty miles from Sanity when the guys pulled into a truck stop to eat. Arlise told them she hoped they choked and drove on here."

Gina hesitated, her head bowed, directing her remarks at the table. "By the time Arlise pulled in, the party was over and everybody was lights out, except for AnnaLeigh. The miniblinds at the back of the motor home were closed, but—'' she looked up ''—the outline of a man having sex with AnnaLeigh was as clear as if they'd been wide open.''

"Oh, shit."

"Uh-huh. The kind that hits the fan."

Hannah thought a moment. "Except if Reilly caught AnnaLeigh in bed with another guy, why didn't he kill her—or both of them—right then and there?"

"He didn't catch them. It was midnight before Ernie and Reilly drove in."

The flame-thrower glare Hannah leveled at Gina's travel trailer should have torched it. *"Do you mean Arlise told Reilly what she saw?"*

"No, no, no. She didn't even tell Ernie until after the show last night. Someone else must have seen them, and blabbed about it. When Reilly heard—and he would have—as jealous as he was already, he must have just snapped."

Hannah mulled over that possibility. Reilly had demanded to know where AnnaLeigh had been when she walked into the motor home yesterday afternoon. He'd also noticed she wasn't carrying a purse and hadn't bought anything on her shopping trip—both signs of a jealous man and–or one who didn't trust his wife farther than he could throw her.

Maybe AnnaLeigh hadn't been sick the morning of the parade. Her symptoms would apply to a few beers and a hearty romp in the sack. At least, as best as Hannah could remember, she was reasonably sure they would.

"I presume only The Shadow knows who the shadow belonged to," she said.

Gina made a noise in her throat. "The double standard strikes again. You can rule out Vincente and Ernie. Other than them?" She hunched her shoulders. "There's a few guys in the crew that'd play while the cat's away. Plenty of townies were hanging around that night, too. Having a quickie with one of them would have been safer."

The trailer's metal storm door banged behind Arlise. A sock-footed cherub in overalls with golden ringlets bucked in her arms. Nicky's "Mommy— Mommy—down—pu' me down," was as insistent as Arlise's "Did you tell her yet?"

Gina plopped her son on the table and nuzzled his neck. "Yeh-yus." Her soprano chirp was common to mothers of babies and small-dog owners such as IdaClare Clancy. "Mommy told Hannah everything, didn't she, Nicky-nick? Oh yes she did."

The giggling little boy waddled around for a peek at the stranger in his midst. Hannah plastered on an exaggerated smile and finger-waved at him.

Goodbye, happy camper. Hello, Walter Matthau in miniature. Whimpering, "Mom-my," he stood up on Gina's thighs and buried his face in her hair.

"He's at that age," Arlise said. "Bashful around people he doesn't know."

Yeah, right. David would have the kid slapping high fives, down lows and on the sides in a nanosecond.

Jeers and laughter sounded behind her. The crystalline notes of a hammer dulcimer lilted from the fairgrounds. A reedy voice, amplified by a megaphone, invited one and all to attend the circus's afternoon matinee.

Arlise fiddled with the bill of her cap, then coughed into her fist. "I, uh, got a little carried away before I went in to get the baby. Spending most of my time around horses and Ernie, sometimes I'm not real good at talking to people."

"You care about Reilly," Hannah said. "That's nothing to apologize for."

"He deserved better than he got."

Hannah caught Gina's eye. So had AnnaLeigh, they agreed silently.

Arlise leaned sideways. "What the…" She scooted a hip's width, then blanched. "Stand by, ladies and gents. There's a ballyhooly heading straight for us, and Vera and Frank look madder'n hops."

"Uh-oh" didn't begin to describe the seismic foreboding that hummed through Hannah's bones. A host of possible causes scrolled through her mind. Number six hundred and forty-four had just ticked past when Frank Van Geisen said, "Ms. Garvey, I think these belong to you."

She reeled in her legs to pivot around on the bench. Froze in midspin. Gawked. Feeling her head tip as though her neck were testing its horizontal capabilities seemed vaguely significant.

Standing before her was a flushed and furious Vera Van Geisen and her ever-stoic husband. To Vera's right, a uniformed security guard gripped the arm of a green-haired Delbert Bisbee. Gargantuan trousers were hitched armpit high by a pair of suspenders. His face was painted a chalky, streaked white. Clipped to his nose was an orange, hollowed-out Titlist golf ball.

To Frank Van Geisen's left, another security guard restrained Leo Schnur. His ensemble included a hideous, knee-length floral polyester dress, accessorized by argyle socks and wing tips. A Prince Valiant wig, complete with bangs, hugged his bald head. Leo's crowning glory, however, was the horned, Valkyrie headdress used in annual productions of *O'Valhalla,* an original stage play written by one of the residents to celebrate the Vikings' mythical expedition to central Missouri.

"What's your game, huh? Sabotage?" Frank said. "First, three of your spies come a whisker from setting off an elephant stampede."

Vera, seething with rage to the roots of her overpermed, overbleached hair, chimed in, "Then we catch *these* two sneaking around, peeking in windows."

Delbert said, "We never—"

Hannah made a slashing motion at her throat. Leveling a wait-till-I-get-you-alone glare at the prime perpetrator, she stood and said, "I can't tell you how sorry I am, Mr. and Mrs. Van Geisen, but you have my word, there'll be *no more incidents* of this kind."

"Your word?" Vera's laugh was short-lived and snide.

"There better not be," Frank said, "or we'll have you arrested." At his nod, the rent-a-cops freed their prisoners and started away.

"Let's make ourselves perfectly clear." Vera's eyes scanned the small crowd that had formed. "If any member of the Van Geisen troupe sees you or your friends one inch inside our midway, we *will* press charges. Is that understood, Ms. Garvey?"

"Yes, Mrs. Van Geisen. It is."

The woman turned, took a step and reversed herself. "Oh, and you can tell your *father* to stop calling my office, too. Tell him he'll rot in hell before any of *us* pass the hat to pay his bail."

13

Please leave your name, number...

David cradled the telephone receiver. Unless Hannah was screening calls, she was still somewhere besides home.

Nothing's wrong, sport. It's a pretty day. Weekends are prime for drive-bys wanting to tour Valhalla. No reason at all for that scratchy feeling behind your breastbone.

David inserted the last of a burger in his mouth and grimaced. From the first bite, it had been chew and swallow, or choke. What appetite he might have had evaporated during the three-hour pounding at Woroniecki's office. He just needed a blood-sugar boost to stave off the shakes and cold sweats.

Feet crossed on Marlin Andrik's desk, David leaned back in the chair and closed his eyes to let the grease settle. Telephones to computers to scanners to Josh Phelps's subdued voice droned in Surround Sound. All of it white noise compared to the cussing, stomping, unholy hissy fit Claudina Burkholtz would throw if she found him.

Make that gets to me, he corrected. After all, his

Crown Vic was parked in plain sight at the curb. Except, unlike his office at the courthouse, the wrath of Claudina couldn't be visited on him without a key card to The Outhouse's front door.

He did feel a tad guilty about his almost last-minute cancellation of the debate she'd arranged with Jessup Knox at the fairgrounds. God knew he'd dreaded it, but scotching it wasn't premeditated. Why, he'd ironed his uniform, buffed his boots and everything this morning.

When Claudina cooled off, she'd understand the limit to the number of fools a man could suffer in one day....

The smell of smoke awakened David from a nap he didn't know he'd taken. "If I were you," Andrik said from the molded-plastic armchair on the visitors' side of the desk, "I'd see a doctor about those adenoids."

David yawned, scrubbed his face with his hands and peered between his fingers at the wall clock. Near as he could guess, he'd been 10–45 for eleven whole minutes.

Andrik graced him with a rictus smile. "Don't get up on my account. Seeing things from the dirtbag side is doing wonders for my sensitivity."

"Jesus, Marlin. You're a real comedian today."

"Must be on a roll. The first thing Beth said this morning was, 'You've gotta be kidding.'"

He tamped out his cigarette. Only two butts had been in the plant saucer when David sat down for his picnic. Either the detective had been in the field all morning, or he'd quit smoking again. For him, cutting back to a pack a day was the same as abstinence.

"How's Toots holding up?"

"I haven't talked to her today. Telephone tag."

Marlin looked skeptical and concerned, but didn't press. He knew about walls and the position Reilly Boone had put David in. Talking about it wouldn't shake any bricks loose.

"I just came from the Short Stack," he said. "Claudina's working the lunch shift and told me to tell you, you're off the hook."

"She's lying." David chuckled. "Thinks she can decoy me out of my 'fraidy hole and over to the café. She probably has a fork tucked in her apron pocket to stab me with when I get there."

"Not this time, boss." A smirk wasn't part of Marlin's facial lexicon, but his eyes had a wicked glint. "One of Jessup Knox's band of merry nimrods called after she got your message. Elvis can't make the gig, either."

"Isn't that dandy." The chair's swivel mechanism howled as David swung his legs off the desk. "Instead of feeling guilty about canceling, now I can feel guilty for not eating at the café and contributing to her tip jar."

"You were there in spirit." Marlin wiggled his fingers. "You owe me five bucks, Caspar."

"Good man." David reached back for his wallet.

"I talked myself hoarse giving that deposition. What was Knox's excuse?"

"Well, it seems that at approximately 10:00 a.m., a tree took a notion to throw itself right in front of that hot-to-trot Stealth Jessup Jr.—aka, Chip—got for his sixteenth birthday."

David's lunch turned leaden. "Was he hurt?"

"Uh-uh. The car's DOA, though." Marlin's non-smirk deepened. "The EMTs had a helluva time getting Chip out of it. The kid was two clicks past shit-faced."

"Drunk? At ten o'clock in the morning?"

"Hear-tay par-tay down on the river last night, dude. Chip should score as high on his SATs as he did the Breathalyzer."

A sigh of relief bellowed David's cheeks. A slug of watery soda left from lunch didn't quite wash the sour taste from his mouth. He loathed Jessup Knox, but the man's heart must have bled dry when he heard about the wreck.

Chip was a nice kid. Spoiled, but had none of the cocky, you-can't-make-me swagger that would be comical if it wasn't so obnoxious. "Thank God he didn't kill himself—or anyone else."

Marlin nodded, "Amen." He had two teenagers at home. Few things in life brought on a religious conversion faster.

"Who bought the beer?"

"Chip had a fake Louisiana ID in his possession.

Won't say who supplied it or where he bought the booze.''

"Aw, c'mon. That boy couldn't pass for twenty-one with a ski mask on.''

"Knox said he'll persuade the details out of him.'' Marlin's hand raised to his shirt pocket, hovered, then dropped.

Yep. He'd quit smoking again. "You realize who'll wind up catching the blame, don't you?'' Marlin said.

David shrugged, as though his shoulders were broader than they appeared. "Boys'll be boys,'' he said, exaggerating his opponent's drawl, "but young and foolish is one thang. Sheriff Hendrickson turning blind eyes to those sellin' alcohol to our young'uns is another. It's gotta stop, folks, and as a father myself I'll get *that* job *done*.''

"Spooky.'' Marlin flinched. "If I didn't know better, I'd think you were writing his speeches for him.''

"Easier to get elected, than reelected.'' David's tone dismissed Jessup Knox as a conversational topic. He tapped the accordion control file labeled with AnnaLeigh Boone's name and case number. "Got time to bring me up to date?''

"Sure.'' A flip-top box of Marlboros and lighter made their inevitable appearance. "Except I thought you wanted distance from this one. Because of Hannah.''

"I do.'' David straightened reports in the file folder he'd left open on the desk. "And it's impossible because of Hannah.''

"Jimmy Wayne thinks he saw her at the circus, bright and early."

"Am I surprised?"

"IdaClare Clancy and the pair she runs with were there before Hannah was."

David groaned and rested his brow on the heel of his hand. "Delbert and Leo?"

"Uh-huh. Marchetti and Rosenbaum." Marlin coughed. Or laughed. "Hey, that's catchier than 'Cagney & Lacey.'"

David just wished they'd stop trying to be Cagney and Lacey.

Truth be told, he admired all five Mod Squad members. They laughed easily and often, squeezed sixty seconds of living out of every minute and had come within an inch of solving three previous homicides using old-fashioned, by-guess-and-by-golly horse sense.

It was their habit of committing misdemeanors to clear felonies that worried him.

After Andrik described the latest near disaster, he gave David his impressions of the interrogation not covered in the reports, and the additional interviews from that morning.

"How did Reilly react to the Polaroids we found?"

"He didn't. I saved them for last, hoping the medical examiner in Springfield made good on that preliminary he promised, before I ran out of darts to throw. Reilly slapped the photos on the desk facedown. No comment."

"You're satisfied then," David said.

"I don't have to be. Cops arrest. Prosecutors file charges." Smoke streamed through Marlin's lips. "I gave Mack Doniphan what we had, and he thought it justified second-degree homicide. Could go to first-degree, with a piece or two of solid evidence. Judge Messerschmidt agreed, and set bond at the recommended amount."

"A hundred and fifty thousand's kind of steep," David said.

"Doniphan considers Reilly a flight risk. For several reasons."

Marlin responded to Phelps's leavetaking, then walked his chair forward to lean on the desk. "A carnie will snitch for pocket change, but circus people are a commune on wheels. Very defensive of each other and leery of everyone else, especially us."

"They're suspicious of townies and cops because townies and cops have always been suspicious of them."

"'Gypsies, tramps and thieves,'" Marlin sang. Cher had nothing to fear from his rendition. "The mentality's a bum rap and likely always has been. Problem is, the 'us against you-all' attitude gives Boone a couple of options, flight to avoid prosecutionwise.

"With AnnaLeigh dead, so is the magic act and his future with the Van Geisens, but Boone could hire on as an animal handler with another outfit. I'm told he's a horse whisperer, only his spiel works on anything with four legs.''

Reilly's body language and voice had galvanized when he'd told David and Hannah about his beginnings as a trainer, particularly when he mentioned Caroline demanding he beat the animals for frightening her.

Arthritis might not handicap a trainer as much as a magician, but… "Circuses have a mighty tight grapevine, Marlin. Would another troupe knowingly harbor a fugitive? Especially a guy accused of murdering one of their own?''

Cigarette butt number four smoldered in the ashtray. "Maybe not.'' Marlin strode toward the coffeepot. "Which brings up the other option.'' He hoisted the carafe at David. The sludge at the bottom scarcely rippled.

"No, thanks.''

Marlin continued. "According to the Brooks County sheriff, the Boones and other circus people have wintered around Molalla, Texas, for years. Quite a few retired there. Reilly could hightail it south with a sob story about needing money—say, AnnaLeigh's in the hospital, or whatever—and be in Mexico before anyone found out differently.

"He speaks the lingo,'' Marlin added. "Circuses are hot stuff down there, and who'd give a damn if he's a fugitive.''

David considered another possibility. "That works as well as a flight plan before the fact as after. Maybe

Boone dreamed in Spanish when he dreamed up AnnaLeigh's fatal 'accident.'"

"Damn straight."

Looking through Andrik rather than at him, David said, "How Hannah figures into it I don't know, but—" He recoiled. "Unless…"

"Boone capitalized on a golden opportunity," Marlin finished. "Give himself a .32-caliber divorce in the podunk county where his daughter's sweet on the sheriff, who would surely to God balk at accusing Dad of murder, then adios, amigos, before the hammer falls."

"He'd face extradition."

"On a single homicide charge in central Missouri? When burros fly."

David's head swayed from side to side. "Is Reilly that shrewd?"

"To take instant advantage? You tell me. First wife dies the night she rides a green-broke horse. No net, turnbuckle breaks, second wife falls to her death. That smells worse than this coffee."

"Reilly wasn't directly involved in either accident," David reminded. "Shooting AnnaLeigh outright deviates from any pattern."

"You *assume* he had no direct involvement in the others. Phelps hasn't had much luck gathering the info. Yet."

"Yeah, but…" Absent was a sense of loose ends plaiting into a neat, logical braid.

"Money's the motive," Marlin said. "I'll stake my badge on it."

"I'm not arguing motive, other than how Anna-Leigh's life insurance fits in. Would Reilly bolt and leave that money behind?"

"Greed versus self-preservation divided by risk," Marlin said. "He had to know, even if he skated on a homicide charge, the insurer wouldn't pay off without a private investigation."

"Which could take years," David allowed. "And with no statute of limitations on murder, could provide enough evidence for a charge later."

"It happens. Boone could have a wad of cash stashed at their house in Molalla, too. Gamblers don't always lose, you know."

The phone rang. Marlin said, "Hold that thought."

David stared out the window at the trees on the courthouse lawn hula dancing on the wind. Memory audibilized the *plang* of the flagpole's swaying pulley. Vehicles puttered around the square as though four consecutive turns was a road hazard.

A compelling case had been built against Reilly Boone, at least as compelling as the second-degree manslaughter charge that had almost been levied against David.

Maybe that's why he kept trying to punch holes in the evidence. Find nits to pick. Andrik had joked about sitting on the dirtbag side of the desk. Exactly a week ago, David had sat in that chair proclaiming his innocence, feeling the weight of circumstantial evidence bear down on him, and knowing his interrogators believed it and not him.

A cop must maintain objectivity. Once compromised, a vicious circle begins. Each error and miscue seems like proof of impaired judgment. Self-doubt generates more errors and miscues. Sooner or later, you either hesitate and get yourself or another cop killed, or overcompensate and kill somebody else.

My interests are conflicted, all right, David thought, but is it because of Hannah? Or a hairline crack in my belief system?

If he wanted to get psychological about it, taking Andrik's chair might not have been unconscious. Andrik letting him keep it might not have been, either.

"Uh-huh...sure," Marlin said into the receiver. "Late. Whatever. I won't. Love you, too. Bye."

Folding a sticky note, he slipped it in his jacket pocket, muttering something about honey-dos. "Now, what the hell was I—oh, yeah. The discrepancy in the bank account."

Another two hundred thousand and change. Large sums of money and Reilly's name did crop up in the same sentence with astonishing frequency.

Marlin said, "The Bank Secrecy Act says cash deposits or withdrawals in excess of ten grand must be reported to the feds. It's supposed to red-flag drug traffickers and others who use banks like the corner washateria. Like they've never heard of offshore Laundromats."

He started around the desk. "My new best friend,

Jerry What's-his-name at Cattleman's Union Fidelity, swears AnnaLeigh made the withdrawal fourteen months ago.'' From the file, he produced a fax with the Cattleman's letterhead. ''This signed copy of the form corroborates that.''

Beside the form, Marlin laid a faxed photocopy of a check AnnaLeigh had endorsed and the account's signature card. ''I'm not a handwriting expert, but...''

David adjusted the desk lamp. ''I see what you mean. The letters are smaller, closer together in AnnaLeigh's signature on the form. The slant is more pronounced, too.'' He frowned. ''But people don't write their names the exact same way every time.''

''True, but there are stronger similarities in the endorsement and signature card than on the form.''

''You think Reilly forged it?''

''Who else had reason to? Probably did it after Jerry What's-it had a sudden urge to bend down and tie his shoelaces, then got a cut for his trouble.''

Marlin ticked off on his fingers, ''The motor home was financed. The Boones rented the house in Molalla. In the past fourteen months, AnnaLeigh didn't lease a villa on the Riviera, buy a Jaguar or invest in the stock market. If she withdrew the money, where'd it go?''

David splayed his hands. ''Blackmail?''

''Two hundred grand for three crappy Polaroids? Jesus. A hundred bucks, maybe. And why would *she* dummy the monthly statements? It was her money.

She inherited it from her mother's estate. Besides, AnnaLeigh was the family bookkeeper.''

A related question David had put on hold prowled along the fringes of his mind. Bookkeeping. Something to do with…

''Those credit card late fees. If the personal account was short and AnnaLeigh thought she had a two-hundred-grand nest egg, wouldn't she transfer money to the checking account to avoid them? And if she tried, she'd have known the balance had shrunk over a year ago.''

Marlin gestured as though it was a point he'd forgotten to include. ''Reilly told me—and others corroborated—that circus mail delivery is sometimes Murphy's Law personified.

''Before the troupe hits the road, they send forwarding notices with the outfit's headquarter's address to their post office, creditors, yada-yada. The outfit then submits a list of forwarding addresses to the post office, based on the schedule to coincide with what town they'll be in on Tuesdays and Fridays.

''Usually the boss clown picks up the mail, but Frank Van Geisen is their postman. He collects the outgoing, then sorts and delivers the incoming.''

David said, ''I can guess where this is leading. A screwup anywhere along the line has a domino effect.''

''Delays are expensive, too,'' Marlin said. ''Credit-card companies don't give thirty-day grace periods anymore. Even with a permanent address, you're lucky to have two weeks to make a payment before you're nailed with a late fee.''

David's eyebrows raised in mute agreement. Absently, he scratched the bony ridge where his ribs met. Some people felt weather changes in their joints. His purveyed nebulous warnings that something somewhere was amiss.

Marlin hiked a hip on the corner of the desk. ''Look, I didn't dump the puzzle out of the box, and *boom,* there's a picture of the Grand Canyon in five hundred, interlocked pieces.''

''I know. Putting enough together in under a day for Doniphan to file charges is impressive as hell.'' David smacked his lips. ''But you're nowhere near ready to pop the top on a brewski and celebrate.''

''No. Not yet. This isn't a hoist-one-for-justice kind of case.'' Fingers tapped and twiddled a need for existence, other than as a cigarette holder.

''Why not?'' David added, ''Hannah's relation to the suspect excepted.''

''Because critical as the first twenty-four hours always are, that's all we get on this one. If we miss something, it's gone. No second chances, no followups. By sunrise tomorrow, there won't be anything left of the crime scene, or primary witnesses besides tire tracks and garbage bags.''

''Do you think you missed something?'' David asked.

''We always do. And defense attorneys always find them.'' Marlin's expression would frighten young children. "It's an extra piece of the puzzle that bugs me. The medical examiner may send it down the tubes, if he ever finishes the friggin' lab report."

David didn't know what he was referring to, but his tone discouraged questions. Marlin played his own hunches. If they didn't pan out, no explanation was needed.

"Gotta detour to the supermarket for milk, bread and a box of Ding-Dongs," he said. "Then it's back to the circus for more fun and games. Hell, if the little woman's craving chocolate, I might as well grab a six-pack for later."

His scowl averted to the ringing phone. "Now what? If Beth's out of..." He answered with a charming, "Yo—Andrik. Yeah, he's— Wait, hang on a sec." Covering the mouthpiece with his palm, Marlin said, "Janice Ford, for you. Says it's urgent. Want the call transferred over here?"

David's arm shot out. "Yes."

The detective's eyes narrowed. He knew Mercy Hospital's pretty, young lab tech had pursued David for months. "Do I need to take a whiz?"

"I'd appreciate it if you would."

David waited for the bathroom door to slam, then cleared his throat. "This is Sheriff Hendrickson."

"Oh—uh—hi, David. It's me, Janice." She laughed. "Gosh, I thought the guy that answered at your office told you who it was."

Pulse beating loud in his ear, he struggled to keep

his voice pleasant but businesslike. "Force of habit, I reckon."

"I know just what you mean. Half the time I answer my phone at home, 'Lab, Janice speaking.'"

"Uh-huh." Paper crackled as David whipped through the file folder.

Pause. "Well, I won't keep you—I know how busy you are—but I have the test result you wanted on that Jane Doe. I'm really sorry it took so long."

"No problem, Janice."

"Since the sample was extracted instead of drawn, I typed it twice, to be certain. Both came back AB, which is rare. Only about five percent of the population have it."

"Okay…" The sheet David had searched for was found on the second pass. "What if Jane Doe's father is type O?"

Her silence extended a good five seconds. "I—um—gosh, David. Neither parent can be type O if the child is AB."

"You're sure."

"Absolutely. A hundred and ten percent sure." The lab tech's voice was so bright, David almost laughed. The next bulletin to scorch Sanity's gossip hot line would be *Blood test proves David Hendrickson is not the father of Jane Doe's baby.*

A toilet's *kawhoosh* harkened Andrik's return. And another you'd-better-not-be-two-timing Hannah look.

"Thanks, Janice. I really appreciate your help." He

gritted his teeth. "Oh, and the bill for the test should be sent to me, and not the county."

"It will be," she assured. "I entered the charge in the computer myself. Is there, um, anything else?"

There wasn't, and never would be. Marlin, of all people, should know that.

The file folder slapped shut. David pushed back in the chair then stood. The expected rush of vindictiveness and anger at his suspicions proving correct hadn't materialized.

It would, though, and he'd welcome it. Needed its heat to thaw the icy cavern in his gut. He'd asked Luke Sauers the wrong question hours too late. He'd acted without asking Hannah, at all.

For Marlin's benefit, David forced a smile. "I s'pose the sooner I take off the sooner you can get back to work."

The detective's eyes flicked to the phone, then back to David. "Where you headed? Valhalla Springs?"

"After a while."

Marlin didn't like David's answer. He punched a code to release the door's lock mechanism. "Give Toots my best. When you get around to her."

The message behind the message stung like hell. David ignored it, as he did the fact that anything pertaining to Reilly Boone pertained to the investigation. Right or wrong, Marlin Andrik ranked third on David's needs-to-know list.

Once inside the shuttered courthouse's east entrance, he wound up the staircase, one purposeful step at a time. His senses perceived the fusty air, voices reverberating from above, his parched mouth, his shadow framed within rectangles of sunlight on the risers. A single thought permeated his mind: Reilly Boone would have one chance to give him a straight answer.

Dispatcher Allen Reece buzzed him through the department's secondary entrance. Reece nodded hello while speaking into a stand microphone and typing vital statistics for a license check into the computer. The dispatcher's plywood, half-walled workstation crammed with computer and communications equipment looked like a third-world NASA.

A high counter with slots for blank forms partitioned the small office adjacent to the jail's booking area. Video monitors bracketed below the ceiling surveiled the visitors' area, cells, hallways and processing rooms on the oh-shit side of a steel entry door.

Jim Lyndell, the turnkey, sat facing the monitors. With a backward glance, he scrambled from his chair. "Been real slow since lunchtime, sir. Busy before that, though."

"You winning?" David indicated the arm Lyndell held behind his back.

"No, sir." The two-month veteran of the department's most thankless job blushed to the roots of his crewcut. He tossed his Game Boy into a cubbyhole in the counter. "Sorry, sir. It won't happen again."

Eyes trained on the monitors' black-and-white images, a vise tightened around David's chest. Cells built for single prisoners held three, and in one case, four. Orange, county-issue coveralls separated the convicted and the yet-to-be-tried from those awaiting arraignment.

Some sat, or sprawled, on cots and bunks. Others talked among themselves. A restless few did knee bends and vertical push-ups against the bars. The visitors' room was empty. Hallways, processing room—clear.

"Where's Reilly Boone?"

"The magician?" Lyndell grinned and flapped a hand. "Oh, he got bailed out a while ago."

"Who posted it? Why wasn't Andrik notified?"

The jailer backpedaled a step. "I did, Sheriff. Honest." Lyndell sorted through a stack of paperwork piled in a metal basket. "Detective Andrik wasn't in his office. I left a message on his voice mail."

Which Marlin hadn't checked before waking David from his nap. If he had, his gored-bull bellow would have peeled the paneling off The Outhouse's walls.

David took a stapled sheaf of forms from the jailer.

"Boone was released at 11:07," Lyndell said, the answer redundant to the printed information. "His daughter posted bail. Nice lady—"

David slapped the paperwork on the counter and stalked out. With every step, the litany in his brain grew louder.

Ten thousand dollars. Hannah paid a bondsman ten fucking thousand dollars—cash—to get that lying son of a bitch out of jail.

14

Hannah stared into the shelved cavern that was her refrigerator. Napoleon Hill, the late great motivational speaker, once said, what the mind can believe, the mind can achieve. Or something to that effect.

If she stood there long enough and really concentrated, maybe she could achieve groceries. Nothing fancy. She had a full jar of pickles. All she needed were a few things to go with it. A pound of pastrami or smoked turkey would be nice. A little cheese, some lettuce, a tomato, potato salad, a loaf of bread…

"Great place you got here," Reilly said for the fifth or sixth time. "Cozy."

Her "uh-huh" coincided with a stomach growl. Food sources, both cash-and-carry and prepared to order, were as close as Main Street. So was an encounter with residents who'd last seen Reilly onstage, screaming his dead wife's name. The alternative was a solo supply run to the mercantile. Except she wasn't comfortable with leaving him alone, even for ten or fifteen minutes.

Which made no sense, but what *had* in the past twenty-four hours?

God, how she missed the rational, logical, nonimpulsive Hannah of old. *She* would have driven from the circus's midway to Price Slasher for groceries, *then* stopped by the First National Bank of Sanity to cash in a third of her net worth in CDs and rack up a whopping penalty for early withdrawal, to bail out and bring home a man she'd met only yesterday, who'd been charged with first-degree homicide.

Live and learn. Next time the compulsion struck to aid, abet and feed a felony suspect, she'd have her priorities straight.

Malcolm wedged himself between her thigh and the door. He sniffed, looked up, then sat down on his haunches as though expecting the movie to start at any moment.

Hannah's eyes flicked from a carton of eggs to a tube of refrigerator biscuits. The cupboards were Mother Hubbard–like, too, but a menu idea suggested itself. Ingredients and dog removed from the refrigerator, she reached into the cabinet for a jumbo-size can of spinach.

"Ever heard of a dish called Moses in the Bulrushes?"

Reilly's lips parted in surprise. "Not since I asked your grandma what in Sam Hill she was spooning into your mouth, I haven't."

No one insulted the bizarre and often delicious concoctions that flowed from Maybelline Garvey's imagination and stove. She believed anything could be rendered edible if it was boiled, baked or fried long enough. Exceptions were smothered in cream of mushroom-soup gravy before serving.

"What did Granny say?"

"She dared me to take a bite. I told her it tasted a lot better than it looked, and that I'd be glad to polish off the plate when you were through." Reilly's smile widened. "When you were, Maybelline scraped the leavings into the slop bucket, set it in front of me and said, 'Have at it, boy.'"

A sheet of aluminum foil sufficed as a cookie sheet for the biscuits. Both were made of the same metal, but one had to be washed afterward and the other didn't. A culinary no-brainer.

"Granny must have appreciated the compliment," Hannah said, "or she'd have dumped the bucket on your head."

"She did, when I asked her for a fork. You laughed till you spit up all over yourself."

Hannah could guess what happened next. A dose of castor oil for her, and Reilly scrubbing the cracked linoleum floor until the sound of kneecaps grinding down to cartilage got on Maybelline's nerves.

Memories dropped on the turntable of Hannah's all-occasion, mental Wurlitzer. Sweetened through the ages like wine? Well, plenty of them had, thank you very much. As for the others, it would be a bitch finding something to rhyme with "sour like vinegar."

While Hannah flattened the spinach in the bottom of a skillet with a wooden spoon, Reilly stroked Malcolm's fleecy throat. The Airedale-wildebeest's tongue lolled out the side of his mouth; the dog was virtually orgasmic with bliss. Reilly just looked sad and thoughtful and tired.

She laid down the spoon on the theory a watched vegetable never simmers. Cooking was said to be relaxing by people who did it often and well. She did neither, and imagining the slam of a Crown Victoria's door at two-second intervals would trip-wire the Galloping Gourmet.

David had no right to be angry or to feel betrayed. Okay, yes, he did, because of the protective, emotional cocoon she'd wrapped herself in.

As for Reilly, it wasn't as if she'd tossed a rope through the jail's window for him to shinny down. Bail was made to be posted. Reilly would have done so himself if he'd had the money, and he had given Hannah his word he'd pay her back.

Her problem. Her decision. Her money. End of discussion. Until the inevitable actual one with David.

She checked the biscuits' progress through the oven window, then refilled Reilly's coffee mug. When she slid it across the counter, he stayed her hand.

"Sweetheart..." he began.

She'd rather he wouldn't call her that. David, Delbert, Jack Clancy, Andrik—all had pet names for her. She liked them. Even Toots, though she'd never disappoint Marlin by telling him.

Sweetheart grated. Jarrod had called her that, inflected with his slightly mocking, definitely superior

British accent. The whisper of Kentucky twang and affection in Reilly's voice couldn't revise history.

"I'm sorry, Hannah. I swear to God I am." His eyes raised to hers, the irises more black than brown, and halved by skin folds drooping over the lids. "I'm sorry for lying to you."

Rusty, capped-off fuel pipes spiked the concrete service island in front of Clyde Corwin's filling station. Ghostly outlines of the Texaco star were still visible on the spavined canopy and the lollipop-shaped sign beside the road.

A portable billboard advertised Flats Fixed, Small Enjin Repair, Tun-ups, Etc. Whilst U Wate. One of the double bay doors was open; a late-model pickup was reared up on jack stands. Clyde would never win a spelling bee, but how many national champions could turn a rotor?

The Crown Vic's tires crunched to a halt alongside the cinder-block building. Paint was peeling off the exterior walls like shed scales. The plate-glass window was blanketed with taped-up sale bills, reward posters for lost pets, church bulletins, weight-loss come-ons and garage sale flyers.

No pit bulls bared their fangs as David tramped through calf-high weeds to the impound lot. The cattle gate with sheet metal wired to the lower half stood open. No motor home of any make or model was parked inside the pitiful excuse for a fence.

"Good as I'm getting at predictions," David said,

"I ought to buy a turban and a deck of tarot cards and emcee my own infomercial."

Reminding himself of the stern lecture on anger management he'd delivered to himself after storming from the courthouse, he rolled his shoulders as he walked toward the clank of tools on concrete.

The proprietor was crouched on a wheeled mechanic's stool, his arms sunk to the elbows in the pickup's fender well. "If'n you're here about my letter," he said without looking up, "save your wind, Sheriff. I've done quit the impound business and that's that."

"Well, now, Clyde, you have me at a disadvantage, since I haven't had time to check the day's mail yet."

"Hmmph. Didn't mail it anyhow." The grate of metal on metal echoed off the walls. "After that girl at the bank notaried 'em for me, I plunked a copy on your desk, personal, same as I did Commissioner Gray's."

David folded his arms at his chest. "I'm here, and the letter's at the courthouse, so how about giving me the gist of what you said?"

Clyde scooted backward, an obstinate look on his grimy face. "It says, as of ten o'clock this morning, I ain't runnin' no impound lot for the county no more, and that all them vehicles best be gone off'n my property by noontime Monday."

"Is that why the gate's open?"

"Yes, sir. I give notice, right and proper. Don't

care who takes them cars away, neither, 'long as they're gone by Monday.''

"You have a contract with the county, Clyde.''

"Ain't you listenin', man? Not no more I don't.'' Clyde's chin buckled. "Weren't ever nothin' in it that said I had to put up with folks killin' my dogs for pure spite.''

He wiped his hands on a shop rag, then dabbed his temples. "I already done buried five—every one a bloody mess from that poison eating 'em inside out. It woulda been kinder for them murderers to put a bullet betwixt their eyeballs.''

No argument. Clyde's pit bulls had been a continual source of complaint, but nothing justified poisoning a dumb animal and leaving it to die in agony. "The two dogs you found this morning are all right, aren't they?''

The mechanic blew his nose in the rag, then shoved it back in his pocket. "The vet says King, my stud male, will come around 'afore the day's over. He ain't so sure about the litter of pups Queenie is carryin'. If she loses 'em, I'm out another eight, nine hundred dollars. Maybe more.''

His arm swept the bay. "This place was a goin' Jesse till them convenience stores, and those hurry-up lube joints priced me outta business. Nobody can make a livin' competing with them, and I can't sell the building for nothin' else, lest I pay to have the underground fuel tanks dug up first.''

"It's a catch-22, all right,'' David agreed.

"Ye-ap. Didn't know them Communists had a name for it, but that's what it is." Clyde stood like a man who'd spent more years bent over an engine block than upright. "I make enough off small jobs for taxes and insurance and some left to eat on, but them dogs pay more'n impound fees ever thought about."

"I realize that, Clyde, but—"

Grease striped the man's palm. "You can't afford to post a deputy at night. I can't afford no private one, nor to lose another dog. I ain't makin' trouble, Sheriff. I've just had too much of it my own self and I can't take any more."

David made a mental note to talk the commissioners out of suing Corwin for breach of contract and other willful violations thereof. Ray Bob Oates would argue against a lawsuit, too, but in this instance, the sheriff's opinion would have greater impact.

Finding another lot keeper wouldn't be difficult, but... "It'll be darn near impossible to remove those vehicles as fast as you want them gone, Clyde."

"I won't be responsible for 'em whilst they're here," he warned. "I ain't lockin' the gate, neither. Sure as I do, without the dogs to stop 'em, somebody'll bust it down and steal parts right and left."

David shook his head. "I want that gate locked on the off chance there's one or six people who haven't heard you fired yourself yet. If any damage occurs, we'll thrash it out later."

"I don't like that a bit, Sheriff."

"Keep pushing me in a corner and you'll like it a helluva lot less, Clyde."

A toe of the mechanic's boot excavated a pock in the concrete floor. "Aw, it ain't you I'm riled at. Jessup said he'd install security lights and cameras—as a favor— before I ever bid that contract. Then he promised this morning he'd put 'em in as soon as he's elected. Let the county pay for it, he said."

Clyde lifted a shoulder. "My old lady'd skin me alive, but he ain't gettin' my vote. He's like them fellers down to Cape Canaveral. Always promising the moon and forgettin' who's payin' for the gas to get there."

David would have to remember to tell Claudina that one, but not the source. "Before you go lock that gate," he hinted, "how many vehicles have gone through it today without a release from my department?"

Clyde had the decency to appear sheepish. "Two. Dub Arpel's wife took his F–150 'cause she didn't have no other way to get to work."

The last time David had seen Arpel he was curled up on a jail cot, sleeping off his bimonthly binge. If Sanity's engine remanufacturing plant paid every Friday, the tool-and-die operator would never spend a weekend at home.

"Let me guess," David said. "The other was a motor home and trailer with Texas tags."

"Uh-huh. I disremember the owner's name, but it

matched the registration and his license, and his spare key fit the ignition.''

"Was anyone with him?"

"A woman driving a Blazer—'94, maybe '95 model—dropped him off. I didn't get a good look at her.''

David had suspected—make that, hoped—someone from Van Geisens' had helped Boone liberate his motor home. He started for the bay door. "Lock that gate, Clyde. *Now*. No more unauthorized releases, or you'll answer to me. Clear?"

"Yes, sir."

"Be in my office Monday...10:00 a.m. sharp. We'll work something out with Paul Gray about the contract.''

"Lied?" Hannah repeated. The kitchen dimmed, as if the sun were retreating to another galaxy. With exaggerated precision, she set the coffee carafe on its warming plate, then turned around. "What did you lie to me about, Reilly?"

"I don't know what possessed me—"

"What did you lie to me about, Reilly." Her fingernails yielded to the inflexible counter.

"Shame," he answered, his voice soft yet laced with steel. "That's why I lied, so as not to feel it, but all's I did was swap one kind for another.

"I told you I ran away from home to join the circus.'' Reilly shook his head. "My daddy sold me for fifty bucks to an animal trainer he met up with, scouting for bear cubs or a mountain lion kit to put in his act.

"There was nine of us kids. Too many mouths to feed and a new one every year. Me being the oldest boy, I ate too much and grew too fast. There wasn't enough work at the mine for the men, much less a puny, half-starved kid."

Hannah couldn't speak, couldn't see through the shape-shifting kaleidoscope of welling tears.

Reilly sat back, his features rigid, his face as pale and rough as bleached hide. "I saw a movie way back when. Don't recall who was in it—Burt Lancaster, maybe. 'Spect I was too busy cobbling his shoes onto my feet to care.

"He was book-smart and lived in a middlin'-nice house, but he wanted an adventure—to see the world a little. It broke his mama's heart when he ran off and joined the circus. Years later, after he got famous, oh, how proud she was for making something special of himself, and her and the whole town."

Reilly sawed a finger under his crooked nose. "That's what I wanted you and Sheriff Hendrickson to think I did. That I'd had me a never-ending adventure, instead of being sold off like a damn plow mule."

Was there anything more vile than parents selling their own child? The knot in Hannah's throat swelled so hard and huge that pain shot through her temples and across her brow. Lashes damp and heavy, she refused to cry. If she started, she wouldn't stop. She'd held in too much for too long. It would all crash down on her at once if she let it.

"Oh, Reilly...I'm so sorry—"

"Don't be, sweetheart. It shames me then and now to be a mule, but I've had those adventures and I've seen the world and that's more than a lot of others can say."

He straightened his jacket lapels. "Boone's not my birth name, either. I changed it from O'Donough—legal—'cause I didn't want Pa's if he didn't want me."

Perfect. Hannah tipped back her head, her lower lip trembling, stretching into a smile, then a grin. Born in Kentucky, reborn a Boone. As in Daniel, the state's favorite adopted son and hero. Peachy freakin' perfect.

A hand brushed her arm. For an instant she shrank from his embrace, but he wasn't a stranger anymore and he'd never been a threat.

Cheek resting near his shoulder, she closed her eyes and breathed in stale sweat and smoke, cleaning fluid and lanolin. And she wondered how a daughter was supposed to feel, and wished—yes, *wished*—she'd known for so long, the thought wouldn't occur to her.

The circus had been a foreign country to Caroline. Different, yet strangely similar to the emotional place Hannah found herself in. Nothing was familiar or natural. She didn't speak the language, didn't know the customs, the rules, the mechanics of a father-daughter relationship.

Burrrrr-ff.

Startled, she stepped back. "Malc—" Her head whipped toward the cooktop. Grabbing the spoon, she stirred the spinach that was simmering nicely and in no danger of scorching.

"Shoo," she commanded, waving her other hand. "Both of you, back on the spectator side of the bar. Cooking is hard enough without mad dogs and Irishmen pestering me while I'm doing it."

"I'd be happy to help," Reilly said.

"Uh-uh." She looked over her shoulder at the biscuits. Her lip caught between her teeth and her gaze lingered a beat or two longer than necessary. "Everything's under control."

"No," Frank Van Geisen said. "Nobody here's seen Reilly since that deputy hauled him off last night."

He motioned for David to follow him a few yards from their travel trailer. "Vera's in there right now, talking to the gal in charge of the committee that booked us about packing 'er in after the matinee." Frank grimaced. "Nothing short of chains will keep my wife here if she finds out Reilly's on the loose."

"Why?"

"Because she's scared to death of him. Has been for years, I guess. Said she thought Reilly had...well, *reformed* is as good a word as any, when he quit drinking. After what he did to AnnaLeigh, Vera says there's no tellin' what he'll do next.''

David groomed the phantom mustache he'd shaved off before he left Tulsa. Fearful didn't jibe with the troupe's combination CEO, stage mother, Dear Abby and dictator when circumstances warranted.

''You didn't know your wife was afraid of Boone until recently?''

''I knew Vera didn't much care for him,'' Frank said. ''Her and AnnaLeigh hit it off like peas in a pod. Always had their heads together about something or other. Except Vera may forgive, but she doesn't forget.''

''What do you mean?''

''Reilly's first two wives—Darla and Jeannie. They were friends of Vera's, too. It's like she told that Detective Andrik, she gave Reilly the benefit of the doubt, but just could never quite trust him.''

From the corner of his eye, David saw Vera profiled in the trailer's window. She was talking into a cell phone—arguing, by her gestures. A memory bubble floated to the front of David's mind. ''What did she buy yesterday?''

Frank's lack of comprehension was apparent.

''When she invited AnnaLeigh to go shopping with her after the parade. What did Vera buy?''

''They didn't—'' His eyebrows met and became one. ''Groceries, maybe. I dunno. You'll have to ask her.''

''You didn't go to town with them?''

"No, sir. One of us has to man the ticket booth." Frank grinned. "Besides, do I look crazy enough to go shopping with two women?"

They exchanged a couple of sexist remarks on the subject, then David asked, "How about you and Reilly? Did you get along all right?"

"Oh, yeah. Me and him used to jackpot for hours on end."

"Beg pardon?"

Frank laughed. "Sit around telling stories. Reilly's got a million of them. So's Johnny Perdue. A man can learn a lot listening to them. Walking circus encyclopedias they are, sure enough."

"Jackpot, huh?" David smiled. "For a minute, I thought you meant you were Reilly's gambling buddy."

Van Geisen was as Joe Average as a typical witness description. Early to mid-fifties, medium build, brown hair, hazel eyes, no prominent scars, no distinguishing characteristics.

Except for his habit of flicking his thumb with his ring finger when he was thinking. Not thinking about lying, necessarily. More like a kid who breezed through eight years of math then flunked algebra because right answers suddenly counted against him if he arrived at them the wrong way.

David shifted his weight to the opposite foot and his demeanor to good ol' boy. "I'll be honest with you, Frank. I realize things look dire for your friend, Reilly Boone. No question about the smoking gun being in his hands, and we've got enough motives to loan some out to the less fortunate.''

He paused, his jaw craning upward. "It's also true that Detective Andrik and the county prosecutor aren't prone toward errors in judgment..."

"But you don't believe he killed her, either," Frank blurted, his hands as still as a stopped watch.

"Of course he doesn't," Vera said, startling her husband. "Who would want to believe that his girlfriend's father is a murderer?"

She twined her arm around Frank's and gazed up at him. "We've been preoccupied with our own worries, but can you imagine the awkward position this has put Sheriff Hendrickson in?"

Frank twitched but said nothing. Vera's lips drew back in a tight smile. "I laid out your yellow tux for the matinee. I thought it would be more cheerful."

By her husband's expression, he'd need a lungful of nitrous oxide to approach mildly amused. "What about the evening show?"

"Nothing has been decided yet," Vera said.

"That's funny," David said. "I took a call from Miz Janocek, the Dogwood Days committee chairlady, on my way over here. From what I gathered, she's counting on you to fulfill the terms of your agreement."

Her voice cordial yet crisp, Vera replied, "If that's why you're here, I don't see how our negotiations with the Dogwood Days Committee has anything to do with you."

"They don't, ma'am. Not directly." David pulled his notebook from his shirt pocket. "The whereabouts of Reilly Boone and his vehicle do though."

"What? I thought he was in jail."

"He was, until he made bail and collected his motor home and trailer from the impound lot. I figured he might have come here."

"Here?" Vera's sunlamp tan faded to a sickly white. Her eyes widened and skittered. "No, no... That can't be. Reilly has to stay locked up. It's too dangerous..."

"Now, honey, there's nothing for you to worry about," Frank said.

She shoved him backward. "Don't 'now, honey,' me. If Reilly finds—" Vera whirled around. "This is an outrage, Sheriff. Everyone in this troupe cooperated with you. Gave you and your men carte blanche, despite the inconvenience. Despite our financial losses. And now you tell me a killer—a *murderer*—is walking around free?"

The woman hadn't yelled, but David's ears heated as though she'd screamed like a banshee. "A suspect can't be detained once his bail is paid, ma'am."

"Ten thousand dollars, wasn't it? I'd love to know how Reilly paid it. He doesn't have any money."

Vera advanced a step. "Hannah Garvey posted it, didn't she?" Lips moving in silent condemnation, she looked back at her husband. "We're tearing down. Right now. If the sheriff won't protect us, we'll have to protect ourselves."

Frank's eyes met David's, held, then slowly averted to his wife.

"I can't let you do that," David said. "We haven't finished our investigation."

"We might, just *might* be able to recoup some of our losses if we make Topeka ahead of schedule," Vera said, thinking aloud and obviously liking what she heard. "There's nothing he can do, legally, to keep us here."

Reflex guided David's leftward pivot. Moving up behind him was a bare-chested Johnny Perdue and three other clowns known as PeeWee, Jazz and Chino. Fats, the bandleader, lumbered from the big top, with Ernie Fromme and twin dog trainers Priscilla and Drucilla at his heels.

Lord almighty. If somebody'd blown a whistle, David wasn't attuned to the pitch.

Addressing the circus owners, but with his voice loud enough to be heard by the sudden multitudes, he bluffed, "You're right, ma'am. Legally, I can't stop all of you from leaving the county. What I can do is arrest you and Mr. Van Geisen as key witnesses in an active homicide investigation."

David eyeballed Perdue, Fromme and several others for effect. "And anyone else that may apply to."

"Oh, really? Try it, Sheriff, and our attorney will—"

"That's enough, Vera," Frank said. "We'll tear down after the evening show and not before. AnnaLeigh deserves that much."

"Are you— *Who do you think you are!*"

"Will that give you and your men enough time, Sheriff?" Frank asked.

"It depends somewhat on whether we receive straighter answers to our questions. If we don't..." David's gesture implied their stay in Kinderhook County could be extended indefinitely.

"You arrested Reilly Boone," Vera said. "What else could you possibly need from us?"

"Being charged with a crime isn't a conviction," David shot back. "Boone's lawyer will petition the court to drop the charges, if he hasn't already. It's standard procedure."

Vera clutched at her sweater. "You can't let him do that."

David's chuckle was neither good-humored nor at her expense. "The decision isn't up to me. We need evidence, every scrap we can lay hands on. Facts, not more rumors and innuendo."

"We've told you everything we know, Sheriff," Perdue said.

"I believe the gentlemen heading this way might disagree with you, Johnny." David nodded at Andrik and Josh Phelps, the young lieutenant struggling to keep pace with his hatter-mad superior officer.

Head lowered and shaking, the boss clown's sigh was as doleful as his stage makeup. Perdue had reportedly "just left" everyplace Marlin had been told to look for him that morning.

Retribution for the dodge wouldn't be pretty. Too bad David couldn't stay to watch.

"Fancy meeting you here," he said to the detective.

"Great minds, and all that shit."

"Boone hasn't returned to the scene. That leaves two guesses."

"Yeah. Toots and Texas." Marlin edged nearer. "By the way, back at the office, I was, uh, out of line to—"

"Forget it. I have."

"You checking out Hannah's place next?"

"Uh-huh. I started to call her from the courthouse then decided against it."

"I tried a few minutes ago," Marlin said. "Got the machine."

"Did you leave a message?"

"No. You can revise the one I told you to give her though." Bogart's famous sneer was a distant second to Marlin Andrik's. "The part about my best is okay. Just add something about how I'm gonna kick her ass big time for bailing Houdini out of jail."

As David walked to his cruiser, he wished that was all he had to tell her.

Reilly waggled his fork at the platter where a fried egg remained atop a nest of spinach. "Want the last one?"

Arrgh-argh. A "Yes-sir-ee, Bob, lay it on me" in Malcolm-speak.

"He wasn't talking to you, doofus." Hannah motioned "Help yourself" to Reilly. "Either my cooking has improved, or you were starving."

"Better'n Granny used to make."

High praise indeed.

Malcolm growled canine curse words and slumped back down on the floor.

"What is he, about two, three years old?" Reilly asked.

"That's the veterinarian's estimate. David rescued him from a puppy mill–dognapping ring who sold animals for lab experimentation."

Hannah racked her plate, butter knife and fork in the dishwasher. She could feel Reilly thinking that Malcolm looked like the aftermath of lab experimentation. If he had, he covered it by asking, "Did you name him?"

"No," Hannah said, "but whoever did definitely captured his essence."

The edge of the spatula she wielded banged against the skillet's ossified egg white, spinach and bacon bits. Well, hell. They could land robots on Mars, but couldn't make a disposable frying pan. Which this one would become if a long soak didn't melt the gunk.

"He'd be easier to train if his name was shorter," Reilly said. "For the same reason commands are one syllable."

Hannah laughed as she stacked his plate, the platter, utensils and their coffee cups. "Train? Malcolm? If that isn't an oxymoron, I've never heard one."

Moron being an integral part of the dog's vocabulary, the topic of discussion stood, his upright ear swiveling from Hannah to Reilly.

"Any animal can be trained, sweetheart."

"To do what? Malcolm already pees and poops outside." Dishes rattled into their appropriate slots. "There's nothing wrong with being an underachiever. It makes the rest of us look like overachievers without breaking a sweat."

While a bubble volcano erupted in the sink, she wiped off the stove top, counters and coffeemaker with the efficiency of someone who seldom ate directly from microwavable food containers.

"Watch this," Reilly said. Palm aloft, he chanted, *"Sitz, sitz,"* as he walked backward into the breakfast room.

Malcolm hunkered beside the bar stool, his anvil head bobbing and his neck stretching out like a charmed cobra.

Reilly stopped.

Malcolm tipped over and crashed nose first on the hardwood floor.

Hannah jammed a fist in her mouth.

On command, the Airedale-wildebeest resumed the position. Grudgingly.

Reilly's arm dropped. *"Komm."* A finger pointed downward. *"Sitz."*

Malcolm came. Malcolm sat. Malcolm gulped the biscuit Reilly saved as a reward.

Hannah breathed. "I saw it, but I don't believe it."

"All you've gotta do is speak their language."

"Malcolm speaks German?" Hannah's eyebrow dipped. He'd never responded to Leo, other than whiffing his crotch, but Malcolm did that to everyone. Except David.

"Lots of animals savvy German better than English," Reilly said. "K-9 dogs—the pure, European-bred McCoy, like shepherds and Belgian Malinois—are trained in it, and not just because it's handier for the breeders."

Hannah's knowledge of German was limited to obscenities. Anyone who'd lived in Chicago as long as she had, who couldn't curse in twenty-five languages, never took cabs.

"There has to be more to it than that," she said. "Malcolm doesn't know German from Hindu."

Reilly winked. "A magician never reveals his secrets, sweetheart." No sooner than he said it, his features went slack. He turned and stared out the French doors at the motor home parked parallel to the deck.

Platitudes wended through Hannah's mind. Solicitous, empty phrases that served no purpose but to create sound when silence became too loud for a bystander to bear.

Malcolm padded over and licked Reilly's hand. Angling for another treat most likely. Reilly smiled down at him and stroked his head, telegraphing appreciation for the condolence Hannah mistook for greed.

"I don't mean to impose," he said, "but I could use a shower and a shave before I tackle that mess in my trailer." His smile widened. "The water tank in that rig is surely hot by now, but the donniker is stingy on elbowroom."

She had a better idea. Better for her purposes, anyway. Which was searching the motor home and trailer. For what, she didn't know, besides a motive for killing AnnaLeigh and framing Reilly for her murder.

Marlin and David had already searched it cop fashion, but maybe they'd missed something. Maybe they'd concentrated on evidence of guilt instead of proof of innocence.

Yeah, and maybe doing it again was a fat waste of time, and that was running out, fast. The real killer had to be connected with the circus, and Van Geisens' would be on the road in a matter of hours. All Hannah needed was privacy and a lot of help from her friends.

"After your shower," she said, "why don't you stretch out on my bed for a nap?"

He took his keys from the table. "Naps are for babies and old folks."

Hannah followed him out on the deck, stepping over the hose and extension cords connected to the cottage's exterior faucet and outlet. "I take naps when I'm tired."

"Okay, so they're for babies, old folks and women."

A streak of Delbert must reside in all men of a certain age.

Reilly jiggled the motor home's door handle. "No damn reason for that deputy to tear up the lock. I gave him the keys when he served me with the warrant."

He swung open the motor home's door, then paused. "I don't believe Sheriff Hendrickson was party to it, but wait'll you see what his deputies did to the inside."

Hannah expected fingerprint powder strewn like black talcum over every horizontal surface and numerous vertical ones. Nothing prepared her for upholstery split at the seams, cushions stripped of their covers, drawers dumped on the floor, gaping cupboard and cabinet doors and emptied closets.

"I promise you, Reilly, no member of the Kinderhook County Sheriff's Department had anything to with this."

A pair of socks and underpants were added to the black T-shirt and trousers he excavated from a clothing pile. "Then, who did? Detective Phelps had the keys, and Andrik had the motor home towed to the impound lot after they searched it."

The man in charge of the lot hadn't impressed Hannah as Mensa material, but trashing a vehicle in his possession was beyond stupid.

"I don't know who did it," she said, "but I think

I know why. If you'll let me, I'll do my best to find out the what.''

Reilly gathered toiletries from the hallway and bathroom like Easter eggs and dropped them into a leather shaving kit. "Come again?''

"Did you kill AnnaLeigh?''

He froze, then pivoted on the balls of his feet. Disbelief, hurt and bewilderment shone in his eyes. "No, Hannah. I didn't.''

"Did you know she asked me to meet her after the show last night?''

His brow corduroyed. "No.''

"Any idea why she'd want to talk with me alone?''

"To get better acquainted? But why sneak around about it?'' He pondered a moment. "Lest she thought it'd be stealing time with you away from me.''

If he was lying and was that proficient at it, would he be charged with homicide? Hannah's gut and head voted no. Her heart recused itself.

"I think somebody ransacked your motor home searching for something that would implicate them in AnnaLeigh's death. That somebody also must have had access to your rifle and the gunpowder, and pre-loaded it before you went onstage.''

"Who?'' Reilly clutched Hannah's arm. "How do you know that?''

"I don't *know* anything. It's pure speculation, but it's the only thing that makes sense. To me. If I can find *what* the somebody was looking for, we'll know the *who.*''

"What if they already found it?"

Hannah inhaled, then released the breath as a soft groan. Hers and the gumshoe gang's banishment left no options. If caught on circus property again, the Van Geisens would make good on their threat, and who could blame them?

"All I have to offer is a hunch," she said, "and the hope it pays off."

15

David and Reilly Boone stared at each other through the screen door. Both were surprised. Neither pleasantly.

The magician was barefoot, his hair damp and comb-tracked. He motioned, said, "Come on in," then stepped back, tightening the belt of his velour robe.

Malcolm gallomphed from the direction of the bedroom, his tongue flapping and tail wagging at odds with his gait.

Boone pointed at the floor. *"Sitz."*

Damned if Malcolm didn't dig in his toenails and tuck his butt, as pretty as you please.

"Where's Hannah?"

The magician gave David an "Oh, she's around, I haven't disposed of the body yet" look. Not smart, which Boone realized a second too late. He jerked a thumb toward the breakfast room. "She's out back, in the motor home. I'll get her for you."

"Don't." David could see the rig's sidewall through the French doors. "It's you I came to talk to. First."

David had never been one to throw his weight around, but he was aware of the height advantage and the seventy pounds that went with it. So was Reilly Boone. More's the better.

"All right then." Boone padded toward a club chair. "Have a seat, Sheriff."

His near nakedness, proprietary attitude and the scent of Hannah's soap and shampoo surrounding him like an aura chipped at the margins of David's self-control. The bastard had even snookered her dog.

"I'll stand," he said. "This won't take long."

Boone rested his hands on his hips. Curious. Wary. Defiant.

"Do you know what your blood type is?" David asked.

"My wha— Well, yeah. Sure. It's type O."

"The same as mine," David said. "And forty percent of the rest of the population."

Eyes fixed on Boone, he reached up and unpinned his badge. "This is where things get personal, my friend. Not between you and Sheriff Hendrickson. Strictly between you and *David* Hendrickson. Understood?"

The magician watched the shield detach from the uniform and disappear in David's fist. If the man was breathing, there was no outward sign of it.

"Hannah's blood type is AB, Mr. Boone. In case you didn't know, that's rare. Only five percent of the population has it."

The badge's insignia imprinted David's palm. Its brass surface was no longer cool to the touch. "There are two bona fide facts about blood types. They don't lie and they don't change."

The color began to leach from Boone's face.

"A lab technician—an expert—told me another real interesting fact a little while ago." David barely restrained the urge to ball the man's robe in his other fist. "A man with type O blood can't have a daughter with AB."

"No!" Boone staggered backward. "You're wrong—"

"Uh-uh. Blood tells. Blood doesn't lie. Hannah Garvey is *not* your daughter. No kin to you at all. No way. No how. Never was."

The shield's blunt, brass edge cut into the bends of David's fingers. His throat constricted, his voice lowering to an icy rumble. "And you damn well know it."

"No, no. She's *mine*. I swear to God, she is. Me and Caroline's." Boone sat down hard on the arm of the chair. "I held her when she was a baby. Sang her to sleep. My little girl. My beautiful little baby Hannah."

Tears pouring down his ravaged face, Boone stared up at David. His hands spread and shook like a beggar's. "Loving her, searching for her, praying to Jesus I'd find her is all that's kept me going."

Choking, almost strangling on his own voice, he said, "I'll do anything you want. *Anything*. I already lost her once. Don't, please, for the love of God, take my daughter away from me again."

David turned his head, the drumming in his ears so

loud he couldn't think. He wanted the hate to come back. Willed it. Demanded it.

All he felt was pity for the sobbing wretch. He had come there to destroy Boone with his own lies. Instead, he'd destroyed him with the truth.

The metal step squeaked. The motor home took a slight tilt to the left. "Andrik told me to give you his best."

Hannah spun around.

"He also said he's going to kick your ass for bailing Reilly out of jail."

She rubbed the elbow she'd bonked on the galley's dividing wall. David's smile might be a ruse. Except he looked haggard rather than angry. His eyes were more blue than gray, too. And his Smith & Wesson was still in its holster.

As omens went, all of the above seemed auspicious.

"C'mere, woman." He held out his arms.

She filled them and wrapped hers around him. "Good thing you're wearing body armor. Might save you a couple of cracked ribs."

"You missed me, huh?"

Like a flower misses sunshine. Like lungs miss air. "Yeah, I guess. A little, maybe."

"How many months has it been since last night?"

"Rough estimate?" Hannah bowed her back. "Nine thousand, four hundred and twenty-six." She kissed his chin, her tongue flicking the hint of a cleft. "Now start making up for it."

Lips parted and descending to hers, he hesitated, and pulled away. "We have to talk, Hannah."

It wasn't a tease or an "Oh, by the way."

"Not in here, though," he said. "Let's take a walk."

Her heart sank. The ol' walk-and-talk. In the context of a relationship, a metaphor for the proverbial plank. In any context, no wasn't an option. Stalling only delayed whatever the inevitable might be.

"Okay, but I need to call Delbert first. I left a message for him to come help me, uh…" Her arm swept the cabin. "Help straighten up."

David glanced around. Until that moment he'd only had eyes for her. "Holy Moses. Did Reilly do this?"

"No." Hannah steeled herself for his shift to cop mode. "It was trashed when he picked it up at the impound lot."

"Which it hadn't been released from yet."

"I kind of wondered about that."

"Uh-huh." David motioned "scoot." He strode down the hall, barricaded midway by jumbled linens, then barreled back. "Damn it, Hannah—"

"Yes, I should have called you or Marlin to report it. No I didn't, because it's a waste of time to redust for prints that aren't here, since whoever broke in would have been smart enough to wear gloves."

"Now, where have I heard that one before?"

"Well, I was right, then, too." Teeth clenched against further petty remarks, she added, "Sorry."

"Anything missing?"

"Reilly didn't think so, other than the stuff you and Andrik seized as evidence."

David stepped out to examine the door lock.

"His key won't work on the equipment trailer's lock at all," Hannah said. "Its hasp is dinged, too, as if somebody tried to hacksaw it off, then gave up."

Another challenge for Delbert and his handy lock-pick gun, and an even worse time to inform the sheriff that he owned one.

David's jaw cocked to one side. His eyes darted as though watching beads clack together on an abacus.

She slipped her hands in the back pockets of her jeans. Counted to twenty. Tried to curl her fingers into fists. Yeah, sure.

A full minute later, David muttered, "Gotta see a vet about a dog. Andrik's still third on the list."

"You're talking to yourself again."

"Heard that before, too." David tugged her hand from her pocket. "Now, I'm going to talk to you."

"But I haven't called—"

"If Delbert shows up, he'll keep. What I need to say won't."

They didn't walk far, just to a weeping willow, under which Hannah planned to spend summer afternoons in a hammock, with a book and a gallon of sun tea.

David began. "It wouldn't have been right to kiss you before..." He closed his eyes and exhaled frustration. "Last night, after you left with Delbert, I did something I knew was wrong. I had plenty of chances to stop myself, too, but I didn't."

A cool, oily emptiness seeped through her. A familiar feeling, but never, ever as intense.

"No excuses," David went on, "but when you love somebody, it's just so damn easy to believe you know what's best for them that you don't bother asking what she thinks is best for herself."

He finger combed the hair brushing her cheek back from her face. "Problem is, once you start playing God with someone else's life, you can't stop, back up and pretend you never started down that road."

Giving her the thinnest of smiles, he said, "I know I'm rambling. It comes from being afraid one thing I have to say will mean I lose you, and knowing the other is going to hurt you."

"If it does, I can take it," Hannah lied. "Been there, done that. Life goes on."

Kevlar vests don't deflect verbal bullets. Hers scored a direct hit.

"All right then. Those cotton balls Johnny Perdue cleaned the scrapes on your knees with? I dug them out of the trash and took them to a lab tech at the hospital. Asked her to determine what my 'Jane Doe's' blood type was."

Her? As in, a previous commitment you realized you weren't quite finished with yet? "Why didn't you *ask* me, David? I'm type AB. I carry a wallet card, because it's rare."

"I was busy playing God, remember? Reilly had already consented to a blood-alcohol test at the hospital."

He snorted. "I told myself, no conclusions would

be drawn from it. Odds were, it wouldn't prove or disprove anything. Just because it was your blood, and your decision to make, there was no sense asking what *you* wanted.''

"Oh, David." Hannah's head wobbled from side to side, relief tasting sweeter than the kiss he'd denied her. "I already knew Reilly wasn't my father. Oh, I wanted him to be, so much I tried my hardest to *make* him fit the part."

Eyes lowered, she whispered, "But he isn't."

David couldn't have been more shocked if she'd slapped him. "You *knew?* How? When?"

"I think I knew all along, but not for certain until an hour or so ago. Even then, I rationalized that something must be missing in me not him."

She told him of Reilly's confession, his misplaced shame and of how an O'Donough became a Boone. "Then he hugged me, and I hugged him, and I expected this...this *epiphany* to wash over me, and all of a sudden he'd be 'Dad,' or 'Daddy,' and I could think it and say it and it would feel and sound like the most natural thing in the world."

David started to take her in his arms, but she resisted. "No, it's okay. I'm okay. Honest, I am."

Tracing the etched letters on his name plate, she said, "See, we have a bond, Reilly and me. Not blood, but...well, I do kind of love the old guy.

"He loved my mother, and he bought me ice cream when I was little, and somehow it doesn't matter that I didn't remember him. He *cared* about me. He cared what happened to me, and he still does. He always will.''

David's hand almost crushed hers. Labored breaths ruffled her hair. Concentrating on the field of stitched, buttoned-down midnight blue, she said, ''As for playing God, you're no George Burns, but it'd take more than that to lose me. All I ask is that if any revelations are made to Reilly, they'll come from me.''

A half sigh, half groan escaped David's lips. He braced a forearm against the tree, his knuckles raking his brow.

''What's the— Oh, no. You didn't—'' Yanking her hand free, she pushed away from him. ''You *told* him, didn't you? About the blood test.''

''I thought—''

''Busted. Endgame. That's what you *thought*.'' Willow leaves rained from stripped branches. ''Who else did you tell before *me,* David? Marlin? Phelps? The entire department?''

His face flushed. ''No one. I intended to talk to you first, then Reilly answered the door and—''

''You couldn't very well pass up a chance like that, now, could you?'' She laughed bitterly. ''Hey, gotta rip while the rippin's good.''

''That's a cheap shot, Hannah. How could I have known what intuition—and damn it, that's all it was—had already told you? I thought you believed he was your father with your whole heart.''

''You thought this. You thought that.'' The man's ego was monumental. Colossal. ''How could you *know?* Well, here's a news flash. You could have asked me, but you didn't. Not yesterday afternoon. Not last night. Not once have you asked what *I* believed."

David stared toward the lake, his features rigid, a nerve in spasm below his temple. His silence wasn't a ploy. He wasn't stonewalling until her temper cooled, or got tired of waiting and walked off or tired of fighting and declared a truce. He was the quarterback and it was Monday morning.

"I was at The Outhouse when the lab called and watch-what-you-wish-for slammed head-on into greatest-fear-realized. I hied to the jail to ask Boone flat out why he lied to you. Except he and ten thousand dollars of your money were already gone."

"And with it," Hannah said, "any doubt that I believed everything he'd told me."

"Yep." David made a kissy noise. "Rip into him? When he answered the door, sashaying around like the lord of the manor? Hell, yes, I did. Enjoyed it, too, until he begged me not to take his baby girl away from him again."

He turned to look at Hannah. "Then I knew who the real liar was."

"From a few bloody cotton balls doth a shit load of awful truths come."

"Not funny. Not the least bit."

"It wasn't meant to be." Arms winged, she balled her hair in her fists. "Good God, there are enough victims of circumstance in this to form a freakin' rock band. Yourself included. The Jumping Conclusions."

Hair and hands shot skyward. "And that's not meant to be funny, either."

David's expression concurred, but his mouth crimped at one corner.

"Just because I defend my mother doesn't mean I have any illusions about her. But lie to Reilly about me?" Hannah shook her head. "I'll bet he never asked if he was her baby's father. Which isn't to say Caroline wouldn't have lied, to keep the voluntary child support rolling in.

"I remember those mysterious windfalls. The fridge and the cabinets emptied faster than they filled, but I never asked where the money came from, either. I was afraid she'd tell me and it would be bad, or she'd lie and I'd know it. Also bad. Maybe worse."

David said, "What about you, though? Whether Caroline lied outright, or by omission, to Reilly, why didn't she tell you he was your father? Why didn't *somebody* tell you, just to save you from being hurt?"

Her ribs compressed, her stomach churning a warning not to give David the means, the power to gouge out her soul, tear it apart and cast the pieces back in her face.

Trust versus secrets. Fear had guided Caroline's choice, too.

"My mother loved Reilly Boone until the day she died," Hannah said. "No question about it in my mind. She *wanted* Reilly to be my father, but couldn't be sure he was. In fact, on a gut level, she was more certain he wasn't.

"To tell me, Granny, Great-aunt Lurleen, Great-uncle Mort—anyone—that he was was like daring God to destroy that glimmer of hope that the man she loved and couldn't live with was her baby's father.''

Confusion and skepticism leavened David's expression. ''But if even Caroline doubted that Reilly is your father, then who is?''

''I don't know, David. I never will. But I think I know how I was conceived.''

She clasped her hands behind her back and spoke to the sky. ''Mama wasn't pregnant when she ran away with Reilly. The time factor doesn't jibe. She didn't get pregnant after she got back to Effindale—same reason. It's total speculation, but I refuse to think she slept with someone else when she and Reilly were together.''

''That leaves the yahoos Caroline bummed a ride from after she delivered her 'the circus or me' ultimatum to Reilly.''

It mattered if David believed what she was about to say. Then again, it didn't. Caroline had always told her daughter the truth. Hannah simply hadn't listened.

''When Reilly didn't drop that tent rope, Mama had no choice but to carry out the 'or else.' She was hurt, angry, in the middle of nowhere, with no money and nowhere to run, except home to Effindale.

''The times were different, then. Any young, beautiful girl who climbed into a car with three strange men was asking for whatever she got.''

Hannah snorted derisively. ''Really, it isn't the attitude that's changed much. People just aren't as quick to say such a thing out loud.''

Nails digging hard into the backs of her hands, she said, "One of those men must have raped my mother. One of them is my biological father."

A wisp of cloud skimmed into view. She smiled at it, the hard edge diminishing in her voice. "When I asked about my father, Mama always told me I was hers. I heard it as 'Shut-up and quit pestering me,' but she was telling me the only thing she knew to be true. I was *hers*. She wanted me to be Reilly's, too, but knew in her heart I wasn't. There was no name she could give me. Except her own."

David's hand caressed her cheek. She closed her eyes, absorbing the warmth of his touch, the comfort in it, the wondrous sense of peace.

"And you've done it, and her, proud," he said. "I just wish to God—"

"That you hadn't told Reilly?" She turned her head to kiss his palm. "I'd have rathered you didn't."

"We talked for quite a while before I came out to the motor home. You always have been, and always will be, his little girl."

"I know. Had I decided to tell him, he wouldn't have believed me, either. As long as Reilly has me, he has Caroline. As long as I have him, I do, too."

"That's why you posted his bail."

"No. It isn't."

David frowned. "Then why? Ten thousand dollars is a lot of money, sugar. I'm reasonably sure you aren't a millionaire."

Hardly. On the pivotal Saturday when she deliberated whether to resign from Friedlich & Friedlich, she calculated her earnings over the past twenty-five years in comparison to her net worth.

Conclusion? She'd squandered hundreds of thousands of dollars buying and maintaining a lifestyle that smacked of success, but she never stopped feeling like a perpetual understudy, in rehearsal for someone's else's role.

She'd saved pennies on those dollars for posterity. And she didn't care. Poverty didn't scare her anymore.

Actually, she still *was* poor. She just had a better address, a nicer wardrobe and statistically higher odds of undergoing quadruple-bypass surgery, so she could keep proving what a successful, liberated, career woman she was.

The two words chosen for her resignation memo were appropriate but obscene. She'd settled for *I quit*.

"I posted Reilly's bail because he didn't kill AnnaLeigh," she said. "I'd have paid yours if you'd been charged with a murder you didn't commit."

David's eyes replied, Like hell. I'd have refused it.

"C'mon, Sheriff. Be honest. You don't believe Reilly did it, either." Hannah arched her eyebrows. "And don't give me a bunch of crap about evidence."

"Evidence isn't crap."

"Nor is it the be-all and end-all, or you and Reilly might have shared a jail cell and I'd be applying for bankruptcy."

David fidgeted and made gutteral sounds, which answered her question before he answered her question. "I'm maybe not completely, entirely, a hundred percent convinced. Just between you and me, I think Marlin has doubts, himself."

Hannah didn't quite shriek, "Then why did you charge Reilly with homicide," but her tone approached shrill.

"Like a certain chief of detectives put it, cops arrest. Prosecutors charge."

"But—"

"The clock is the enemy, Hannah. Not us. Instinct needs follow-up time we don't have." David nodded at the motor home. "Andrik will be mighty interested in that B and E you didn't report, though. There's implications to it I need to check out first. I also suspect Marlin has an ace up his sleeve he won't show unless it plays out."

She rolled her eyes. "Far be it from him to admit it if it doesn't."

"Yeah, well, Nancy Drew, I suspect the reason for his butt-kick message is that you trumped one of them when you bailed Reilly out of jail."

"I did? Oh, I did not. Marlin's just—"

David loomed over her. "Waiting on me at The Outhouse for a brainstorming session."

Her mouth opened in protest but his lips smothered it, his tongue slowing to erotic, bone-melting strokes as his hands slid down her back. Pulling her to him, his fingers kneaded her bottom, and she felt his erection lengthen, swell, harden. She moved against him...wanting him, needing him...here...*now*.

Relaxing his hold, his lips parted from hers with exquisite reluctance.

Hot, breathless, her head spinning, she stammered, "I-if that's a goodbye kiss, what say we start there next time and work backward to hello."

"Might could." His lopsided grin had a stuporous quality to it. "Only someday we're gonna tarry for three or four hours in the middle."

A delicious shiver raced from her nape to her toes. "Then we'll start over again."

"And again..."

"And where we'll stop..."

David kissed her quick and tender. "No stops, sugar. Ever. Nothing but time-outs in between."

16

"AnnaLeigh and Johnny had been having an affair for years," IdaClare said, loudly enough to be heard from one end of the motor home to the other.

She strained on tiptoe to push stacked plates into the galley cupboard. "Another outfit offered Johnny a higher salary—and Van Geisens is financially shaky—but he stayed to be with AnnaLeigh."

Hannah craned her neck at the windows, as if vocal vibrations might pry them open again. After David left, she'd found Reilly, the militant non-napper, sleeping crossways on her bed in a just-resting-my-eyes-a-second sprawl. She'd covered him with the afghan and muted the doorbell chime and phones so he'd stay that way.

Still, combining a top-of-the-lungs Code Name: Gamma meeting with a search-and-scrub mission was risky.

On the other hand, Delbert had brought a bowl of his homemade "killer guacamole," a bag of tortilla chips and virgin margaritas in keeping with the group's secondary interest: refreshments. The snack deviated from standard dessert fare, but met, if not exceeded, the high-calorie, high-fat, irresistibly scrumptious criteria.

"Who told you about AnnaLeigh and Johnny?" she asked.

"I don't know their names, dear. We were trying to be…" IdaClare appealed to Marge, who was whip-stitching the lounge's split seams until they could be professionally repaired. "Oh, what's the word?"

"Sneaky." Marge squinted one bifocaled eye to thread a crescent-shaped needle.

"That isn't it," IdaClare said. "It's longer and it starts with a C."

Rosemary sang out from the donniker, "Covert?"

"No…"

"Is the clandestine, I think you mean," Leo suggested, peering around the side of the cockpit's swivel chair.

"Clandestine," IdaClare repeated with gusto. "Doesn't that just sound exotic? It always makes me think of—oh, what's that movie?"

"Casa-blan-ca," Delbert snarled from the bedroom. "Now, if you can remember the rest of your dad-blasted report, get on with it, for Christ's sweet sake."

Leo said quietly, "So cranky, Delbert has been all day. His stomach, it does not agree with him."

"Who does?" Marge stage-whispered.

A disembodied "I heard that" echoed from the rig's farthest reaches.

Contributing to the conversation by back-and-forthing along the hallway like a duck at a shooting gallery must be getting tiresome. Specifically, a green-headed mallard duck, due to Delbert's ignorance of food coloring's resistance to shampoo, detergent, diluted bleach and a lardacious cleaning compound known as Goop.

He'd assigned each senior Sherlock—aka Task Force Gamma—an area to search and straighten. An A and E operation, in Master Detective–speak, meaning "assimilate and elutriate."

Hannah, their meetings' perennial moderator, was the "floater." She helped where needed, sorted miscellany and prevented bickering from escalating to flame wars.

Returning a scrapbook to its storage box, she hauled another into her lap. "These two nameless roustabouts you followed to the Laundromat," she said to IdaClare. "What else did they say about this alleged affair Johnny and AnnaLeigh were having?"

"It isn't alleged," Marge said. "Mr. Bacon, the cook we talked to at the circus, told us they were having one, too."

"Not *Mr.* Bacon," IdaClare corrected. "Bacon. I swear, those circus people have more nicknames than Carter has oats."

Rosemary yelled, "Chino is my favorite."

"Figures." Delbert sniped from beyond. "That's his real name."

"Meanwhile," Hannah said, "back at the Laundromat…"

Over the clank of silverware being shuffled into drawer dividers, IdaClare said, "Well, the one with the earring told the one with the beard that Johnny and AnnaLeigh must have had a fight before they got to Sanity, because Frank Van Geisen had to coax AnnaLeigh to the party at the dining tent—er, top.''

Marge added, ''Reilly didn't pull into town until late. A mechanical breakdown on the highway or something.''

Rosemary appeared in the doorway, plundering a cosmetics tote. ''Earring said Johnny was mad because he and AnnaLeigh could have made an appearance at the party then snuck off for a while. Except she just wanted to go to bed. By herself.''

''Or so Earring thought,'' IdaClare said. ''Frank and Vera kidded AnnaLeigh into being sociable, having a drink with the rest of the troupe. AnnaLeigh completely ignored Johnny, then went back to her motor home. After the party broke up, Beard saw her lights on and thought AnnaLeigh and Johnny were— uh…'' She made an ugly face. ''Well, having relations is close enough.''

''Need help with another word?'' Delbert inquired, chuckling wickedly.

''Say it and you'll blow soap bubbles for a month.''

To Delbert, such presented a challenge, not a threat. Hannah grimaced in anticipation of the F-word, in past tense, thundering down the hallway like a train through a tunnel.

When it didn't, she presumed the economy-size bottle of dish detergent in the galley and no exit at Delbert's end of the coach had zipped his lip.

"No sooner than Beard saw what he saw," Rosemary said, "Johnny strolled from Clown Alley to smoke his pipe."

"Beard tried to divert his attention," Marge went on, "but Johnny saw what Beard saw and *freaked*." She glanced up at Hannah. "That means he went crazy."

"Gotcha."

Marge plied her needle to another rent. Rosemary about-faced for the donniker. IdaClare wiped fingerprint powder off the cupboards with a damp cloth. The sound of continued assimilation and elutriation wended from cockpit and bedroom.

"Okay," Hannah said. "So, then what happened?"

"Nothing, dear."

"That's it?"

"Well, it's probably not the end of what happened," IdaClare allowed, "but Beard and Earring threw their clothes in baskets and rushed out of the Laundromat to their truck. We couldn't very well jump in with them to eavesdrop on the rest."

"They were a bit suspicious of us, anyway," Marge said. "We kept poking quarters in the washing machines, but I think they began to wonder why we never took anything out."

"Baloney." Rosemary popped back into the cabin. "Every time a machine stopped, I raised the lid and went on and on about bloodstains being hard to wash out." She flapped a hand. "Beard and Earring never suspected a thing."

Except a midwestern branch of Murder, Incorporated, disguised as three little old ladies.

"My stars and garters." IdaClare examined the smudges on the pink Pink Floyd sweatshirt she'd bought at a yard sale because it matched her high-top sneakers. "I hope this nasty fingerprint stuff washes out."

Hannah assured her it would, then said, "I don't recall you saying why you followed Beard and Earring to the Laundromat in the first place."

"After that security guard—such a sweet young man, wasn't he, girls?—walked us to my car and explained about restraining orders and everything, we were about to vote on how to sneak back in, when Rosemary saw Earring and Beard's truck pull out of the back lot."

"No," Marge said. "Frank left in his truck before they did."

A hip shot closed a galley drawer with a bang. "In the interest of time," IdaClare said, "I'm trying to leave out extraneous details. We do have a wedding rehearsal in a little while, you know."

"Hear that, Leo?" Delbert said. "Extraneous details. By cracky, when some people borrow a book, they *read* it."

Leo swiveled to yell back, "A hundred times already, I tell you. The detective manual, I am reading. IdaClare, maybe she reads faster than me."

"Hmmph."

Hannah asked, "Do you have any idea where Frank went?"

"The post office." IdaClare shrugged. "That's why we didn't tail him. We were talking to Bacon when Frank gave a last call and picked up the mail bin in the dining tent—er, top."

Hannah mulled over the semi-alleged affair between AnnaLeigh and Johnny. Why hadn't Gina Zandonatti or Arlise Fromme mentioned it? To protect Reilly? Johnny *was* his best friend.

No, unless it was sheer gossip, they'd stayed mum to protect Johnny. After all, Hannah was an outsider and he was Boss Clown.

The list of nonparticipants in the Thursday-night sexcapade now included Earring, Beard and Johnny. Intuition said a connection existed between AnnaLeigh's unknown lover and her death. What, was a blank. The who might fill it.

The circus's male contingent numbered at least thirty. However, a somewhat conceited woman with a notoriously jealous husband wouldn't have sex with a flunky with less to lose than she did.

Hannah's index finger seesawed on her chin. If that supposition was on target, "Maybe the mystery man AnnaLeigh was having sex with was Frank."

"Eww—ick." Marge's rouge vanished behind a genuine blush. "Sorry, that just sort of slipped out." Her nose crinkled. "Really, though, I can't see AnnaLeigh getting hot and bothered about him at all. He seems nice, but he's just a...*Frank.*"

"Don't be so hasty," Rosemary said. She motioned at Hannah, indicating the bathroom was clear and clean. "You can't judge a book by its cover, you know."

"What's that have to do with sex?" Delbert squeezed past her into the cabin. He looked from her beatific smile to Leo's moony one. His lip curled in disgust.

"I heard Frank did favors for AnnaLeigh all the time," he said. "Took her to run errands, critiqued the new act she was working on, delivered her mail to her door. Women eat that kind of stuff up with a spoon. Works like a charm."

Four female voices chorused, "Oh, really?"

Delbert backpedaled. "Not on gals like you. You ladies are too savvy to fall for that, but AnnaLeigh wasn't in your league." Sincerity oozed from every pore. "Few are."

Wowser. Trust a Renaissance man to stick his foot in his mouth and pull out a glass slipper.

"Maybe Frank bent over backward to be nice because AnnaLeigh was a prima donna," IdaClare said. "Rumor has it she'd always been moody, but had swung from cheerful to depressed to irritable since the season started."

Marge added, "One young lady we talked to, Felicity something-or-other, said AnnaLeigh acted like she didn't want to be there. Very restless and impatient."

"Someone else told us she didn't practice their act enough to suit Reilly," Rosemary said. "AnnaLeigh was an above-average magician, but before his hands failed him, Reilly was one of the best in the business.

He pushed her to get better. She called him a slave driver.''

"Jehoshaphat." Delbert made a give-me-a-break gesture. "AnnaLeigh was hard to get along with. Big deal. Probably just going through the change."

"Why, you—" Rosemary socked him on the shoulder. "That's sexist, demeaning, insulting, and *wrong*. There happens to be a three-month supply of birth control pills in the medicine cabinet."

Rubbing his arm, Delbert apologized for his unfortunate remark. Hannah figured he was most sorry for standing too close to Rosemary when he made it.

IdaClare had rinsed and retired her cleaning rag. Leo had completed A-and-E-ing the cockpit. Marge had already searched the upholstered pieces, although whoever damaged them would have removed anything cached there.

Well, hell. The equipment trailer's lock had yielded to Delbert's illegal entry tool, but why waste more time pawing through it? Somebody had ransacked the motor home for something. An incriminating something. Which had likely been found and destroyed.

Or was the vandalism a ruse? Hannah stared down at a feature article clipped from the *News-Messenger* in Fremont, Ohio: Lady Magician Amazes Children of All Ages. AnnaLeigh had struck a showgirl pose for the photographer. Her beauty and presence would have earned her a prima-donna label had she sold major appliances at Sears.

Why was everything so complicated? Not a puzzle. No connecting pieces, no framework. This was a game of fifty-two card pick up. Blindfolded. In a stiff wind.

"What's the matter, ladybug?" Delbert knelt in front of her. "Are you mad at me, too?"

She sighed and shook her head. The last scrapbook closed with a dull thump. "Could Reilly have killed her after all, Delbert? Concocted this elaborate, topsy-turvy fun house of a plot in advance—including paying somebody to trash the motor home—to throw everyone off?"

Absently, her thumb rubbed a paper cut on her knuckle. "The cops operate on logic. We usually end up there eventually, but go off on all kinds of tangents en route."

Delbert said, "But Code Name: Gamma is all tangents and no route."

"Bingo."

The other gumshoes huddled up for the powwow in progress. Hannah surveyed their smudged, stained clothing and her own. The dirty half dozen. And for what?

"A crime, the more simple it is, the less probable to be caught." Leo stuck out his tongue at Delbert. "Somewhere I read that."

"Well, it's true. Killers trip themselves being extra cagey. Try to second-guess and outsmart the cops before the fact, and they trap themselves."

IdaClare huffed. "Anyone who's ever watched *Murder, She Wrote* on TV knows that."

Hannah agreed. "But what if the killer complicated

the complications on purpose to such an extent, no logic can be made of it?''

"There's logic somewhere, ladybug. The line's as crooked as a bucket of snakes, but it points at the murderer.'' Delbert patted her knee. "And it ain't Reilly Boone.''

"Really?'' Rosemary gasped. "Then who is it?''

"Hell, I dunno. That scenario I was cookin' last night sewed up Boone tighter than those cushions, but like Hannah says, it's too elaborate.''

"I liked it,'' IdaClare said.

Delbert sat down on the floor and folded his legs, tailor fashion. "I'll bet what we've got here is an established motive—God knows what. The means was thought out in advance, an idea whose time hadn't come yet. It might never come, but the killer had an out if it did. Something set the wheel to turning. Opportunity clicked in place. Luck was mixed in, too.''

Marge nudged IdaClare. "Did you understand any of that?''

"I—well, yes. Delbert thinks whoever killed AnnaLeigh planned way ahead to frame Reilly. The reason we can't make heads nor tails of it is because the killer had plenty of time to plant red herrings.''

Marge groaned, then nudged Leo. "Did you understand any of *that?*''

"Yes, it is the—''

"Oh, never mind.''

"My money's on this Perdue character,'' Delbert said. "When AnnaLeigh got her new act together, she was replacing Reilly with a female assistant. Instead of forced retirement, maybe she was going to leave him for Johnny. Or Johnny believed she was.''

"Until Johnny saw her relating with somebody else," Rosemary said.

Marge snapped her fingers. "And thought, if I can't have her, nobody else can.''

Johnny Perdue did fit the as-much-to-lose criteria, Hannah thought. "Except AnnaLeigh was *married* to Reilly. Meaning he already had her.''

"Scratch the names off the scorecard, ladybug.'' Delving into the pocket of his striped, orange shorts for visual aids, Delbert assigned a quarter the wife role, a roll of antacids the husband's and a golf tee the lover's.

"Wife cleaves unto Lover." The quarter and the golf tee skipped across the carpet together. "Wife tells Lover she wants him, but has to stay with Husband till her career's on track, since she and Lover cleaved about the same time she took center stage.''

He placed the quarter between the antacids and the golf tee. "Lover puts his career on hold to wait for Wife. Wife uses Husband to further hers. Lover pushes. Wife says 'Be patient.'''

A pair of nail clippers dive-bombed the quarter. "New Lover horns in on Wife," Delbert said. "Old Lover sees Wife has played him for a fool, figures Wife had no intention of leaving Husband. Husband still has Wife. New Lover is getting his. Old Lover has squat. To hell with that.''

The quarter disappeared. Delbert stabbed the roll

of antacids with the golf tee. "Two paybacks for the price of one."

Ouch. Shakespeare could have learned a few things about symbolism from Delbert.

"Here's the sixty-four-thousand-dollar question, though," Hannah said. "How do we unravel this mess?" She consulted Leo's watch. "Within the next four hours."

"Why do we have to?" Rosemary asked. "I know how stressful this must be for you and Reilly, but it'll be weeks, maybe months, before he'll go to trial."

"Because Van Geisens folds the tent tonight," Delbert said. "If the cops don't snag another suspect before then…"

"Oh, dear." IdaClare fussed with the hem of her sweatshirt. "I'm afraid we don't have even that long. Not with Leo and Rosemary's wedding rehearsal."

Plastering on a wide, fake grin, Hannah draped one arm over the bride's shoulders and the other around the groom's. "Tell you what. If you lovebirds let me skip the practice run so I can search the equipment trailer, I won't hold you to your promise of making Malcolm the ring bearer."

"Malcolm?" Horrified, Leo rocked forward as far as his belly allowed. "My darling Rosemary. *This* is the surprise at the wedding you would not tell me?"

His darling blanched. Stammering pronouns, Rosemary's eyes darted between IdaClare and Marge.

"Heavenly days, Leo." IdaClare laughed. "Why, that's the silliest thing I've ever heard."

Marge caught the chuckle bug. "A dog for a ring bearer. Can you imagine?"

"Precious. Absolutely precious." IdaClare clapped with glee. "If Malcolm's in the wedding party, Itsy and Bitsy have to be flower girls."

"Sure—uh, why not?" Rosemary patted her bosom, as though her heart was racing. "Maybe we can teach Walt Wagonner's cat to sing 'Oh, Promise Me.'"

Leo, Delbert and Hannah joined in the laughter, though they had no earthly clue what had set off the other three.

Twenty-four hours would pass before Hannah gave it another thought. By then, the answer would be right in front of her.

17

Hannah sat down on a flat-topped trunk, one of several she'd evicted from the equipment trailer. Elbows on knees and chin on the heels of her hands, she pondered how many climbers had trudged midway up Mount Everest before asking a Sherpa what the hell they'd gotten themselves into.

Insects swarmed and tinked off yard lights mounted beneath the eaves and the jerry-rigged clamp lamp attached to the top of the trailer's door. Garment bags rode the deck railing like oblong saddles. Surrounding her in the yard were weird and wonderful *objets d'*illusion: giant scimitars, baskets, large hoops and small ones and some that glowed in the dark. There were nested boxes, collapsible platforms, daggers, swords, playing cards, glittery drapes, silks from scarf- to sheet-sized and numerous items whose purposes were unknown.

Malcolm weaved around and through the magician's bazaar, his tail swaying when he sniffed his new friend Reilly's scent. Padding over to Hannah, he stared at her, then *moomphed* as though she'd taken an unscheduled coffee break and her paycheck would be docked if she didn't get back to work.

Hannah pointed at the grass. *"Sitz."*

Tongue dangling and dripping, Malcolm looked down then up again. His eyes telegraphed an internationally recognized *Huh?*

"Good boy." She kneaded the ruff around his neck, jingling the tags clipped to his otherwise invisible collar. "Smart dogs are highly overrated."

The cottage's interior was gloomy, save for the light above the kitchen sink and the banker's lamp on her desk.

She'd tiptoed in a few times to use the half bath off the great room, cadge a soda from the fridge or a munchie. Hearing snores drift from the bedroom was at once homey, kind of precious and a smidge disconcerting. Much like the cottage's groans, rattles and bumps had been those first nights after her move.

Did David snore? Strange not to know for sure, but Armegeddon could have occurred last night and she wouldn't have known until she wakened and noticed a lot of ashes.

Did she snore? Oh, God. Oh, *shit.* What if she did? Jarrod said she did, but being a twenty-four-carat dick head, he was probably not what one would call a reliable source.

Anyway, why was it socially acceptable for guys to do warthog impressions, and horrifying for women to make the slightest, most endearing little *wuffles* while they slept?

Hannah frowned at Malcolm. Yeah, well, if she did, at least he couldn't tell anyone about it.

She stood, stretched, then rested her hands on her hips. "An optimist would say the trailer is half-empty. What I'd truly love to know is how the cops searched it and put everything back so fast."

The gumshoes had offered to come back after the rehearsal, but she'd declined their help. Rosemary and Leo had other things to do on the eve of their wedding—although Hannah refused to speculate on what. IdaClare, Marge and the committee they'd recruited were hauling out at dawn to decorate the community center for the reception. Delbert had a hot date with Blanche Ehrlich—a potential candidate for his harem, to replace Maxine "Poison Ivy" McDougal.

"The sooner you sort through the not-empty half," Hannah told herself, "the sooner you can stuff the stuff back in, grab a spoon and dig into that carton of butter brickle in the freezer."

From the simple to the sublime, all the props were cheats. "They aren't called magic *tricks* for nothing," Reilly had said, "Except tricks aren't magic. Anybody can make a dove out of a hankie. Only a showman can make you *believe* the hankie turned into a dove."

The old saw about magicians never revealing their secrets added to the mystique. In Reilly's opinion, the pros who'd raised a ruckus about a series of TV shows exposing tricks of the trade had fallen for the oldest one in the book: misdirection.

"Just because I've watched *E.R.* a coupla times," he said, "don't make me a brain surgeon."

He also credited audiences with performing a fair share of the work. Most people who fork out money for show tickets hope to be fooled. It's a fun, safe escape from reality, and who doesn't want to believe in magic? Die-hard skeptics who think they can spot sleights of hand are the easiest marks simply because the hand *is* quicker than the eye.

If it isn't, the hand doesn't belong to a showman.

Hannah carried out a vinyl-upholstered board and returned for a dollhouse stored at the rear of the trailer. Constructed of balsa, the miniature house was two stories tall, but had no interior walls. The roof was hinged, as were the sidewalls, she discovered when one flapped open.

In the midst of stepping from the trailer, Reilly yelled from the deck, "Hannah, are you out here? Do you know what time it is?"

The dollhouse flew from her arms. The roof yawned wide an instant before the corner of a trunk sheared it off. The beheaded house crashed to the ground, wobbled a pirouette and splintered apart.

Turning slowly to look at Reilly, Hannah said, "Well, it ain't Howdy Doody time."

"Don't worry about that piece of junk." He sucked in his belly and poked his black turtleneck into his slacks. "AnnaLeigh never got it to work right, anyhow."

"What kind of a prop is—er, was it?"

"A close-up. For stage shows, or cameras simulcasting on screens. There's dolls that go with it—different sizes. The trick's to make 'em disappear and reappear, each one bigger than the last.''

"I'm sorry I broke it.''

"What you shouldn't have done is let me sleep so late. It's almost twenty of nine.''

Hannah started to tease him about his nap, but his expression stopped her. He seemed tense for a man fresh from a long snooze. ''Is something wrong?''

"Nah. I just don't like having to tear out here to ask if I can borrow your Blazer.''

Before she could reply, he said, ''Vera called this afternoon, 'bout when I got out of the shower. Told me to meet her and Frank at the ticket trailer. Nine, sharp. Said if I'd sign a contract release, she'd give me my paycheck.''

Hannah scanned the props scattered across the lawn. ''Help me stash anything Malcolm could destroy, and I'll drive you into town.''

"I don't have time. When Vera says nine, she doesn't mean five after.'' Reilly leaned over the deck railing. ''I need the money, sweetheart. Besides a hundred-some in my billfold, Detective Andrik confiscated every dime I had to my name.''

Hannah gnawed her lip. ''I'll get you there. I know the road better than—''

"I've driven every vehicle in creation, over roads you wouldn't walk on, in all kinds of weather.''

"I'm sure you have, Reilly—''

"I'm not gonna wreck your truck.''

"Of course, you—''

"I ain't gonna jump bail in it, either."

Hannah stiffened. "The thought never crossed my mind. What did is that you going to the fairgrounds alone is asking for trouble. Begging for it."

"Aw, forget it." He stomped across the deck. "I'll unhitch the trailer and drive my own damn rig."

As he breezed by, she reached and caught his arm. "What's going on, Reilly? Why can't I go with you?"

Chin thrust out, he refused to meet her eyes. After a moment, he blew out a sigh. "I've got goodbyes to say, and I want to say 'em in private. This ain't the same as when a troupe breaks up for the winter.

"I need to talk to Gina and Arlise and Johnny about—well, there's some things I want to do for AnnaLeigh's funeral. Want to ask 'em if they think she'd like 'em all right."

He looked at Hannah. "Then, after all's said and done, I want a little time alone in the big top...with my wife."

Voice failing her, Hannah nodded, her arm dropping to her side. Why did murder take precedence over death? How could logistics and speculation and cold, impersonal facts overwhelm sorrow and mourning and grief?

Because concentrating on the circumstance dulled the pain of loss? It did, no question about it, but like a hankie that magically becomes a dove, the mental misdirection was still a cheat.

Hannah smiled, then kissed Reilly's cheek. "I'll go get the keys."

* * *

"What are we missing?" David asked, pacing The Outhouse's narrow width.

Desk chair swiveled to face the back wall, Marlin glowered at crime-scene sketches, enlarged photographs, time-lines, and the dry-board where they'd what-iffed and wiped off a dozen possible scenarios.

"It isn't what we're missing, pard," he said. "What we've got is fifty pieces more than the five hundred we need for the puzzle."

"Okay." Turning, David walked toward the wall. "Which ones make a picture of the Grand Canyon, and which ones are palm trees?"

A pencil Marlin had champed down to the lead speared into the trash can. "Damned if I know."

"At the risk of pissing you off," David said, "I wish you hadn't put Phelps on suspension. Yet. With Cletus coming down with food poisoning on the way back from Springfield, three heads might've been better than two."

"Not with Phelps's stuck up his ass." Marlin's voice went falsetto. 'But sir, I didn't have time to inventory Boone's trailer last night before it was towed to impound. I was going to do it today, then I thought since Boone was in jail, recanvasing witnesses was the priority.'"

David couldn't help laughing. "Since when does Phelps sound like Julia Child?"

"Since I gave his testicles reason to undescend. Shouldn't take more than a month for them to realize they're not tonsils."

David shoved his hands in his pockets. Phelps deserved the suspension. He just hoped the rookie didn't resign because of it. Jimmy Wayne was taking up what slack he could. There were two other rookies more junior than Phelps on burglary and theft detail.

Glancing over his shoulder at the desk nearest the window, David thought, Get well soon, Cletus.

"As long as you're up," Marlin said, "get rid of those Polaroids."

David moved to detach them from the wall. "Still messing with your mind?"

"Yeah."

Marlin's hunch had paid off. Toxicology results had shown the presence of Rohypnol, aka the date-rape drug, in AnnaLeigh's bloodstream. The beer remaining in the can found crumpled in the motor home's galley had also tested positive for Rohypnol.

The tranquilizer was legal in sixty-four countries and had been prescribed as a sedative and an anti-convulsant for years, but was banned in the United States in 1996. Why three-quarters of the planet used Rohypnol as prescribed, and the DEA had documented evidence of abuse in three-quarters of America, defied explanation.

"Reilly couldn't have slipped her that roofie," Marlin said for the umpteenth time. "He didn't make it to the party Thursday night."

"And if he'd given it to her before Fromme's truck broke down, AnnaLeigh would have conked out behind the wheel before she made it this far."

Marlin nodded. "Then whoever drugged her beer set her up to be Playmate of the Month. Live action."

David laid the Polaroids on top of a file cabinet. "If you wanted these out of the picture, so to speak, why are we still talking about them?"

"Because it bugs the hell out of me."

The detective yanked another pencil from the holder. David doubted if eating wood-flavored graphite was any healthier than inhaling tar and nicotine.

"I keep seeing the look on Boone's face when I showed them to him," Marlin said. "If he didn't kill AnnaLeigh, that's a shitty thing to remember her by."

"Somebody took a lot of trouble and an awful lot of risk to plant a motive," David said. "Theoretically, everyone in the troupe had access to the rifle, the fake and real gunpowder and the ammo. I can't figure out why whoever preloaded it thought he needed to ice the cake twice."

Marlin stood. Arms winged, he clasped his hands behind his neck. Had his skull been transparent, synapses firing like spark plugs would have been visible. He moved to the section of the wall papered with bank statements and photocopied faxes.

"What if Boone wasn't lying?" he said.

"About what?"

"Much of anything." Marlin twisted at the waist. "He's an ex-con, a circus bum and a cocky old bastard. Evasion would be as natural as breathing."

"Yeah, well. What's your point?"

"Blackmail."

David gestured disbelief. "Is this déjà vu? Or did I dream suggesting that nine hours ago?"

"You meant the 'Pay up, or I'll show these to your

husband' kind. How about the 'Shut up, or I'll show these to your husband' kind?'' Marlin waggled his eyebrows. "What d'ya think?"

"I'll let you know soon as I divine what you're talking about."

"What if the photos weren't taken to frame Reilly. What if they were taken to coerce AnnaLeigh into doing—or not doing—something. When she told the blackmailer to go screw himself, he went to plan B."

David's gut whispered, *Oh, yeah. Now you're on the right track.* "Which was preloading the rifle and letting Reilly take care of the problem for him."

"Uh-huh. Except, why let those nasty-ass photos go to waste? Why not twist the knife and make AnnaLeigh look like a whore while he's at it?"

"Jesus H. Christ." Head shaking slowly, David said, "That's low. Evil."

Marlin's voice was calm, controlled and subzero. "To trick a guy into blowing his wife's face off, then wave pictures of her screwing another man under his nose?"

He hauled back and punched the file cabinet. "I want that son of a bitch, David. Like yesterday."

Malcolm lunged at a jagged chunk of the shattered dollhouse. Prize clamped in his teeth, he whirled and bounded away, delighted by his cleverness.

Hannah said, "Come back here with that."

He stopped, snickered, then started off again at a trot.

If a splinter lodged in his throat, it could be fatal.

She dropped the garbage bag and leaped to her feet. *"Sitz, damn it."*

Lo and even behold, Malcolm reversed forward thrusters, tucked his butt and skidded to a halt.

Hannah congratulated him on his understanding of two-word English commands, then grasped the board. "Okay, now drop it."

Not.

She tugged. "You can't eat wood, you doofus."

Malcolm pulled back. *Arrrr.* Translation: Can so.

"Let. Go. Mal. Colm."

Rrrr—rrr—rr.

In desperation, she warned, "I'll tell Reilly…"

Abracadabra. Malcolm licked his now-empty chops and panted up at her. Treat time.

Instant gratification didn't allow for fetching a bone biscuit from the kitchen. Hannah reached in her pocket for a roll of breath mints. "Here you go, big guy. Yum-my."

He wallowed the disk around on his tongue, made a *yeow* face common to humans tasting their first habanero pepper, then bolted for his water bowl on the deck.

En route, he keelhauled the broken dollhouse. Probably on purpose. Oh, well. She'd have had to break the larger pieces before bagging them, anyway. Hannah threw the board into the open sack and knelt to clean up the rest of the mess.

Whoever designed and constructed the prop must have been a master carpenter as well as a magician. Spaces and compartments between the interior and exterior walls, inside the roof, the fireplace's chimney and under the floor were invisible until the impact effected a cutaway perspective.

The dolls Reilly mentioned were stored in various nooks and crannies. Choreographing their appearance, disappearance and change in size was basically a variation on the age-old shell game. With a bazillion times more dexterity and showmanship applied.

Finger probing one of the hidey-holes, she said, "I couldn't whip a doll out of here, even if I wasn't trying to be slick about...it."

Her nail scraped what felt like paper. Prying it from the balsa-wood wall, she tweezered it out with her fingers.

A love letter? She glanced at the empty driveway, like a child who'd happened across a parent's guilty secret and was afraid of being caught red-handed.

Two sheets of standard printer paper were folded together and knife-creased to reduce the bulk. Her heart rate doubled as she scanned the top page. Skittered wildly when she read the second.

She ran for the cottage. The French door's screen *zinged* on its track. She yanked the kitchen phone's receiver from its hooks. Hand shaking violently, she misdialed. Cursed. Jammed down the disconnect toggle. Redialed.

"Answer. Please, please."

Second ring. Third.

"Come on-n-n. Answer the—"

"Hello?"

Hannah screamed into the mouthpiece, "Reilly

borrowed my truck. I've got to get the fairgrounds—
now. Hurry—please! Fast as you can.''

Marlin slammed down the receiver. "Damn it."
His spun around, his face livid, sweat glistening on
his brow.

David needn't ask why Andrik was too enraged to
talk. From Marlin's side of the conversation with the
prosecuting attorney, David gathered there were no
legal means to delay, much less prevent Van Geisens
from leaving their jurisdiction.

"Restraint of trade, my ass," Marlin howled. "Un-
lawful restraint. False arrest. Illegal seizure. Like I
give a shit about the fuckin' Fourth Amendment. Let
'em sue. Sue our friggin' pants off.''

David's fist smacked his open palm. "There has to
be a way. Health department violations. Animal control. Stall 'em up with a DUI checkpoint. Some—''

Marlin stabbed a finger at the phone. "Didn't you
listen to a word I said? I *asked* Doniphan about check-
points, inspections—*any* ticky-tacky hundred-year-
old statute on the books we could throw at them."

Rapping his knuckles on the desk, he heaved a
sigh. "Sorry. Just blowin' off steam. Or trying to."

"I know." David's ribs felt like barrel staves.
"Seems like everybody has rights except AnnaLeigh
Boone."

"Yeah. The dark side of 'protect and serve.'''

Dark? Well, not exactly. Unjust. Maybe hypocrit-
ical. Slanted a tad too advantageously toward the perpetrator instead of the victim, sure. But dark?

David watched Marlin's expression alter from furious to calculating. As long as cops like Andrik cared, the system's grays wouldn't fade to black.

All available officers blared simultaneously from the handset on David's belt and The Outhouse's scanner.

911 report of a felonious assault—a stabbing—at the fairgrounds. Victim inside the ticket trailer adjacent to the circus tent.

David and Marlin sprinted for the door.

Victim's status unknown. Ambulance en route. Suspect last seen on foot, running east. Suspect described as a white male, mid-sixties, red hair, dark shirt, dark trousers. No height, no weight given by caller.

Struggling to catch her breath, Hannah reached for the desk phone. After locking a reluctant Malcolm in the garage, she'd propped the trailer's doors shut then run through the cottage, flipping off lights, checking doors, grabbing her shoulder bag from the dresser in the bedroom.

Finger poised above the keypad, she squeezed her eyes shut. David's cell-phone number. *What was it?*

He'd only had it a few days. She'd only called him on it once. Think, *think*. It was written on the back of his business card…somewhere at the bottom of her purse.

Headlights strafed the front of the cottage. She hung up the phone and dashed out the door just as the Edsel rolled to a stop in the circle driveway.

"I love you, Delbert Bisbee." The seat-belt tongue clicked in the buckle. "Now, step on it."

An earlier boast that his classic car could go from zero to sixty in twelve seconds was proven twelve seconds after they pulled through the gates and onto Highway VV.

"Sorry to spoil your evening," Hannah said.

"You kiddin'?" Delbert's grin rivaled Snoopy's when he piloted his Sopwith Camel. "It's just getting started."

"If Van Geisens isn't packed up and gone before we get there."

"Hmmph." Delbert pulled back the windbreaker folded over his lap. Arm raised like a waiter carrying a service tray, he juggled the gumball flasher on the flat of his hand.

"Want to dog along behind the pokey Joes," he asked, "or clear the decks?"

"That thing is illegal."

"Uh-huh. So's murder, ladybug."

An excellent argument. Hannah mounted the device on the dashboard as Delbert instructed, then plugged the cord into the cigarette lighter.

"Make sure the control lever is set to the left," he warned. "All we want is a half rotation. If that beam swings full around, I'll be blind as a bat."

Winking crimson light splashed the dashboard, the interior, and reflected off the windshield. Even with its arc halved, the gumball's glow was as bright as a miniature UFO.

A 1958 turquoise Edsel Citation with a Continental

kit extension being used as an emergency vehicle must not have struck the driver of the Aerostar in front of them as odd. The van peeled off onto the shoulder, as did the Subaru in front of it and several oncoming vehicles.

The heavy car's acceleration was as smooth as velvet. Hannah couldn't see the speedometer needle for the gumball's glare. Just as well.

"Now that we're cruising," Delbert said, "mind telling me what this bum's rush is all about?"

"I think I know why AnnaLeigh was murdered. If I'm right, it may be why she wanted to talk to me. Not because of Reilly, per se. Because I'm an outsider."

"Makes sense. We knew it had to be an inside job." Delbert aimed a sidelong look. "So, what's the motive?"

"A one-year, two-hundred-thousand-dollar promissory note at fifteen percent interest, extended for an additional sixty days, at twenty percent."

"Holy mackerel." He whistled through his dentures. "Big bucks and Mafia-style interest. When does it come due?"

In a quiet voice, Hannah answered, "Today."

18

David's Crown Vic, Marlin's unmarked Chevy and a patrol unit pitched and yawed across the field.

David didn't have time to think about Hannah's Blazer parked in a dark patch of open ground before he spotted an assault in progress. Two men were wrestling a third to the ground. The light bar on the ambulance idling in the midway silhouetted five or six more men running toward the fight.

"Sheriff's department," David yelled as he bailed from the cruiser. "Break it up." Feet planted, he leveled his Smith & Wesson.

Andrik and Deputy Bill Eustace took identical stances on either flank. A three-on-eight situation is no time to play nice.

"Show me your hands," David said.

Marlin's Glock waved at the new arrivals. "Hold it right there."

One of the fighters, a bearded worker named Pete Peterson, lofted his arms. "We didn't do nothin' wrong, Sheriff."

"It's him you want," said the second, indicating

the man lying facedown. "He killed Frank Van Geisen. All we done was catch him."

"Frank's dead?" The man on the ground rose on
all fours. Grass clung to Reilly Boone's hair and black
shirt.

"Like you didn't slit his throat." Peterson kicked
at Reilly. "Gina saw you tear outta the trailer with
the knife in your hand, you murderin' bastard."

"She couldn't have. I just *got* here."

The combatants were separated and subdued, and
the late arrivals dispersed. Deputy Eustace began taking witness reports from Peterson and the other man,
Jude Whitney.

Arrested and Mirandized for the second time in less
than twenty-four hours, Reilly's gloved hands were
cuffed behind his back.

"Where's Hannah?" David asked, escorting Reilly
to the cruiser.

"She's home. Look, I swear, I didn't kill—"

"Then what's her truck doing in the parking lot?"

"She let me borrow it. Call her and ask, if you
don't believe me."

David and Marlin exchanged relieved looks.

"What's with the gloves, Boone?" Marlin asked.

"Huh? Oh—well, I always wear 'em when I drive.
The swellin' in my hands, it makes my skin tender,
slick-feeling. The warmth eases the pain some, too."

David opened the cruiser's back door. "In you go,
Reilly. Watch your head."

During the short drive to the midway, Reilly
claimed and re-claimed his innocence. Swore he'd

just arrived and was walking toward the ticket trailer when Peterson and Whitney jumped him.

"Save it." David shifted the Crown Vic into park. "We'll get your side soon enough. Better make yourself comfortable back there. I may be a while."

"But, I didn't do—"

Slam.

EMTs hustled a gurney from the trailer. Frank Van Geisen's shirt and a leg of his trousers were soaked with blood. How he could lose that much and still be alive David didn't know, but paramedics didn't bust their tails trying to save a corpse.

Vera screamed and burst from the crowd huddled near the ambulance. Throwing herself over Frank's body, she cried, "Oh God— Oh, please don't let him die."

The gurney tipped, swayed with her weight. The frantic EMTs struggled to right it, to keep moving, yelling, "Get her off, get her off."

David ran forward, but was on the wrong side of the gurney. Ernie Fromme grabbed Vera's shoulders and pulled her away. Arms windmilling, she screamed, "Let me go." As Fromme dragged her backward, Vera whirled around and collapsed against him, sobbing.

Grim-faced and silent, the spectators fell back to allow the ambulance room to maneuver. David followed Marlin into the trailer.

The detective halted just inside the mobile office. The room was approximately ten by twelve feet and crammed with equipment, file cabinets and shipping cartons. Blood smeared the chair and floor and splattered the papers and money strewn across the desk.

It was hard to tell if Frank had grappled with his assailant. In such a confined space, the EMTs' efforts to stabilize and remove him could have caused some of the damage.

"You were right," Marlin said.

"About what?"

"I shouldn't have suspended Phelps yet." Marlin made a twirling motion. "Exit stage left, boss. I'm sealing this scene until Jimmy Wayne can get here. No way am I working it solo, with a shitload of cash lying around."

David agreed. Evidence was fragile, but it didn't sprout legs and walk away. Assisting Marlin left no one to canvass witnesses. The longer they talked among themselves, the more embroidered their stories would become. Like nature, memory abhors a vacuum, and the mind is wide open to suggestion. What gaps remain automatically fill with plausible deductions.

At the bottom of the steps, Marlin said, "While I'm tying a yellow ribbon 'round—"

"Sheriff Hendrickson." Vera Van Geisen spoke David's name as though threatening him with it. She was shaking, her eyes puffy and red-rimmed. A slash of blood darkened her cheek and matted her hair where she'd lain on her dying husband's chest. "How many of us does Boone have to kill before you lock him up for good?"

* * *

The oncoming ambulance's lights flashed then strobed. Its siren keened then chirped. The tanklike, top-heavy vehicle careered into and out of First Street's turn lane, all but shoving cars from its path.

Delbert swerved onto the paved shoulder. The ambulance roared by with an ear-splitting wail. Hannah swiveled to watch it through the rear window. Her stomach knotted. They weren't far from Old Wire Road, but the ambulance could have come from anywhere.

"But it didn't," she said. "Something's happened at the fairgrounds."

Delbert pulled back into the driving lane. He didn't ask how she knew. Even confirmed misogynists respected women's intuition. Especially when they respected the woman possessing it.

A county patrol unit and an unmarked Ford blew past them, just beyond the city limits. Gripping the steering wheel, Delbert floorboarded the Edsel. Hannah gripped the seat's leather upholstery. *Hurry.*

Slowing for the turn into the fairgrounds, Delbert warned, "We're not doing a park-and-walk," as if nipping her protest in advance. "We're heading straight for the big top."

"Good."

A saner person would have been terrified by his vehicular slalom around picnic areas, the closed Dogwood Days booths and cinder-block rest rooms. Hannah planted her feet on the floorboard, her eyes riveted on the scene unfolding before them.

The midway was ablaze with light. Bright yellow

crime-scene tape X-ed the ticket trailer's door. A deputy and a city cop were talking to a group of performers assembled near David's cruiser. Some looked angry, their gestures punctuating their remarks. Others stood mute, their expressions dazed and confused, unmindful of, or resigned to, being jostled by the vocal minority.

Hannah saw the object of their wrath slumped in the Crown Vic's back seat. "Oh, no. Not again."

Delbert nosed the Edsel between two of the big top's guy lines. "It's better than him being in the back of that ambulance, ladybug."

"Here's some typical female logic for ya." Her fingers raked through her hair. "Now that I *know* it wasn't Reilly, I'm not so sure."

Delbert snorted. "Well, Vera Van Geisen wasn't in it, either. You could spot her a mile away. Appears she's giving Jimmy Wayne McBride holy hell, too."

A borealis of purple, green, saffron and crimson glinted off Vera's sequined tunic. McBride was nodding, hands raised and palms out, placating her and shielding himself from her wildly waving arms.

Marlin was taking dictation from Gina Zandonatti. Her husband, Vincente, held little Francesca. Arlise Fromme cuddled Nicky. David was talking with Johnny Perdue, the other clowns surrounding them like bodyguards. Hannah hadn't met, nor could she recognize every member of the troupe, but Frank Van Geisen was nowhere to be seen.

Delbert unplugged the gumball on the dashboard, then cut the ignition. Still, a pinkish haze clouded

Hannah's vision. She told herself she couldn't pick King Kong out of a crowd, let alone a nondescript circus owner.

Delbert said, "Vera isn't part of the show, is she." A statement, not a question.

"Not as a performer, no. She manages the business end and most of the ticket sales."

"She's awful gussied up for traveling."

Mr. Fashion Conscious was attired in teal, maroon-and-black-plaid slacks, a marine blue, long-sleeved, collared sports shirt banded vertically in orange and a navy Valhalla Springs windbreaker. Date-wear à la Delbert.

The dome light switched on. "You want to stay here and guess what's up, or c'mon and find out?"

They didn't venture far before the answer man, all six feet three inches of him, intercepted them. David looked askance at Delbert's hair color, and not happy to see either of them.

"What happened?" Hannah asked. "What's Reilly been arrested for now?"

David hesitated. "Understand, I don't have time for subtlety or an argument. Okay?"

Blunt but not harsh. In other words, prepare for the worst and leave Reilly's defense to an attorney. Fair enough.

"Frank Van Geisen was stabbed in the throat while he was counting the day's receipts inside the ticket trailer. A witness saw Reilly, with what was thought to be a knife, run from the trailer and toward the parking lot.

"Several of the men chased after him. They lost him, saw him again about the time we got here, and tackled him. Deputy Eustace found a bloody letter opener between the trailer and the field where they caught Reilly."

Bile scorched a path up Hannah's chest. Reilly had figured out who killed AnnaLeigh. An eye for an eye. Biblical justice.

"Is Van Geisen dead?" Delbert asked.

"He was alive when the EMTs hauled him out of the trailer," David said. "I don't know how serious the stab wound is, but he's lost a lot of blood. Vera got hysterical when she saw him. Thought Frank was dead and threw herself on top of the gurney."

"Hmph." Delbert rocked back on his heels.

Hannah said, "Who's the eyewitness?"

"Gina Zandonatti. She doesn't want to be, but she is."

David started to put his arm around her. The sheriff side of him must have advised against. "I'm sorry, Hannah, but from dispatch's description of the assailant, I knew it was Reilly before I arrived at the scene."

"How?" Delbert said. "How'd a description go out on the radio before you ever got here?"

"The 911 caller that reported the assault also described...the assailant." David's lips compressed. He turned and looked at his cruiser.

Vera's voice carried from the midway. "I demand to be taken to the hospital immediately. My husband may be dying—may be dead, for all you know. You can't keep me from him.''

Hannah took the folded papers from her purse. One hour. A lousy sixty minutes. If only she'd found them earlier, Reilly would have been cleared of the homicide charge against him. If only she'd listened to her gut, insisted on coming with him.

"Whatcha got, Toots?" Marlin said, startling her. "A permission slip from Bisbee?"

Her bafflement must have been obvious, for he jerked a thumb at the Edsel. "To borrow the *QE II*. I hear he won't let a mechanic touch it until he signs a liability form."

"I didn't borrow it. He drove me—" Hannah whirled a complete circle. No Delbert. Anywhere.

"He'll turn up," David said, his tone suggesting handcuffs and leg irons.

"So did the motive for AnnaLeigh's murder." Hannah held out the promissory note. "That's why Delbert and I came here. I found this in one of the props in the equipment trailer."

"Oh, yeah?" Marlin glared at David. "Phelps just got himself demoted to jailer. Maybe for life."

Ignoring the apparent inside nonjoke, Hannah said, "If I'd found it sooner, none of us would be here."

David's eyes raised from the paper. "You know what this is, don't you?"

Nodding, she bowed her head. "The reason Reilly tried to kill Frank. He must have realized Frank preloaded the rifle to get rid of AnnaLeigh before the note came due. A default transferred fifty-one percent ownership of Van Geisens to AnnaLeigh.''

Marlin said, ''It explains the two hundred large missing from AnnaLeigh's account, too.''

''Except Reilly didn't know where the money went.'' David pointed at the bottom of each sheet. ''This was AnnaLeigh's deal. Reilly's signature isn't on it.''

Marlin shook a cigarette from the pack directly into his mouth. ''Thanks, Toots. I need a Rubik's Cube–style *attempted* homicide to go with my Rubik's Cube homicide, like I need a new—'' The click of his lighter finished the sentence for him.

She'd assumed the promissory note would be Reilly's proverbial death knell. Off the hook for AnnaLeigh's murder; right back on it if Frank died. Hope seeped in at David and Marlin's reaction. Puzzlement, not Vs for victory.

She stared at Reilly's profile, distorted by the curvature of the Crown Vic's window glass. ''What time was Frank attacked?''

David said, ''About nine o'clock.''

''Define 'about.' Five minutes before? Ten after?''

''Right at nine, give or take a minute each way.''

''According to Gina Zandonatti,'' Hannah said.

''Uh-huh.'' Cigarette ash danced on the air like dingy dust motes. ''Along with plenty of others who heard her scream.''

''Reilly didn't leave my cottage until at least eight forty-five, Marlin. He couldn't have driven here from

Valhalla Springs and stabbed Frank in fifteen minutes.''

David said, ''You're sure he left at eight forty-five.''

''Within a minute of it, yes. Absolutely. It was eight-forty when he came out on the deck, upset because he'd slept so long.''

She explained about Vera's phone call, the scheduled meeting and the argument about borrowing her Blazer.

The detective's fingers closed around her right wrist, then the left. An eyebrow cocked.

''No, I wasn't wearing a watch.'' She sighed. ''And I probably wouldn't have checked it if I had been.''

David studied the black-cased, gadget-fraught model he wore when in uniform, as though he was counting off seconds.

''I know what you're thinking,'' Hannah said, ''and you're right. Reilly telling me the time wouldn't establish an alibi.''

''Not good enough for a cop to swallow,'' Marlin agreed, ''but it probably sounded a couple of clicks north of clever to Reilly.'' He exhaled over his shoulder. ''Look, I wouldn't want this to get out, but we don't catch many Einsteins.''

''Okay,'' Hannah surmised aloud, ''then explain why Reilly would use me as his alibi to kill Frank, at the exact time he told me he was meeting Vera?''

David said, ''Vera told us Reilly set the meeting

time. He called Frank this afternoon, demanding the wages they owed him.''

''Great. Fine. He said. She said.'' Hannah waved at the trailer. ''Why don't you ask Vera about the loan? Maybe Reilly, who isn't Einstein, typed it up and forged everybody's signatures to it. Wanted to give AnnaLeigh her very own circus as an early Christmas present.''

Neither man seemed taken aback by her outburst. Yeah, well, they were accustomed to them.

David handed the papers to Marlin. ''Go for it, Andrik. Miz Van Geisen doesn't hate you as much as she does me.''

''The hell she doesn't.'' The Marlboro's ember glowed orange in the grass. A soft-soled oxford ground it to shreds. ''What I originally moseyed over here to tell you was that I told Eustace to transport Vera to the hospital.''

David spun on his heel. ''You did what? Why? You and Jimmy Wayne haven't even had time to work the crime scene yet.''

''There's your reason right there, kemosabe. She was harassing the crap out of Jimmy Wayne. He couldn't get away from her. It was making the natives restless, too, yelling about being kept from Frank's deathbed.''

''Sir? Uh, ma'am?'' One of the stunt bicyclists, a boy of about twelve, pointed in the direction of the backyard. ''Mr. Bisbee told me to come and get you.''

Marlin said, ''You can tell Mr. Bisbee—''

"He wants to show you something, sir. He said to tell you it was real important."

"Lead the way." Hannah looked from David to Marlin. "Delbert has his moments, but he wouldn't have sent someone to find us on a whim."

They trailed the boy through the midway, the campground, then into the sheltered picnic park area adjacent to the river. Surrounding a trash barrel like Macbeth's witches were Delbert, Johnny Perdue and his minions. Flashlight beams illuminated their faces with a macabre, orange glow.

"This had better be good, Bisbee," Marlin said.

"See for yourself."

David and Marlin joined the crowd around the barrel. Johnny aimed the flashlight downward. Delbert stirred the interior with a tree branch.

"Well, I'll be damned," David breathed. His head jerked up. "You didn't touch anything, did you?"

Delbert looked insulted. "Of course not. Any danged fool knows better'n do that, for Pete's sake."

"If you gentlemen would excuse me." Hannah peeled Marlin and David apart.

"Sure, Toots. Knock yourself out. Just don't—"

"Touch anything."

Hands clasped behind her back, she bent at the waist, then froze. A wig, a shade darker than Reilly's hair, and a pair of bloody gloves lay atop a bed of soft-drink cans, charred meat, chip bags and food wrappers.

Johnny said, "I thought Bisbee was nuts when he asked us to help him search all the trash cans."

"*You* thought he was nuts." Jazz chuckled. "It wasn't you he told to climb in and root around in the Dumpsters back at camp."

The look Marlin gave them said they weren't necessarily wrong. He snapped on a pair of latex gloves. "Hesitant though I am to ask, where'd you get the idea to paw through the garbage?"

"Well, Detective, it was like this." Delbert grasped the lapels of his windbreaker. "While Hannah and the sheriff were talking, I surveiled the scene of the crime. Kept wondering why all the circus people were in work clothes, except for Vera. I supposed maybe she hadn't gotten comfortable yet, but that didn't explain why she was so dressed up in the first place."

"Uh-huh." Marlin pulled a brown paper sack from his sportcoat's pocket, dropped the bloody gloves inside and folded over the top.

"I also wondered how Reilly got from Valhalla Springs to here in half the time we did with a, uh—" Delbert's eyes flicked to David "—with a faster car. Along with how the 911 caller described the assailant to where the sheriff knew it was Reilly before he saw him."

David nudged Hannah. She motioned for patience. She telegraphed that circling a point until the listener is on the verge of screaming was not exclusive to retired postal supervisors.

"Lastly," Delbert said, "I wandered over to the sheriff's car and gave Boone a lookie-loo. Black shirt, black pants. Same as Vera, except for her fancy overblouse. Like I told Hannah when we got here, you could see it a mile away.

"It just so happens nobody else was wearing a long-sleeved black shirt." Delbert flapped a hand at Jazz. "Him and a few others are wearing black T-shirts, but not long sleeves."

Holding the wig upside down, Marlin told Johnny, "Shine that light inside this thing. Yeah, there you go."

David said, "And what might all this have to do with group Dumpster diving?"

"Well, criminitlies, Sheriff. Have I gotta spell it out for you?"

"Bisbee figured if Vera fixed herself up to look like Reilly to throw the blame on him," Jazz said, "she must have stashed her disguise pretty close to camp."

"Hey!" Delbert went bug-eyed, as though he'd been electrocuted. "Andrik asked *me*, not you, by God."

Jazz grinned. "Yeah, but we've got a show to do in Topeka tomorrow afternoon."

"David," Marlin said. "C'mere. Seems the ol' geezer just might be right."

"Old geezer!"

Marlin's tweezers clamped a curly, blond hair extracted from the wig's lining. "I wouldn't call it conclusive, but it just might get that way in a hurry."

Hannah cleared her throat. "Not to rain on anyone's parade, but why would Vera want to kill Frank?"

Delbert bellowed, "Because she's *married* to him."

Marlin shrugged. "Works for me, Toots."

False dawn washed the world beyond the third floor room's windows with a lavender-gray haze.

Frank Van Geisen lay semisupine in the hospital bed. His fingers were flying over a laptop's keypad with a vengeance. The IVs attached to each arm didn't seem to hamper him, any more than the thick gauze bandage taped to his neck.

Beside his bed, a court stenographer recorded his every word as it appeared on the screen. Just because the man couldn't speak, and might never again, didn't mean he couldn't dictate a statement for the authorities.

Marlin and David stood in the hallway, their feet spread and arms crossed at their chests. If there was such a thing as an afterglow, apropos to police work, they were basking in it.

"It still blows my mind," Marlin said, "that you thought of deputizing Claudina over the phone."

"It probably wasn't legal."

"So? A civilian can testify to what she saw with her own baby blues."

Marlin glanced at the nurses' station and lowered his voice. "But don't you know, Bill Eustace like to shit when Claudina told him she was his backup?"

The chief dispatcher had arrived at the hospital in one of her trademark neon-print muumuus and orchid jelly shoes. Bless her. David had hollered "Mayday" and Claudina had responded. He wouldn't have cared if she'd shown up in a nightgown and bunny slippers with curlers in her hair.

"I didn't have any choice," David said. "Eustace couldn't go to the ladies' with Vera, and the department can't seem to hire any female deputies to save ourselves."

"If Claudina would lose about a hundred pounds, I'd sponsor her for the academy."

"I've told her the same thing, Marlin. Only with a little more tact. She says she already dropped two hundred when she divorced that scuzzball she married."

The detective cocked his head. "What about Toots? Do you think she'd be interested?"

"The woman has a perfectly good name," David said. "And no, she's not interested."

"You asked her?"

David smiled. "After tonight, it wouldn't surprise me if Claudina put herself on a diet. You'd have thought she'd lassoed all ten of the FBI's Most Wanted when she walked in on Vera scrubbing the bloodstains from her shirt in the bathroom sink."

Marlin shot him a think-I-didn't-catch-the-dodge? look, but didn't press. No doubt he'd broach the subject to Hannah the next time he saw her. First she'd make some smart-ass remark on the assumption he was teasing, then be flattered to her toenails that he was serious. Then she'd decline, citing a prior commitment.

The soft tick-clack duet continued in the hospital

room. The printout of Marlin's interview comprised ten double-spaced pages. Frank would likely double that with his statement.

David couldn't begrudge the man his say, no matter how long it took. Even on the page, Vera shouting, "No one is taking Van Geisens away from me. Not AnnaLeigh. Not you. *No one*," as she plunged the letter opener into Frank's throat sent a chill through David.

Seeing Frank was still alive when the EMTs carried him from the trailer, Vera hoped her hysterics would delay help long enough for Frank to bleed to death.

"The guy's a certified drone," Marlin said, "but I can't help feeling kind of sorry for him."

"I do, too, except for him being deaf, dumb and blind to every dirty trick Vera pulled over the years. Damn shame she had to graduate to murder before Frank's conscience cried uncle."

"If it did," Marlin said.

"It about had to, didn't it? If he didn't tell Vera he was going to call me and confess as soon as the teardown started, she wouldn't have had reason to kill him to shut him up, then pin it on Reilly as a bonus."

They stepped out of the way of a nurse pushing a portable electrocardiogram. She acknowledged Marlin with a nod, then batted her lashes at David. The detective's eyes rolled ceilingward.

David said, "I suspect Mack Doniphan will charge Frank with a dozen accessory-to-commits and after-the-facts. Then he'll drop most, if not all of them in lieu of him testifying against Vera."

"To be admissible, Frank will have to divorce her first, won't he?"

"I'm not sure, but I don't think he'll have much problem proving alienation of affection."

"Or irreconcilable differences." Marlin scratched at the stubble bluing his jaw. "Cruella De Vil and the Drone. Guess I have to make that Cruella and Drone De Vil, though, huh. The poor slob could barely remember the name he was born with."

Frank had changed his surname to Van Geisen when he and Vera married and took over the circus from Vera's parents and uncle. The elder Van Geisens retired to their native Austria and died there several years later. A cousin kept Vera supplied with Rohypnol, the only medication she'd ever found to combat chronic insomnia.

"I'm not blaming the victim," Marlin said, "but AnnaLeigh shouldn't have played with fire."

"Nope. Bailing out Vera with a loan she couldn't repay to take control of the outfit was no smarter than dummying the bank statements to keep it a secret from Reilly. That may be why AnnaLeigh's signature was different on that Bank Secrecy Act form. She was so excited at the prospect, she couldn't write her own name."

Marlin grunted. "Reilly wouldn't have gone for the deal in a million years. Which is why AnnaLeigh didn't tell him."

David clapped the detective's back. "That's why you've gotta have honesty in a relationship."

"Yeah, right. Spoken like a true, friggin' bachelor.'' Marlin flinched, peered around, then jerked his chin, as though a dearth of witnesses absolved him of cursing in a hospital corridor. ''Oh, well. Like they say, all's well that ends well.''

''Beg pardon?''

''Reilly and Frank. Winding up partners.''

''Helluva way to get there,'' David said.

''It's poetic justice, man. Think about it. Even if Reilly knew AnnaLeigh planned to dump him, the age difference had finally caught up to them. What was he gonna do? His hands were too arthritic to be Houdini anymore.''

Marlin moved to hold up the wall with a shoulder. ''Ah, but what he didn't know was that AnnaLeigh had maestroed a piece of Van Geisens, Incorporated, that's now legitimately his.

''With Vera locked up—let's hope, for life—Frank needs a road manager while he recuperates. It's a good bet Reilly will become the permanent ringmaster, too, thanks to Vera's Zorro number on Frank's voicebox.''

Marlin sucked his teeth. ''Plus, there's Anna-Leigh's funeral arrangements.''

Judging by the detective's exaggerated shudder, for David to remain ignorant on the subject would be the wiser course. Unfortunately, Marlin's cooperation was essential, and he wasn't about to let it slide.

''Junior Duckworth thinks he's a shoo-in for the Believe It or Not award at the next funeral directors' convention,'' Marlin said. ''If dressing AnnaLeigh in one of her X-rated outfits isn't a first, putting a cadaver on ice for six months ought to do it.''

"On ice?" slipped out before David could stop it.

"Well, you can't have the funeral now. It's circus season. Reilly's having AnnaLeigh frozen, then shipped to Molalla, until everyone in the trade is off the road and can pay their final respects.''

It was David's turn to shudder. He believed that at death the soul left the body and went to a finer place, but freezing the remains seemed downright gruesome.

Marlin said, "I haven't had the heart to tell Junior yet, but burying performers in costume is traditional. Other than AnnaLeigh being female, the postmortem Popsicle-thing has already been done, too. The ME in Springfield told me Carden's Circus froze their elephant trainer a while back, until the troupe came home to give him a proper send-off.''

"Cradle to grave, I reckon circus folk just have their own way of doing things.''

"Yeah." Marlin paused a moment, shaking his head. "Vera's on ice in the county jail, AnnaLeigh's on ice for real and the has-been magician and the mute ringmaster ride off into the sunset together.''

He wheezed out a chuckle. "Honest to God, if that ain't poetic justice, I don't what is.''

David thought about it and decided he might be right. As partners, Reilly and Frank might restore Van Geisen Circus to its former glory.

But for all the pain and heartache AnnaLeigh and Vera had caused so many people, it was still one helluva way to get there.

19

Hannah couldn't remember when she'd last slept past four in the afternoon. Not without a hundred-plus degree fever and whacked out on too many jiggers of NyQuil.

Fair compensation, she supposed, since Reilly hadn't left until after dawn. Nor had she remembered to switch the phone ringers and door chime back on before she'd gone to bed.

Jack Clancy was going to fire her one of these days. Or have her arrested for trespassing. Possibly both. Then what would she do?

"Well," she told Malcolm, "I can either run away and join the circus, or apply for the police academy."

If adoring, Hershey Kisses–eyes could talk, his said, *For a clown or a cop, you make a great operations manager.*

"Oh, yeah?" She slip-knotted the belt of her ugly, favorite chenille robe. "Now I don't feel so mean about locking you up again."

Malcolm had never strayed beyond home turf, but the lakeside nuptials might be too close and too tempting to resist. She wouldn't put it past IdaClare to sneak Itsy and Bitsy into the ceremony, either. The Furwads from Hell always got Malcolm in trouble, then sat back on their pouffy little butts and looked smug.

"So, really, Malcolm, when you think about it, this is for your own good. A noble sacrifice, even."

With a granola bar in her robe pocket for a bribe, Hannah lugged a gallon milk jug full of water and a heaping bowl of dry dog food down the back steps.

Malcolm stopped several feet from the threshold, wise to the deeper meaning of dinner and drinks migrating from the utility room to the garage. *I'm not gonna, and you can't make me* radiated from eighty-five pounds of lock-limbed, giant Airedale-wildebeest on the paw.

Peeling the wrapper from the granola bar, Hannah drew it under her nose like a wine snob does a cork. Malcolm salivated. She squatted on her heels and cooed synonyms for "yummy." He crept inside, his nose aquiver. She flipped the treat toward the back wall. He went for it. She ran out and shut the garage door behind her.

She refused to hazard a glance at the area where the motor home and trailer had been parked. First things first. Such as, getting over the feeling that her cottage was suddenly larger than it had been yesterday.

"I can't stay, sweetheart, but I'll be back as soon as the season's over. I promise."

When Reilly whispered that in her ear and hugged

her tight, Hannah remembered him telling her exactly the same thing the day he bought her ice cream in the park.

"Cross your heart?" she'd said when she was a little girl of nine, or maybe ten, and again as a grown woman of forty-three.

Smiling, his eyes glistening just as they had before, Reilly etched an X with his fingertip on his shirtfront, and held his palm aloft. "Cross my heart."

And once more she believed him.

The strange and rather wonderful sense of the past melding with the here-and-now enveloped her again as she slipped into the strapless, formfitting, midnight-blue velvet gown. She'd worn it the night she was Cinderella to Jack's Prince Charming, except try as they had, the shoe wouldn't fit.

"It is a pretty dress." She turned this way and that in front of the cheval mirror. Her palms glided down the butter-soft fabric, following contours as though confirming that her head hadn't been surgically implanted on another woman's not-half-bad body.

Grinning, she cocked a knee through the side slit and flapped a hand at the mirror. "Aw, c'mon, girlfriend. Admit it. You look hotter than a firecracker on the Fourth of July."

Her eyes averted to the bedroom door, expecting to see David, or Delbert, or a *Candid Camera* crew standing there, watching her make a fool of herself with herself.

Moving to the dresser, she opened the jewelry

box's bottom drawer, a quickening at her solar plexus warning that she'd given away, sold or lost the gown's matching cameo choker. She knew better, but was learning the wisdom in "You don't miss what you had until it's gone."

She fastened the ribbon around her throat, then tossed her head, letting her hair brush her bare shoulders. There. Cinderella redux.

"And so help me God, Hendrickson. If you don't make it to the wedding and see me looking my ultimate spec-freakin'-tacular best, you won't live to regret it."

She picked up Caroline's photograph. "Will he, Mama?"

The spittin' image Reilly saw, and Hannah finally wanted to see, laughed back at her. Lying flat on the dresser was a glossy publicity photo of the Amazing Aurelius she'd swiped from one of the scrapbooks she'd flipped through yesterday afternoon.

Had she asked, Reilly would surely have given it to her. She'd simply taken it, in secret, like the snapshots of her he carried in his wallet. If that type of impulse was the stuff of a psychiatrist's doctoral thesis, so be it. Finding traces of Reilly's features in her own would keep a shrink in Mercedes convertibles for life.

Hannah jumped at the doorbell's three-note chime. She laid Caroline's picture beside Reilly's on the dresser, then winked at them. "My coachman awaits."

Delbert gawked at her, backpedaled, then managed to pucker enough for a wolf whistle. "I always knew you were pretty, ladybug, but tonight you're a *knock-out.*"

She returned the visual up-and-down. His hair had faded to a seafoam shade, which complemented his tapestry cummerbund's pastel hues. "Well, you're mighty spiffy in that tux, yourself, Mr. Best Man Bisbee."

"Hmph. If you're into high-toned pallbearers, I s'pose I look all right."

He seated her in his flower-bedecked golf cart, careful to tuck the hem of her gown around her feet. Hop-skipping around to the driver's side, he threw the gear-shift into reverse. Then forward. Then barked a landscape timber with the tires on the way out of the driveway.

"Delbert? You're nervous, aren't you?"

"Hell, yes, I'm nervous."

"Why? Leo's the one getting married."

"After five trips down the aisle, coming within a hundred yards of a ding-danged altar gives me the cold sweats."

"Maybe six would be the charm."

The cart left the pavement and onto the grassy easement. "Mark my words," he said. "If I ever take the plunge again, it'll be 'cause the bride's daddy has a shotgun aimed at my privates."

Hannah's chuckle segued to a gasp. Two snow-white tents flanked a blue linen runner leading to a skirted platform. A series of ivy-twined, brass candelabra with hurricane shades flickered behind it, descending in height along the sides of the platform. Above, was a lattice arbor threaded with ivy, baby's breath, bearded blue iris, ribbon and lace.

Quite a crowd was already seated in the curved rows of wooden folding chairs. David was not among them. A sinking feeling slid the length of her. She'd mentioned the wedding to him several times. Now that she thought about it, he'd never mentioned it to her at all.

"David was invited, wasn't he?"

Delbert's eyebrows met. "I wasn't privy to the guest list, but… Yeah—sure. They wouldn't have left him out." His lips pulled back to imply *Not on purpose, anyway.*

Buck up, kiddo. If David doesn't show up, it isn't the end of the world. This is Rosemary and Leo's special day, not yours.

Pushing disappointment to the back of her mind, she said, "The candles…the flowers. I don't think I've ever seen anything so beautiful in my life. How did Rosemary put all this together in three days?"

"She didn't." Delbert pulled up beside the tent on the left. "Finding the geegaws to do it with took three days. She's been dreaming about it for fifty years."

"You know, you really are a romantic."

He pulled the tent flap aside for her. "I never said I wasn't, ladybug."

IdaClare, Marge and Rosemary squealed, "There she is," when Hannah ducked inside.

Rosemary feigned disgust. "Well, I might as well have worn my housecoat. Nobody's going to take their eyes off you long enough to look at me."

Her creamy, matte-satin gown was as simple as it was elegant. From the mandarin collar to its gored, bell-shaped skirt, the design was slimming, graceful and chic.

"I believe you have that backward, Rosemary," Hannah said. "I can't remember when I've seen a lovelier bride."

IdaClare modeled her floor-length, periwinkle suit. The short, asymmetrical jacket was trimmed in rosy satin. Strands of crystal beads and earrings repeated the luscious, two-toned color scheme. As did, of course, her pastel-pink hair.

"What do you think, dear?"

"Perfect."

"That's what I keep telling her," Rosemary said, "but she's afraid it's more grandma-at-a-baby-shower than matron-of-honor at a wedding."

Marge said, "Oh, she knows she looks *fab*. She's just fishing for compliments."

"Speaking of fab," Hannah said, "it's no wonder why you're ahead of me in the processional."

Blushing, Marge twirled in her slate blue suit. The belted, hip-length jacket was trimmed with diamond-quilted lapels and cuffs. The A-line skirt's center slit would have Delbert bobbing and weaving to catch a glimpse of her gams.

Hannah nodded. "Very classy. And I love the shoes."

Marge hiked up her skirt and pointed a toe. Her sling-back heels had been dyed to match her suit. "I don't know. Spikes I'm accustomed to, only they're the golf kind not the heel kind. There isn't much margin for error in these things."

"IdaClare." Rosemary's fingers snapped like a rifle shot. "I won't tell you again. Close that tent flap and stop peeking at everybody."

"I wasn't peeking. I was trying to get some air. It's stuffy in here."

"It is not." Rosemary dabbed her forehead with a tissue.

"Is, too." IdaClare sniffed. "If I have heatstroke because of your silly whim—"

"Whim? Why, it's a rule, for heaven's sake." Rosemary appealed to Hannah. "It's bad luck for the groom to see the bride before she marches down the aisle, isn't it?"

"I, uh, so I've heard..."

"It's supposed to symbolize chastity," IdaClare snipped. "And everybody knows you and Leo have been boinking like bunnies for weeks."

Ye gods. Was anyone in Kinderhook County under the age of ninety-two, other than David and Hannah, who seemed doomed to eternal celibacy, *not* boinking like bunnies?

"You're just jealous," Rosemary said.

IdaClare started to return fire, hesitated, then lowered her head. "Yes, Rosemary. I am." Shoulders hunched, she clasped her hands together, the thumbs steepled. "Not because of Leo. Because of Patrick." She looked up, her lips curving into a brave smile. "He made me promise I'd remarry if the right man came along. Trust an Irishman to do something like that, when he knows he's spoiled you for anyone else."

"Oh, IdaClare. I'm—"

"No, no. Don't you dare fuss over me, Rosemary. I'm so happy for you and Leo, I could bust my buttons. Yes, I'm also jealous and it makes me a little cranky and sad, but you know what? I wouldn't be if I'd never fallen in love with Patrick Clancy."

She blew a raspberry. "Lord a-mercy. I wouldn't trade one year with him for a lifetime with Cary Grant."

Rosemary pecked IdaClare's cheek. "He must have really been special."

The opening stanza of the wedding march drifted through the tent's canvas walls.

"He still is. Just like Leo is to you." Chin up, her cornflower eyes flashed defiantly. "All right. Let's get with it before Leo thinks he's been abandoned at the altar."

In true matron-of-honor form, she began bossing everyone around. "Hannah, peek out the flap and tell me when the preacher's in place. Hush, Rosemary, no one's going to see you. Pouf your bangs, Marge. They're wilting from the heat. The bouquets are on the table. Wait for your escort outside the tent. Mind that runner, but don't walk like you're hip deep in a slough.''

Hannah looked out on the guests, shifting sideward in their chairs for a better view of the wedding party's entrance. The overflow, mostly men, stood two deep behind the rows. Squeezing her eyes shut, she exhaled a ragged sigh. There wasn't a single dark-haired county sheriff in the bunch.

She couldn't ask Rosemary whether David had been invited. If he'd been accidentally left off the hurry-up guest list, Rosemary would be mortified.

That he'd been too busy to call all day, or had called but didn't leave a message on the machine, didn't seem like a reasonable assumption to her now.

She thought about their talk yesterday afternoon. The trust she'd placed in him. The revelations that must have been nearly as wrenching for him to hear as they'd been for her to say.

After being fatherless for her entire life, she was more relieved to have guessed the truth than she was repulsed by it. As for David? He was a good man. The best friend she'd ever had. But he was only human.

Kept, or told, secrets might carry a higher mortality rate than wars.

''Is Reverend Lang there yet, dear?''

''Uh—yes, IdaClare. He is.''

The matron of honor adjusted a bra strap then stepped outside.

Rosemary's gown rustled as she glided across the tent toward Hannah. "Line up behind Marge, and I'll tell you when it's time for you to go."

"What about Leo? Won't he see you?"

"I'll close the flap right after I give you your cue. He's joining the other groomsmen at the altar." Rosemary winked. "The star of the show is walking down the aisle, by herself."

She poked a finger through the opening. "Oh, look. Don't IdaClare and Delbert make a *darling* couple?"

Maybe not darling, but definitely cute.

"You're up, Marge," Rosemary said, and made a shooing motion at Hannah.

Inhaling her bouquet's delicate floral perfume, Hannah chided herself for a sudden case of nerves. Ridiculous, for a what? Ten-time veteran of the bridesmaid-but-never-a-bride routine? No sweat. So stop doing it.

She glanced back at Rosemary. "Who's the lucky man escorting me?"

"You've met Walt Wagonner, haven't you?"

Okay, now you can sweat.

Walt One-g, Two-n's Wagonner had the peculiar habit of always introducing himself by spelling his last name, as though every encounter was their first. The retired *Encyclopedia Britannica* associate editor also bore a strong resemblance to Lurch, the Addam's Family butler.

At Rosemary's cue, Hannah pulled back the canvas, took two steps forward...and three back. From inside the tent, the bride whispered, "Surprise!"

The tall, broad-shouldered man standing before Hannah was born to wear a satin-lapeled, jet-black tuxedo. A white, tuck-pleated shirt deepened his tan and brought out the blue in his eyes.

He was as handsome as sin, strong, stubborn, gentle, overprotective, and if she hadn't already been in love for the first time in her life, she'd have fallen for him all over again.

And did.

Not a word was spoken, nor needed to be. Hannah took the arm David offered, and as they strolled down the aisle, all she could think was, if this is a fairy tale, please don't let it end. This time, I'm sure the shoe fits.

At the altar, David's hand caught hers for an instant as they parted. Marge, who had been escorted by Walt Wagonner, murmured, "If you liked your surprise, wait'll Rosemary and Leo see theirs."

At Hannah's questioning look, she nodded at the second row of chairs. Two younger replicas of Leo were seated on the right side of the aisle, three women and a man of obvious Marchetti extraction on the left. All six hid behind the guests in front of them to keep their presence a secret until the "I do's" were done.

Leo bustled from the gentlemen's tent and scurried past David to his proper station at the head of the aisle.

The music swelled just as the sun slipped behind the distant hilltops. The lake turned a molten coppery-peach, spanked by golden waves. Here came the bride, and the groom whispered, "Rosemary, my beloved," and tears began to trickle down his ruddy face.

There wasn't a dry eye in the house by the time Reverend Lang pronounced them husband and wife. Leo laid such a smooch on his bride, his glasses fogged over and she had to assist him from the platform.

The happy couple whooped with joy when the younger Schnurs and Marchettis converged on them, expressing gang-hugging, weeping approval of their union.

In accordance with Rosemary's wishes, the newly-weds led the processional to the community center for the reception. When Hannah took David's arm, he said, "I know everyone has told you how beautiful you are in that dress, but trust me, sugar." He kissed her temple. "It isn't the dress. It's the woman wearing it."

Swallowing hard, she choked out, "This ol' thing?"

David's head angled sideward. Slowly, but devastatingly, his mouth crooked into that lazy grin. "You're about a whisker shy of losing it, aren't you?"

"Uh-huh."

"Thought so." His fingertip traced her neck. "Can

always tell, when that big ol' vein starts bulging fit to bust.''

"Hendrickson, you are—'' Such a dork, she finished to herself, laughing too hard to say it aloud. A perfectly marvelous dork, because above all else, he knew when and how to make her laugh.

She still was when they entered the building, which had been transformed from a nicely appointed, albeit functional, meeting room into a candlelit Shangri-la.

Acres of glittery, blue net billowed from the ceiling. White vapor skimmed the floor created by small, oscillating fans blowing over blocks of dry ice. Tiny amber lights twinkled like fireflies in the branches of silk ficus and palm trees.

"Wow," David said, guiding Hannah to a bistro-size table. "IdaClare did all this?"

"With a lot of help from her friends. Present company excluded.'' She winced. "Other than show up, I didn't do anything to help with the wedding.''

"Nothing to feel guilty about,'' David said. "Rosemary was a nervous wreck before the ceremony, for fear you'd guess I was your escort. She was as excited about her surprise as she was the wedding.''

Hannah picked at an imaginary flaw in the tablecloth. "Well, I, uh, did wonder why you weren't seated with the guests.''

"And jumped to the wrong conclusion.''

"Yes, David. I did.''

His head moved slightly to one side and he gave an almost imperceptible nod. "Give me a minute.

Maybe I can think of some way you can make it up to me.''

At a familiar scent, Hannah leaned nearer the flower-ringed, votive centerpiece. Midsummer night's dream. Her favorite.

Glancing around, she noticed the other tables were decorated with cream-white candles, and seated six or eight.

"Are we being antisocial?"

David must not have heard her over the hired combo striking up the Anne Murray classic, "May I Have This Dance for the Rest of My Life." The bride and groom, Delbert and IdaClare, Marge and Walt took to the floor. All of them waved, "C'mon" at the smallest table in the room.

Hannah was motioning "Thanks, but I'd rather not," when David stood and held out his hand. "May I?"

Oh, God. Oh, no. "You know how to waltz?" she asked, her voice hiking an octave as though she'd inquired, "You know how to knit?"

"Trust me. There's nothing to it."

"But I've never—"

David pulled her from the chair and into his arms. "Look up at me. Come closer. A little more…oh, yeah…a perfect fit."

After a few self-conscious steps, Hannah relaxed, feeling as though she were floating on air. Gazing into David's eyes, the warmth of his hand at the small of her back, they swayed and swirled in two-as-one synchronicity.

He bent and kissed her, his lips sweet and soft. The other dancers, the hundred guests chatting around them, and the waitstaff circulating flutes of champagne, all ceased to exist.

Their lips parted, but only by inches, his eyes searching hers. "By the calendar, we haven't known each other for very long, but I suspect you'll agree we've waded more hell and high water than most couples do in ten years."

Hannah smiled. "Boredom hasn't been much of a problem for us."

"And you know, I'm pretty fond of doing things the old-fashioned way."

"Uh-huh."

"So, I had a talk with Reilly before he left town this morning."

"I'm glad. He's rough around the edges, but he's one of the good guys, too."

"And with due respect," David went on, "I spoke with Delbert this afternoon."

"Oh?" A feathery sensation began in her middle. "You did?"

"With Cynthia, things just happened. I always felt like I'd missed out. Now I'm glad I did, so you can be the one—the only one—I've ever asked…"

Hannah ceased to breathe, mesmerized by the intensity in his eyes, the huskiness of his voice.

"I love you, sugar. You're all I've ever wanted, all I'll ever need in this life."

Bodies motionless, David's arm tightened around her, their hearts beating as one. "Will you marry me?"

* * * * *

To be continued...WEST OF BLISS

Author Note

Dear Reader,

Okay, it's true. Thus far, each book in this serial/series has contained a preview of the succeeding title's first chapter. Which means, if you read *East of Peculiar* or *South of Sanity,* you expected to flip a page and find out Hannah's answer to David's proposal.

Except, did you *really* want to know quite that fast? Did you, perhaps, take a moment to mull over, wonder and guess what Hannah said *before* you turned the page?

Well, of course you did. At least, that's what I'd have done. Quite possibly, I'd have stuffed the book under a sofa cushion, so it couldn't wave its cover at me and go, "Pssst, pssst—over here. C'mon, just a little peek."

But no matter how long I resisted temptation, I still wouldn't be a hundred percent sure I wanted to know—and simultaneously *dying* to find out—because that would spoil the fun of not knowing.

After all, time does fly. I'd tell myself that November 2001 really isn't *that* long to wait. Then, in a lead-me-from-temptation sort of way, I'd wind up wishing the excerpt to *West of Bliss* hadn't been included in the first place.

So, it wasn't.

And now you're howling, "How could you *do* this to me?"

Not to pass the buck or anything, but Hannah hasn't told me yet, either. As soon as she does, I swear, you'll be the first to know.....

Sincerely,

Suzanne LedVetter

New York Times Bestselling Author

JAYNE ANN KRENTZ

The Wedding Night

Owen Sutherland's whirlwind courtship has left Angie Townsend breathless and in love—and hopeful that the fierce rivalry that had divided their powerful families would finally end. But now, nestled in their honeymoon suite, Angie suspects she may also be a fool. A sudden, hushed phone call warns her of the terrible truth: her marriage is a sham, nothing more than a clever corporate raid orchestrated by her powerful new husband. The very husband reaching out to lead her to their wedding bed...
Is Owen Sutherland a calculating stranger...or the man she's married for better or for worse? Until Angie knows for certain, her wedding night is on hold...indefinitely.

"A master of the genre—nobody does it better!"
—*Romantic Times*

*Available the first week
of December 2001
wherever paperbacks are sold!*

SUZANN LEDBETTER

66797	SOUTH OF SANITY	___ $5.99 U.S.	___ $6.99 CAN.
66597	EAST OF PECULIAR	___ $5.99 U.S.	___ $6.99 CAN.

(limited quantities available)

TOTAL AMOUNT $_____
POSTAGE & HANDLING $_____
($1.00 for one book; 50¢ for each additional)
APPLICABLE TAXES* $_____
TOTAL PAYABLE $_____
(check or money order—please do not send cash)

To order, complete this form and send it, along with a check or money order for the total above, payable to MIRA Books®, to: **In the U.S.:** 3010 Walden Avenue, P.O. Box 9077, Buffalo, NY 14269-9077; **In Canada:** P.O. Box 636, Fort Erie, Ontario L2A 5X3.

Name:_____
Address:_____ City:_____
State/Prov.:_____ Zip/Postal Code:_____
Account Number (if applicable):_____
075 CSAS

  *New York residents remit applicable sales taxes.
   Canadian residents remit applicable GST and provincial taxes.

MIRA®

Visit us at www.mirabooks.com

MSL1201BL